# THICKER THAN WATER

Copyright © 2013 by A. Unger.

ISBN:     Softcover     978-1-4836-3423-4
          Ebook         978-1-4836-3424-1

All rights reserved. No part of this book may be reproduced or transmitted in any form or by any means, electronic or mechanical, including photocopying, recording, or by any information storage and retrieval system, without permission in writing from the copyright owner.

This is a work of fiction. Names, characters, places and incidents either are the product of the author's imagination or are used fictitiously, and any resemblance to any actual persons, living or dead, events, or locales is entirely coincidental.

Rev. date: 04/27/2013

To order additional copies of this book, contact:
Xlibris Corporation
1-800-618-969
www.Xlibris.com.au
Orders@Xlibris.com.au
503739

# THICKER THAN WATER

## A NOVEL OF SUSPENSE
### BY A. UNGER

# CHAPTER 1

>>JERUSALEM, 2007

A large van cruised down the quiet street.

It was close to nine o'clock in the evening. The street was dark. The eyes of those sitting inside the vehicle, however, shone brightly.

"Excuse me, are you looking for someone?" A courteous passerby, his curiosity aroused by the van, guessed that they were searching for a specific address and not finding it.

"The Fuchsman family," answered the driver, who looked very grand.

"There are two families here by the name of Fuchsman," the man immediately replied. He seemed to be quite familiar with the comings and goings of his neighbors. "One lives here, in this building," he pointed at the next building, only partly lit up, "and the other lives at the end of the block."

The driver's eyes glided over the quiet, half-dark building. "No, that's not the family we want." He eased the van forward and rolled slowly until the end of the street. The curious pedestrian wanted to follow the van, to check what was causing such a festively dressed man to visit the Fuchsmans at such an hour. Politeness, however, kept him in his place on the sidewalk, watching the receding vehicle confidently pull into the parking lot of the last building on the street.

Belatedly, he noticed the family sitting in the van. Next to the driver sat a young *bochur*, wearing a well-cut suit. Another few members sat in the back. Something was definitely happening.

He made his way to the end of the street. He had to know what was going on. After all, if he didn't know, who would...?

But that evening, everyone already knew.

The family and immediate neighbors knew, the many friends, all those who lived on the block – everyone knew that the oldest Fuchsman daughter was engaged. A steady stream of neighbors climbed to the Fuchsman apartment, carrying trays loaded with cakes and confections. Great joy filled the Fuchsman home, as well as the entire street.

• • •

At a quarter to one, Elya Fuchsman finally entered the kitchen, searching through the mounds of cake and drinks for something to eat.

His wife, Devorah, made some space on the table and served him a plate of cake and a cold drink.

"I didn't manage to taste anything the entire evening," he commented, and laid his hat on the chair next to him. "I'm wondering what kind of crush there will be at the *tena'im*, if tonight the door didn't stop swinging for a minute."

Elya took a few sips and put the cup down in front of him.

"Did you discuss a date for the *chasunah* yet?" his wife asked.

"We barely managed to say two words to each other... I actually tried asking him about a general date. I thought that in another four months, before the *yamim tovim,* would be a good time. He made some sort of gesture that led me to understand that he preferred a later date. We didn't manage to speak any more, but if he has a reason to push off the *chasunah,* then we should take it into account."

"Why push it off?" Devorah started putting containers of cake into the refrigerator.

Elya shrugged. "Maybe they need time to digest it. The engagement took them almost by surprise."

"Another four months strikes me as a good time. Not too long, not too short. I want you to speak to him about it. I don't like to push things off for no reason."

On the couch in the large living room, sat the *chosson*'s parents, Shaya and Chana Bleich, tired and happy, quietly exchanging impressions. Shloime, the acclaimed *chosson,* stood next to the large table, looking into one of the *sefarim* he received that night as a gift.

Shaya rose from his seat and pressed Elya Fuchsman's hand warmly. "We feel like we've been *mechutanim* forever... that's a good sign. Everything should continue to go smoothly."

"*Be'ezras Hashem, be'ezras Hashem,*" Fuchsman replied, pretending not to see his wife signaling to him from the kitchen.

"Is there something we still need to discuss?" Shaya asked.

"No, no, everything's fine... everything's fine. Are you making another *chasunah* in the near future?"

Shaya and his wife exchanged a glance. "Another *chasunah*?! No. Shloime is our oldest."

"And a different event?"

Now even Shloime lifted his head from the *sefer* he was perusing.

"No, we have nothing else happening in the next while. Why do you ask?"

"I wanted to know about a date for the *chasunah*…"

"Why discuss a date already?" Shaya smiled. "We haven't even set a date for the *tena'im* yet, nor reserved a hall. What's the rush?"

Luckily, he didn't see Mrs. Fuchsman standing tensely in the kitchen.

"It's good to be organized," Elya answered. "You know, there are a lot of preparations. There's a lot to buy, a lot to sew… After we have a date for the *chasunah*, we can start preparing properly."

"*Be'ezras Hashem*, there'll be a date. It's not a good idea to decide hastily."

"Of course, of course," Elya hastened to agree.

"*Boruch Hashem*, the young couple is engaged. That's the main thing. Everything else is minor."

"Of course," Elya nodded again.

• • •

Next to Yeshivas Mishkan Yitzchok was a bus stop that was constantly populated. Even at 2:15 AM, a time when definitely no bus was expected, there could always be found two or three *bochurim*, for whom the bus stop was the ideal place for important, late-night conversation.

As such, there were spectators to the unusual scene taking place right across the street.

A large van pulled up with a screech of its brakes. At first, no one exited. After a few minutes, the door to the right of the driver opened, and Shloime Bleich, the fresh *chosson*, put one foot, encased in a highly polished black shoe, down in the street.

For long minutes, he sat like that and spoke with those

sitting in the van. He finally emerged fully, his hands loaded with packages that seemed to have been placed there against his will.

When he finally slammed the door to the van shut, the *bochurim* at the bus stop converged on him, quickly followed by many others. It was no simple occasion. The outstanding *bochur* Shloime Bleich, whom everyone lauded as a great "catch", had indeed been caught!

Had the neighbors allowed it, a wild "*mazel tov*" dance would have taken place right there on the street in front of the yeshiva. What actually took place wasn't much different: streams of *bochurim* surged out of the yeshiva building in order to vigorously pump the happy *chosson*'s hand. There was such a throng that the *chosson* wasn't able to move, let alone reach the wide steps of the yeshiva, and from there, his room, in order to at least lay down the pile of new *sefarim* he had brought with him.

In all the commotion, no one noticed that the large van stayed parked near the sidewalk, and that its passengers – Shaya and Chana Bleich – were silently watching the outpour of happiness and love.

"What a wonderful boy," Chana murmured, and, for some reason, rummaged in her purse for an unused tissue.

Shaya looked at his son – that is, at the hat on his head, as that was the only part of him that was visible among the crowd.

"I'm telling you they sensed something," he said. "I'm telling you. The questions that the *mechutan* asked, at the end of the evening, were pointed. He's a good man, but clever. Or maybe it's not a contradiction."

"He's good and clever," his wife agreed. "And the questions he asked at the end of the evening were legitimate. Your answers were also entirely legitimate. Why suddenly discuss a date for the *chasunah* when we haven't even finished eating the cake from the *l'chaim*? It's his right to ask, and it's our right to push off giving an answer."

"No one's talking about rights and obligations, Chana." He sighed and started the motor. "It's clearly our obligation to delay the *chasunah* as much as possible. If I could, I would have asked to set the date for another two years, and I don't even know if that would be enough time for us."

"We have to discuss this, Shaya, to weigh it carefully. Not to decide anything hastily. Maybe we shouldn't even start with all this. Let's set the *chasunah* for the near future, and afterwards we'll see." Chana twisted her head, searching for her son among the solid, retreating crowd, but was unable to find him.

"There's nothing to weigh." Shaya switched gears and the van shot forward. "The matter is not up for discussion. Tomorrow morning, after *shacharis* and a nice donation to *tzedakah*, *b'li neder*, I'm leaving…"

"Shaya, what happened??"

"Wh-what happened??? Where's Naftali?!"

"Naftali…?"

Chana Bleich squinted in the dark room. The numbers 3:06 glowed eerily on the face of the alarm clock.

"Shaya, it's not morning yet. What's going on?! Why are you sitting like that?!"

"Wh…where's Naftali?! Chana, someone's knocking…"

Chana pulled herself out of bed and flicked on the light. Shaya wiped his damp forehead with his pajama sleeve. "Someone's here, Chana. I heard knocking…"

Wordlessly, Chana threw on a robe and went over to the door, though she knew no one was behind it. She opened it a crack and, as she had expected, determined that the stairwell was dark and completely empty.

"No one's here, Shaya," she announced, wanting to add that

if anyone *had* come, it was in his dreams. But she bit back the words, not wanting to upset him.

Shaya groped his way in slippered feet down the hallway to the apartment's entrance. Chana switched on the hallway light, and went to prepare some warm milk for her husband. Squinting at the light, Shaya continued on to the living room and sank heavily into his easy chair. As if by some unspoken agreement, they both knew that there would be no more sleep for them that night. More important matters were on the agenda.

After Chana returned and placed a mug of milk on the coffee table, the two of them sat, wrapped in silence.

"You're sure that wasn't Naftali at the door…?"

Chana drew a deep breath. "It wasn't Naftali, Shaya. It wasn't anybody. I know how badly you wish it was him, no matter what the hour. But it wasn't. You're getting sucked back into that whirlpool Shaya, because of the engagement. That's all."

"I did return. I must return. This is it, Chana, there's no more avoiding it. It happened even earlier than I expected. I can't run away anymore. You agree with me, don't you?"

Chana bit her lip and silently looked away. The room was dim, and the gloomy shadows cast by the branches spilling out of the hanging plant appeared on the wall as so many entangled arms.

"Nowhere does it say that we have to get involved in all that again." Her voice was barely audible. "Why, Shaya? What for? Things are so good for us now and soon, with *Hashem*'s help, they'll get even better. We're before a *chasunah*, everything's going so smoothly – why complicate matters? It's good for us, it's good for Shloime – why dump him into this? He doesn't deserve it. He's such a good boy…"

Shaya was quite for a moment.

"He is a good boy. Everything's good. But we can't just think of ourselves, Chana. There are other people in the picture – they also want things to be good for them."

"I'm not so sure that ripping the story open again will do any good for these people. I have a feeling that that's not at all so – not at all."

"But we can't decide for them, don't you understand?! Shloime is *their* child, not ours. That's the crux of the matter."

Again, a heavy silence fell upon the large room. Chana left to the kitchen to heat up some more milk.

"Chana!"

The strangled cry from the living room brought her dashing back. Shaya was sitting upright in his chair, clutching his chest fearfully.

"Chana, someone's knocking at the door. I'm telling you! It's him. He felt that something happened, and came. I'm telling you. Please - open the door, carefully…"

Chana didn't laugh. Instead, she went over to the door and opened it wide. The stairwell was dark. In order to calm Shaya, she stepped out, looked all around, and even opened the door to the elevator, which had stood empty ever since their return from the engagement, some two hours earlier.

"There's no one here," she stressed. "Naftali doesn't have *ruach hakodesh*, Shaya, even though he's a good man. I also find it hard to believe that he merited *k'fitzas haderech*, and was able to make it here from wherever he is halfway around the world in just a few hours…"

Shaya sank back down in the easy chair. "I'm traveling tomorrow," he said in a cracked voice.

"Where to?"

Shaya didn't answer. It was a good question. Where would he go? To Los Angeles? Lizhensk? Alaska? The world is purportedly small, but one would have to search high and long in order to locate one man among millions.

"I don't know where. Somewhere. Each big trip starts with one small step."

"Small," Chana agreed, "but in which direction? Right, left, north or south? He could be anywhere. You have to do some homework first, to find some sort of clue. The last time you saw him, where did he say he was going?"

...

## >>JERUSALEM, 1989, 12:50 AM

Most decent people don't knock on another's door in middle of the night, so as not to awaken those who are sleeping. They certainly don't ring the bell – and hard.

"Who's that?" Chana, who was preparing the sandwiches for the next morning's breakfast, was frightened.

Whoever it was rang again, as if it was one o'clock in the afternoon and he wanted to return a cucumber, or convince her to buy a carpet. Before she could make it to the door, the bell sounded once more, insistent.

"Just a minute," she called. Did someone not understand that at that hour people were sleeping?!

She opened the door to find the person she least expected to see: Naftali Bleich, her husband's brother who lived in Haifa. They met about once a year, at a family *simcha* or, unfortunately, under more tragic circumstances.

She greeted him with surprise.

"Call Shaya," he stated flatly. No please, no excuse me, not even a hello.

"Shaya's asleep already." There was a question in her voice.

"So wake him up – now."

Without another word, Chana went to the bedroom. Shaya

was partially awake, and annoyed. Who was ringing the bell at such an unearthly hour?

"Who's collecting *tzedakah* now? Tell him to come back tomorrow..."

"Shaya, it's not - - -"

"Not *tzedakah*? So, who is it – someone selling eggs? It's not right to come so late. People are sleeping!"

"Shaya, it's not eg - - - it's your brother, Naftali. He's at the door..."

"What?!"

Shaya sat bolt upright. "Naftali? Are you sure?"

Chana peeked out of the bedroom towards the entranceway and living room. The door to the apartment was closed, and Naftali was gingerly perched on the edge of the couch, as if it was upholstered with a bed of thorns, nervously playing with the buttons on his watch.

Shaya got up and quickly wrapped himself in his shirt.

"I'll be right there," he called. "What's going on, Naftali?"

"I'm waiting for you," Naftali called back tersely. "Come as you are. As quickly as you can."

Dressed in a shirt and pajama pants, his head sporting the wrinkled yarmulke he wore when sleeping, Shaya made his way to the living room, intensely curious.

"Something to drink?" Chana asked. "A strong coffee?"

"Nothing," Naftali returned, "and could you please leave the room and close the door."

Chana was taken aback by the request, but she instinctively honored it and turned to leave.

"Quickly, Chana," Shaya called after her as he pulled up a chair opposite Naftali. "Can I sit, or is there no time for that, either? Why did Chana have to leave the room?"

He waited for an answer, but none was forthcoming. Instead,

Naftali reached for his brother's hand and jiggled it, back and forth, back and forth, without stop, as if expecting Shaya to understand his distress without his expressing it.

Shaya, somewhat bewildered, rested his hand on his brother's shoulder. Naftali comes to him in middle of the night, demands to speak with him right away, and now, when the opportunity to speak is there, he's quiet?

"I… I don't know how to begin to say this, Shaya. I, I… I just ask that you don't get angry at me."

"I might get angry," Shaya replied, "but you're going to tell me what's going on anyway. What happened? Is somebody sick? Did someone die? Disappear? Lose his mind? What's the story?!"

"None of the above," Naftali said quickly. "All right, maybe we'll start from the end. I have to leave the country immediately, now."

"What are you saying?" Shaya let out a low whistle. "Why? They discovered that you're a secret agent?"

Naftali sighed. "Shaya, really. I can't afford to joke right now. I have a ticket, and at seven I'm boarding the plane. I mean, we are – Rochel and I."

"And Shloimy," Shaya finished for him.

"No. That's just it – he's not."

"What do you mean?" Shaya didn't understand. "Naftali, listen to me. I can't understand a thing from some disjointed pieces of information. Please, sit down and explain to me exactly what's going on, from start to finish, and what I can possibly do to help. Chana! Please bring some coffee and cake."

"It's a long story," Naftali begged. "Very long, and I have no time. Shaya, please understand. Rochel and I took a taxi here, with our suitcases, on our way to the airport. I didn't come here to tell you some interesting stories in the middle of the night.

We're on our way to catch a flight. As soon as I have some time, I'll tell you everything. We have to leave for a month or two, and then we'll be back, *be'ezras Hashem*." Naftali paused to sip his coffee. Not because he had time to drink, but because he couldn't bring himself to refuse.

"The problem is," he continued, his voice breaking, "the problem is, we can't take Shloimy with us. There's absolutely no way. He's only two – a baby. All this bouncing around is not for him. I wanted to ask you -" he coughed, almost choking on his words. "To ask you to take care of him for a short while… for the next month or so…"

Chana, about to leave the living room with the empty tray, froze.

"One minute, I'm trying to understand." Shaya's voice reached her ears with an unnatural clarity. "You're leaving your baby and going overseas, without knowing when you'll return? Naftali, there's something I'm not getting…"

Chana waited to hear some sort of answer, but the silence was deafening. Turning, the tray still in her hands, she caught sight of Naftali leaning against the wall, his hand covering his face.

No one spoke. Shaya couldn't find any words, and Naftali, trying his best to choke back the tears clogging his throat, was incapable of speech.

There was a soft knock at the door.

Chana opened it cautiously, bracing herself for additional surprises.

Her sister-in-law, Rochel, stood in the doorway, her face shuttered, a bulging bag hanging heavily from her shoulder. In her arms lay a peacefully sleeping toddler. Shloimy.

# CHAPTER 2

"Do you have a playpen?" Rochel asked quietly.

"A playpen?" For a second, Chana was confused. "Oh, actually we do. What *hashgachah*! My neighbor was looking for a place to store her playpen, and found somewhere – in my storage room. I know she'll let me use it. I'll open it right away."

Chana retreated into the apartment. Rochel followed her silently, the small, precious bundle in her arms.

"I'll set it up in my work room. Is that all right?" Chana asked. "It's a dark, quiet room."

"That's fine."

Within a few minutes, Shloimy's little bed was ready. Chana showed her sister-in-law into the room, offered her a chair and disappeared. She didn't want to know how a mother takes leave of her only baby – a forced parting for an unknown duration, a good-bye that was allowed to take her, at most, five minutes.

"Our flight is leaving in another few hours." She heard Naftali's voice, low and cracked. "We're late as it is. Rochel?"

He went into the hallway and touched the door that was just barely open.

"Rochel, you're… you're okay, right?"

Chana, standing with her back to the wall, felt something hard rise and ball in her throat. The words that so badly wanted to leave – "Let her be", "Give her another minute to hug her baby" – were stuck inside. And when the ball burst forth in a waterfall of tears, the words were no longer able to be said.

Naftali stepped quietly into the dark room. Chana stood outside, burying her face in two wet hands. Shaya remained in the living room.

Downstairs, on the dark, silent street, the taxi waited. Naftali and Rochel quickly slipped inside and slammed the doors.

"One minute! Just a minute!" Shaya suddenly yelled. So it really was true, all that was happening there?! It wasn't a dream? His brother was really leaving his child by him and was about to disappear?!

"Naftali!!" He banged wildly on the window.

Naftali waved goodbye. Waved and waved. The taxi started to move.

"Naftaliiii!!!" he shouted. The yell echoed on the quiet street, bouncing back to him from all sides.

"Naftali, give me a telephone number, an address, something!!!"

Naftali gestured helplessly, as if to say, "I don't have." After a second, he relented and opened the window. Shaya shot towards him.

"Don't look for me, for now," Naftali pleaded. "At least for the next few months… the next year. I don't know what will be, but I know that it's likely to harm me, us. Promise me!"

Shaya didn't have a chance to promise. Naftali, who knew that if he said any more he'd break down, closed the window. The taxi eased a bit more forward, and then, with a roar of its motor, sped on its way.

• • •

At five thirty in the morning, Chana woke up. She didn't understand what woke her. The alarm clock was set for seven thirty. She didn't yet have a baby that greeted dawn with his cries.

Suddenly, Chana remembered, and a chill ran down her spine: She *did* have, she did have a baby. He wasn't hers. He was her sister-in-law's. A sweet little boy of two years was sleeping in her work room, completely unaware of what storm was rocking his secure little world. His father and mother had picked up and traveled to some place out there. They left a bag, large and filled with clothing and diapers, bottles and pacifiers. They left his teddy bear in his arms, and large, wet tearstains on his clothes. But now, when he was calling "Ima" and wanted his bottle of cereal, Ima wasn't there to gather him into her arms. Ima was far away, and no one, not even she herself, knew when she would return.

Shaya also awakened. When he heard the cries of little Shloimy, something suddenly fell into his consciousness and his head dropped back onto his pillow.

"We have to go to him," he whispered. "Do you know how to prepare a bottle for him?"

Chana didn't know. In all the confusion of parting, that was the last question to enter her head.

"You heat up water, I think," Shaya said. "Or milk."

Chana and Shaya didn't know how to heat up milk. They usually drank coffee. They didn't even have a proper utensil. How did you heat it up? On the stove?

"First of all, we have to calm him down," Shaya said. But the minute Chana carefully opened the door to the room, the toddler recoiled in the strange playpen and screamed, "Ima!!!" twice as loudly.

"Come, sweetheart," Chana attempted. The baby continued to cry. What should she do with him? Pick him up? Talk to him? Rock him? Or maybe she should first prepare his cereal. But how?

"Shaya, put up the kettle," she requested. "And look for cereal in the bag."

"What does it look like?"

Shaya dumped out the entire contents of the bag on the couch in the work room. A respectable mound of items piled up and rolled in all directions.

"Is this cereal?" Shaya held up a square box.

"I don't know. What does it say?"

"Baby Fresh, without alcohol."

"Alcohol?" Chana wrinkled her forehead. "What else does it say?"

"Refreshing."

"I don't know." Chana held a squirming Shloimy and tried to stick the pacifier into his mouth. "Look for something else."

"And what's this?" He held up a ring of keys. "Chana, they left us the keys to their house! Why did they think we'd need them?!"

"Because I suppose we will need them…"

"Here, Chana!" Shaya called happily. "It says: milk powder."

"Great. But how do we prepare it?"

"What's the problem? It's all written right here."

Shaya hurried to the kitchen. The kettle was whistling.

"It says to put it into lukewarm water," Shaya called out. "And the water in the kettle is boiling hot."

"So cool it off."

"No problem." Shaya took down another two mugs and

poured water from one to the other, back and forth, as he had seen his mother do years before for his little brother. In the other room, little Shloimy wailed, firmly rebuffing any attempt of Chana's to approach him. He chewed the pacifier angrily.

"Nu, what's happening?"

"I'm cooling it." The counter was already completely covered with cups, and each time Shaya stuck his pinky in to check, the water was still hot.

"What are you doing? You're not allowed to touch it – it's food for a baby!" Chana yelped, as she entered the kitchen, the rebellious toddler squirming in her arms.

"So how do you check if it's good? How much do we need to cool it? Maybe we should just put it in the refrigerator?"

"Maybe. I think you have to drip some on the back of your hand."

Shaya turned the bottle upside down. Nothing happened. He shook it, but only a few drops dribbled out. He twisted the lid. The back of his hand was covered with water. So was the back of his leg. And the floor.

"Shaya, really!"

When the bottle was finally ready, Shloimy absolutely refused to taste it. He cried, twisting his head back and forth and spitting out the little that managed to enter his mouth.

"He doesn't like it," Shaya guessed. "Should we add sugar?"

"Can he have?"

"I don't know. Why not?"

Why not? Neither of them knew. Shaya took the bottle to the kitchen and poured two heaping teaspoons of sugar into the mixture.

But little Shloimy refused the sweet concoction as well.

"How much sugar did you put in?"

"Two teaspoons."

"That's not too much?"

"Why should it be too much? Let it be sweet for him."

"All right, he doesn't want it," Chana concluded the round of coaxing.

"He wants to cry," Shaya added his own conclusion.

"Me, too," Chana informed him.

They both looked at the little boy. His face was red and his hands were balled into fists.

"Why don't we ask him what he wants," Chana suggested.

"But he's just a baby!"

"He's two years old. He knows how to talk."

"He knows how to scream," Shaya corrected. "At least that's what he's been doing until now."

The two of them looked helplessly at the toddler standing in the playpen, gripping the top bar with all his strength and yelling, "Ima, Ima," with complete faith that, if he only screamed loudly enough, his mother would come.

• • •

## ≫JERUSALEM, 2007, 4:30 AM

Chana stirred Shaya's cup of tea. That was the order: first warm milk, and then tea to get the milk moving, and after that, coffee, because if you're already drinking something, let it be something strong.

Suddenly, she froze in terror. She clearly heard someone playing with the handle to the front door.

It seemed that something still remained of the telepathic connection between Shaya and his brother, though it had lain dormant for years already. Could it be that Shaya didn't just wake up in middle of the night, that he wasn't imagining that his lost brother was opening the door and simply entering?!...

"Hello…"

The terrific fear that gripped her just a moment before was matched by the tremendous relief that flooded her heart.

"Shloime!"

Shloime closed the door gently.

"You're still awake?!"

"Come, *chosson*, come," Shaya said. "What's happening? The weight of marriage is already disturbing your sleep?"

"Uh, no." Shloime sat down on the couch and leaned back tiredly. "The *bochurim* in yeshiva didn't leave me alone. At one point I just picked up and left. But I didn't imagine that you're still up. What happened?"

"It's from all the excitement, Shloime," Chana said from the kitchen.

Shloime looked at his father's tired eyes. "I hope it's just excitement, and not worry," he commented.

"Worry? Why worry? What should we worry about? Everything is so wonderful, *boruch Hashem*."

Still, the deep crease remained firmly etched between his father's eyes.

"Drink something, Shloime. Drink, and go to sleep."

Shaya stood up and began to pace about the living room. From the armchair to the table, from the table to the large windows covered with drapes. From the drapes to the massive bookcase filled with *sefarim*.

"Ima," Shloime called, "am I imagining it, or is Abba overwrought?"

"Abba's excited, Shloime. His son is engaged, no? And what's with you? Should I make up your bed?"

But in the room, hovering somewhere between the aroma of milk and coffee steam, sandwiched between the half gloom and his father's pacing back and forth, something tickled Shloime's fine-tuned senses. Was it really just excitement?!

"Bring him some cake from the *l'chaim*," Shaya said suddenly. "With lots of cream, you hear? With lots of cream and chocolate. No, don't bring one cake. Bring a platter of cakes. We don't have much time left to spoil him…"

"Until a hundred and twenty," Shloime said automatically.

"You hear?" Shaya continued. "Bring it in. There's not much time left…"

• • •

## >>JERUSALEM, 2007, MONDAY, 11:30 AM

"To the U.S.?" the travel agent asked, and tapped on her keyboard.

"To the U.S.," Shaya confirmed, and mopped his forehead with his already wet handkerchief.

"When?"

"Yesterday."

"We won't have a ticket anymore for yesterday, sir," the agent replied courteously, the sarcasm in his words completely lost on her.

"He just means that it's very urgent," Chana explained.

"I'm checking right now if there's an available seat."

Chana played with the buckle on her pocketbook. "You know the prices for last minute tickets, Shaya," she whispered.

"I know, and you know." He exhaled noisily.

"It's a lot of money," Chana murmured, as if he didn't know.

"Money? Money??? You're thinking now about money?"

"You're the one who's always thinking about money," she defended herself.

"So leave that to me this time, as well."

"Package?" the agent looked over her computer at Shaya.

"What package? I don't have to send a package."

"No, sir." Travel agents have patience, so much patience! "I meant to ask if you want a vacation package. A direct flight, reservations in a hotel, a car, a direct return flight, including---"

"He's not going on vacation," Chana quickly interjected. "Now's not the time."

Shaya looked at Chana for a minute and then turned to the agent. "I'd like such a package. How much does it cost?"

"For how many days?"

"I don't know."

"Approximately?"

"I don't know."

"Shaya, you have to know," Chana whispered.

"Fine, let's say two months."

"Vacation for two months?"

"No, not vacation."

The agent wrinkled her forehead. "Shall we organize ourselves?" she suggested.

"How about a week," Chana suggested. The agent grabbed at the piece of information, and her fingers flew over the keyboard.

"Two thousand and two hundred dollars, including flights there and back, six nights in a hotel and a car."

Chana bit her lip.

"But a week isn't enough," Shaya recovered. "I need more, a lot more!"

"How much more?" the agent attempted politely.

"I don't know…"

"I suggest you think about it," the agent said, motioning at her telephone that was blinking non-stop from a slew of incoming calls.

Shaya and Chana moved to a side bench. The travel agency was buzzing with activity, phones were ringing, faxes were arriving, and Shaya told Chana that she simply didn't understand.

"What's a week?" he asked in annoyance. "A week! A week will fly by before I even find myself. When will I manage to find my brother?!"

"But it will cost a fortune."

"And how much does a child cost? Did you ever see a price tag?"

Chana sighed. "And who has to pay the price?"

"Fine, when I meet Naftali, I'll give him the bill…"

When they stepped out of the air-conditioned travel agency into the burning heat outside, there remained in Shaya's checkbook a stub for seven hundred and eighty dollars, the price of a one way ticket to the U.S. He knew when he was leaving; he didn't know when he was returning home.

"And preparations for the *chasunah*?" Chana asked as she opened the door to their car.

"There are no preparations for the *chasunah* until there is a *chasunah*."

A shudder ran through her body.

"Shaya, in another four months Shloime is marrying Suri Fuchsman, whether his biological father stands with him under the *chuppah* or not."

"Would *you* want to be stuck in some far flung place when your child was getting married, without your even knowing about it???"

The two of them sat in the motionless car.

"Where are we going?"

"Where are we going?" Shaya scratched his forehead. "Let's go to the Kosel. Davening can only help…"

Chana glanced at her watch. She had another three minutes until two o'clock. At two, she was to meet Shaya outside in the square. Meanwhile, she had another three minutes to say one more chapter of *Tehillim* and ask for another few things. Oh, how many things she had to ask for...!"

She had already given *tzedakah* to whoever asked. She had already kissed the holy stones. She had already shed a respectable amount of tears – if the number of crumpled tissues in her hand were anything to go by. But *tefillah* is the fuel of life, what kept them going, moving them forward, *be'ezras Hashem*.

*Hashem, watch over our Shloime, that nothing should happen to him. That his gentle soul shouldn't be shaken up; that he should come to his wedding day happily and calmly, and build his bayis ne'eman on a solid foundation.*

True, they had erred. Maybe it was lack of time, maybe hastiness, perhaps too little emotional strength to reopen the painful affair. Now, though, the reasons weren't important; the problem existed in all its glory. Shloime had gotten engaged before they had worked out a solid plan of action.

Shaya was coming. She saw him talking on his cell phone., "What did you say? The *tena'im* is on Sunday...?"

# CHAPTER 3

"They're setting a date for the *tena'im*. They're the parents of the *kallah*, but they're allowed to consult with us first," Shaya fumed, and slipped the small phone into his pocket.

"It doesn't enter their mind that we have something more important to do than to come to our oldest son's *tena'im*, and – between you and me – they're right."

"But on *motza'ei Shabbos* I have a flight to America!"

"So push it off. It's a sign from *Hashem*."

"Oh, so now *Hashem* is sending you signs?! I must fly on *motza'ei Shabbos*. The flight can't be pushed off for even one day. As it is, time is short – very, very short."

"Shaya, just don't tell me that you won't be at the *tena'im*. If I was the Fuchsmans, I would raise three eyebrows, not two. Do you really want them asking questions? The questions they asked after the *l'chaim* weren't enough?!"

The two of them walked from the Kosel square towards their car. Hundreds of people passed by them, each one busy with his own personal affairs and the *tefillos* for which he had come.

"There's nothing to talk about. You're pushing off the flight. If you ask me, it should be pushed off for a few days. It will look strange for the *mechutan* to pick up and travel immediately after the *tena'im*. If you leave after a bit of time, they'll understand that you're traveling to collect money, or do some shopping or something like that. They won't be suspicious."

"But I don't have another few days!" Shaya's voice rose in anger.

"Shaya, don't get upset. Your heart…"

"My heart isn't here anymore, don't you understand? I don't even know where, but my heart is with my brother, who deserves a bit of *nachas* in this world that turned its back on him – and even that he might lose if we don't find him in time…"

• • •

## »HAIFA, 1990

Shaya Bleich climbed the steps in the Haifa stairwell. He really should have come a long time ago. They were missing so many things: Shloimy's vaccination booklet (Chana wanted to take him for his shots as the kind-hearted aunt who was doing the busy mother a favor; without the vaccination booklet, though, no nurse would believe her), and some other papers that could be of use to them. But he hadn't come.

What had made him come just now? True, Shloimy was now three. He had to be registered for *cheder*. As part of registration, the school would ask to see their identity card. But Shloimy wasn't on his and Chana's ID cards. Faigie, the sweet baby that was born to them a few months earlier, was registered on their cards as their oldest child.

The complications were now setting in. He, and maybe even

Chana, had anticipated them, but they had both preferred to suppress them. Shloimy stayed at home with Chana, and lately, also with the baby, as much as possible. He was getting older, though, and needed to play with friends and to learn, not just stay with Ima and the toys. And perhaps *cheder* wasn't actually the reason, but it definitely got him moving. It was time to straighten out Shloimy's official registration.

Shaya sat down on one of the chairs in the dinette and looked around, remembering the funny, yet sad, story that little Shloime'le had told him just yesterday.

*"We were walking outside," the words tumbled out of Shloimy's mouth, "and I was holding on to Faigie's stroller nicely. And we met so many cousins…"*

*"We met the last person we needed to meet," Chana interjected. "Guess who?"*

*"Miriam Rochel Tova Henya," he responded, without even stopping to think. This aunt, whose name was usually shortened to "Marta", was the most dangerous relative to meet in the city, or on the block, or – truthfully – anywhere.*

*"And what happened?!"*

*"Of course, she looked us all over very carefully, asked a few questions about the new baby and why we named her after only one grandmother and not both, and then she asked about Naftali. She said she hadn't heard from him in a long time. I told her what we tell everyone, that Naftali and Rochel traveled abroad on a* shlichus, *and that Shloimy is staying with us in the meantime."*

Shaya stood up and went into the bedroom that had been Shloimy's. The room was a complete mess, untouched for nearly a year. The drawers of the changing table were open, with clothes spilling out of them. The doors to the closet were also opened wide, and toys were jumbled on the floor. It looked as if Rochel had wanted to pack everything possible and, due to the heavy emotional and time pressures, simply grabbed whatever came to her hands.

"*She studied Shloimy with her sharp eyes,*" Chana went on, "*and said, 'I don't understand. You just pick up and leave a child? They first have a* shlichus *to raise the boy, no?!'*

"'*We're just doing our job,' I said, and hugged Shloimy tightly.*

"'*And their parents? What do they say about this?' she continued to interrogate me.*

"'*Their parents know,' I said, and that must have been the only completely true statement in the entire conversation.*"

Shaya tried to fold the clothing and put it away somewhat neatly.

"*Aunt Marta wanted to know where the* shlichus *is. And for how long? And why specifically them? And that her son, Moishe, is marrying off a child and wishes to send them an invitation, so she wants to know the address. I took out my notepad and gave her the fake address that we invented. She'll never know if the invitation got there or not. Even if she gets it back in the mail, we can always say that she didn't write the address correctly on the envelope…*"

Yesterday, Chana had laughed. But Shaya, presently standing in his brother's empty, abandoned apartment, opposite the sink containing remains of cocoa and armies of ants, wasn't laughing at all.

Feeling uncomfortable in the absence of the owners of the apartment, he gingerly walked from room to room. On the bulletin board in the kitchen he found little notices, so full of day-to-day life: Pick up clothing from the seamstress. Pay babysitter thirty shekel. Don't forget to buy Savta a birthday present. Take Shloimy to the ENT, next Tuesday at six PM. All the notes were already yellowed.

On the utility porch, he found piles of clothing. Someone had to come take care of the house. That someone should have been them – and a little earlier.

The living room was actually tidy. Maybe that was because Naftali and Rochel hadn't needed to pack *sefarim*, or their silver. Even so, the door to one cabinet was ajar – the cabinet that held all their documents.

Shaya took a deep breath.

• • •

## »JERUSALEM, 2007

Shaya Bleich and Elya Fuchsman made up to meet in one of the *shtieblach* in the city center. Fuchsman preferred to meet in his house; it would be an honor for him to host his *mechutan*. Bleich, however, maintained that he would anyway be in the city center to run some errands.

When Elya Fuchsman arrived at the *shtiebel*, a *minyan* was gathering for *ma'ariv*. He looked expectantly at the doorway. Another man entered, another young *bochur*, another full-bearded Jew. They were nine. And there was the tenth.

"*Shir hama'alos*," the *chazzan* began to chant. Shaya Bleich burst into the *shtiebel*, huffing and puffing. At the last minute, he signaled to Fuchsman that they would speak immediately after *davening*. He stood in a corner and buried his face in the wall.

"I see you're very busy," Elya Fuchsman remarked after *davening*. The two of them leaned against the wall of the *shtiebel*. "We heard many wonderful things about you the past few days," Elya said.

"*Boruch Hashem*," Shaya smiled with *nachas*. "Just as we've heard about you."

The conversation meandered along, touching briefly on the presents the *chosson* and *kallah* would respectively receive, continuing a bit in the direction of various financial issues, until

Shaya remembered to ask, off-handedly, "When is the *tena'im*?"

"On Sunday," Fuchsman immediately replied. He was very surprised. "They didn't tell you?!"

"Sunday," Shaya repeated thoughtfully, or pretended to appear thoughtful. "I'm not sure that Sunday will work for us. You understand... Sunday is right after *Shabbos*, and the *Shabbos* after the *l'chaim* is a bit, you know, tiring. Many people come to wish '*mazel tov*', they bring lots of cake. I'm afraid my wife might be too exhausted. It's better to come to the *simcha* – especially as it's our first *simcha* – refreshed."

It was Fuchsman's turn to hesitate – genuinely.

"You're sure it's such an issue?" he attempted. "It's just that we received the impression that it was okay, and we already hired a hall and catering..."

"A hall and catering can be found easily," Bleich said. "I would prefer moving the *tena'im* to a different day, if possible."

"Certainly," Fuchsman assured him, somewhat confused. "If it's so important to you, of course we'll take it into consideration. To when do you want to push it off? Monday?"

"No."

"Tuesday?"

"No, no."

"So when? Would you and your wife like to set the date?"

"I'd like to push it up to Thursday – that is, tomorrow."

Elya Fuchsman didn't realize how his mouth dropped open. Bleich, noticing, said hastily, "That is, of course, if it's not too difficult for you. If there's any problem, I take it back..."

"No, no," Fuchsman raised his hand. "Whatever's possible – will be done. I just didn't think that's how it went... We're novices when it comes to *mechutanim*. But I don't think it should be a problem... It took me a bit by surprise, that's all. But it's really not a big deal. We'll organize everything a bit more quickly. It actually wouldn't hurt us to learn, in general, how to get things together... The *chasunah* itself is not that far off. By the way, Rabbi Bleich, my wife asked me to find out – it's important to her – when, approximately, were you thinking of making the *chasunah*?"

There it was again. Shaya rummaged in his pocket. He was positive that his handkerchief had been in the left pocket, but there was no handkerchief in the left pocket, and in his shirt pocket there was only a packet of notes about all kinds of things.

"The *chasunah*? Ummm..." He had to look like he was considering. He had to.

"We were thinking along the lines of another four months," Fuchsman offered.

"Uh, could be."

"Is that good for you?"

"Could be. I just don't have a calendar in front of me right now---"

"I'm not up to calendars. I wanted to ask in general. We'll set the exact date later on, all right?"

But Shaya Bleich didn't want to set it later on. He wanted to find his handkerchief in order to wipe away the beads of sweat rolling into his eyes.

"Fine," he said. He knew he couldn't avoid it forever. It was unheard of for a couple to get engaged and not set a date for the wedding.

He then told his *mechutan* that if there was a problem, the *tena'im* could be held in the *shul* near their house. It had a spacious hall, and the entire community used it for their celebrations. The *mechutan* heard, and seemed relieved. Perhaps it was a good idea anyway to use the hall, and save money. Why pay for no reason?

And when the conversation moved back along the safe, familiar lines of money and payments, Bleich mopped his forehead once again. He did it. The flight on *motza'ei Shabbos* would remain on *motza'ei Shabbos*. Chana would need a good few minutes to recover after hearing how he had moved the *tena'im* forward three days, but he was beginning to see the first signs of *s'yata d'shmaya*.

Afterwards, in the safety of his car and the darkened streets, he allowed himself to release a long sigh. He had one more task to take care of before he lifted his wings and flew off – for an unknown length of time.

• • •

## >>JERUSALEM, 1990

Three year old Shloimy jumped happily between the suitcase and clothing and objects piled about.

"Shloimy, please don't step on Abba's ironed shirts," Chana requested. "And no, not on Faigie's Shabbos dress, either. Yes, I know that you're terribly excited," she sighed, half to herself, "but could you find a different way to express it, other than skipping like a goat between all the things I need to pack?"

"We're going to Savta, we're going to Savta!!!" The happy Shloimy knew no other way to show his joy, besides the one employed by all children his age: jumping and cavorting about. Not every week, nor every month, did they travel to Saba and Savta who lived in Kiryat Gat. The truth is, the last time he visited them was with his parents, when he was almost two. From then, even though Shaya and Chana ached to spend *Shabbos* with the Bleich parents, going with Shloimy put them off. They hadn't been there in over a year. Savta Bleich had visited Chana after she gave birth, and another time or two after that, but that was all.

"You're sure it will be okay?" Chana asked Shaya as they sat on the bus, the children on their laps. Shaya didn't have to ask what she meant.

"We can hope," he answered. "Look, we're not hiding anything from them. There's nothing to be afraid of. They know that Naftali and Rochel left Eretz Yisroel for reasons that aren't known to us, either, and that no one knows when they'll return. They appreciate what we're doing for Shloimy. There might be some cloud of pain in the background, but I don't see any reason to worry."

And indeed, on the surface, everything appeared fine. Saba and Savta were waiting at the bus stop, and scooped the children from the steps of the bus into their arms. Saba Bleich took the suitcase, and Savta the two tots. The house was all ready to grandly receive the honored guests.

"How are you, Shloime'le? Saba carried the little boy to the bookcase and let him take the Aleph-Binah by himself. "You already know the whole *aleph-beis*?"

Shloimy didn't yet know the entire *aleph-beis*, but he did know that he had come to a loving place. He didn't really remember Saba and Savta. He hadn't seen them in more than a year – a very turbulent, significant year for him. However, aided by many candies and much chocolate, almost any three year old can be convinced that he's in the right place.

Chana relaxed. The elder Bleichs weren't angry that they hadn't visited for so long. They understood. And the pain and uncertainty that they must be feeling were well hidden.

The Friday night *se'udah* passed pleasantly, and by *Shabbos* morning, Chana felt comfortable enough to sit with her mother-in-law for more intimate conversation. Faigie was sleeping, and Shloimy played near them with the toy garage.

"So, Shloimy," her mother-in-law decided to open the conversation by way of her grandson. "Do you like Chana?"

The little boy turned his head in surprise. The older Mrs. Bleich looked from him to her daughter-in-law, whose face had turned as red as Shloimy's toy fire engine, and, a minute too late, grasped her mistake.

"Who's Chana?" Shloimy asked. He left the fire engine and looked at his grandmother questioningly.

"Oh, it's not important," she answered him, flustered. That was her second mistake. To children, "not important" actually signifies something very important, indeed.

"I think Savta meant Faigie," Chana hastened to say lightly, though she felt anything but light. "You like our little Faigie, right?"

"Of course," Shloimy said, "Even though she cries all day…"

Later, when Chana, completely beside herself, told Shaya about the incident, he didn't take it to heart.

"Shloimy forgot it already," he soothed her. "Let it go."

"But how could she let herself make such a mistake?"

Shaya could actually understand his mother. "Look, Chana, we've been living with Shloimy for more than a year already. We're so used to him being part of our family, that sometimes even I find myself quite sure that I'm his father. But my mother is seeing us together for almost the first time. She's not yet used to the arrangement, don't you see? It's a logical mistake."

"Maybe we're the ones who made a mistake," Chana sighed, "when we told them everything."

"It wasn't possible not to tell them, Chana. They're parents. They would have turned the world upside down and discovered the truth. If we wouldn't have told them, we would've hurt them, and eventually ourselves, as well. Besides, how long do you think you could hide things, especially from family? I wouldn't be surprised if at some point someone says something to Shloimy, or whispers something behind his back. Shloimy's a smart boy. Between you and me, I'm not looking forward to that day."

• • •

## >>JERUSALEM, 2007

The wide steps of the yeshiva were made of gleaming marble. The glass doors were framed in wood, and through the frosted glass, Shaya could see the shadows of *bochurim* milling about during the evening break.

He pushed open the heavy door. A few *bochurim* threw him a glance. The gaze of some of them lingered. They probably recognized him.

He hesitated near the door for a few minutes. In general, he found himself to be increasingly pensive lately. He, the man of vigor and action.

"Are you looking for somebody?" one *bochur*, walking by, asked politely.

"Shloime Bleich."

The *bochur* gave a low cry of admiration. "Many people are looking for a *bochur* like that, but don't find…"

Shaya couldn't hold back a smile. "I'm his father."

Now the *bochur* came over and shook Shaya's hand firmly. "*Halevai* someone should promise me a son like that."

"*Boruch Hashem*." Shaya stroked his beard. "Is he here?"

"He's probably in the *beis medrash* now. *Seder*'s over, but he usually stays late…"

Shaya went down to the study hall. It was enormous. Just then it was empty, save for a few swaying backs, visible mainly near the pillars. Shaya stepped quietly through the rows of tables, trying not to disturb those learning.

"Shloime." He tapped the *bochur* lightly on the back.

Shloime lifted his head. Upon seeing Shaya, he stood up, his face questioning.

"Shloime," Shaya said briefly, "we have to discuss something important."

"Now?"

"Now. Absolutely."

Without a word, Shloime closed his *sefarim*.

"Let's go outside," Shaya said.

"Where are we going?" Shloime followed his father out of the *beis medrash*. "Home?"

"No. Let's go for a drive."

"A drive? To where?" His father had never been a man of many words, but this time he was being especially stingy!

"Somewhere where no one will disturb us."

# CHAPTER 4

>>HAIFA, 1990

Rather weak-kneed, Shaya eyed the open cabinet in his brother Naftali's living room.

He might very well be about to find some paper that would shed light on the whole mystery.

Unable to shake the feeling that someone was watching him, he went over to the cabinet.

As in all the rooms in the house, definite disorder reigned in this cabinet, too. A few binders lay on the floor. Shaya gathered them up, noticing how extremely organized his brother had been (had been? G-d forbid. Still was.). In one binder were filed, in chronological order, all the bank statements and telephone, gas and electric bills. Another binder held all the receipts that Naftali and Rochel had ever received. Perhaps they would be needed for something or another. The contents of each binder was written on it in large letters.

Shaya reverently returned all the binders to the shelf. It was hard to imagine that in middle of the hurried packing Naftali had needed some gas or electric bill. He arranged all the papers. Everything was so organized and ordinary. He found nothing strange or suspicious.

Only after straightening up from crouching next to the cabinet did Shaya see another binder, closed on the table.

No label was written on this binder. It was gray. Shaya opened it with shaking fingers.

Nothing.

The binder was completely empty. Shaya closed it, and opened it again. One could think that it hadn't served any function, if not for the fact that it looked rather used, and its edges were frayed.

Shaya sighed. There's no way to find something among nothing. He could only assume that inside the gray binder had been all the answers he was seeking, and that Naftali had simply packed it all up and taken it with him to who-knows-where.

Shaya closed the binder again, added it to its cousins standing on the shelf, and closed the cabinet. He sighed, half in relief and half helplessly, and was about to finally leave the living room.

A second before he left, however, he discovered that not all the evidence had flown off with his brother. One piece, small and square, waited for him on the floor.

• • •

## >>JERUSALEM, 2007

Without saying a word, Shloime kept pace with his father's quick strides out of the building. Outside, directly opposite the yeshiva, Shaya's car was parked. He opened the door and entered, waiting for Shloime to follow suit.

But Shloime, instead of going to the opposite door and entering, went over to the window.

"Will it be long, Abba?"

"Could be. Why?" Shaya turned the key and the motor sprang to life. He knew that the world was about to change, but Shloime didn't know that, and was busy with day-to-day affairs.

"I'll be back to sleep in yeshiva tonight?"

"It's hard to know."

Shloime didn't ask any more. Lately his father had been strangely preoccupied. He had a strong feeling that his engagement had a large – maybe even decisive – part in it.

"We're going to Saba and Savta?" he asked, when the car started to glide in the direction of the exit from the city.

"That's right," Shaya said without looking at him.

"Something happened to them?" Shloime became a bit alarmed.

"*Chas v'chalilah. Boruch Hashem*, no."

"So then why---" Shloime didn't really mind if they were hiding something from him. He had never been the sort to stubbornly listen to the secrets of the adults. But this time – this time something fluttered inside his stomach, pushing him to keep asking.

"Come, let's talk about something else, Shloime," his father said, leaving him openmouthed.

"Fine." Shloime recovered quickly and decided to go along. "Let's say that you just want to treat me to a trip. Now that I'm engaged, we both have lots of time to do all that we never had time to do…"

But his father wasn't in the mood of jokes.

"Tomorrow night is the *tena'im*," he said, careful not to level his gaze at his son, who was absorbing surprise after surprise, "and on *motza'ei Shabbos* I have a flight to America. It's important to me that we speak now. To bring up some memories…"

The dark drive passed mostly in silence. Shaya uttered some pleasantries, while Shloime racked his brain to discover the reason for the trip. Visits to Saba and Savta were reserved for *Shabbos* and *Yom Tov*, especially *Yom Tov*, because it was hard for his aging grandparents to host the large family for an entire *Shabbos*. He understood that there was a connection between Saba and Savta and his upcoming marriage. Maybe there was some sort of family will that had to be passed from generation to generation, and now was the time to pass it to him, so that he could, *be'ezras Hashem*, pass it along to the next generation…?

"Why are you traveling to America, Abba?" Shloime tried a different subject.

"Saba and Savta will explain."

Shloime straightened in his seat. What was going on? Every question received a riddle for an answer. How on earth were his elderly grandparents connected to his father's trip?

...

## >>HAIFA, 1990

Shaya bent down. A light blue piece of paper lay under the chair.

He picked up the note.

At the top of the paper, underlined, was the word 'receipt'. This receipt, it seemed, differed from all those collected so neatly in their particular binder.

"I, the undersigned, confirm that I received the sum of $50,000 from M.L."

The signature wasn't Naftali's. Shaya tried to decipher the scrawl, unsuccessfully.

True, the piece of paper said something, but it left a lot more unsaid. Perhaps it even supported the theory that Naftali's flight was due to financial difficulties. There had always been, though, strong ties between Naftali and the rest of the family. If he had needed money, he knew he could always turn to them. It couldn't have been only money. There was something here that Naftali wanted to hide from them, for which reason he didn't let them know that he was in trouble, and didn't ask for their help. And even when he needed to flee, and leave Shloimy with them, he absolutely refused to give the reason.

Maybe Naftali had had business dealings – and maybe he still had? Maybe he had opened a business and was looking for an investor? So why didn't they know anything about it?! The first address for help is siblings, parents – family. Why did he approach them only after…?

• • •

## >>KIRYAT GAT, 2007

"Abba, you're sure we can knock on Saba and Savta's door so late?"

Shloime's simple wristwatch (he would receive the gold one the next day, at the *tena'im*) showed that it was already eleven thirty at night.

"Definitely," his father nodded. "They're waiting for you. For us."

Shaya knocked on the door. Before the third knock they could already hear the shuffling of Savta Bleich's slippers.

"Shaya'le?" she called from behind the closed door. "Is that you?"

"Who else?" Shaya called back, the shadow of a smile hovering in his voice for the first time that night.

They could hear the clicking of the lock. One, two, three.

Shloime counted four turns until the bolt was finally removed and the door opened.

The house was lit up, quite unusual for so late at night. On the table was an assortment of refreshments. Saba Bleich sat at the head, looking in a *sefer*.

"Sit, sit," Savta urged them. "Sit down and eat something. How's everything, Shaya? And how is our *chosson* doing? What a *simcha*, what a *simcha*. And the *kallah* – what a *kallah*! You know, there are many wonderful girls, but…"

Shloime knew his grandmother. She tended to talk round and round. This time, though, he felt that most of the chatter was an attempt to cover up something heavy and mysterious in the air. This whole sudden visit to his grandparents, at such an hour, demanded explanation, and here everyone was acting as if every Thursday they hopped over to Kiryat Gat to taste Savta's *cholent*.

But Shloime didn't mind playing along. He had patience, and he believed that eventually all his questions would be answered. He took up Savta's invitation to sit beside her on the couch, listened attentively to some interesting stories and tasted various cakes and cookies, until Savta suddenly remembered.

"Shloime'le, I wanted to ask you – maybe you can help me? You know, my memory isn't what it used to be… A little while ago, I tried to organize my albums, and I saw that I'm getting really confused. There are so many grandchildren, *b'li ayin hora*, and as much as I try to remember who everyone is, and which family they belong to, I can't seem to get it all straight… Especially with the pictures of everyone when they were babies. They all look so similar… You have a good memory, no? So come help me a little."

And Savta Bleich opened the cabinet under the bookcase and removed a few large, heavy albums.

Shloime thought of the *sefarim* he had left in yeshiva, piled neatly on his *shtender*. Organizing albums? Wasn't that a job for girls before *Pesach*?

But Savta requested. She opened the first album, moved it over to Shloime and asked, "You see this baby? Yes, the one in the sailor suit. Who is that…?"

Shloime took the album and inspected the picture carefully, as if it was the small letters of a difficult *Rashi*.

"This boy… ummm… who is this boy? The truth is, all the kids look alike. But he looks a bit like my brother Ahre'le, no?"

"Right, right," Savta was suddenly overtaken by a fit of coughing. "That's right. Maybe it really is Ahre'le?"

Shaya sat next to the table, seemingly talking with his father, but his ears, his heart and all his senses were tensely attuned to what was happening on the couch. It was true, many times he and Chana had said that Ahre'le strikingly resembled Uncle Naftali.

"One minute, but something here doesn't make sense," Savta objected. "Look, Shloime. Look at this boy's hair. When Ahre'le was two, he barely had two and a half hairs, and this boy – who looks to be about two – has such long hair! It can't be Ahre'le."

"Aha," Shloime said. What a contradiction. What a problem. "So who could it be?"

Shloime got the impression that Savta would be truly bothered if the picture wouldn't be in its proper chronological place in the album.

"Maybe we could figure it out based on the house." Shloime carefully removed the picture from the album and brought it close to his eyes.

"I don't recognize this boy," he commented after thoroughly inspecting it. "It must not be from our family."

"So maybe I'm a bit washed out," Savta said and took the picture from him. "I don't have such a huge tribe of grandchildren. I have two children – your father, and Aunt Gitty, who has only girls. So who is this little boy who stole his way into my album?"

"Maybe it's my brother, Shmiel," Shloime suggested. "He doesn't really look like the boy in the picture, but one could change a lot since they were two."

Savta "studied" the picture again.

"No," she decided. "It can't be Shmiel. Shmiel has big eyes. Right, Shaya? Very big. And this boy has regular eyes, like all the children."

"Ah," Shloime said, trying to catch his father's eye. *This was why you brought me here, Abba, in middle of the night? For this I left the pile of* sefarim *abandoned on the* shtender? *In order to sit next to Savta on the couch and help her organize her albums...?*

"Ima," Shaya said suddenly, "Maybe you could look in the album for some more pictures of this boy. Maybe they'll help you identify him better."

"That's an excellent idea," Savta said enthusiastically, and opened her album again.

"Abba---" Shloime tried.

"One minute," Savta stopped. "Shloime still hasn't tasted the jelly and coconut cake. Shaya, please pour a drink for him. What is this here? He'll yet say that we don't know how to receive guests..."

Shaya passed the plate of cake. He left the pitcher of water by him, in the meantime. Just in case.

"All right, Savta," Shaya tried to shorten the process as much as possible. "Come, let's look for this boy in the album. I'm sure we'll find him."

"I'm sure we will," his grandmother repeated after him. She turned a few pages, turned pack a few pages. He noticed that her fingers were trembling. Time isn't kind to anyone, and even less with the elderly.

"Here," she said and stopped on one of the pages. "Here's the boy, a bit smaller. And here someone's holding him…"

• • •

## >>JERUSALEM, 1991

Urgent knocks, almost banging, brought Chana running to the door. Ever since the nocturnal visit two years earlier, she had developed a specific fear of hurried knocks at the door.

"Chana," the neighbor from the first floor spoke quickly. So quickly, that her words tumbled over each other. Chana managed to make out only "downstairs", "car" and "Shloimy".

"Shloimy???" Chana flew into the back room, scooped up Faigie from her crib and deposited her in her neighbor's arms, and raced down the steps.

In the street – there was turmoil. Huddled mothers, crying children and some cars whose drivers had gotten out. But where was Shloimy?!

"Where's Shloimy???" she yelled hysterically. Now she also saw an ambulance.

Someone pushed her inside. Her four year old Shloimy was there, together with another boy.

Shloimy – oh, *boruch Hashem*! – was half sitting, half lying. He wasn't crying, wasn't scared. He tried to smile at her, tried to explain in his childish words.

"We came off the van," he said, "and a car came. It didn't see us, we ran quickly --- it hurts me here, on my leg…"

A pleasant faced paramedic explained in a bit more detail: "It's a mild injury. It probably happened from his fall on the street and not from the car. These school vans, I'm telling you…"

"So what happened to Shloimy?" That's what interested her.

"Nothing serious. But we'll take him to the emergency room anyway, just to make sure that it really is only a light injury."

Chana tried to breathe in relief, but suddenly an unreadable expression flitted across her face.

"I don't think there's any need to," she said. "Can you check him here and see if everything's okay? It's a shame to bring the boy to the emergency room for no reason."

Had he not been tactful, the paramedic would have raised an eyebrow. "I don't think it's a good idea. In any event, an injury from a car is something that needs to be checked out at the hospital."

"But you yourself said that that it's from his fall, and not from the car. If the car would have injured him, he wouldn't be smiling at me now, right Shloimy?"

The paramedic hesitated. "Mom, I think it's worth going to the emergency room anyway. It will take a few hours – it's not so bad. The main thing is for us to be sure that everything's okay."

Chana gave in. She couldn't insist anymore without it looking strange, even suspicious. She sat next to Shloimy in the ambulance and feverishly tried to plan her next steps.

"Name of the boy?"

"Shlomo."

The receptionist wrote routinely. For her, everything was lines and lines of technical details.

"Father's name?"

Chana looked to the side. Soon they would take Shloimy for an x-ray, but meanwhile he was right next to her. They didn't even give him a bed. The emergency room in that hospital was always overcrowded.

"Excuse me," she said to the receptionist, leaving her a bit stunned with the pen in her hand and the form in front of her. "I must buy my son a drink, he's terribly thirsty. Shloimy! Come, let's buy you some juice."

"But Ima, I just drank," he answered, waving the empty water bottle in his hand.

"Excuse me," Chana said again, aware that she wasn't making the best impression, "I simply must buy myself something to drink. You know how it is here, you get dried out."

And Chana disappeared. She had to. Shloimy, quite bored, was standing right next to her as she gave over his details. It wasn't the first time she had to fudge information. At the pediatrician, for example, she was Shloimy's mother, beyond a shadow of a doubt. At one visit to the dentist, she herself filled out the card with Shloimy's information, and wrote the father's name as "Yeshaya" in clear letters. She assumed they wouldn't ask to see his ID card. And so it was.

But the emergency room was much more official. She knew that. She was afraid of that.

"Excuse me, doctor," Chana asked a doctor who was passing by, "when are they taking him for an x-ray?"

The doctor looked down at Shloimy. "As soon as we can. Wait a bit."

But Chana couldn't wait a bit. She had to go finish giving over the details, and couldn't do so in front of Shloimy and his sharp ears.

"Oh!" Shloimy called suddenly, unaware that he was actually saving her, "Ima, here are fish!"

"How nice!" Chana was genuinely amazed. There was an aquarium. "You sit here for a few minutes, Shloimy, and watch the pretty fish, while I go take care of some things." Whoever had placed the aquarium in an attractive corner of the emergency room had intended to entertain the children, not to save their parents.

"Yes, I'm sorry," she returned, breathless, to the receptionist. "Regarding Bleich, Shlomo."

"Yes." The receptionist found the paper. "Father's name?"

"Ima!" Shloimy called. Again he was next to her! "There's a red fish and a gold one, and…"

"Naftali," Chana said. That's it. She couldn't run again to buy a drink.

Afterwards, after the card was completely filled out, and a bed was available for Shloimy, and he finally, with his mother's help, was lying in it, Shloimy remembered to ask something that was troubling him.

"Ima, who's Naftali…"

The next evening, when Shloimy would be home and already peacefully asleep, Chana would tell Shaya that they needed to put an end to it.

"Legal adoption. We have to do it. It's impossible like this. It's impossible to live with excuses. Shloimy is bigger, and the need to adopt him has grown, as well. What will be tomorrow? And if we want to open a bank account in his name? And if we have to travel abroad with him, for whatever reason, how will we get him a passport? And if---"

"We can't adopt Shloimy legally, Chana. I already looked into it." He would stop her mid-stream.

"What does that mean – can't?!"

"In order to adopt Shloimy," he would patiently explain, "we would have to prove that his parents aren't fit to raise him. There's a board that checks everything. If we say who his parents are, we're likely to complicate matters for them. They'll start asking questions: Why aren't they here? Why can't they raise him themselves? Do you want to get them – and us – into trouble?"

# CHAPTER 5

>>KIRYAT GAT, 2007

"One second, Savta," Shloime said even before seeing the additional photos, and asked to see the original picture again. "I don't know why I didn't see it. This boy is me, isn't it? Everything fits. When I was two, I had long hair, my eyes are blue, and the picture was taken in our house. I was thinking so much along the lines of somebody else, that I simply didn't recognize myself."

Savta forcibly restrained herself from looking at Shaya. He, too, kept his eyes studiously away from his mother's.

"What do you say!" she exclaimed. "Never mind you – you wouldn't recognize anything other than the tiny print of the *gemara*. But me? That I, your grandmother, shouldn't recognize my own oldest grandson?!"

"That really isn't good," Saba murmured. "I think you have to put together a separate album for Shloime and give it to his *kallah* as a present, maybe after the *chasunah*. She has to see how cute he was already then, when he was two."

"What a wonderful idea!"

And Shloime saw Savta pull out an empty album and start to collect pictures of him from all the other albums.

"Now?" Despair crept into Shloime's voice. "Savta, you're planning on doing this now?!"

"Of course now," Savta said gaily. "When then? Right this minute, when you yourself are here and can help me arrange the pictures in chronological order. Alone, I'd get confused, and put a picture of when you're two before one of when you're one."

"Savta," Shloime avoided looking at his watch so as not to offend her, but even without looking, he knew it was late. Very late. "I think that Ima could help you with this better than I could…"

But it was as if Savta hadn't heard, or wasn't paying attention. She piled together all the pictures of Shloime and began to arrange them in the album, one next to the other.

"You have to find pictures of when he was really tiny," Saba advised her from his seat next to the table. "I think we have a picture from his *bris*. That should be the first picture."

Shaya felt an irrepressible quiver run from his toes to his knees. This was it. The truth was about to be revealed. There was no going back.

• • •

## >>JERUSALEM, 1991

A private investigator cost a fortune. Both Shaya and Chana knew that.

"We have money put away for emergencies. I don't know a bigger emergency than your brother and his wife flying off in middle of the night and disappearing without a trace."

Chana was sunk in thought. Shaya had always been the thrifty one, while she was quick to spend. But now it seemed to her that he was being too hasty. Maybe there were things that they themselves could discover, even without a private investigator? Maybe specifically because they were family, there were things that they could get to, that someone from the outside – no matter how professional – couldn't?

"You really think we've exhausted all avenues?"

"I think that there are no avenues," Shaya rejoined, helplessly. "A man and his wife pick up and disappear. They give us not one word of explanation. No address, no phone number, not the slightest lead. Where are we supposed to begin to search? Maybe among the bottles and pacifiers that were in Shloimy's bag back then, when they brought him?!"

"I have a feeling that even had they wanted to, they couldn't have given us an address or a telephone number, because they had none," Chana commented. "But I have a different idea."

"Let's hear."

"We can check the phone calls that they made in the last few days before they left."

He heard. There was something to what she was saying.

"And how will we check? The conversations weren't recorded."

"True, but maybe we can get the numbers and see if we recognize any of them. And even if we don't, we can call them and get some sort of lead."

Shaya digested her words quietly. It was in interesting idea, but still too vague. Not too practical.

"How will we get the numbers?"

"We'll ask Bezeq." It was so plain to her.

"And why should Bezeq tell us?"

"Why not? Why should they mind?"

Shaya sighed. "No one minds anything, Chana. Everyone loves us and is desperate only to help us. But there are rules, and they have to be followed. I think you can only get a printout from Bezeq if you own the line. And we don't."

"So we have to arrange that Bezeq should give it to us, too."

"Oh, Chana, it's a pity you're not running the world."

"I've heard of instances where they've entered someone else's phone."

"So did I. Someone particular did it. It's called the police."

• • •

## >>JERUSALEM, 2007

Mrs. Fuchsman sat by the large table in the dining room. An open notebook lay next to her. It was almost new, but a respectable number of lines had already been filled with endless lists. A wedding was such an exciting event. Was that why she was swamped with so many errands?

True, Suri was the Fuchsman's oldest daughter, and Devorah had no more experience marrying off children than did Chana Bleich, but she knew from her friends that it was an all-encompassing project with an endless amount of details to be seen to.

At that hour of the evening, when all the children were asleep, and her husband hadn't yet come home, she finally had a bit of quiet to begin organizing the list of jobs before her.

They had to sew lots of clothes; to find, of course, an apartment for the young couple; to set it up with furniture and appliances; to reserve a caterer; arrange flowers…

But they couldn't start anything without a date.

Devorah peeked at her watch. It was quite late, but not too late to pick up the phone and call the *mechutanim* and finally settle this important issue.

"Hello, good evening," the voice of her *mechuteniste*, Chana, sounded definitely awake.

After the required pleasantries, Devorah Fuchsman got straight to the point. She explained the importance of the matter in three sentences, and when she finished, she waited for a "yes", or "um", but none was forthcoming.

"Mrs. Bleich?"

"Yes, you can call me Chana… just, my husband isn't home, and I can't decide anything like this without him."

Was Devorah only imagining the sudden tension in the conversation?

"I understand… when will he return?"

"I don't know… he'll be back very late tonight." Shaya and Shloime had gone to Kiryat Gat. Who knew when they would return. She was just sitting there on the couch, saying *Tehillim*, as far removed from sleep as if it was first thing in the morning.

"I understand…" It seemed to Devorah Fuchsman that she understood another thing or two, such as that Mrs. Bleich would keep manufacturing excuses, if she'd only continue asking her about the date.

"So we can discuss it tomorrow evening," she said.

"Could be," Chana replied. Shaya had called her and very briefly told her that the *tena'im* had been pushed up to the next evening. It was interesting how calmly the very organized Mrs. Fuchsman had received that bit of news, and why she wasn't saying anything about it.

"Fine," Devorah felt she had to say, "It's not really urgent. We can speak next week, too, after the *tena'im*."

But, to her surprise, Mrs. Bleich had what to say about that, as well.

"I'm not sure. Next week my husband is traveling to America."

"Oh my, what a crowded schedule," Mrs. Fuchsman said in wonder. "I assume he's traveling in connection to the wedding?"

"Yes." Definitely. True, not directly connected, but definitely strongly connected.

"For a few weeks, I assume?"

"I don't know."

Devorah Fuchsman tried to understand. "You don't know how long he'll be away?"

"No."

"He has a lot of things to take care of, I understand." Devorah wasn't so sure anymore that she understood.

"Yes," Chana said wearily, "a whole lot…"

• • •

## >>KIRYAT GAT, 2007

Saba rose from his chair. Only Shaya remained sitting by the table, his face turned towards the wall. Most definitely not towards Shloime, though his desire to see his face was fierce.

"Here," Saba said, stooping over the album, "This is the first picture of Shloime'le, from his *bris*."

Shloime had never seen any picture from his *bris*. Ima always lamented the expensive camera that Uncle Tzvi – Aunt Gitty's husband – had used to record the entire event. After the *se'uda*, it had simply disappeared, with the film of pictures inside. Not one picture remained, Ima said regretfully, from the exciting event.

And now, interestingly enough, it seemed that there were pictures from Saba and Savta's camera! How could it be that they had never shown them to him?!

He saw a tiny, red baby, swallowed up by a giant white pillow, lying on the knees of an elderly, distinguished looking Rav. Next to him stood someone entirely unfamiliar to Shloime, crowned with *tallis* and *tefillin*.

He lifted his head and gave Saba a questioning look.

"Are you sure this is a picture from my *bris*?"

Shloime was confused. Someone was making a mistake. At his *bris*, his father should have been wearing *tallis* and *tefillin*, nobody else. Or maybe he wasn't so well-versed in all the *minhagim*?

Savta looked at Saba. Saba looked at Shaya. Shaya lowered his gaze.

"Yes, Shloime," Shaya finally said, his voice hoarse. "We're sure."

"But that can't be." Shloime looked for a date on the picture. If that red baby was him, the date on the picture should be eight days after his birthday. But the camera that had taken the picture, like most cameras then, didn't have the date function.

"Who is this man in *tallis* and *tefillin*?" Shloime tried to understand what was going on.

"His name is Naftali Bleich. He's my brother." True, Shaya had planned that his parents, who weren't in the eye of the storm like he and Chana were, would help him with the difficult job of setting the facts straight before Shloime. When it came down to it, however, the two of them sat dumbly on the couch, leaving him no choice but to answer.

"Your *brother*???"

Shloime knew that his father had a sister. Aunt Gitty. He knew that his Kiryat Gat grandparents had two children, not three.

"Abba, you have a brother?! But who is he? Where is he?! How come you never told me...???"

Either Shloime still didn't make the connection between this brother and himself, or he was trying to bury it with a thousand questions.

Shaya didn't know how, but at one point he found himself sitting opposite Shloime, with the two of them alone in the room.

It was just the two of them.

Shloime held the picture in his hand, looking from it to his father, and back again.

"So this *bris* is the *bris* of this Naftali's son?"

"Correct."

"This is m-my *bris*...?"

Shaya nodded. Slowly. Up-down. Up. Down.

Later, the two of them sat in the car. All was dark. Shloime was quiet. The silence stretched endlessly. Shaya recognized his son's body language. His lips pressed in a thin line, his head slightly inclined, one finger playing with one of his *peyos* – it was as if he was wearing a large "Do Not Disturb" sign.

Shaya turned the steering wheel with his left hand, and with his right, rummaged among the tapes. He had the tapes of a chazzan that Shloime enjoyed a lot.

"Not now," Shloime requested. "Please."

"There's a bag of cookies on the back seat," Shaya tried.

He gave up, and the car moved smoothly towards the highway leading to Jerusalem. The quiet, broken only by the low hum of the motor, bothered him.

"Tell me about Naftali," Shloime requested.

• • •

## >>HAIFA, 1991

Shaya was beginning to get annoyed. What kind of husband was he that listened to each capricious idea that fell into his wife's head? Chana spoke of a printout of outgoing calls. It was a good idea. The telephone company categorically refused to give him the printout. He thought to give up the idea, to try a different direction, but Chana dug in her heels.

"Go there," she said, "to their house. Feel about. Maybe

you'll find some papers with telephone numbers written on them. Maybe a list of errands to be done. Something. We've waited enough. We've waited a long time for a sign of life from them – in vain. Now it's time to act."

He didn't think that "to act" meant to poke around the empty apartment like a cat looking for some leftover food, but she claimed that every amateur investigator knew that the first place to search was the last place where the person who had disappeared had been.

So what did he do? He didn't know why, but he simply picked himself up and went. The drive from Jerusalem to Haifa afforded him time to build his hopes, which were all dashed by the two rounds he made of the rooms in the apartment.

There was nothing there. The previous visit, he had more or less tidied the mess, and now he regretted it. Had he been smarter, he would have looked for significant clues before straightening up the place.

Under the telephone, on a small shelf, lay a small personal telephone book. Shaya leafed through it. Nothing unusual. There were the phone numbers of the entire family, the dentist, and work. There were no stray notepapers. Rochel had been an extremely tidy woman.

He snapped the phone book shut in annoyance. *Why, Chana, why did you send me here? To waste my time…?*

He returned to the living room, where all the folders of documents, which he had combed thoroughly the last time he came, were. Should he open the cabinet again, and waste more time searching after the wind…?

Here was the wind. Here it was.

At the back of the binder holding the telephone bills, there were sets of papers stapled together in perfect order. Every two months, Naftali had received, apparently by his request, a printout of the incoming and outgoing calls from the telephone company. Thorough man that he was! He never paid a phone bill without first going over all the calls and noting to himself with whom he spoke too long, in order to balance the next bill.

Shaya flipped through the papers. The last printout Naftali received was dated two months before he left. That printout wouldn't help him much. A printout of the last few days would be much more focused. But there was no such printout. Naftali couldn't have filed it when it came, because he was already gone.

So where was the printout now?

Shaya tapped his forehead. Silly question.

As if shot from a cannon, he burst from the house into the stairwell. He sprinted down to the ground floor, and from there, one more flight. This visit, and last visit, he had entered the building from the main entrance, while the mail boxes were located by the back, lower entrance.

The mail box was full, but not overflowing, as a box that hadn't been emptied in an entire year should have been. One of the more considerate neighbors had realized, apparently, that the owners of the box were absent, and decided to gather the mail for them until they should return.

Shaya stuck his fingers into the box, and pulled out what was there.

A gas bill. An envelope from the insurance company. Advertisement brochures. An electric bill. Shaya slit open the electric bill. The neighbor seemed to have been satisfied gathering the mail that was scattered about the box, but hadn't tried to remove the mail that had been stuck inside when the box had still been empty. The electric bill was dated exactly one year ago.

There was something else in the box. A large envelope. Shaya's heart pounded furiously.

It was a telephone bill. Shaya tore open the envelope and

removed a thick sheaf of papers. He put the bill aside and took only the papers that bore the heading "outgoing calls".

His heart racing, Shaya flew up the steps and reentered Naftali's apartment. He slammed the door behind him and placed the pile of letters and papers on the table.

He riffled wildly through the papers. He then sat on the edge of a chair in order to do the job levelheadedly. Nothing was going to explode from the papers. At the very most, he would find some unfamiliar phone numbers that wouldn't teach him a thing.

He took the last page. There was a chart showing, next to each number dialed, the date and time of the call, and the duration. Shaya looked at the date of the last call.

One day. One day before Naftali and Rochel flew off and disappeared into thin air. He checked a few lines above the call, and found that on that day many calls had been made to certain numbers, but none of them were overseas.

He tried calling Chana from the house phone, in order to share his findings with her, but the line was disconnected. *Nu*, of course. The phone bills had continued to arrive, even in the owners' absence, demanding payment for the maintenance of the line. But there was no one to pay. The debt swelled. Had Naftali taken problems like this into account when he upped and left? If not, was it possible that from then until now he hadn't given it a thought? If so, what on earth had pushed him to fly off in the dead of night, tossing his entire life over his shoulder?!

Shaya put the papers in his bag. He ran his eyes over the house one last time, wondering when his next visit would be, and quietly locked the door.

Was the lead they were seeking, he thought, as he strode briskly down the street, waiting among those papers…?

...

## >>JERUSALEM, 2007

Shloime stood facing his parents. He knew that their time was short. In another minute, the *mechutanim* would come over to say good-bye, and his father would once again return to his everyday affairs. His younger brothers and sisters, busy with a merry game of tag around the hall, could also approach at any minute.

An onlooker would see the most natural picture in the world – the *chosson* going over to his parents at the end of the *tena'im*, to exchange impressions and good wishes.

"Ima?"

For the first time since the previous day, Chana stood face to face with Shloime. She couldn't look at him directly, at the boy who, for eighteen years, had thought he was hers. What was he feeling now? Was he confused? Uncomfortable? Perhaps angry that they had kept the truth from him for so many years? And maybe, as she wished to hope, he was filled with feelings of gratitude…?

Last night, even before Shloime and Shaya returned from Kiryat Gat, exhaustion had overwhelmed her. She had prepared a plate of cookies for Shloime in his room, along with a hot drink. A few minutes before she fell asleep, she heard the door open and Shloime drop like a rock into his room. Shaya, too, dropped into his old armchair, drank boiling hot coffee and filled the ashtray. Filled it and filled it.

She knew that Shloime didn't sleep the entire night. His bed, which he stubbornly refused to switch for a larger, more comfortable one, creaked noisily. Occasionally, Chana woke up and looked at the clock, not understanding what had woken her at three, at four, at five. Until she heard the creaking.

At five thirty in the morning she heard the door close gently. Shloime had gone to *daven*, and from there to yeshiva. Only towards evening did he return home, to get ready for the *tena'im*, and then Chana was busy, or tried very hard to be busy with every technical thing that would prevent her from directly facing Shloime.

She imagined that, sooner or later – probably sooner – Shloime would have a conversation with her. He would initiate it. It wouldn't be an easy conversation for Chana. It would be full of memories. Full of tears. She wouldn't initiate it. It was enough that she would have to go through it.

Shloime, too, lowered his gaze. The hall's bright lights shone on the gleaming floors.

Eighteen years. Almost his entire life. For eighteen years he had been sure that he was the oldest son of Shaya and Chana Bleich, his dear parents to whom he owed the world. And suddenly he finds out, in a very well planned conversation, that his parents were really his uncle and aunt. A very dear uncle and aunt, an uncle and aunt who were like parents, but only an uncle and aunt.

Last night (When had it been? He hadn't slept the entire night, or at any point during the following day), he had driven with his father. A long, nocturnal drive, from Kiryat Gat to Yerushalayim. Abba had told him all that he needed to know.

At first, he wasn't capable of speaking. He had always known that he was reserved. That wasn't why he was quiet, though. Rather, it was because something enormous was sticking in his throat. It was the shock.

"Naftali is my brother," Abba said, "my dear, beloved brother, my sweet brother. We don't know where he is today. *Halevai* that we did."

"Oh, so he wasn't *niftar*? And my mother?!"

Shloime was taken aback to see his father take his hand off the steering wheel for a second and pass his sleeve over his face.

"No, he wasn't *niftar*. At least not that we know of. It's eighteen years already since we've heard from him. From the day they left you with us, we haven't seen or heard from them again. Ever."

"So where are they…?!" Shloime didn't realize that he was shouting.

"I told you, Shloime'le. *Halevai* that we knew."

"How could such a thing be???" Shloime's voice rocked the car.

"It can't be," Shaya replied. "If someone would have told me such a story, I wouldn't have believed him. The problem is, it's my story. Mine and my brother's, whom a day doesn't go by without my thinking of him…"

"But a thousand things could have happened to them in the meantime. They could have circled the world three times and had ten children. And in all this time they didn't pick up the phone even once, didn't send a letter, a message, regards, something…!" Shloime tried to forcibly wring from his father that which he absolutely couldn't give him, even with all his good will.

"Nothing, Shloime'le. Zero. There could be two reasons for this – one bad, and the second terrible. The first could be that because of the reason that they fled, they couldn't make contact in order not to incriminate themselves, or in order not to be discovered, or something like that.

"The second reason could be – and I hope and pray, and beg *HaKadosh Boruch Hu* that it's only a bad dream – that they are no longer with us. Because if I was the father of a two year old child whom I left behind, I would have dug a tunnel all the way to *Eretz Yisroel* to get to him. If this reason is incorrect – and *halevai* that it is incorrect – then they must be sitting there, against their will, thinking about you every minute, yearning – yet chained…"

# CHAPTER 6

Shloime looked right and left. No one was in hearing distance, but what he was about to say was worth another check that truly no one could hear.

"I thought that maybe it's possible to go back in memories," he said quietly, almost in a whisper. At first, Shaya and Chana didn't understand what he was saying, and their expressions said as much.

"I mean…" Shloime said and was immediately quiet, as one of the waiters was crossing the hall right near them, "I mean that it's possible to try and refresh my memory. I don't remember – that is, I know I don't remember, but maybe there are ways to retrieve things that I knew at a young age. Before I was two."

Chana looked at him with round, wondering eyes. What did the boy mean? To go back? The *tena'im* had just ended, his real life was about to begin – he need only look forward. What did he mean? Which memories? Which memories could be troubling a young *chosson* on the night of his *tena'im*?

"No, he wasn't *niftar*. At least not that we know of. It's eighteen years already since we've heard from him. From the day they left you with us, we haven't seen or heard from them again. Ever."

"So where are they…?!" Shloime didn't realize that he was shouting.

"I told you, Shloime'le. *Halevai* that we knew."

"How could such a thing be???" Shloime's voice rocked the car.

"It can't be," Shaya replied. "If someone would have told me such a story, I wouldn't have believed him. The problem is, it's my story. Mine and my brother's, whom a day doesn't go by without my thinking of him…"

"But a thousand things could have happened to them in the meantime. They could have circled the world three times and had ten children. And in all this time they didn't pick up the phone even once, didn't send a letter, a message, regards, something…!" Shloime tried to forcibly wring from his father that which he absolutely couldn't give him, even with all his good will.

"Nothing, Shloime'le. Zero. There could be two reasons for this – one bad, and the second terrible. The first could be that because of the reason that they fled, they couldn't make contact in order not to incriminate themselves, or in order not to be discovered, or something like that.

"The second reason could be – and I hope and pray, and beg *HaKadosh Boruch Hu* that it's only a bad dream – that they are no longer with us. Because if I was the father of a two year old child whom I left behind, I would have dug a tunnel all the way to *Eretz Yisroel* to get to him. If this reason is incorrect – and *halevai* that it is incorrect – then they must be sitting there, against their will, thinking about you every minute, yearning – yet chained…"

# CHAPTER 6

Shloime looked right and left. No one was in hearing distance, but what he was about to say was worth another check that truly no one could hear.

"I thought that maybe it's possible to go back in memories," he said quietly, almost in a whisper. At first, Shaya and Chana didn't understand what he was saying, and their expressions said as much.

"I mean…" Shloime said and was immediately quiet, as one of the waiters was crossing the hall right near them, "I mean that it's possible to try and refresh my memory. I don't remember – that is, I know I don't remember, but maybe there are ways to retrieve things that I knew at a young age. Before I was two."

Chana looked at him with round, wondering eyes. What did the boy mean? To go back? The *tena'im* had just ended, his real life was about to begin – he need only look forward. What did he mean? Which memories? Which memories could be troubling a young *chosson* on the night of his *tena'im*?

Shaya thought he was beginning to understand. It was a good idea, a huge idea. An idea that was a bit fuzzy about the edges. A good idea, though, is the kind of thing that's always refreshing.

"I need an explanation, Shloime," Chana said sharply.

"I mean regarding the past, the… regarding all that we don't know, Ima. About all that was, about my parents that ---"

Chana was quiet. Only yesterday Shloime had fallen into the eye of the storm, and already he was having ideas and making plans?

"There is something, a way to bring forth existing memories that a person doesn't remember. There is such a treatment. Maybe they'll manage to retrieve from my brain memories of those days and then we'll have some information. Look, there's no document anywhere, or letter, and no one knows what really happened and why they suddenly ran away. And where. Maybe it's in my memory…"

"You mean – *hypnosis*?" Chana's eyes grew rounder and rounder.

• • •

## >>JERUSALEM, 1991

"Are you going to dial?"

The telephone was on the table. On a fresh, white paper, Chana had written the last phone numbers that had been dialed from Naftali and Rochel's house, as they appeared on the print-out. Soon she would prepare a folder, brown and new, put these papers inside and write "Naftali and Rochel" on it in thick black marker.

"I should dial? Really?"

He had traveled to Haifa and back in order to get these phone numbers. Now, when they were lying on his table, he drew back in hesitation.

"I think it's worth it," Chana said calmly. "What could happen? The worst is an alligator will run along the line and bite you. We've known worse than that."

Shaya knew he wasn't afraid of the alligator. He was afraid to touch the lead that would possibly connect him to his brother. He was afraid of what might be said to him there, on the other end of the line, good or otherwise.

"Zero three," Chana intoned, mimicking the talking clock, "five seven, seven two, two five."

"Stop," Shaya said in annoyance. Chana got the hint and left to the kitchen. He preferred to do it when it felt right to him, without pressure. She had nothing to do in the kitchen. The sinks were clean, as always; lunch was cooking. Even the window was polished. She sat down on one of the chairs and waited.

She heard the telephone beep. One beep, and another beep. Chana counted eight beeps and her breathing quickened.

"Hello," she heard Shaya's voice, struggling to remain steady. "With whom am I speaking?"

Somebody said something.

"My name is Yeshaya. I'm just ---"

Shaya was quiet again. Whoever was on the other end seemed to have cut him off.

"Yeshaya Cohen," he said.

Another question. It sounded more like an investigation.

"Fine, I'm sorry. I guess I got the wrong place. Thank you."

Shaya put down the receiver and Chana flew into the living room.

"We made a mistake," he said. "We should have first checked out whose number it is. I can't ask anything or reveal any details to someone I don't know, who maybe isn't connected to the matter at all, and who might harm me or Naftali, or both of us."

"But how will we discover whose number it is," Chana sighed, "without saying who we are and the reason we're asking? Things are getting complicated again."

The two of them sat in silence. He waited for her to come up with some brilliant idea that would pave their way out of the predicament. She was hoping that he would pull some rabbit out of his hat, but the hat was hanging in the hallway, with only an old lining peeking out of it.

"We need to get our hands on two things," she said wearily. "The name and address of the number's owner. Even the name could be enough for us. Even if his name is Levy, with some tedious legwork we can find the Levy of this number in the 03 area."

"And if the apartment is rented? And if he moved? There are a thousand possibilities."

But there was one more possibility that they didn't take into account.

...

## >>JERUSALEM, 2007

There are many things one could speak about on the way back from a *tena'im*. One could speak about the great excitement; about the guests, who came and who was missing; even about the food, and how much was left and where to store the leftovers.

Shloime and his parents returned home. They had sent the other children ahead. At first, the streets were teeming, but the closer they got to the edge of the city, the streets became darker and quieter.

The three walked in silence.

"We'll make every effort," Shaya tried, "that we haven't yet made – if there is such a

thing – to locate your parents, Shloime. I understand your

feelings. You want to turn the world over, and perhaps you could. But I'm not sure it's worth it."

Chana slanted a quick look at Shloime. He looked like a good boy who mistakenly got entangled in the wrong story. A determined sort of good boy, though, who was telling himself that if he's already involved in the mystery – he'll do anything to solve it.

"One time," Shaya said, "I'll tell you a few stories about what we did to turn over the world. We almost succeeded, and then we feared that the world would bury us underneath it…"

Shloime was quiet. He twisted the new gold watch he had received around his wrist. He hadn't even set it yet. What time was it then in the place where his parents were – his parents, about whom he had heard only yesterday, and for whom today he was already pining…?

"We'll think again together," Shaya promised. "You have a big advantage over us. You want what's best for your parents even more than us, and you're also young. Youth – means full of energy."

"Also a bit rash," Chana commented wisely.

"Oh, don't worry," Shaya said. "Shloime won't do anything without first consulting with us. He's relied on us all these years. I hope he doesn't plan to start doubting…"

"*Chas v'shalom,*" Shloime said.

"Shloime, you do believe that we love you and want what's best for you, no?" Shaya glanced at him.

"Oh, of course." Shloime stopped twisting his *peyos* a minute.

Again it was quiet.

Chana wanted to ask Shloime to promise that he wouldn't do a thing without their approval. Or at the very least, without first letting them know. If she would ask, Shloime would do it. But she didn't ask. This boy of hers, walking so close to her on the sidewalk, with the same clothing and the same movements as always, had suddenly become a stranger.

• • •

## >>JERUSALEM, 1991

Chana would soon return. That would be wonderful, since little Faigie was screaming non-stop, and Shloimy, asleep in his bed, was beginning to move around. It was impossible to expect him to continue sleeping when his little sister was making so much noise.

Shaya took Faigie into his arms. Maybe she had a stomach-ache? Maybe it was something else. He went into the hallway on his way to the kitchen.

Ah, he heard footsteps. It was surely Chana coming. Shaya went, holding the wailing girl, over to the door. He almost turned the handle, but the footsteps stopped and no one tried to enter. Meaning, it wasn't Chana. What a shame.

Shaya went to the kitchen to prepare a bottle of milk. When he returned to the hallway, again trying to make out Chana's redeeming footsteps, he found a white envelope on the floor.

Together with Faigie, he bent down and picked up the envelope. It hadn't been there before. Had the wind blown it there from the shelf of documents? He glanced over his shoulder. The curtain was still. There wasn't even a breeze.

The envelope was completely white. There was no sender or addressee written on it. No stamp. Nothing.

Shaya wasn't used to people shoving envelopes under his door. And for some reason, it didn't enter his mind to flinch – even for a second. He sat down on the couch, sitting a winded Faigie on his lap, and deftly opened the envelope.

**STOP SEARCHING FOR**
**NAFTALI AND ROCHEL BLEICH.**

That was it.

Shaya turned the note over, searching for some sort of sign. He held it up to the light, but there was nothing, other than what was written very clearly.

The letters were printed. There was no greeting. No signature. Nothing…!

Had he had a bit of experience, he wouldn't have touched the envelope and paper with his bare hands, in order to be able to lift from them fingerprints that would take him one giant step forward.

That's how Chana found him, sitting stunned on the couch, the letter in one hand, and the other hand supporting Faigie, who had fallen asleep on his shoulder.

"This is someone very clever," she said, her face a bit pale.

"Clever? It's clever to write such a note?"

"No. If he noticed that we're searching for Naftali and Rochel, despite the fact that that we told absolutely no one about the search, he must have long arms. The truth is, Shaya, it's beginning to scare me."

"There's nothing to be afraid of, Chana," he said automatically, though some color drained from his face, too.

• • •

## >>JERUSALEM, 2007

It was a modest waiting room, with two chairs upholstered in blue. Shloime sat down on one of them and took out a small pocket *Gemara*. Not for long.

A man of average height, his hairline receding and his demeanor inviting, came out to him.

"You are Shlomo Bleich," he said, and stuck out his hand. "I'm very pleased to meet you. You already impressed me on the telephone. You can come in."

Shloime, if he had expected to see a dim room with pictures of the heavenly spheres hanging on the walls, was proven wrong. The room more resembled a lawyer's office than that of a psychologist who would soon hypnotize him.

The psychologist placed a large sheet of paper on the table and picked up his pen.

"Tell me about yourself," he requested.

Shloime leaned back in his chair.

"I can say a lot about myself. Why don't you ask me direct questions so we'll get to the point more quickly?"

"This is the point." Shloime gathered that the smile was a steady fixture on the psychologist's face. "I want to hear what you have to say about yourself. It's important to me."

Shloime removed his pen from his pocket and began to play with it. Where should he start? From the beginning, or should he start from the end and go backwards?

"The reason I came to you is because of some huge changes in my life recently," he said. "First of all, I got engaged and I'll be getting married in a few months. In middle of all that, I found out that my parents aren't really my parents, but my aunt and uncle. My biological father is my adoptive father's brother."

"Hmm, interesting," the psychologist said, and began to write.

"When I was two years old, my parents suddenly fled Israel, leaving me with my aunt and uncle. They disappeared without a trace. My parents, who tried to find them, were unsuccessful all these years."

"An interesting story," the psychologist remarked, without stopping to write.

"Right now, the main thing I want to do is to try and find my parents – whatever it takes. What I want from you is - - -"

"One minute, one minute," the psychologist interrupted him.

"Let's go in order, my young man. Tell me your first memory."

Shloime stopped. His first memory? He had a few vivid childhood memories, but they weren't in any sort of chronological order. He remembered his *upsherin*, which must have been when he was three, but his first lesson in riding a bike – was that when he was four or five? Before or after the time he locked himself on the porch and couldn't get into the house? When he had two younger siblings or three?

"The order doesn't matter," the psychologist said calmly. "Tell me what comes to mind."

Shloime felt a bit awkward. He, a grown *bochur*, a *chosson*, who generally didn't make small talk, was sitting and telling a stranger what happened to his pants when he climbed a tree for the first time in his life and couldn't get down. And that man was listening carefully and even writing down what he said, as if they were *chiddushei Torah*.

• • •

No one went with Shaya Bleich to the airport to see him off. Not his wife, none of his children. He ran around the terminal, dragging his large suitcase behind him.

What had Chana packed? Everything but the kitchen sink. She was so confused, and felt so helpless; she wanted to pack everything, but didn't know where to start. How long was Shaya going for? It was impossible to know. Where was he going? He was flying to America, but she couldn't know where he would go from there, and when, and what the weather would be like in places that she didn't even know where they were. So what should she put in for him? Warm clothing? Light clothes? A coat? Sunscreen? And what about food? Maybe he wouldn't find kosher food wherever he would be. So what should she pack? Lots of canned goods? Crackers? That's what he would live on? And how much should she pack? How much could he *shlep*?

"Somebody else has to pack your suitcase," she turned, her hands spread in despair.

"Chana, don't get so excited. Meanwhile, I'm going to places that have a concentration of Jews. And even in those places which don't, there are Chabad houses everywhere, with kosher food. And there are clothing stores across the globe. Don't worry. Instead of packing up the entire house, say a few *kapitlach* of *Tehillim*.

But he was also very unsettled. The taxi came to pick him up at eight o'clock in the evening. He said good-bye to the children, trying very hard to make the trip seem like no big deal, making not the slightest mention, of course, of its purpose.

Chana accompanied him downstairs, where Shloime was waiting. He took leave of his father with a fierce hug and tearing eyes.

"*Hatzlacha rabba*," Shloime said over and over. "Hashem should give you loads of *s'yata d'shmaya*. *Bli neder*, I'll go to the Kosel each day."

Shaya tried to move forward to the patiently waiting taxi. Shloime looked at him beseechingly.

"I'll be very happy to hear of any progress, even the tiniest bit."

"And I'll be very happy to tell you, Shloime'le," Shaya promised. He put his suitcase into the trunk.

"You'll be around when I'm gone, right?" he wanted to make sure. "So Ima won't feel alone. You're the oldest. You'll make sure to be around, right?"

Shloime promised. He was the oldest – at least that's what everyone knew.

*Thicker Than Water* << 75

The taxi pulled away. Shloime went upstairs, making sure to wipe any suspicious traces from his face. Chana also went upstairs, and for the next few hours busied herself with every job in the world, urgent and not, in order to calm herself.

"Ima, I think you already cleaned the stove this morning, no?" Shloime came into the kitchen and sat down.

"Could be." He knew the stove was just a means and not the end. "Do you want me to make you something? A sandwich, maybe, or some salad?"

"Yes, Ima," he answered, to her surprise. "I want the biggest salad you can make me, from all that you can tell me about my parents. A hundred stories, a thousand stories. Everything you can tell me, I want to hear."

Chana was taken aback. After some thought, though, she agreed that it was the best thing with which to occupy themselves just then.

"I met your mother when she joined the family, not long after me. Abba is about one year older than Naftali; they were always very close."

She spoke, and the words rang oddly in the kitchen. For years upon years they only spoke about Naftali and Rochel in hushed secrecy, and suddenly now she was sitting and saying those names to Shloime, out loud.

• • •

## >>JERUSALEM, 1991

"So now what?" Chana asked, "We should stop searching?"

"This note," Shaya said thoughtfully, "is, on the one hand, frightening, and encouraging on the other. It seems that our poking around, minor as it was, was quite focused, and whoever was supposed to, felt it and became pressured."

"Who could it be?" Chana was consumed with curiosity. "You think it has anything to do with the telephone call that we made? I can't think of any other possibility. Who could have known about the search and sent us such a firm message?!"

"Maybe it's connected. Maybe not."

They were both quiet. The patter of little feet came from the hallway. Shloimy.

"I can't find him," he wailed. His eyes were puffy, his hair messy.

"Who?" Chana took Shloimy onto her lap and hugged him.

"Meir'ke, my teddy bear. He was lying next to me in bed and now I can't find him."

Together, Chana and Shaya went with Shloimy to his bed. The two felt an especial need, due to the circumstances, to protect him.

"Here's Meir'ke," Shaya picked up the bear from where it had fallen behind the bed. "Lay nicely, teddy, next to Shloimy, and we'll cover you both."

*Halevai we should find your parents so easily*, thought Chana and Shaya, each one separately. Just move something, find, hug, and relax.

# CHAPTER 7

*Daven mincha*. That was the first thing Shaya had to do after extricating himself from the airport. A taxi brought him to the closest Jewish neighborhood and stopped in the middle of the block next to a building that looked like a collection of *shuls*.

Shaya paid and dashed to take his suitcase, sidestepping the driver who wished to help him. It was almost *shki'ah*.

When he entered, stowing his suitcase in a corner, everyone was already standing for *shmoneh esrai*. Shaya found a place for himself and lost himself in prayer, the only familiar thing to him there.

After *davening*, he hurried to collect his suitcase and himself. First thing, he needed to find a place to stay.

An older Jew, short and quick-motioned, caught up to him on his way out, literally in the doorway of the shul.

"A visitor," he said, rather than asked.

"Yes, yes," Shaya replied. "Maybe you know where - - -"

"From *Eretz Yisroel*," the man continued to inform him.

"R' Nachman," someone tall and smiling said from behind them, "this fellow just arrived from the airport. Why not give him a few minutes to breathe before asking him a-l-l of your questions?"

"To breathe? He breathed," R' Nachman rejoined. "I saw that he breathed before I came over to him. So where are you from, eh? Yerushalayim?"

"That's right," Shaya said and pulled up the handle of his large suitcase.

"A collector? You don't look like it. Maybe collecting money for your child's *chasunah*?"

"No," Shaya said. He moved his suitcase a bit.

"You can come to me," R' Nachman offered generously. "All visitors come to me; I have a lot of room in my house."

*No*, Shaya said in his heart. *I prefer to go to a hotel and pay whatever they'll charge me, rather than stay in your house that has a lot of room, but that also has a lot of questions that require a lot of answers that require a lot of energy. That doesn't work for me right now.*

"You did your homework?" R' Nachman continued from where he had left off. "Because, you know," he said secretively, or at least pretended to be secretive, because his voice was loud enough to awaken donors from their grave, "I have a lot of information. Anything you want – or don't want – to know, I know. You know what? I'll tell you something. Just don't tell anyone, you know…"

Against his will, Shaya was drawn after R' Nachman, listening to the story that he must have told thousands of people, who promised not to tell anybody.

While telling the story, which wasn't very interesting, R' Nachman felt a need to point out important landmarks every few yards. "Here, this is where Shloimke Friedman lives, who not so long ago did a *shidduch* with Freilich, wealthy, important people. Everyone's breaking their heads what Freilich found in his son. What he found in Freilich, everyone understands. Everything he doesn't have and never will have. Here's Mordechai Feingold's house. There was lots of money there, until he made a few mistakes and went bankrupt. He sold his house and ran away. He couldn't show his face in *shul*. This is Senderovitz's bakery. Look, look inside. You see the old man? That's him. He built the bakery and kept it going for decades already. He lives from it. Who will take over after a hundred and twenty? He has three sons. Such good-for-nothings, none of them can even roll a *bilke*. This is Eisenshtark's house. The one who had a break-in and they stole from him all the records of all the debts people owed him. He has a *gemach*, you understand? Here, this is the house. You see, here on the corner. No, don't look. They'll say I talk about people..."

Shaya's head moved back and forth like a sprinkler. Eventually he gave up on following R' Nachman's commentary.

"And this," luckily, R' Nachman stopped, "is my house."

R' Nachman's house was large and inviting. The mistress of the house, who, it appeared, was familiar with her husband's habit of bringing home all visitors who popped up in shul, placed a plate of pastries before him and politely asked if he would be staying overnight.

"Of course," R' Nachman said, "and for breakfast."

Shaya realized that he was doomed. He tasted the pastries, and only when his arms leaned on the table and his head fell forward, did he realize how tired he was.

"Have a cup of tea," R' Nachman offered him the thermos. "A cup of tea will revive you. You understand, so Bloom, the ones who live so modestly, and no one knows that they have a chain of hotels and a chain of restaurants and factories – that means, no one knows except for me, of course – moved away. I did a bit of checking. You know, it's not nice to check up on people. But I didn't understand why they moved, so I found out - - -"

Shaya's head fell forward, almost knocking over the cup of tea.

...

## >>JERUSALEM, 1991

"We don't have to stop searching," Shaya said determinedly. "I find this note very encouraging. It tells me that we're on the right path."

"Right and risky."

"For a brother you take risks."

They both knew that. They sat in silence.

"We'll continue searching. We can be more discreet, maybe we'll try a different tack, but we won't stop. We can't. Agree with me that this note tells us that they're in trouble. Someone is keeping very careful watch over them."

She agreed.

"Maybe we should take a private investigator," she said. "After all is said and done, we're not the biggest experts in searches."

"And we'll pay him," he said.

"A fortune," she said.

Again they were both quiet. *When* davening *that money should go to only good things*, she thought, *we mean that it shouldn't go to weird, inexplicable things like this.*

"We'll get the money." Right then he didn't even think about from where.

"And if we don't find them in the end?"

"Why be pessimistic? We do what we can."

"Then the money will go down the drain."

"No. The money will go to our conscience and reassure us

that we did everything possible."

"It's always possible to do more."

"No, not always. There are clear limits what's allowed and what isn't. It's also forbidden to redeem captives for more than they're worth."

"They're not captives."

"Okay, enough," Shaya begged. "I can't talk about this without getting depressed. Without feeling like some fish in the water that lost his fins and can't swim. Please bring me the telephone. I'll speak to a few people and I'll find us a private investigator. It's either now or never."

...

## >>JERUSALEM, 2007

The window in the psychologist's room was covered, of course, with a curtain. It was almost completely opaque. Someone outside couldn't see what was happening inside. And whoever was inside could get only a hint that it was light outside and the world was continuing as usual.

Shloime fingered the couch underneath him. Everything was fine. The psychologist promised him that everything would be fine. Except for a slight fogginess, something akin to waking up from a dream, he felt regular.

"Something to drink, Shlomo?"

"No, thank you very much. Thank you. I'd prefer to address the issue."

"To address the issue," the psychologist murmured after him. "Ahem, the conversation under hypnosis was very interesting, Shlomo. You are an exceptional young man. An intelligent young man. Restrained. Sensitive. Rational."

"Thank you."

"I wrote down, of course, every word that was said in this room - as I told you I would, before the treatment."

"May I have the papers?"

"Are you sure you really want that?"

"I'm positive. Didn't you say before that I'm an intelligent young man?"

"Are you emotionally prepared for every word written here?"

"I hope so. Any particular bombs are supposed to fall on my head?"

The psychologist paused. "There were things that you said which were unclear to me. Perhaps you'll be able to make sense of them, discover what's behind them, and perhaps there will be revelations that will impact you."

"I'm curious. Can you at least give me a hint?"

"We don't work that way, Shlomo. I usually create a printed transcript of the conversation, after I process it, and also add my opinion. Look, let's not be unprofessional about this, Shlomo. We're dealing with the emotions."

"And when can I receive the transcript?"

"At your next visit, Shlomo. I have to prepare it properly. We're not hasty, correct?"

"It's very important to me."

"Oh, of course. I'll be happy to help. Let's meet next week, on whichever day is good for you."

Shloime came out of the building and sank down on a low stone fence nearby. Normally, in the neighborhood where he lived and where his yeshiva was, he wouldn't perch himself on a fence in such an undignified manner. But here, in such a remote neighborhood, he didn't think anyone he knew would pass by. He was able to just sit limply on the stone fence and mull over the secrets he had told the psychologist.

Someone coming down the street behind him noticed the

figure of a yeshiva bochur, in all his glory, sitting on the stone fence. A second's focused gaze, and he continued on. Shloime continued to sit, unaware that certain eyes had photographed him and stored the picture in their memory.

• • •

Yisroel Yitzchok Fuchsman purposely hadn't wanted to learn in the same yeshiva as his brother. Not because he didn't like or admire his brother; quite the opposite. His older brother, Avrohom, was an especially talented boy, as opposed to Yisroel Yitzchok, who knew how to learn and was well liked, but who wasn't particularly brilliant. He could delve deep into the *sugya*, but his wasn't from the sharpest brains in the *shiur*, and he knew it. Not wanting to always stand in his brother's shadow, he chose a different, less prestigious yeshiva for himself where he could grow and stand out in his own way.

His parents honored his decision. There were many yeshivas, almost as many as the types of boys that there were, and each boy found the right place for him. His future brother-in-law, Shloime Bleich, whom everyone couldn't stop praising, also learned in a different yeshiva. His parents stressed time and again that they were choosing a *chosson* for Suri based on the boy himself, and not according to what looks good on the resume, like learning in a specific yeshiva.

Yisroel Yitzchok now climbed the huge marble steps leading to the elite yeshiva in which his brother Avrohom learned. He purposely came then, as his brother would be in the dining room eating lunch, though he knew the topic was important no matter what it was interrupting.

"Fuchsman, you have a guest," one of those sitting around the table noted.

Avrohom rose quickly.

"Yisroel Yitzchok, what's the matter?"

"Let's go outside."

Outside there was nothing. Only a wide street. The two of them walked towards one of the buildings in order to stand in its shade.

"I have some important information," Yisroel Yitzchok said.

"So, let's hear what the secret agent has to report to the Bureau of Intelligence," Avrohom laughed. Yisroel Yitzchok? Information? Important?

"It has to do with Shloime," Yisroel Yitzchok said briefly.

"Shloime? Which Shloime?" For a minute, Avrohom didn't understand what he was talking about.

"Shloime Bleich," Yisroel Yitzchok replied, impatience stealing into his voice. "Shloime, *nu*, Suri's *chosson*…"

As soon as Avrohom realized which Shloime he meant, his face brightened. Ah, what a magnificent *bochur* Shloime Bleich was. His sister, a wonderful girl in her own right, couldn't have found for herself a better *chosson*. A *talmid chochom*, refined, friendly. And not that Avrohom relied on rumor; he himself checked into him, and even after they got engaged, spoke with him many times. Each time anew, he found himself enjoying the knowledge, the intelligence of his future brother-in-law.

"One second, what about Shloime?"

Yisroel Yitzchok huddled closer against the wall of the building. The day before, towards evening, he had an emergency appointment with Dr. Shmidt, the dentist whose clinic was at the opposite end of the city. Numerous times, Yisroel Yitzchok had asked his parents to switch dentists. Not because Shmidt wasn't a good dentist, but because the trip to his clinic was as long as the *galus*.

"Yesterday," Yisroel Yitzchok related, "I left Shmidt right before it got dark, and you can't imagine what I saw."

"A cat," Avrohom attempted.

"Come on, really…"

"Something really way out?"

"Exactly so."

Avrohom tried to think what it could be.

"Shloime," Yisroel Yitzchok intoned.

"Okay," Avrohom said, not understanding what the big issue was, "so you saw Shloime. Did you go over and say hello?"

"Of course not. I passed by behind him. He didn't even know that I saw him."

"Okay," Avrohom said again and glanced at his watch, "I understand that you didn't come here in order to waste my time, Yisroel Yitzchok. What is it that you want?"

• • •

## >>JERUSALEM, 1991

Chana baked two cakes, even though Shaya kept telling her that the food wasn't the point. She put the children to sleep exactly on time, scrubbed the house, and at ten to eight already filled the kettle with water.

"My heart is pounding," she confessed to Shaya, who was roaming the house restlessly.

"Why? He won't investigate you."

"I don't know. A private investigator sounds like somebody you have to be careful of."

"But his name is Mendel Lederman, and he's a pleasant person."

"Shhh, don't speak so loudly. Maybe he's at the door…!"

Lederman truly was pleasant. The *tzitzis* draped over his dumpy figure made him look like the shul's candy man, or, at the very most, a wandering *maggid*. When he came inside, his smile came in with him.

"Mendel," he held out his hand to shake Shaya's.

"*Sholom Aleichem.*" Shaya showed him into the living room, where everything they would possibly need was already on the table.

At first, Chana kept busy in the kitchen. When she came to the living room, however, loaded with a pitcher and glasses, Lederman requested that she stay.

"What we're about to tell you," Shaya began with a deep breath, "isn't known to anyone in the world. Our own parents don't know exactly what happened, and also the parents of - - -"

"Slowly, slowly," Lederman said, and spread a sheet of writing paper before him. He took a pen from behind his ear and uncapped it.

"I know very little about you. Before you start telling me things that no one in the world ever heard or knew, tell me who you are, what you are, what you're looking for in this world and why it's worth it for *HaKadosh Boruch Hu* to leave you here."

Shaya and Chana looked at each other.

"We're very regular people," Shaya said, "and we would never have met you if not - - -"

"You would have never met me," Lederman murmured. "Who promised you? Maybe someone hired me to search for you? Maybe one day I would have stood opposite you and told you that the game was up? Maybe you're starring in one of my big investigations? Be careful of exaggerated self confidence, my friends. You, where do you come from? Tell me everything. Everything that you know about yourself. Also everything that I don't need to know. What do you do when you wake up in the morning?"

Mendel Lederman's booming voice brought a sobbing Shloimy from his bed.

"That's your son?" he asked, after Shloimy went back to bed with a bottle of cocoa.

"Yes. No." Chana said.

"Meanwhile he's our son," Shaya tried to explain briefly. "And that's why - - -"

"Fine, it really doesn't matter whose he is. The main thing is he's a cute kid. He has intelligent eyes. But please, *rabbosai*, we haven't yet started to fill anything in. I have enough to investigate. I don't want to investigate you as well. I want to receive the information that's coming to me. What do you do for a living? What have you always done for a living? Everything, everything matters."

Chana left the room for a minute to bring the cakes. Her head was spinning. This wasn't how she pictured their private investigator. But he came very well recommended.

"Mrs. Bleich?" He called to her to come right back.

• • •

## ≫JERUSALEM, 2007

"I saw Shloime there," Yisroel Yitzchok said, lowering his voice dramatically, "sitting on a fence, as if he was waiting for someone."

"Maybe he was waiting for the bus."

"But there's no bus stop there. I know. I know the place very well," Yisroel Yitzchok said. "And besides, he didn't look at the street, not even once. He just sat there staring into space, like some loafer."

"I see you've managed to analyze him well in the few seconds that you saw him," Avrohom said, a touch annoyed. "Maybe he also had to go to some doctor or another."

"So why didn't he go straight home?"

"Maybe his father was supposed to come pick him up," Avrohom tried lowering the drama. He really didn't understand what the whole big deal was about.

"His father isn't in the country now. He went to America."

"So maybe someone else was supposed to get him." Avrohom looked at his watch again. He wished they would end this pointless discussion of an even more pointless topic. His lunch was getting cold.

"I don't know," Yisroel Yitzchok said, shaking his head. "But something didn't sit right with me. A *bochur* who's a *yorei shomayim* sitting on a fence in such a place, swinging his legs and waiting for someone to come pick him up – it doesn't *klap*."

Avrohom shrugged. "I don't understand. Perhaps my ears aren't so sharp; I don't get what doesn't *klap*. Let the boy live his life in peace and do what's good for him. If his parents are responsible for him, that's enough for me. Everyone has his job. And the two of us, you and I, have to learn, not be busy keeping tabs on people."

"I told Abba and Ima," Yisroel Yitzchok said, as if he hadn't heard Avrohom's last words.

"*Nu*, and what did they say?"

"They *davka* listened to me."

"And now they're very worried?"

"No, not really," Yisroel Yitzchok said, and shifted his disappointed gaze. "I think that they don't fully understand what there is to be afraid of. I know *bochurim* from up close, you understand? I know where such a thing could lead a *bochur*. And this *bochur* is meant to be our Suri's husband."

"You're turning mice into elephants," Avrohom said shortly. "I also know *bochurim*."

"So you don't want to have anything to do with this, I take it?"

Yisroel Yitzchok wanted to know.

"Absolutely not."

"Fine," Yisroel Yitzchok said resolutely, or maybe it was with affront, "I'll deal with it."

# CHAPTER 8

>>JERUSALEM, 1991

Mendel Lederman, private investigator, gathered the papers scattered on the table into a neat pile.

"Is there something you still haven't told me?" he asked, though he had already asked that question at least three times.

Chana and Shaya shook their heads. They had related everything, reliving that abrupt day.

"So I'm free to go now?" he asked. They were already used to his droll nature.

"When will we meet again?" Shaya tried being businesslike.

"In another day or two, year or two, whenever it works out."

Their eyes widened.

"I don't know how this file will roll," he tapped the binder under his arm. "There are things that move quickly and there are things that move slowly. Some things crawl and some don't move at all. I have no way of foreseeing what will happen this time. I do all that I can, recruit the best professionals, use the most advanced methods – and you, my fine people, *daven*. It helps."

• • •

## >>JERUSALEM, 2007

Shloime's behavior that day seemed odd to Chana. He came home, tired and in a rush, went into his room and asked that nobody disturb him. For good measure, he closed the door to the small room and locked it. That wasn't like Shloime, who always had a smile for everyone – certainly for his siblings – and whose door was never closed.

"Shloime?" She knocked hesitantly on the door. "Is everything all right?"

"Everything's wonderful," he said, and she heard the plea in his voice that he be left alone.

Inside the room, after making sure that no one could see him, Shloime closed the shutters and turned on the light. He then took from the inside pocket of his jacket the sheaf of papers he had received from the psychologist.

There were lots of crowded lines. Shloime adjusted his desk lamp and began to read.

The questions asked by the psychologist were in bold type. His answers were in regular type. It was strange to Shloime to read the things he said, to know that he said them, but to not remember it at all.

**"Sit back and relax. Close your eyes. Breathe deeply five times. One. Breathe out, and feel how, with each exhale, your muscles are loosening. Two. Relax your face, your neck, shoulders, that's right. Three, your arms, four… your legs, the soles of your feet until your toes. When I say five, you will be completely relaxed.**

**"Five. Now you are completely relaxed. Let your thoughts**

flow without stopping them. Pay attention to your breathing."

Shloime couldn't help smiling as he imagined himself sitting in the blue armchair and obeying all the instructions.

"I'm going to ask you to tell me what happened on the day that your biological parents brought you to your aunt and uncle's house. Continue to sit quietly. Everything will be under your control. Any time you feel that you don't wish to continue, simply stop. I will count from ten to one. When I reach one, you will be two years old, in the house where your biological parents lived. Nod your head if you agree."

Now, too, Shloime nodded his head without realizing it.

"Ten, nine, eight; you are more and more relaxed; you are completely loose; seven, six, five; more and more. You are sinking deeper and deeper. Four, three; even deeper. Two. And deeper. One. Where are you now?"

"In my room…"

"And what are you doing?"

"I'm lining up my cars. A green car, a blue car, a yellow car, another blue car. Another ye - - -"

"And what else?"

"Ima comes to the room."

"How does Ima look?"

(The psychologist wrote: "Hesitation".)

"She has a robe that's black."

"And if you look a bit higher?"

"She isn't smiling."

• • •

## >>NEW YORK, 2007

When Shaya Bleich woke up, the sun's first rays were shining through the window. He surveyed the room, not understanding where he was.

"Aidel!" He heard grumbling from outside the room. "I can't find my *gartel*. What did you do with it? Again you tied back the gate to the yard so it shouldn't creak?!"

He could hear the lady of the house rushing about, looking for the lost *gartel*. At the same time, it seemed that R' Nachman was searching for the *sefer Ohr Hachaim Hakadosh* in order to learn from it before *davening*, and couldn't find that either.

"Aidel!" He banged on one door and another, looking for his wife, and not finding her as well. "It's impossible like this – that things shouldn't be organized before I go *daven*."

Shaya had the feeling that it wasn't his wife who was responsible for the scattered items, as much as it was the absentmindedness of R' Nachman himself. He deliberated if he should get up and join his host on his way to davening, but the memory of their shared walk the previous day didn't give him much desire.

When he finally left his room, the house was filled with the voices of children. A mug of coffee and some cake were waiting for him on the table, next to the morning paper. Shaya's English wasn't the best. It definitely wasn't good enough to read the newspaper. He moved the paper aside. Underneath was a community telephone book that R' Nachman must have forgotten on the table.

He flipped through the names. Even though everything was written in English, Jewish names aren't hard to read.

Abramov. Brandwein. Deller. A long list of Cohen and Levy. Shaya took another sip of coffee and leafed backwards. Interesting – maybe there was someone there by the name of Bleich?

He pulled the book closer. There was Black. And Bloch. If there was Bleich, it should have been between them. But there wasn't.

A cute boy sat down next to him with a huge bowl of cereal and milk.

"*Du redst Yiddish?*" Shaya turned to him.

The boy shook his head. He understood Yiddish, but English would be easier for him.

"Is there a Bleich family here?"

Bleich, Bleich… the boy strained his memory. There was a Bluth. And a Bloch. He didn't know any Bleich.

"There was a Bleich family here a number of years ago," his mother said from where she was busy next to the oven, "and they left."

Shaya was suddenly wide awake. Maybe this would be a lead?

"Did you know them?" he asked.

"A bit. For a while Mrs. Bleich prepared food for the *chesed* organization that I run. Then she stopped. Their daughter was in nursery with our daughter."

"Do you know where I can reach them?"

She raised an eyebrow. "Their phone number is probably listed in the old phone book. Maybe the people living there now would know where they are. Do you want to call them and ask…?"

• • •

## >>JERUSALEM, 2007

Devorah Fuchsman, the *kallah*'s mother, slammed the door to the taxi and hurried into the house. It had probably been a mistake to decide to sew all the clothes for the wedding instead of buying them. Buying might mean more running around and spending more, but all that paled in comparison to the headache of sewing.

She burst into the house and shut the door with a bang.

"Who's home?"

For a minute there was quiet, and then suddenly the unexpected figure of Yisroel Yitzchok appeared in the doorway of one of the back rooms.

"Yisroel Yitzchok, what are you doing home at this hour?!"

"I was waiting for you."

She put her packages down on the couch in the living room. "Each thing today took longer than I planned. And we still haven't gone to look for a suit for you, Yisroel Yitzchok, and for Avrohom and Uri. There's no time for anything, and the *chasunah* keeps getting closer."

Yisroel Yitzchok went to the kitchen and brought a drink for his mother.

"When you have a chance, Ima, I wanted to talk to you."

"Now is as good a time as any, Yisroel Yitzchok. I assume it's something important if you came home special from yeshiva and waited for me."

Yisroel Yitzchok wasn't sure how to begin. He wandered around the table and finally sat down on a chair and played with the edge of the tablecloth.

"It has to do with Suri's *chosson*, Shloime."

Her face tensed. "It seems to me that we spoke about this already, Yisroel Yitzchok – Abba and you and me – and we asked you to leave it alone."

"But I can't leave it alone, Ima," he said heatedly, "It bothers me all the time. I'm really worried. You took for Suri a *chosson* about whom you heard wonderful things – and what if the praise was exaggerated? What if his friends just wanted to be good to him? Such things have happened…"

She tried to organize her words.

"Yisroel Yitzchok, listen carefully. Abba did not choose Suri's *chosson* based on rumors. You can rely on your father. When it comes to business deals, he always checks fifteen times; all the more so when it comes to a *chosson* for Suri, he checked one hundred and fifty times.

Yisroel Yitzchok picked at the tablecloth.

"Soon is the *chasunah*, Ima. And the closer it gets, the more I'm afraid. I want to make sure that everything is really all right, and that I'm worried for no reason. Do you let me?

"What does that mean?"

"I want to do a test. Something that will make it one hundred percent clear that there's nothing to worry about."

Devorah shrugged her shoulders. A test – how exactly would he do a test? And what exactly would it entail? Would he secretly follow their dear *chosson*'s every move twenty four hours a day? Set up ambushes? She didn't like any of that at all.

"I don't allow anything, Yisroel Yitzchok. We believe one hundred percent that Shloime is a choice *bochur*. Suitable for Suri. Suitable for our family. What kind of nonsense has gotten into your head?!"

"Ima, let me," Yisroel Yitzchok literally begged, "just so I should be calm. And that you should be calm…"

• • •

Shloime folded back page number four and went on to page number five.

It was all baloney. It had seemed like such a good idea at first. He believed that the hypnosis would bring forth great secrets, but he had learned almost nothing new from the transcript of the conversation.

He couldn't say that the psychologist didn't do a good job. But it isn't possible to retrieve from the brain what isn't there. And it seemed that the memories from before he was two, with all of their effort, simply weren't in the brain. They hadn't been forgotten; they had simply never been imprinted.

What the psychologist had thought was a revelation was really a playback of the stories that his mother had told him over the past few days of their sudden leaving of home; of his parents, who had been (and still were – still were!) refined, pleasant people, for whom this whole story was completely out of character; of the welcome in a new, strange place.

There were a few interesting details. It would be worth checking with Ima if they were correct. Did his father have a black, trimmed beard? Had there been an electric train in his room? Was there a large picture of an important Rav hanging next to the door to their house?

But all those details didn't really matter. If they were true, it would be interesting, at most. It wouldn't, however, bring him even one step closer to his goal.

Ima said that his parents had brought him after midnight, when he was sleeping. But if the description in the transcript was correct, then he must have been awake when leaving the house, and had fallen asleep on the way.

**"What is Ima doing, with the big bag on her shoulder?"**
"She's standing next to the door."
**"And what is Abba doing?"**
"He's in the room."
**"What does Ima say?"**
"Don't know. She's not saying anything."
**"And what do you think will happen now?"**
"Ima will open the door."
**"And Abba, what does he say?"**
"Abba is standing next to the closet and takes something."
**"What does he take? Is there any way you can know?"**
"No."

**"And afterwards?"**
"Ima goes down the steps. She holds my hand."
**"And Abba?"**
"Don't know."
**"And afterwards, during the ride, Abba is there?"**
"Yes, he's there."
**"Does he say something?"**
"Yes."
**"Do you remember what he says?"**
(The psychologist wrote: "quiet", "increased concentration".)
"I don't understand what he says…"
**"Do you remember the words? Or maybe even a few words?"**
"He says… uh, he says…"

• • •

## >>JERUSALEM, 2007

There was no way, but it happened.

Yisroel Yitzchok couldn't believe his eyes. He sat on the bus, in the third seat next to the window, because his favorite spot – the front seat – was taken when he got on.

At the central bus station many people got on, most of them adults. The driver, as usual, urged everyone to get on, closed the doors and then took the fares while driving.

Yisroel Yitzchok didn't usually look at the faces of those entering the bus, especially at the central bus station. One after the other, there passed by him various sorts of shoes, baskets and bags, and eventually also a long, black coat.

He lifted his eyes, but the owner of the coat had already passed him. He turned around.

It was him, without a doubt. Shloime Bleich. It was impossible to mistake him. His blond hair beneath his hat, his height.

His straight posture. The bus was full, and there was no place for Shloime to sit. He stood, holding on to a pole, between a shopping cart and a stroller, showing his full profile to his future brother-in-law – though he was completely unaware that they were sharing a bus.

*Very good, R' Shloime Bleich. We'll have an interesting ride, and what follows will be even more interesting.*

Today the dentist would have to accept the non-arrival of the nice Fuchsman boy for treatment. There were more important things in the world.

...

## >>NEW YORK, 2007

When R' Nachman returned from *davening* and all that went along with it – long, important conversations with whomever he chanced upon, a visit to the bakery to pick up some danishes for breakfast and updates on all the news, even tomorrow's – he finally sat down to breakfast with his new guest from *Eretz Yisroel*.

Shaya had already finished *bentching* and was trying to plan his next steps, but that didn't bother R' Nachman. He spread the newspaper out on the table and shared with his guest every piece of news that could possibly interest him.

"They say the situation by you is catastrophic, what?"

"It's hard," Shaya agreed. "But it's *Hashem's* land. There's *hashgachah pratis* every step of the way."

"The government is limping along, and nothing's moving, eh? And the Arabs, what's with them? You're from Yerushalayim, right? There are terrorist attacks there every other day. We over here know and hear everything."

Shaya sighed.

"Everything is expensive by you, that we know," R' Nachman continued, "and they also have stores open on *Shabbos*."

Shaya shifted in his chair. "*Eretz Yisroel* is the place to live."

"So what are you looking for here?!"

The question caught Shaya unawares.

"You didn't come to raise money," R' Nachman said and mixed another spoon of sugar into his tea.

"How do you know?"

"Because this is not how you come raise money. Whoever comes to raise money comes prepared. He arranges a place to stay in advance. He sets up a driver; starts to work. He doesn't waste a minute. And you sit here like the whole world is waiting for you."

Shaya decided not to reveal, definitely not at that point, the real reason he came to the U.S.

"I came to tour," he said.

"To tour," R' Nachman repeated after him. "The *meraglim* who went to tour the Land got punished for it. And what do you have to tour here? Didn't you say before that the place for a Jew to live is Eretz Yisroel?"

Shaya hesitated.

"There are all kinds of constraints," he finally said.

"Constraints, shmonstraints. Listen R' Yid, from me you won't hide anything, or my name isn't R' Nachman. What's this telephone number written here?" He jabbed at the piece of paper on which his wife had written the phone number of the Bleich family that had lived in the neighborhood some years earlier.

"Ah, this? This is the number of a family Bleich that once lived here. Any Jew, whether his name is Weiss, Wolf or Cooperwasser, anywhere he goes, the first thing he does is look for relatives, no?"

• • •

## >>JERUSALEM, 1991

Two weeks passed without Chana and Shaya Bleich receiving any sign of life from Mendel Lederman.

"That's how it goes?" Chana asked Shaya. "He's not supposed to be in touch with us at some point?"

"He said it could take a while, and I really believe that it will. He has practically nothing to work with. He has to start from almost zero."

But Lederman actually called that evening.

"I'll be coming to you tonight," he said briefly. "Tell your wife, please, Mr. Bleich, that I expect to receive exactly what I got on my last visit."

"What did he get last visit?!" Chana strained to remember.

"I think he means the jelly cookies…"

When Lederman came in, Shaya tried to read from his expression what kind of news he had for them. His face, though, was round and smiling as usual, and completely uninformative.

As opposed to the previous visit, Lederman didn't open his thick folder. He didn't even remove his pen from behind his ear.

"I'm very sorry to disappoint you," he said, and broke a jelly cookie in two.

They both leaned forward anxiously.

"I put aside almost all my other work and focused completely on this file, because it touched me, and because you're nice people, as I've already told you.

"I tried getting information every way possible. And every way is possible. But, to my great distress, and, I believe, to yours as well, I have failed in my mission. This file will remain, at least as far as I'm concerned, locked and sealed like the wall around Jerusalem under siege."

Chana lowered her head and breathed in the heavy disappointment that filled the room.

"You just – couldn't find anything?!" Shaya asked.

"Right," Mendel Lederman said. "There are things that even a professional investigator like myself can't do and, unlike others, I'm not embarrassed to admit it."

Chana stood up to get a tissue. She couldn't control the tears that flooded her eyes.

"And just like that, after two weeks, you pick up your hands and say 'I can't'?" Shaya wanted to know.

Mendel lifted his eyes to meet Shaya's, and for the first time since they met him, he wasn't smiling.

"Excuse me if I sound a bit rude," Shaya went on, "but it's strange. You said that it could even take a year, and suddenly after two weeks you're stopping everything?!

Chana, curious, came back and peeked from the doorway to the living room. She saw how Mendel Lederman took a deep breath and agitatedly played with the zipper of his briefcase.

"Do me a favor, Shaya Bleich," he said edgily, "and don't ask me any more questions. As far as I'm concerned, I don't even mind if you don't pay me. I, in any event, am removing my hands from this file this very minute."

"Just one more question," Shaya said. Chana was surprised. She had never known that Shaya could be so assertive. "One more question: Are you stopping to deal with this file willingly, or is someone forcing you to stop?"

Mendel Lederman didn't answer. Actually, he did answer.

"Allow me, Shaya Bleich, to not answer the question."

*Thicker Than Water* << 103

# CHAPTER 9

Mendel Lederman's hasty departure from their home left Shaya and Chana clearly overwrought.

"Someone is looking over our shoulder," Shaya said, and glanced behind him just to be sure no one was there, "and knows our every step and tries to foil it. Someone wants that we absolutely shouldn't find Naftali and Rochel…!"

"But Lederman is on our side," Chana said. "Why can't we get him to tell us who it is?"

"I believe that if he was able to, he would have cooperated with us. Maybe he's being threatened. Maybe this person," he shuddered, "is from the underworld, which no one wants to touch with a ten foot pole. You can't ask Lederman to put himself into danger for a client."

"So really," Chana said, gathering the forlorn refreshments from the table, "really, we're back at a dead end. Much more blocked than before. There's really no way out…"

• • •

## >>JERUSALEM, 2007

After a few stops, the bus began to empty. Shloime finally spotted an empty seat at the back of the bus and hurried to grab it. He usually wasn't from those who rushed to sit specifically, preferring to leave any available seat for those older and more tired than he. This time, though, he had something important to do during the ride; something that was difficult to do while standing.

He removed the folded sheaf of papers from the inside pocket of his suit coat. Between his last visit to the psychologist and now he had read them over and over, searching between the lines for veiled hints and hidden significance.

A few seats ahead of him sat his charming future brother-in-law, Yisroel Yitzchok, though Shloime was unaware of it. He opened to page number six, whose upper corner had been folded down.

**"And afterwards, during the ride, Abba is there?"**

"Yes, he's there."

Shloime remembered that that was where he had stopped, more or less.

**"Does he say something?"**

"Yes."

**"Do you remember what he says?"**

("Quiet", "increased concentration", the psychologist continued his impressions.)

"I don't understand what he says…"

**"Do you remember the words? Or maybe even a few words?"**

"He says… uh, he says…"

("An effort to concentrate. Eyes focused upwards. Intense attempt to connect")

*Thicker Than Water* << 105

"I don't see his face…"

**"Is he sitting in the inside seat?"**

"Maybe. I don't see his face. I hear him talking."

Here the psychologist refrained from asking any more leading questions. It seemed he preferred to let Shloime's brain concentrate on retrieving the information.

"One Jewish soul!"

(The psychologist wrote: "relief", and then: the patient makes a desperate effort to retrieve more information.)

"To save her, to sacrifice…"

("Sigh of relief", the psychologist noted, "impression of having exhausted the memory's ability.")

**"And do you know who has to be saved, or sacrificed, Shlomo?"**

"No, no. I don't know. Abba didn't say…"

The bus stopped. Shloime glanced outside and shot, at the last second, out the open door. It was so not like him to be so absorbed in something, even something important, and not to notice that he had arrived at his stop.

He walked quickly. He had two minutes to cover a five minute distance, and his psychologist was a stickler for punctuality. As he hurried along, he definitely didn't notice someone trying to keep pace with him, while, at the same time, taking care that Shloime shouldn't see him.

• • •

## >>NEW YORK, 2007

"Mmmm," R' Nachman said and took another sip of tea, "you're looking for the Bleichs who used to live here and moved? Chances are, they're not related to you."

"Why is that so obvious to you, R' Nachman?"

R' Nachman cleared his throat calmly and then, as if he was opening his notebook and reading from it, he began to explain:

"This Bleich family lived three blocks over, in a small house. The father – his name was Yitzchok, if I'm not mistaken, and I'm usually not mistaken – worked with a printing house. When it closed, they picked up and left. Their son – I remember him, a cute kid – would sit on his father's shoulders in shul. I'll tell you exactly how old he was, because his *pidyon haben* was the same exact day that my brother's son got engaged to the daughter of the wealthy Pietrokovsk - - -"

"Ahh," Shaya said in disappointment. "So I guess they weren't my relatives."

Now it was R' Nachman's turn to ask how it was so obvious to him.

"Oh," Shaya said in confusion, "I… I… if his name was Yitzchok, then it's hard to believe he's my relative. You understand, we're a small family, and we don't have any Yitzchok."

"*Nu*, nu," R' Nachman said, "I wouldn't say that that's proof."

But Shaya had already gotten his proof. If this Bleich family made a *pidyon haben* for their oldest son here, in the United States, they definitely couldn't be the parents of Shloime, their oldest, whose *pidyon haben* had been in Eretz Yisroel.

"Are you sure that there was a *pidyon haben*?" he asked.

"If I say something, then I'm sure of it," R' Nachman said, somewhat offended.

Shaya was sunk in thought. Maybe Naftali and Rochel had another son, and in order not to arouse any suspicions, made him a *pidyon haben* even though he wasn't their oldest?

"Tell me about them," he requested.

R' Nachman liked that sort of request.

"The truth is I don't know much. He was tall, and knew how to *daven* nicely for the *amud*. They hosted their relatives a lot.

His parents came to them literally every third *Shabbos*. I remember his father, a nice Jew, I think he worked in - - -"

"Okay, okay," Shaya said and stared at the bitter dregs of coffee remaining in his mug. *This is not the way to conduct an investigation, Yeshaya. You don't sit with your host and search through the telephone book. If this is how you plan on continuing, you can go home right now and save yourself a lot of money.*

"So you don't want to meet with Bleich?" R' Nachman asked. A strange guest he had. One minute he's very interested, and the next minute not at all.

"No, it's not so important," Shaya said and stood up.

• • •

## >>JERUSALEM, 2007

"Ima?" Suri knocked softly on the door. "There's an urgent phone call for you from the dental clinic."

Devora Fuchsman shook off the cobwebs from her afternoon nap. The dentist? That's right, Yisroel Yitzchok had an appointment today. He was supposed to have gone there straight from yeshiva. Could he have forgotten?!

"Hello?" she said, trying her best not to sound too hoarse.

"Hello, this is Dr. Schmidt's secretary speaking. Your son Yisroel was supposed to be here at four o'clock."

"That's right. He left for the clinic," Devorah said. Suri, standing next to her, saw how she was gripping the receiver.

"I understand," the secretary said. "In any event, he never arrived. It's a shame you didn't let us know about the cancellation. You know that our clinic charges for non-arrivals without twenty four hours notice."

"But there was no cancellation," Devorah said. "We made up yesterday that he would go to the clinic today. Maybe there's traffic?"

"I have no idea," the secretary said, "and now it's five o'clock. It's not always a good idea, Mrs. Fuchsman, to rely on children too much. Most parents accompany their children to the clinic." Devorah could hear the implied rebuke.

"Yisroel Yitzchok isn't a child," she mumbled. "He's sixteen years old. I really apologize. Of course, we'll pay... right now I'm more worried about my son than the money..."

Suri noticed her mother's trembling hand as she laid down the phone.

"What happened? Yisroel Yitzchok never showed up at the clinic?!"

"It's very strange," Devorah said. "He's usually so organized. He should have left yeshiva at three, and an hour is enough time for the bus ride."

She stood there helplessly for a few minutes.

"There's no choice," she finally said. "Abba will have to go out there. Yisroel Yitzchok isn't the type to wander off, which makes me ten times more worried. It's not a religious neighborhood, if you know what I mean..."

Ten minutes later, Elya Fuchsman left his office and folded himself into his car. On the way, he listened to the news. There was a recent accident, but on the other side of the city. There was no mention, either, of any unusually heavy traffic, and definitely not of a nice sixteen year old *bochur* who was supposed to have shown up at the dentist and disappeared on the way.

The car moved smoothly along the highway leading to the neighborhood where the clinic was located. A large bus pulled up to the bus stop, right in front of him. Fuchsman stood behind the bus, waiting to see who got off.

Two dusty boys, returning from school. An elderly man gripping baskets from the *shuk*. The bus, with a roar of its motor,

*Thicker Than Water* ≪ 109

pulled away from the stop. Yisroel Yitzchok wasn't there. The question was where was he?

As he drove, Elya Fuchsman tried to remember where the clinic was located. He recalled coming once with Yisroel Yitzchok – maybe for the first visit – but how was he supposed to remember now where it was? All the houses looked similar. He navigated the quiet streets, their streetlamps going on in the evening gloom.

He called Devorah for the exact address.

"Look in the street, too," she told him, trembling. "He never showed up at the clinic."

"Maybe he lost his way?" he asked, his eyes following a youth dressed in a suit similar to Yisroel Yitzchok's.

"But Elya, he's been there many times already. And he's not a child."

"You think someone kidnapped him?!" he chuckled. "Maybe for ransom…"

There was hardly anyone on the street at that hour. Elya glided after the owner of the long coat. Maybe he knew something.

Seeing that the youth was about to turn into a side street, he honked.

The boy turned around. Elya squinted. No, it wasn't Yisroel Yitzchok. Yisroel Yitzchok was shorter, with a completely different carriage. But he knew that youth – he knew him very, very well…!

• • •

## ≫NEW YORK, 2007

R' Nachman walked by the closed door of his Israeli guest, his shoes clicking. A few minutes later, he walked by again. The door was always closed. What was his guest doing in there?

Reading *k'pitlach*? Making a *cheshbon hanefesh*? Eating *kigel*?

The time for lunch was long past. His guest, Bleich, was surely hungry. From when breakfast was over, he had closed himself in his room and hadn't left.

R' Nachman wasn't sure what to do. The slap of his shoes against the floor seemingly wasn't enough. Should he knock? His guest *was* a guest, considerate of how the house was run, and if he closeted himself in his room, he must have a real reason to do so. He was in there for a good few hours already. Maybe he was sleeping, making up for the time difference? But he hadn't seemed especially tired at breakfast.

Inside the room, Shaya Bleich sat on a chair next to the small table put in there for guests. His suitcase was on the side. Before him were a pen and paper. He had been sitting like that for quite some time, but there was only some doodling on the paper. Not anything that even remotely resembled the beginnings of a plan of action.

*This, Yeshaya, you should have done before traveling. True, when you're actually there it's easier to hit upon a lead than from a distance, but to come without a plan of action, or at least a general outline? What are you, Shaya Bleich? A complete fool?*

*Logic says that if they wanted to remain hidden, they would be called by any name except for Bleich, or something similar. If so, clever man that you are, under what name will you look for them? And if circumstances forced them to change their name a few times? Almost twenty years have passed since then. Almost a generation. People fleeing from somebody (Who? Who???) could go through quite a lot, until they themselves could forget who they had been so many years earlier.*

So what should he do? What should he do?!

He could really use another head to help him try and find his way out of the tangle. It was always easier with two. His wife,

Chana, was always the one who joined him, usually proving herself. But maybe right now it wouldn't be wise to involve her. She would hear the despair in his voice.

He glanced at his watch and counted seven hours ahead. It was quite late in the evening at home. Shloime would be home already, and wouldn't have gone to bed yet.

It was actually Faigie who picked up the phone.

"Abba! How nice!"

Faigie didn't show any sign of curiosity about his sudden, odd trip. Were his children so well raised that they didn't question anything that their father did? Or maybe Chana had told them some sort of cover story?

"Can you give the phone to Shloime?"

"One minute," Faigie said, "I'll check if he's here."

Faigie came back quickly, awkwardness in her voice. "The door to Shloime's room is closed, Abba. I tried knocking, but I didn't hear anything. It looks like he's inside and can't come to the door."

What was that supposed to mean? Since when was Shloime's door closed…?

"Try again, Faigie," he requested. "Tell him I want to talk to him…"

• • •

## >>JERUSALEM, 2007

Slowly, Elya Fuchsman opened the door to the car. The motor was running, the key was inside, but he climbed out.

"R' Shloime???"

His future son-in-law. Suri's *chosson*. From all the people in the world, he would not have expected to meet him here.

"*Sholom aleichem*," Shloime said, slightly embarrassed, and put out his hand. "What an interesting person to meet, in an interesting place…"

"You're going to the doctor or something like that?" the *shver* inquired delicately.

"Something like that," Shloime nodded.

"I'm looking for Yisroel Yitzchok," his father-in-law said, managing to surprise him. "He was supposed to be here in this neighborhood an hour ago already, at the dentist, but the secretary called and said that he never came."

"Really?" Shloime looked surprised. "Yisroel Yitzchok is a responsible boy."

"Very responsible," his *shver* agreed.

Only a few houses away, Yisroel Yitzchok stood bent over, hiding behind the green wall of a dumpster. This was certainly an interesting, unexpected development that could definitely work to his benefit!

He assumed that his father, whom he could see, but not hear what he was saying, had come to look for him. If that was the case, his absence from the clinic *had* made waves. They must have called his mother, who then called his father, who bothered himself to come all the way out to look for him.

Logic dictated that he reveal himself and put an end to his father's and everyone's worrying. But if he revealed himself now, Shloime might suspect that he was following him. His tailing Shloime was about to yield some very impressive results. He couldn't ruin it just now.

Over an hour ago, he followed Shloime off the bus. Shloime almost ran, and he ran after him, keeping to the building courtyards in order not to be seen. He saw Shloime disappear into one of the doorways, waited a few minutes and then went over to read what was written on the small metal sign at the entrance.

"Dr. Gavriel Narkiss, Psychologist".

If so, then their *chosson*, the wonderful, brilliant, steady *bochur*, regularly saw a psychologist. Aha. His gut feeling hadn't misled him. His parents had refused to consider there being the slightest flaw with their incredible *chosson*, but it seemed as if there was some kind of imperfection. Even more than an imperfection.

From his hiding place down the street, Yisroel Yitzchok tried to listen to the conversation between his father and Shloime. He couldn't hear what they were saying, but from their hand motions it was obvious that they were enjoying their conversation, and that his father didn't begin to imagine the real reason why Shloime was in this place at this hour.

Abba invited Shloime to join him in the car. A bit hesitantly, Shloime accepted the invitation. It was clear that the hesitation was from embarrassment; Abba would take him home, though, or to yeshiva, saving him a lot of time.

Wait, if they were leaving, Abba might continue looking for him for hours. He wouldn't come back to that street, since he had already been there without finding him.

Yisroel Yitzchok wanted to come out of his hiding place and run over to his father. He had to. But his legs wouldn't obey him. Would he give up in one minute all he had accomplished? For more than an hour he had sat patiently in a place where he could see Shloime leaving the building, without being seen. And finally, after his patience had almost completely given out, the dear boy had left with measured steps, stuffing some papers into the inside pocket of his coat.

It seemed to Yisroel Yitzchok that Shloime was slightly unsteady, but he wasn't sure.

The car began to move. Now he certainly wouldn't raise his voice and call after it. His eyes followed the receding lights, knowing that he would now have to pull himself to the bus stop and travel close to an hour to get home. Abba and Ima would continue to worry that entire time. But when he came home with the important information he had gathered, they would surely forgive him, no?

•  •  •

## ≫NEW YORK, 2007

"I told him, Abba," Faigie came back to the phone, feeling even more uncomfortable. "He said he'll call you soon. He can't talk now."

Shaya felt a blend of anger and curiosity.

"Fine," he said impatiently, "Give me Ima."

"Ima's not home."

Shaya banged on the table in exasperation.

In the hallway, R' Nachman was planning to leave to *mincha*. He walked by the closed door for the umpteenth time, deliberating whether to remind his guest that it was almost *shki'ah*. He heard the nervous drumming of a pen against the table.

"I don't understand," he heard his guest say in a loud voice, almost yelling. "I just left the house and already there's mayhem. Where's Ima? And what's going on with Shloime? What's with the other children? I don't understand what's happening here, Faigie."

The guest was quiet. He must be listening to an answer. But not for too long.

"Shloime went somewhere and came back? Where did he go? I want to know."

There was a short silence.

"What does that mean he'll call me soon and tell me everything? What's wrong? He's out of breath from running home, and now he can't talk? What did you say?? I didn't hear you…"

R' Nachman peeked at his watch. *Shki'ah* always made the

hands on the clock race forward.

"What did you say?? He has important information that could help me...?!"

# CHAPTER 10

>>NEW YORK, 2007

Shaya banged down the phone. He didn't like this game. Was Shloime able to come to the phone and talk to him or not? Was he able to give over his information or not?

The paper filled with angry scribbling. He felt like coloring the entire paper, from top to bottom, with black crayon. Groping in the dark – that was an apt description of his feelings. A man sits in one spot on the face of earth, not at all sure that that spot was any better than any other spot, and thinks how to find his brother, one man out of six billion people. What were the chances of his finding him in exactly that place, at exactly that time? Less than one in six billion, that was certain.

If only he had a lead. He would grab it and hang on tight. A hint of a name, of an address, a small sign.

Suddenly Shaya remembered a forgotten detail: his brother Naftali had a birthmark the shape of a peach pit on his upper left arm. His mother used to jokingly say that one day, before Naftali was born, she had a craving for a peach. She asked his father to stop at the fruit and vegetable store on the way home and pick up a box of peaches. "But Abba," she would always say, "doesn't see past his '*dalet amos*'. He just didn't see the store." And Naftali was left with a souvenir on his arm. When Naftali was little, the mark was small. When they were older, they wore only long-sleeved shirts, so Shaya only saw the mark when they *davened* together during the week. When they entered yeshiva and hardly ever *davened* together anymore, the mark was forgotten.

*Nu, so now what will you do, Shaya Bleich? Walk through the streets scrutinizing everyone's face, and whoever seems like a likely suspect, you'll kindly ask him to roll up his sleeve…?!*

The small telephone next to him rang. As he looked at the telephone and saw the number of his home in Israel, Shaya noticed in alarm the waning sunlight. No, he couldn't answer the phone now, even if it was Shloime, wanting to finally give him "the important information that might be able to help him". He rushed out of the room in a panic, catching up to R' Nachman by the front steps.

• • •

## >>JERUSALEM, 2007

"So you're back." Elya Fuchsman's presence filled the living room.

"I'm back," Yisroel Yitzchok said breathlessly and sank into one of the armchairs.

"Very nice," his father said, and his sharp look said exactly the opposite. "So, as the kids say in their games – and it seems that you haven't yet outgrown them – 'where have you gone and what have you done'?"

Yisroel Yitzchok desperately wanted to drink something. It

had been quite a long time since he ate or drank. But his father's withering glare disallowed anything except an immediate answer.

"It has to do with Shloime," he said.

His father's eyes narrowed.

"You're late because of Shloime? What else are you going to throw on Shloime, Yisroel Yitzchok? Completely groundless suspicions, and now the fact that you're late? Maybe he's also responsible for your getting up late in the morning?!"

"Abba," Yisroel Yitzchok said, "I have something important to tell you."

"Something important." It was impossible to miss the heavy sarcasm. "More important than being away for hours, sending your mother out of her mind with worry. No, don't go in to her now. You don't deserve to see how she looks after worrying about you so."

Yisroel Yitzchok looked down.

"It really was wrong of me to be so late. I should have called, but it didn't work out."

Elya was quiet. Yisroel Yitzchok squirmed under his gaze.

"Actually, why did you come back?" Elya asked.

"Because… because I finished what I had to do."

"Ahh, important business you have."

"Abba," Yisroel Yitzchok tried to stand up, "could we talk later?"

"No!" Elya shot, "We'll talk now. I want to hear everything – from the very beginning to the very end."

Yisroel Yitzchok hesitated. This was his big moment, and he knew it. It was a pity Ima wasn't there, too, but it wasn't the end of the world. The main thing was to give over the facts calmly and impartially, in a way that made it sound credible.

"Shloime was on my bus."

"Okay."

"He got off a few stops before the dental clinic. I got off after him. I wanted to know where he was going."

"What's it your business where he's going?!"

"I felt that… that it was important."

"Okay." Yisroel Yitzchok sensed that it wasn't at all okay. According to his father, it was the first in a string of follies.

"I followed him. I saw which building he went into. Downstairs, at the entrance to the building," Yisroel Yitzchok paused for effect, "there was a psychologist's sign."

"Very nice," his father said wearily. "You're so bent on finding something wrong, though I don't understand why. Did you notice if there were other signs next to the one of the psychologist?"

"No," Yisroel Yitzchok admitted, "I didn't notice."

"It's possible that there were?"

"It's possible."

"Perhaps there was a sign for an ENT and Shloime goes to him because he suffers from adenoids?" Elya asked, not without sarcasm. "Maybe there was also an orthopedist and Shloime, who, let's say, broke his leg last year, came to him for a checkup? These guesses could be correct, or are they unrealistic?"

Yisroel Yitzchok dipped his head quietly.

"You thought you had a 'scoop', eh?" Elya asked, and added, "And now go in to Ima. I think you owe her an apology…"

• • •

## >>JERUSALEM, 1991

Chana Bleich opened the mailbox and removed a stack of letters. With Faigie in one arm, and Shloimy holding on to her hand, she was unable to look at them just then.

In the house, in all the tumult of lunchtime, the pile of letters was relegated from the table to the shelf. Later, Faigie "tidied" them up, "sorting" them according to appearance. The colorful envelopes she placed under the couch, and those that were plain white she tried to shove under the bookcase.

"Ima," Shloimy came to tell her, "Faigie's making a mess."

Chana went into the living room and, at the last minute, saved the letters from being shoved permanently under the large bookcase. Anything that went underneath it was gone forever; there was no way to retrieve them.

Chana rescued the letters from Faigie's active hands and placed them in a pile on a high shelf over the breakfront. An electric bill, property tax, two bar mitzvah invitations and one wedding invitation, an envelope from the bank. She went back to washing the dishes from lunch.

"Ima!"

Shloimy called her again. Again, she wiped her hands on her apron.

"Ima, I think there's another paper there, under the bookcase."

Chana went to look. It was easier for little Shloimy to see what was doing under the bookcase, and he indeed saw the corner of a white envelope peeking out at him.

"All right," she said, "I'll bring a wire hanger. Maybe that will help us pull out the envelope."

Together, Chana and Shloimy tried sliding the envelope out from under the bookcase, but, as if to tease them, it got pushed further and further in as opposed to coming out.

"Okay," Chana sighed after a few failed attempts, "let's stop now. In any case it's not helping. Tonight I'll ask Abba to move the bookcase."

But at night, the day's events tend to be forgotten. That which is routine enjoys attention from force of habit, but everything else gets washed away with the tide.

The envelope remained under the heavy bookcase. Chana

completely forgot about it. *Erev Pesach*, when she did a major mopping in the living room, pouring buckets of water, no envelope came floating out. The bookcase was solid and heavy, loaded with *sefarim*. Who even thought to ever move it from its place…?

• • •

Shloime tried calling. He tried again and again. He didn't understand what was going on. Only a minute ago, his father was looking for him, and now he wasn't answering. Shloime didn't even think of *mincha*, completely forgetting about the time difference.

Perhaps Abba was angry at him. It really did border on chutzpa to have Faigie tell Abba that he couldn't come to the phone.

"Faigie!"

"What?"

"Did Abba sound angry when you spoke to him?"

"Angry? I don't know. He sounded like he didn't understand what was going on."

Of course Abba didn't understand what was going on. He couldn't guess that Shloime was hiding in his room, finally in his own quiet little corner, trying to digest the new information that threw light on the entire mystery.

The psychologist had highlighted the phrase "to save her life" as the key phrase from the transcript of their dialogue. He claimed that if Shloime was looking to solve the riddle of his early childhood, this was the beginning to the solution. A lead, as they called it.

Whose life could it be?

He tried to think of a likely candidate. Someone for whom his parents would have had to flee Israel and hide. Savta? It was hard to believe. Savta was a very straight person, with no past or present hidden affairs (he hoped). It couldn't be his mother, because his father said these words in third person in front of her, making it sound like he meant someone else.

Faigie? Also impossible. Faigie hadn't even been born yet.

It had to be somebody else. Someone whom he didn't know, but his biological parents knew and were worried about.

The realization suddenly hit Shloime full force. It was so obvious, so compelling, that he simply took a step back.

It had to be someone extremely important to his parents. Otherwise, they wouldn't have been so busy with her. Someone that he must not know because he had been very young, a toddler really. That was it. He now knew the secret.

The phone rang. Abba was on the line. He surely wanted to finally hear which new information Shloime had to tell him.

"How are you?" his father asked him. His voice was completely devoid of any anger. It was as full of warmth as usual, maybe even more so. "I need you here with me now. Things aren't moving along as I expected. Actually, right now they're not moving at all."

"And if I would be with you, how would that help? I'd be able to push harder?" Shloime smiled.

"Your mind could push. And besides, two isn't just one plus one. It's one times two."

Shloime was quiet. He wanted to share his discovery with his father – even though at that point it was just a feeling – but he was afraid. That is, he wasn't afraid to share it; he was scared that his father would have facts that would immediately refute his theory, and again he would be left with nothing.

"Faigie said that you have something important to tell me?" his father asked.

"Yes, that is... I think it's important. Maybe it's even a lead."

*Thicker Than Water*

"A lead with some meat on it, I hope."

"Yes, that is… I thought of something that could have caused my parents to disappear."

"*Nu*, let's hear." Shloime could see Abba's fingers out there, drumming on the table in anticipation.

• • •

Yisroel Yitzchok knew he would check it out. Not that day, nor the next, but the next time he visited the dentist he would go to the clinic that Shloime had visited and check if there were other doctors there, or if it was solely the psychologist's clinic.

Meanwhile, he knew, he wouldn't get an ounce of support from his parents. Just the opposite. Abba and Ima viewed these theories of his as, number one, suspecting the innocent. And not just any innocent, but Shloime, their first, esteemed *chosson* – the one and only. Besides for that, they saw it as doubting Abba's capability to judge the character of their new *chosson*.

But what should he do that the gentle, dove-eyed Shloime seemed to him, from the very first minute, to be hiding something? Yisroel Yitzchok trusted his intuition implicitly, and besides, he was a responsible, unbiased brother. In a place where there were no men, or there were men but they were closing their eyes, he would have to be the man.

He had never waited so eagerly for a visit to the dentist. His next appointment was in another week. Ima would surely warn him up and down to leave on time and come home on time, and, of course, not to wander around on the way.

But he was mistaken.

The night before his appointment, his mother casually told him that his father would drive him to the clinic the next day, wait for him – despite the precious time it would take from him

– and bring him back home. After the previous week's fiasco, Yisroel Yitzchok had lost a lot of points by her, she said regretfully, and she couldn't rely on his age and responsibility until he proved otherwise.

Yisroel Yitzchok was up in arms. True, last week he had done something inappropriate, but he had apologized profusely a few times and thought that he was forgiven. Ima could be sure that it wouldn't happen again. But that Abba should go with him? What was he, a six year old?

"Right now," Ima said, "that's about the age where I would put you, at least when it comes to responsibility." No, it didn't bother her that he felt slighted. Her peace of mind was more important to her, and if Yisroel Yitzchok viewed the escort as a punishment – well, she didn't think a small punishment would do him harm.

Yisroel Yitzchok, on the other hand, though he didn't voice it, thought that it was terrible. Abba wouldn't drive him to any other street. He wouldn't be able to go and check what was really written there at the entrance to the clinic. He wouldn't be able to verify his assumption. After all, why was he going to the dentist…?

What would be…?

• • •

"That's nonsense, Shloime. I'm sorry."

Shloime was silent. He guessed that his father would try to refute his presumption, but with such certainty?!

"An older sister?! I'm willing to take guesses into consideration, but not inventions. If I hadn't been at your *pidyon haben*, and if I didn't remember it as if it took place today, you would have what to tell me. But you are the *bechor*, Shloime. There's no doubt about it. Onwards, Shloime, to the next idea. But please, let it be a bit more grounded…"

"Abba - - -"

"What? *Nu*, Shloime, really."

"Abba, I once heard of someone who made a *pidyon haben* for a baby who didn't need it. I don't remember the reason… He asked a Rov, a big Rov, and the Rov told him exactly what to do, and how to do it… That means that there is such a thing. Maybe they had a reason to make me a *pidyon*, so no one should know about… about this girl. Maybe that reason is connected to the reason they ran away. It seems logical to me."

Shloime heard nothing from the other side of the line. Then he heard his father laugh.

"Shloime, Shloime… you have such an imagination. But what should I do, you were born a year after your parents got married. So when exactly was this sister born?"

Shloime fell silent. He knew that, but hadn't taken it into account. How dumb.

"*Nu*, I asked you already," his father said, a bit impatiently, "another idea. But more realistic."

Shloime was quiet.

"You know what?" his father suggested. "It won't work on the telephone. Take a pen and paper, write down whatever comes to mind and fax it to me. Let me check what the number here is."

Shloime absentmindedly wrote down the number.

"What time is it by you?" his father asked. What time was it? Late. His father told him to leave everything and to go to sleep, otherwise he wouldn't be able to get up in time for *davening* and would come late to yeshiva. "You have to take advantage of these days," he said, "the last months in yeshiva. You'll yet miss it."

"Abba," Shloime said suddenly. "Maybe we were twins?!"

"Who?" His father was confused.

"*Nu*, me and this sister."

Abba was quiet, but only for a minute. "Do you really think that's something you could hide from family? From a brother? From parents?!"

"You could hide anything, if you really wanted to," Shloime replied.

"But why would they hide such a thing, Shloime? Why? I think that if I would have such a big *simcha*, the birth of twins, I would share it with the entire world."

"*Nu*, that's exactly the answer we're looking for. Why. Why they hid it. Why they ran away. My heart tells me the two are connected."

"And my heart tells me that you're tired and imagining things, Shloime. We'll talk more tomorrow. Go to sleep now."

• • •

"What are you looking for, Yisroel Yitzchok?" Suri didn't like to be disturbed while sewing, but what could he do if the telephone book was on the shelf right above the sewing machine?

"The phone book," he answered briefly.

If it had been Ima, she surely would have asked why he needed it. Lately, she was checking up on his every move. He felt that her trust in him had weakened. But this was Suri, busy making tucks in a dress, and all she wanted was for him to take what he needed and go.

Yisroel Yitzchok closed himself in his room and opened the book. There was a classified list of psychologists in the yellow pages. He wasn't sure if Shloime's psychologist was listed there, but maybe he was. It was worth a try.

Yisroel Yitzchok went through name after name. Why did psychologists have such unusual names? He looked for one whose address was in his dentist's neighborhood. Would he find it?

• • •

Chana was busy tidying the kitchen at the end of the day. She couldn't sleep peacefully if there was a mug or plate left in the sink.

"Ima, do you have three minutes for me?" Shloime stood in the doorway to the kitchen, tall and tired.

"For you, all the time in the world."

"I need only three minutes," Shloime repeated. "I wanted to know where all the documents you brought from my parents' house are. All the documents connected to my birth."

"In the documents drawer… One minute, your papers we actually kept somewhere else, not with everyone else's papers. We didn't want one of the children to find them and start asking questions. Give me a minute to remember where they are."

Shloime sat down by the table and waited. Chana cut a slice of cake for him. She couldn't see someone sitting by the table without some refreshments. As she moved, she thought.

"The house isn't that big," she gave a little laugh, "and we don't have a safe where we keep our documents… You have to look in Abba's drawers, I think. There's also a small box of papers in the storage area near the ceiling. Do you want me to get it down for you?"

"No," he protested. "I'll do it tomorrow morning, when no one will be here to disturb me and I won't wake anyone up… its fine, Ima."

Some hours later, Shloime had fallen into a fitful sleep. Chana could hear the bed creak each time he turned over. She, too, was desperate for sleep, but sleep refused to come. She told herself that it must be the loneliness, knowing deep down that that wasn't the truth. The loneliness bothered her, but something else bothered her more, gnawing at the edge of her brain, nibbling at her peace of mind.

*That wasn't a good move, Chana. Not good at all. Shloime asked you for his documents, and you, maybe out of pity for his sensitive situation, cooperated with him. You shouldn't have done that. You can't encourage this investigation that Shloime is starting. You know Shloime. When he sets a goal for himself, he keeps at it. Like his father, and his uncle. It will start with available documents and go on to documents that are less available. The next step will be to turn to sources that will put you and his parents in danger. And you asked him not to do anything dangerous. You shouldn't have lent your hand to even this first, innocent step.*

She turned over. *Nonsense, Chana. Shloime's very levelheaded, and now, with Shaya not here, he's that much more reliable. He wants to see the documents, to actually feel the new reality of his life with his hands. What harm could come from rummaging in the storage area, from an old birth certificate…?*

# CHAPTER 11

In the morning, Shloime came home from *davening* and ate a relaxed breakfast. He waited patiently for everyone in the house to leave for school and work, leaving him alone to calmly search for the documents, without any curious questions to disturb him.

It should be quite simple, Shloime thought, as he took the ladder and opened it near the door to the storage area. A small box of documents. They weren't secret documents. His parents had already seen them years ago and didn't seem to have learned anything special from them – a regular birth certificate, the hospital release papers, and what else? He didn't really know which other documents should be there, but he'd soon find out.

The storage area was full of dust. Shloime doubled over coughing and hurried down to change his clothing. Searching through the storage was a job for *erev* Pesach; it would be a shame to ruin his good shirt and pants. He also needed to arm himself with a flashlight and a bit of patience.

At first glance, he didn't see any small box. Maybe Ima was

mistaken, and it was in a bag? There were many bags there. Preferring to assume that his mother's memory was in full working order, Shloime began to carefully remove the large boxes of Pesach dishes.

He paused. He should really sweep the floor first, before the Pesach boxes touched it. Shloime went to bring the broom and shovel. He then went to get a bag for the dirt, and then he brought a disposable tablecloth and spread it out on the floor. He wasn't taking any chances with the Pesach dishes.

He finally climbed back up on the ladder and started to take down the boxes. From the rattling of the dishes inside he guessed that the contents were very breakable. Three boxes were down, allowing him to see more of the storage area.

A small box? No, there wasn't any. There was only a small lizard, its rest disturbed by the flashlight. It scrambled madly and ran right past his face into the hallway.

That was just what he needed. Faigie, and also Ima (though she didn't readily admit it), were deathly afraid of lizards. If he didn't catch it now, it would run somewhere and hide, and there would be chaos until it was found. If Abba was there, he would settle everything with a few reassuring words. Abba, though, wasn't there, and Shloime was now the man of the house.

Shloime jumped off the chair and took off after the lizard. From the storage area to the hallway, from the hallway to the kitchen. He almost caught it with the broom he was holding, but then it scampered under the stove. He knocked the stove heartily a few times, and the frightened lizard fled from there and found refuge under the refrigerator.

He was frustrated. What had he stayed home for? To find some urgent documents, something that should have taken him, at most, five minutes. Meanwhile, he had wasted more than half an hour chasing a lizard!

After the lizard ignored his knocking on the refrigerator, he rolled up his sleeves and started to pull the fridge forward.

He soon saw it dart out from under the fridge, straight into the living room. That was a good place. There weren't many hiding places there, unlike the kitchen. There was more space. He grabbed the broom again and ran after the lizard.

The lizard, though, seemed to have been blessed with healthy instincts, and ran for all it was worth, straight under the large bookcase, which was impossible to move.

• • •

Louis the Fourteenth Street. Yes, Yisroel Yitzchok was almost positive he saw a sign with that street name in the dentist's neighborhood. The clinic itself was on Henry the Eighth Street. It seemed right. The name of the psychologist was Gavriel Narkiss. Yisroel Yitzchok opened his little notepad and carefully copied down the name and address. Even if Abba insisted on taking him to his appointment, there was hope that by the next one, Ima would have calmed down and would let him go by himself.

Yisroel Yitzchok returned the telephone book to its place, managing to disturb Suri again, exactly in the middle of a tuck.

"Can I understand," Suri fumed, "why you're here and not in yeshiva? It seems to me that lunch was over long ago. Your *chavrusa* isn't waiting for you?!"

"I don't mix into your sewing, so please don't mix into my business. I'm a big boy already."

"Right," Suri blew a pin out of her mouth, "we've already heard how big you are. A big boy who goes to the dentist and gets lost."

Now she got him really angry. His voice rose to decibel levels that the Fuchsman house didn't usually hear. He went towards the door, perhaps to assure himself an escape.

"Continue sewing!" he yelled. "Sew dresses for your *chasunah*. Ten dresses, a hundred dresses. And *daven* that you'll really have a *chasunah* to wear all these dresses to…"

... 

## >>NEW YORK, 2007

Shaya Bleich lay in bed. Sooner or later, he'd have to rent a room somewhere, and not rely on the generous *hachnosas orchim* of this family who didn't even know him. If only he knew that he was in the right place. Maybe he had no reason to remain even one minute longer?!

Shloime's fertile imagination seemed to be working overtime. Shaya had no doubt that none of his strange ideas held any reality. Shloime didn't have an older sister. Nor a twin. He clearly remembered the birth of his nephew, the thrilling *pidyon haben*. He knew Naftali. If there really had been some unknown birth before Shloime's – something that was really impossible – Naftali would rather have made up some story why he couldn't make a *pidyon haben* rather than staging it.

Neither was any twin sister born. Had Shloime been influenced by some thriller? Until Naftali and Rochel's mysterious disappearance, everything in their family had been completely normal. True, Naftali had lived quite some distance away, in Haifa, but their relationship had been strong enough, certainly when it came to *simchos*. Shloime's birth was a well remembered event.

What, actually, was pulling Shloime in that direction? Why was he thinking about a sister? Who had planted such an idea in his head?

The question actually intrigued him, but it was already very late at night in Yerushalayim. He would wait until morning to receive an answer.

While Shaya Bleich fell into an exhausted sleep in his room, R' Nachman and his wife sat at the kitchen table for a late supper.

"This guest, Bleich, seems very troubled," R Nachman commented, and sprinkled salt on the vegetables.

"People can be troubled by many things. Nachman! Enough with the salt. It's not powdered sugar, and it's not good for your heart."

Nachman took a spoon and began to toss the vegetables with the salt.

"He didn't come to collect money, though he's soon marrying off his son. I checked it out."

"Maybe he came to do some shopping," she suggested.

"No," R' Nachman said, "Why would he be worried if he came to shop? And why not go out to buy things right away on the first morning? Why waste time sitting here?"

"Fine, Nachman. I think you'd best busy yourself with the vegetables and not with the troubles of others. If he is anxious, I'm glad he has good lodgings and some peace here. At least he doesn't have to work hard for a place to sleep. As far as I'm concerned, he can stay here as long as he wants."

A few rooms away, Shaya Bleich tossed and turned in his bed. Tomorrow, first thing in the morning, he would leave, no matter what. Besides being a burden on this nice couple, there was no advantage to his being there as opposed to any place else. *What did you think, Shaya Bleich? That* HaKadosh Boruch Hu *would drop down a lead from on high and all you would have to do is reach out your hand and grab it...?*

• • •

"*Whaat???*" Suri turned around. The chair turned with her.

"Nothing," Yisroel Yitzchok said from the doorway, "Go back to your sewing."

"I want to know what you said, and what you meant by it. Wait!!! Don't run away."

Yisroel Yitzchok, as he had on many other occasions, regretted what he said. Why did he have to be so reckless? Suri was a *kallah*, sensitive and excited. What he had said was harsh, and he knew it. Especially when there wasn't really anything on which to base it.

"I want you to repeat what you said," Suri demanded again, strongly.

"It doesn't matter," Yisroel Yitzchok said, one foot out the door. "You can forget what I said. That is, you have to forget what I said."

"Listen, Yisroel Yitzchok, you know that no one plays around with me, especially about serious things." Yes, he knew that. Abba and Ima also knew that when they chose Shloime, a serious *bochur* for a serious girl. "Please repeat what you said, word for word. You said something about my *chasunah*, right?"

"Right."

"What did you say about my *chasunah*?"

"I said that... fine, *nu*, there's no need to repeat it."

"You will repeat it," Suri said, very determinedly. Yisroel Yitzchok knew there was no escape.

"I said that... that you should *daven* that you'll have a *chasunah* to wear all the dresses to. Now are you happy?" Yisroel Yitzchok repeated what he had said and felt even more how silly and foolish his words were.

• • •

Shloime stood facing the bookcase, helpless. The lizard, terror of Ima and Faigie, was there. It was the hiding criminal, and he was the police, standing outside and needing to convince it to come out and fall into the trap.

He could guess how to convince those in hiding to come out, but he had no clue how to convince lizards. Should he bend down and whisper to it? Should he bang on the walls of the bookcase? This lizard was no fool. It ran out from under the stove because of banging, and wouldn't fall into the same trap again.

He actually knew that lizards were attracted to light. He walked backwards, so as not to miss the big exit, and removed a flashlight from the drawer. The flashlight threw light under the bookcase, but the lizard didn't seem too impressed.

Shloime went and brought a long, thin stick, like those that his little brothers used in the game 'pick-up stix'. If that wouldn't help, either, he would take a metal wire and comb every inch under the bookcase.

Shloime, thorough that he was, didn't take into account that, though the bookcase was up against the wall, a creature the size of the lizard could definitely press into the space between the bookcase and the wall and remain there for all of time, or until someone took apart the bookcase – something which hadn't happened in the past twenty years. Moving the long metal wire along the floor, Shloime felt it catch on something. He pulled and pulled. It would be great if the lizard, dead or alive, would finally come out, letting him continue with his original plan.

But, like a fisherman surprised by the reality sprung on him, Shloime found himself blinking at something quite different than a lizard – a white envelope, dirty and frayed, looking as if it had planned on being forever buried under the bookcase, until Shloime Bleich came and disturbed its rest.

• • •

R' Nachman wasn't the rich man of the city. He hadn't been successful in business like his neighbors and acquaintances were. In the past, he had been a well-known *rebbe* in one of the yeshivas, and he received a nice pension from them ever since he retired. He and his wife managed with the household expenses, but rich they weren't.

That was the reason that R' Nachman, and even more so his wife, chose hosting guests as their way of giving. Large checks for *tzedakah* they couldn't give, but they were able to set aside a few rooms in their house for guests, for an unlimited amount of time, and were able to handle the expense of feeding them.

*Hashem* led R' Nachman and his wife down the path which they had chosen, and their reputation as hosts spread quickly. The greater their devotion to their guests, the more satisfaction the couple derived from the *mitzvah*.

So it happened that at 2:00 AM, when the street was silent and still, soft knocking was heard at the door to their house. R' Nachman, who had installed a special system that brought the sound of knocking straight to his room, got out of bed and wrapped himself in his robe.

In the darkness stood a tall, thin man, bag over his shoulder, and the embarrassment of knocking at such a late hour on his face.

"Come in, come in please," R' Nachman urged him. "Come inside and make yourself comfortable."

The Jew came inside and R' Nachman poured him a hot cup of tea from the thermos that stood ready for just that reason, and sliced some cake as his wife had taught him to do.

"Where are you from, *tzaddik*?" he asked, after the guest had begun to relax.

"I'm from Netanya."

"From Netanya?! How interesting. Now we'll have two

guests from Israel. What are you looking for here that's missing in Netanya?

"Don't look for money, *tzaddik*. Whoever looks for it usually doesn't find. Those who find always say that they weren't looking... Where do you think you'll look for money here? Under my floors?!"

"No," said the new guest, a bit stunned by the flood of words. "I'm a doctor by profession, an anesthesiologist. I've come to look for a job."

"That's very interesting, what you're saying," R'Nachman murmured. The guest finished his second slice of cake and yawned.

"One second, if you're an anesthesiologist, then surely you'll have no problem falling asleep," R' Nachman joked, lifting the man's suitcase and carrying it to the ready room. "This is where you'll sleep. If you need anything, don't hesitate to ask. Tomorrow morning you'll meet our other guest from Israel, and then you really won't be lacking anything in order to feel at home..."

The next morning, however, the flow of unaccented Hebrew in the kitchen notwithstanding, brought no sort of bonding between the two guests. Though the entire Israel is no larger than one small state in the U.S., its inhabitants could be poles apart from each other.

As the guest interested himself in every detail of his surroundings, asking and answering, Bleich sat and chewed his toast in silence. His plate was half empty, indicating that he woke up that morning without much appetite – which indicated that he wasn't in the best of moods.

"Where are you from? Jerusalem?" the guest asked, and helped himself to another omelet, his third.

"Yes," Bleich said.

"Ah, I have a brother in Jerusalem," the guest said. "Yitzchak

Weiss, you heard of him?"

"Yitzchak Weiss," Shaya said apathetically, "There are three on every block."

"And what's your name?" the guest didn't let up.

"Yeshaya Bleich," Shaya said, and removed his wallet from his pants pocket.

"Oh, so maybe you're related to---"

Shaya slowly removed a stack of bills from the wallet and began to count. The guest's question trailed off, and R' Nachman, busy at the stove, heard the silence that fell and turned around to see Bleich counting out bills.

"You're planning on opening your first business in America today, R' Shaya?!"

Shaya didn't answer. He placed on the table, one on top of the other, one bill and another bill and another, until he reached a sum that satisfied him. He then folded the pile of bills and placed it near R' Nachman's plate.

R' Nachman, one hand holding the frying pan and the other a spatula crowned with a quivering omelet, went over to the table and stared.

"What's this, R' Shaya?" he wanted to know.

"This is what I owe," Shaya said tiredly, and returned the wallet to his pocket.

"What…you owe? You owe me something? I lent you money?! When?! Remind me."

Shaya looked up.

"A debt doesn't have to be specifically from a loan, R' Nachman. I'm here a few days already, eating at your table and being hosted by you. This isn't a hotel, though the accommodations are wonderful. I don't have any institutions funding me, so I have to pay for myself."

R' Nachman's face showed utter horror. He tried shoving

away the pile of bills without actually touching it, as if it was contaminated.

"Tell me, you want me to throw you out of here?!" he yelled.

"I believe that's what will happen one of these days."

"That's what will happen if you don't take away this minute this… this… what you put here on the table. Tell me, you ever learned Torah? You heard of the *mitzvah* of '*hachnosas orchim*'? Or maybe in our world, where everything begins and ends with money, they've already done away with this *mitzvah*…?!"

Shaya sat there stunned. He didn't take the money, but he knew that very soon he would take it. R' Nachman wouldn't let him be until he took it.

"You will stay here as long as you need," R' Nachman informed him, "You hear? Two weeks or two months or two years. As long as you need."

Shaya's fingers groped for his wallet. Such a degree of kindness deserved payment, even if the payment was to take his money back, immediately.

After things calmed down, and the guest was served his fourth omelet, and Shaya's improved mood allowed him to bite into a piece of cheese, the guest repeated his question.

"Ah, Bleich, maybe you're related to the Bleich from Haifa?"

• • •

Suri stood up from her sewing machine. Yisroel Yitzchok had disappeared, but she would find him. And when she found him, she would get from him every crumb of information that he didn't want to share.

As she darted from room to room, her heart was gripped with fear. Did Yisroel Yitzchok know something that she didn't know? Something that perhaps they were hiding from her? And why didn't Abba and Ima say anything? What did that mean, '*daven* that you'll have a *chasunah*'? She had davened long enough for a *chosson* who was a *talmid chochom*, and *boruch Hashem* she had found one. The date of the *chasunah* was drawing nearer. The dresses and robes that were filling her closet attested to that. Now was the time to *daven* for a good continuation, to celebrate with a light heart, to build a home that would last forever. To *daven* that there would be a *chasunah*? What on earth was Yisroel Yitzchok talking about?!

# CHAPTER 12

"*Whaaat???*" The fork fell from Shaya's hand with a clatter. "What did you ask?!"

"He asked if you know Bleich, someone from Haifa," R' Nachman, as host, said.

Shaya decided to be cautious.

"I seem to remember something," he said calmly, his heart beating like a tom-tom under his tzitzis. "When did you meet him? Recently?"

"The truth is that I haven't seen him in years," the guest from Netanya admitted, "maybe even in many years. But when I was younger, I worked for a short time as a *rebbe* in the *cheder* in Haifa, and one of the staff there was a fellow by the name of Bleich. Naftali Bleich."

With his knife, Shaya carved deep scratches in his piece of cheese.

"He was a nice fellow," the man said, wiping his plate with a piece of bread. "We got along well. He would come help me gain control when the boys got too wild… he had a firmness about him, even though he was young."

Shaya's heart slowed. If that was the case, there was nothing unusual about the story, nothing that would make him any wiser. The man had been in touch with Naftali before he had traveled, not after.

"After a few years," he suddenly heard the man next to him say, "Hey, what's this interesting cheese on your plate, with grooves?" He threw a questioning look at R' Nachman, as if wondering why he hadn't been given a taste of this special cheese.

"*Nu?*" Shaya asked urgently, not understanding how it was possible to be busy with cheeses instead of with more important matters.

"What *nu???*"

"What happened years later? You didn't finish saying."

"What didn't I finish saying?"

"The story – about Bleich."

"So Bleich does interest you? You are related to him?"

"Could be." Shaya didn't elaborate.

"All right. So after a number of years, when I didn't work there anymore, and I had even moved, I had a cousin's wedding in Manhattan. I flew out there, where I took a taxi. The taxi driver was very courteous, not like the drivers we have in Israel. You know."

"I know," Shaya said impatiently, hoping that the story wouldn't veer off track again, and that they would finally get to the point.

"I spoke with him about all sorts of things. His English sounded as though he might be a former Israeli. I asked him if he was Israeli, and he said no. I asked him his name, and he said David Stone. You know, in America there are three David Stones to a block, like Yitzchok Weiss in Jerusalem."

"*Nu*, so what does this whole story have to do with Bleich?"

The man chuckled. "Maybe you'll say I have a good imagination, but you don't see two things like this every day. When I was a *rebbe*, I once went into Bleich's classroom while he was teaching his boys how to bake matzos. He didn't just explain it, but brought almost an entire matzo bakery to class and went through the whole process together with his students. That was the only time I saw his sleeves rolled up, and I noticed that he had a mark the shape of a peach pit on his arm. It may sound funny, but this taxi driver, David Stone, who drove with one arm leaning on the open window, his short sleeves flapping in the wind, also had a mark like that on his arm. The exact same mark…"

The guest finished his tale and went to wash his hands before *bentching*. R' Nachman was already engrossed in *bentching*, so neither noticed the involuntary trembling that beset Shaya Bleich's hands, feet and teeth.

The man from Netanya was right. It wasn't his imagination. One didn't see two things like that every day. He knew that his brother Naftali had been a *cheder rebbe* in Haifa for some time. The story of baking matzos in class was typical of him, too.

But a taxi driver? David Stone…?!

"An interesting story," Shaya finally managed to say without his teeth chattering.

"Mmmm," said the guest, who didn't speak after *mayim acharonim*.

Shaya waited patiently. He had a whole list of questions, a very long list, but he couldn't seem too interested. After all, the reason for his being in that part of the world still wasn't known to anyone, and he couldn't know if any word or move of his would harm his brother, himself or them both.

"Where did you say it was? In Monsey?" he asked when the guest finally lifted his eyes from the *bentcher*.

"In Manhattan. It was years ago."

"How many?" Shaya wanted to know. Had to know.

"How many years?" It was hard to remember the exact date of a trip in a taxi. "I have to remember when this *chasunah* was. I think five years. Maybe six…"

"Can you remember exactly?" Shaya was impatient, but tried to keep his expression nonchalant.

"I can ask my wife to find out, if it's really, really important to you." In other words, Shaya understood, 'All I did was tell you a nice story. I didn't mean for you to bother me about it, so please leave me alone.'

But Shaya couldn't leave him alone. He had to hold tightly, though delicately, to the one lead that he had.

"When are you leaving here?" Shaya tried a different tack.

"Today, tomorrow, maybe another two years." The guest laughed, but Shaya wasn't in the mood of jokes. How could he get the information he needed without letting on that it was important? For him to approach all the taxi stands in Manhattan and ask if they knew a driver David Stone, he had to at least have a rough date. If a number of years had passed already, Stone might not work there anymore.

"I'll ask my wife," the guest promised, "and sometime today I'll have an answer for you. What do you say, R' Nachman, can I stay until the end of the day…?"

• • •

Shloime held the envelope over the garbage can with his fingertips, trying to shake off the layers of dust that clung to it. The envelope, as far as he could see, was white, with nothing written on it. That could be for two reasons: either it contained an invitation to the wedding of a couple who was already making a

*Thicker Than Water* « 145

bar mitzvah for their son – or to the bar mitzvah of a boy who already had a number of children of his own – or it was a request for *tzedakah*. Shloime didn't remember when requests for *tzedakah* were much more rare, definitely not arriving in the mail in a closed envelope, as was the present norm.

The envelope was well sealed, but Shloime was patient. Millimeter after millimeter, he slit it open, being careful not to tear it.

What emerged from the envelope, however, didn't make him especially smarter: one lone sheet of paper, typed, that, after glancing through it, didn't teach him much. It seemed to be a letter for his father, sent by someone Lederman. Shloime didn't know of any Lederman among their friends and relatives. Maybe his father would remember who it was, or maybe his mother, he thought to himself and put the paper aside. What's more, the letter – which hadn't been protected from the wear and tear of time and from the enthusiastic floor washings of Ima and Faigie – had many water stains that blurred a large part of the words. If Abba or Ima would want to read it, they would have to work hard, or ask the unknown Lederman to send a new copy of the old letter.

The phone rang. It was his father, looking for his mother. He was surprised to hear Shloime, who should have then been in the thick of *seder* in yeshiva.

"I only stayed for a little while," Shloime said apologetically. He felt uncomfortable telling his father that he was searching for his birth certificate, and that meanwhile, instead of striking gold, all he found was a lizard that disappeared and an envelope covered with dust.

"I found a letter here, Abba," he said, "something that might interest you. It was under the bookcase and, according to the date on it, it was sitting there for quite a number of years."

"A letter? Under the bookcase? What does that mean? Somebody hid it?" Shaya tried to understand. "A letter from whom?"

"I don't know who it is. It doesn't look like someone tried to hide it. It's more likely that it got stuck there by mistake. It's from somebody Lederman."

The name Lederman hit Shaya like a sledgehammer.

"Ah," he said, "Leave it."

"Who's Lederman?" Shloime was curious.

"Someone I once knew. We haven't been in touch for years."

Shloime shook the paper; maybe some words would fall from it.

"Oh, I think it's a receipt," he wrinkled his forehead. "Maybe you bought something by this Lederman?"

"Could be," Shaya said, wanting desperately to strike Lederman from the agenda.

"So I should throw out this paper?"

"Yes," Shaya said, "You could throw it away." 'You *must* throw it away' is what Shaya wanted to say, but held himself back in order not to arouse Shloime's suspicions. If Shloime would know about a private investigator who had tried to find his parents and had suddenly stopped, all his antennas would shoot up. Shloime could not be allowed to meet Mendel Lederman. It was dangerous.

"Should we ask him to send the receipt again?"

"No, there's no need..."

• • •

Suri found her mother in her room, busy on the telephone with preparations for the wedding. She motioned to Suri to wait. Suri sat down on the edge of the bed, chewing her nails, every line of her face screaming that she had something important to say, to ask, to shout.

"Ima," she shot as soon as the phone was put down, "what does Yisroel Yitzchok know that I don't…?"

"What does Yisroel Yitzchok know that… what does that mean? I don't understand the question, Suri."

"There's something that Yisroel Yitzchok, and maybe you too, and maybe some other people, know, and I don't. Something to do with the *chasunah*. I want to know what it is, Ima. Is there a problem with my *chasunah*? Something wrong? Something that was okay and is now going to change? Tell me everything, Ima, please. Don't hide anything from me…"

Devorah Fuchsman tried to string her daughter's words together and absolutely couldn't.

"Why don't you direct me, Suri," she suggested. "Give me some sort of explanation, a hint, something, so that I could understand what you mean, because meanwhile I don't understand a thing…"

"Yisroel Yitzchok," Suri shifted on the edge of the bed as if it was a thorn bush, "told me that I should *daven* that I should have a *chasunah*. So I---"

Devorah was struck dumb.

"Yisroel Yitzchok said that?! When?"

Suri looked at her watch. "About ten minutes ago. Maybe a little less. You understand, Ima, these things---"

"I understand one thing only," her mother cut her off, "and that's that I don't understand a thing. Yisroel Yitzchok!! Come here, right now!!"

But the house was quiet. Yisroel Yitzchok had anticipated the storm and slipped out to yeshiva while he still could.

"He left," Suri said and sighed.

Devorah Fuchsman closed her hand over that of her daughter,

the *kallah*, and prayed that she find the words that would strike every strange, frightening thought from her child's heart. "You know Yisroel Yitzchok, Suri," she said. "He's impulsive. He doesn't think about what he's saying and many times he really feels bad afterwards. I think that in this case he just wanted to tease you, for whatever reason. He knows that it's usually useless to tease you, so he chose the thing most sensitive and important to you, and to all of us. I promise you, Suri, I'm your mother and you can trust me. Your *chasunah* will take place, *im Yirtzeh Hashem*, as planned; you can go back to your sewing machine and finish your dress for *Shabbos sheva brachos*."

"Yisroel Yitzchok may be impulsive," Suri said without lifting her eyes, "but he's not stupid. And he doesn't just toss things out into the air. If he said it, he must have what to base it on. Of course, I believe you completely, Ima, but I want to know why he said it."

"Yisroel Yitzchok's not stupid, that's true," Devorah said, "but sometimes he has a hard time differentiating between reality and fantasy." As soon as the words left her mouth, Devorah regretted them. Words, though, can't be reclaimed.

"Which fantasy?" Suri lifted a pair of huge eyes.

Devorah sighed. She would now have to explain the foolishness that filled Yisroel Yitzchok's head regarding Shloime – and to Suri? It was so unnecessary, so ridiculous. *This, Yisroel Yitzchok, is what we call* aveira goreres aveira.

• • •

Shloime didn't throw out the letter. He put it in his night table, under all the binders and papers.

"Ima, who's Lederman?" he asked his mother in the evening.

"Lederman… Lederman… the name sounds so familiar. Why do you ask?"

"I found an old letter under the bookcase today, that someone Lederman sent. The letter is almost all erased, but the name Lederman is there."

Chana waited until the last of the children left the kitchen and was out of hearing distance. Shloime's questioning look, and the fierce desire to help him, once again disconnected the red lights in her mind.

"Lederman is a private investigator that we took way back to investigate your parents' disappearance."

"Really?!" Shloime's ears perked up. "And what did he find?"

Chana returned to those far-off days. How much hope they had placed in the strong, well connected Lederman, and how painful had been the despair when he informed them that he couldn't get involved, couldn't give them any information.

"Nothing," she said.

"Nothing at all?" Shloime didn't want to believe it. Could his parents' disappearance really be so complicated?! Had they been swallowed up into some black hole…?!

"He said that he couldn't get involved," Chana said briefly. She caught herself, a bit late. She wouldn't tell Shloime that an outside force had threatened Lederman. Such a story would only fire his imagination ten times more. "We saw no reason to approach him again, or any other investigator, who would have probably given us the same answer."

"So you stopped looking?" Shloime asked. Almost demanded.

"No, Shloime. We never stopped. We always searched for information, and we never stopped *davening*, not even for one day."

"So they… they're just missing for almost twenty years…?"

"You can call it whatever you like, Shloime, but no description will change the reality. The pain rips me apart – and Abba even more so – each day, each hour."

Shloime was quiet. He was filled with tremendous admiration for his parents.

"So... so what will be now? If you haven't managed to find them until now, why should you succeed in finding them in the short time that's left before the *chasunah*?!"

Chana sighed.

"I said as much to Abba. He also knows it, but he said he'd never forgive himself if he didn't know that he did everything – but really everything – in order that your real father lead you to the *chuppah*."

Shloime hung his head and played with his *peyos*. Chana began drying the dishes, something she hadn't done in years. Even with her back to him, she could see the wheels in his head whirring.

"So... so really there is information," he said. "It's possible to get information – and perhaps this investigator already had it – but there's some sort of block that's preventing the information from being given over. This block has to be removed."

Chana turned to face him. There was terror in her eyes.

"You're still young, Shloime," she said, almost pleading, "Very young. I beg you not to do anything hasty. Don't try to break down walls that you have no idea what's hiding behind them. Shloime, I beg of you," she repeated, when she saw that Shloime wasn't picking up his eyes, "Shloime, don't do anything on your own. With all your worry and love for your parents. I can't stress enough how terribly important it is…"

• • •

Shaya Bleich remained closeted in his room the entire day, trying to process the information. True, it wasn't certain that that taxi driver was his brother Naftali – and it was very, very difficult to imagine such a thing: his bearded brother, his face so refined and Jewish, his modest brother, driving a car with his short sleeves flapping in the breeze from the open window... On the other hand, how many people have a mark the shape of a peach pit in the same place, on the same arm...?

Only late at night did the guest from Netanya return from a packed day. He went into the kitchen and sat down for supper. Shaya had already eaten supper, but he had no patience to wait for the guest to finish eating. Based on that morning's experience, it could take quite some time.

He went into the kitchen and saw the guest sitting down, a full plate before him and the newspaper fully spread out on the table.

"Uh..." he began. Actually, he didn't even know the name of the guest.

The guest picked up his head. Immediately he remembered Shaya and his request from the morning.

"I spoke to my wife," he said, and swallowed a bite of meatloaf. "She also didn't remember exactly. She just remembered the headache that she had on that trip. She didn't feel comfortable calling our cousins and asking them exactly when the chasunah was, and we threw out the invitation long ago."

"That's all right," Shaya said immediately. "Thank you very much, and please thank your wife for me."

He would have to make do with that. Now he had to get the phone numbers of all the taxi stands in Manhattan. He wouldn't ask any more questions. He would just try his luck, and search until he struck gold.

Something deep inside actually wished that he wouldn't find him. That it shouldn't be his wonderful brother Naftali who was forced to change his identity to a lowly cab driver. Because in his mind, Naftali today was the same Naftali of long ago, and no other identity would suit him. Ever.

...

One of the *bochurim* tapped Yisroel Yitzchok on the shoulder.

"Someone's waiting for you next to the yeshiva office," he said. Yisroel Yitzchok immediately stood up. Who could be looking for him? He strode quickly through the hallways, unable to think of anyone.

Abba. His father stood next to the Rosh Yeshiva's room. His face was grim.

"We're going out now for a little while," he said briefly to Yisroel Yitzchok. "I already spoke with the Rosh Yeshiva. It's extremely urgent."

Yisroel Yitzchok veered into the hallway to take his hat and coat. He could begin to guess what his father wanted to tell him.

The afternoon sun beat down on the street. Yisroel Yitzchok searched for his father's car with his eyes, but didn't see it anywhere.

"We're not driving anywhere," his father said sharply, seeing his searching eyes. "I have some questions for you; let's just find a shady corner. You may deserve a good beating, but not sunstroke."

Shade, if it could actually be called that, was finally found under a tree a few blocks away from the yeshiva.

"Can I understand the meaning of this story with Suri?" his father asked directly.

"What story with Suri?"

His father, though, had no patience for hedging. He pushed Yisroel Yitzchok up against the wall, not taking into account that his son was the sort of person who, rather than breaking from being pushed up against a wall, was driven to acts of desperation.

"Yes, that's what I think," he said boldly. "I have a lot of doubts about this perfect *bochur* that we're bringing into our house. I have a strong feeling that he's hiding something not so kosher, and I quite rely on my feelings."

His father's lips tightened.

"Your feelings, Yisroel Yitzchok Fuchsman," he said quietly, almost in a whisper, and Yisroel Yitzchok knew that the quieter his father spoke, the more dangerous it was, "you can save for other things. When it comes to anything that has to do with the house or the family, you may not feel or rely. Two people run the house and two only: Ima and myself, and we will not tolerate any interference, all the more so such gross interference as your own. You have no idea," Elya Fuchsman filled his lungs, "You have no idea how much anguish you caused Suri – a *kallah* approaching her *chasunah* – with the few reckless, baseless statements of yours. I absolutely forbid you---"

"Abba, they weren't baseless statements."

Had they not been standing in the street, Elya Fuchsman would have exercised his fatherly obligations and slapped Yisroel Yitzchok. As it was, he stuffed his hands deep into his pockets and hissed, "I don't want to hear another word from you on the topic, do you understand…?!"

# CHAPTER 13

"Lederman Investigations, how can I help you?"

The pleasant secretary didn't know Shloime. He asked her if it was possible to set up a meeting with Mendel.

"About what?"

Shloime didn't know how any answer he might say would be received. "About an investigation."

"Most people who call here are calling about investigations," the secretary chuckled.

"I can't be more specific," Shloime said, and for good reason. He knew that if Mendel would know the purpose of the meeting, chances were he wouldn't agree to keep it.

"Has there already been a meeting about this investigation?" the secretary wanted to know.

"Not with me," Shloime said briefly.

In the end, a meeting was set up for Thursday, at two thirty in the afternoon. Shloime gave a fake name. He feared that the name Bleich would cause the meeting to be immediately cancelled. He hoped, though, that sitting face to face with Mendel Lederman, things would sort themselves out differently. He also hoped that when Lederman discovered he had been duped, he wouldn't throw him out on his ear.

• • •

The list in Shaya Bleich's hand was creased. The telephone was slippery in his sweaty hand.

He had already spoken to the dispatchers of thirteen taxi stands. They didn't understand what he wanted at first, and were usually impatient, as well. They weren't sitting there in order to answer questions, but to field orders. Some of them were more polite, some less so. What they all had in common was that none of them knew a driver by the name of David Stone – not today, nor from six years earlier.

One was able to offer a driver by the name of Robert Stone. Another had three Davids who worked for him, but none of them were Stone. Many asked what difference it made, and why he was looking for that driver. Shaya mumbled something, belatedly realizing the need to have some sort of convincing cover story, without which, no one was too eager to cooperate with him.

His list had six more numbers. He would try them, but he prepared himself for the definite possibility that nothing would come of it. At that point, he would seriously consider hiring the services of a private investigator who would be able to discover things that he, Shaya, had no way of finding.

He dialed the number of stand number fourteen.

"Hello," he spoke briefly and quickly, in a voice loud enough to be heard over the background buzz of chatting drivers. "I'm looking for a driver by the name of David Stone, who works for you, or worked for you six years ago."

"Why are you looking for him?" came the immediate question. The voice didn't hide its suspicion and impatience.

"Something very important got lost when he drove me," Shaya said, thinking that if David Stone really was his brother Naftali, then he could definitely describe him as something very important that he lost.

"When?"

"When he drove me."

"Six years ago?"

"Yes."

"And why did you remember about it only now?"

Shaya was slightly pushed into a corner. He didn't have a good answer. Actually, though, why should he have to answer before receiving an answer to his main question?

"First tell me, please, sir, does David Stone work for you or not?"

"We don't give out information about our drivers."

"But I'm telling you that I lost something while riding with him."

"If you lost something, you're welcome to come to our lost and found in order to find it, though I don't believe that what you lost is waiting here for you for six years."

"I'd like to speak to the driver himself," Shaya said in alarm, before the window of opportunity closed.

There was a short silence on the line.

"You have nothing to talk to him about. We don't have a driver by the name of David Stone."

"And in the past you did? It's very important to me."

"It's important to me to end this conversation. Have a good day."

A very good day, Shaya thought bitterly, and hesitated before drawing a line through the name of the taxi stand. He hadn't received a clear negative answer. On the other hand, there had barely been any cooperation.

Shaya keenly felt the lack of a private investigator. People treated investigators differently, both because they knew how to talk to people and because they knew how to find information that they were seeking.

Should he call the next taxi stand, or give up in despair...?

• • •

Shloime shook Lederman's hand and sat down in a chair opposite him.

"Yes, Yitzchok Blau," Lederman glanced at the card in front of him. "How can we help one another?"

"Let's start with a small correction," Shloime said, feeling his heart pound, "Not Yitzchok Blau, but Shloime Bleich."

Lederman looked at him for a minute, with a look that caused Shloime to slightly cringe and doubt the correctness of his move.

"What causes an upright client to present himself with a name other than his own?"

Shloime checked that the door behind him was closed so that Lederman couldn't throw him out, and said, "My parents met with you quite a number of years ago. You had a file with the name Bleich."

Lederman looked long and hard at Shloime, keeping his thoughts to himself. Shloime had the feeling that the man had recognized him from the start.

"Yes," was all that he finally said. And again, "Yes."

"That's why I'm here," Shloime said. "Do I have to remind you of the details in that file, or should we get straight to the point?"

"You don't have to remind me of the details," Lederman said wearily, "because we're absolutely not going to deal with that file. By the way, who told you of my involvement with it?"

Shloime squirmed in his seat. Was it right to say that his parents gave him the information when they had tried their best to prevent him from meeting with Lederman?

"I'm the son of Naftali and Rochel Bleich, who disappeared and still haven't been found," Shloime said.

"Yes," Lederman said with that same thoughtful look, "I know that they still haven't been found."

"I'm about to get married," Shloime said, "and my father traveled to America in order to search for them again. He can't bear the thought of my standing under the *chuppah* without my biological father being there."

"I understand," Lederman said and doodled on the paper in front of him.

"I don't know what happened when you dealt with the investigation," Shloime said. "I was a little boy then. But now I'm asking you, as a son who has no recollection of his father and mother – would you agree to help me find my parents? I have a feeling that it's now or never. Going to the *chuppah* without them would be kind of making peace with their absence. I don't want that to happen. Please understand me, R' Mendel."

Lederman continued to doodle for long minutes. Shloime didn't dare disturb his train of thought.

"With all the good will in the world," he finally said, "and believe me, the will is there, I can't help you, young Bleich. I am simply not able to. If I was able to, I would have already helped back then. Believe me."

"But why?" Shloime asked, leveling his gaze at Lederman. "What's stopping you?"

Lederman didn't answer immediately. He allowed himself

time to think before every answer.

"I can't tell you that either," he finally said.

Shloime felt the frustration spread through him, filling every pore.

"I can't handle the thought," he said, "that somebody knows where my parents are, but can't tell me. Who would stand in the way of a child who wishes to meet his parents?!"

Lederman smiled thinly. "You're very convincing, Bleich," he said, "but if you know me at all, you know that once I give a commitment, I'll never break it. If I cannot release information, I will not release it."

"Commitment??" Shloime asked, suddenly alert, "What commitment? To whom?!"

• • •

Devorah Fuchsman looked at the calendar. That evening they had two bar mitzvahs and a wedding. In the whirl of preparations for their own wedding, they couldn't forget about their relatives and friends. Wait, what was written there in tiny letters, in Yisroel Yitzchok's handwriting?

"Dentist appointment, two thirty."

She tapped her forehead in consternation. She had really planned on switching Yisroel Yitzchok to a closer dental clinic, even if it wasn't as good. With all that was going on, she simply forgot. And this was the result: Yisroel Yitzchok would travel again to that clinic, and again he would return with all kinds of new conjectures regarding their *chosson's* doings. That couldn't happen, it just couldn't. It wouldn't be good for anyone.

The problem was that if the appointment was for two thirty, Yisroel Yitzchok would leave straight from yeshiva. She had to somehow get hold of him right away, and let him know that she was cancelling his appointment.

Devorah dialed the yeshiva's office. The line was busy. Again it was busy, and again. She tried the public phone, but no one was around to answer it, as it was in middle of *seder*.

Devorah quickly ran through her options. If she dropped everything and went to the yeshiva, she would be able to find Yisroel Yitzchok, but she wouldn't be able to get back in time for the other children.

The line was still busy. She knew from experience that it could take a long time. She didn't have a choice; she would have to organize herself immediately, find a neighbor who would agree to have the children until she returned, and catch a taxi to the yeshiva. True, it wasn't accepted practice for mothers to come down to the yeshiva, but then again, neither was it accepted practice for *bochurim* to follow their future brothers-in-law and try to find any possible fault with them.

"Drive quickly," she urged the taxi driver. They would be cutting it close.

But, as if preplanned, a large traffic jam stopped the taxi. Devorah's gaze swung back and forth from her watch to the long line of cars. If traffic didn't free up right then, she might miss him.

Finally, the small taxi was free of the jam and sped forward. The driver did his best, but Devorah arrived at the yeshiva building at 1:40.

"Excuse me," she turned to the first *bochur* she saw outside, "I'm looking for Yisroel Yitzchok Fuchsman. It's extremely urgent."

Just then, Yisroel Yitzchok was sitting in the back seat of the bus that was pulling away from the stop. It seemed to him that he saw a familiar women running towards the bus stop. No, it couldn't be that that was his mother. Ima was at home, serving lunch to his little brothers and sisters. He pressed his nose against the window and fingered the inner pocket of his suit coat. His notepad with the carefully copied name and address of the psychologist rested there securely. Today he would return with real findings.

Devorah Fuchsman watched in despair as the bus pulled away from the bus stop.

She couldn't be sure that Yisroel Yitzchok was on it, but it was highly probable. If that was the case, all her efforts had been for nothing. She could, perhaps, call the clinic and cancel the appointment – not such a proper thing to do less than an hour before the appointment – but even if she did, and knew, more or less, when to expect Yisroel Yitzchok back, he would still have enough time to poke around. He could always claim that the bus came late or that it got stuck in traffic.

There was no choice. Elya would have to drive there now, in middle of the workday, wait for Yisroel Yitzchok at the bus stop, and catch him before he could go anywhere from there. Elya didn't appreciate being disturbed, but this wasn't called disturbing. It was a sort of *piku'ach nefesh*.

• • •

"What commitment?" Shloime asked again, leaning forward without realizing it. "R' Mendel, do you owe anything to anyone besides me? Don't I have preference in receiving information? These are my parents, nobody else's…"

Mendel Lederman was quiet. He knew that the stirring arguments of the boy had momentarily distracted him, causing him to say a sentence that wasn't allowed to be said.

"I cannot add another word, Bleich," he said, angry. Not at the refined, unfortunate boy, but at himself and the mistake he had made. "And do me a favor, don't ask me to. Just as you would want me to keep your secrets, I must keep the secrets of others. Is that clear?"

"But who are these 'others'?" Shloime didn't let up. He couldn't.

"I told you, I cannot say another word. Bleich, leave me alone. You don't want me to throw you out of here."

No, Shloime didn't want to be thrown out, but to pick himself up and leave with things the way they were was simply beyond him. In a move that was completely out of character, he banged his fist on the table in frustration.

"R' Mendel Lederman, listen to the absurdity of it!" His voice rose, "You committed yourself to somebody to keep the file secret. From whom? From me, from the son of the couple that disappeared. Can there be someone more important than me, who comes before me?! That can't be. Agree with me R' Mendel. Maybe my parents left behind another son who is looking for them?"

Mendel Lederman automatically shook his head.

"There is someone who could be more important than you, Bleich," he said. "And with all your pain – and I identify with your pain with all my heart – I am not the address for information. What comes through this doorway," he pointed to the door to the room, "and through this telephone, doesn't leave. That's one of the reasons for my crowded schedule, if you shall. Come, Bleich, let's end this meeting on a positive note." Lederman called for his secretary, who brought a cup of cold water, put his card down before Shloime and shook his hand in parting.

• • •

Elya Fuchsman sounded put out when answering his wife's

phone call. Why was she disturbing him in middle of work? She knew how bothered he got from interruptions. As she spoke, however, he, too, grasped the urgency of the matter and promised to do as she asked as soon as he finished his call on the other line. The drive by car was much shorter than by bus. If he left in the next few minutes, he would surely be there by the time Yisroel Yitzchok came off the bus.

He couldn't know, however, that Yisroel Yitzchok planned on staying on the bus for one more stop, getting off closer to the psychologist's clinic and leaving his father to roast for a long while in his car until realizing that something wasn't right.

Yisroel Yitzchok, then sitting comfortably under the air conditioning vent on the bus, had planned carefully. He hadn't relied on circumstances bringing Shloime to the same bus again today so that he could follow him. He wrote down the psychologist's address, looked at a map in order not to get lost on his way there and even sketched the route in his notebook.

As the trip progressed, he thought to let the clinic know that he would be about a quarter of an hour late. If today, too, he didn't show up on time, the punctual secretary would call his mother again. His mother would become hysterical, sending his father once again to the neighborhood and ruining the entire plan.

Yisroel Yitzchok didn't have a cell phone, but he did have a calling card. He got off the bus as planned, one stop later, and made his way to a public telephone.

"You'll be a bit late?" the secretary asked. "What a shame. Try not to be too late. You don't want the doctor to have to wait for you."

"Oka---"

"Wait, just a minute, what did you say your name was? Fuchsman Yisroel?"

"Yisroel Yitzchok Fuchsman."

The secretary was confused. "I don't understand what's going on here. I have here that your appointment for today was cancelled."

Yisroel Yitzchok was stunned. "What do you mean? I have an appointment for today. I made it a long time ago. I never cancelled it."

"I don't know, Fuchsman. I got here half an hour ago. It could be that the cancellation was made while the other secretary was here. In any event, there is no appointment for you today, because someone from the waiting list took your slot. It's good that you called, so you don't come in for nothing."

No, he wouldn't come for nothing. There was only one logical explanation: his parents cancelled the appointment and didn't let him know about it. He had left yeshiva before lunch and traveled all that way for nothing.

"And when is my new appointment?" he asked the secretary.

She checked the computer. "I don't see another appointment for you, Fuchsman. At least not in the next half a year."

Aha. In that case, everything was clear. His parents were afraid that if he came to the area, he would bring back information about Shloime, information that would ruin their dear *chosson's* pure, untarnished image.

The whole time that Yisroel Yitzchok stood, tight lipped, by the public phone, undecided what to do, Elya Fuchsman sat in his car two streets down. He shut his Palm Pilot in order to focus on the job and not miss the passing bus. And he didn't miss it. One bus passed, and another; all sorts of people got on and off, but Yisroel Yitzchok was nowhere to be seen.

"No sign of him," he said to Devorah on the telephone.

"What, he didn't get off the bus?! The way I figure it, he should have gotten there long ago."

"Well, I guess he figures differently than you, Devorah."

"Do you want to wait another few minutes?"

"I'll wait. And if he doesn't show up, then what should I do?"

She truly didn't know. "Maybe go to the clinic. Maybe he got there some other way."

"You can check that by phone, no?"

Yes, she could. "I'll check and get back to you. Give me a few minutes."

• • •

Shloime Bleich left Mendel Lederman's office, his blood pounding in his ears. He had been so close, and once again he was left dangling.

He didn't even realize that he began the long way home on foot. For half of the way, he couldn't tell the difference between right and left. *Ribbono shel Olam*, there was someone who knew where his parents were to be found – if they really were to be found – and was able, with a few sentences, to solve the question of his life, yet was prevented from doing so.

Slowly, it sank in that he *had* learned a few things at the meeting. First of all, Lederman let on that he had a commitment to somebody not to pass along the information. And if there was someone like that, it meant that there was another party to whom his parents' disappearance was important. From that, two things were clear: number one, there was someone else standing on the other side. His parents hadn't been swallowed up into a black hole without anyone knowing why. Was that encouraging? Maybe, maybe not. Secondly, if the commitment to the other party still existed, then it sounded like his parents were still alive. They were still hidden from him, but they were alive wherever they were. It was hard to believe that somebody would guard their secret so fiercely after their death.

There was more to be learned from what Lederman said, whether intentionally or innocently. His parents didn't leave behind another child who was searching for them. Maybe today there were more children, but those children were together with them. On the other hand, those 'others', to whom Lederman promised that he wouldn't pass along the information, were no less important than he, the biological son, was.

Shloime laid out the family unit in his mind. Who could be as close as him? His parents, Shaya and Chana. A brother was no less close than a son. Saba and Savta Bleich were no less important than he was, either. They were the parents. The parents of Ima Rochel were the same thing, as were her sisters and brothers. He, Shloime, was just another relative. When his parents got lost somewhere, he was just a little boy. He wasn't involved in any searching, and nobody made any commitments to him.

If so, he now had to change direction. If the information was by his parents, or someone else from the family, it would be easier to get it from him than from the investigator. It was hard to believe that it was by his adoptive parents; otherwise, why would his father, Shaya, embark on such an intense round of searching? Were there secrets, though, in the family? Was there something that Saba and Savta, or one of the brothers-in-law, knew, and were hiding from his parents?!

As Shloime's head started to ache from all his thoughts and speculations, he realized that he had been walking for more than an hour. He really hadn't paid any attention where his feet were taking him. It was a pity, too, since he found himself near a teeming shopping center that he would normally have tried to avoid.

His head cleared. He removed his hat for a minute and wiped his sweating forehead, looking for the street that would lead him away from there.

"Excuse me," a bareheaded soldier carrying a huge duffel bag turned to him, "Do you know how to get from here to Tel Aviv?"

Yes, Shloime knew how to get from there to Tel Aviv. He shook off the remaining cobwebs of thought and summoned all his graciousness and ability to explain in order to make it as easy as possible for the soldier.

He had no way of knowing that, precisely during those few minutes, his future father-in-law's car was driving down the street. Elya Fuchsman had not succeeded in meeting Yisroel Yitzchok. He had sat in his car and waited for him for more than an hour. Just a few minutes earlier, his wife had informed him that Yisroel Yitzchok had shown up at the door to their house. Angrily, Elya drove away, determined to put an end to this annoying business for once and for all.

It was impossible to mistake him. In his dark coat, Shloime stuck out among all the colorful characters of the shopping center. Elya Fuchsman didn't let his children roam the place, and it didn't sit well with him at all to see Shloime, the supposedly G-d fearing future husband of his oldest daughter, standing right there, without his hat, speaking animatedly with a bareheaded soldier.

# CHAPTER 14

Had it not been such a noisy street, Elya Fuchsman would have pulled over and offered Shloime a ride home. This time, though, not wanting to be there more than the minute or so that it took to drive through, he just kept on going until the end of the street, stopped and continued to observe the sight of his future son-in-law, the charming young man, standing right in middle of the secular street.

Even after a few minutes, when Shloime began to walk down the street in the direction of his neighborhood, Elya's mind was not at rest. He continued to sit in his car, deep in thought, letting Shloime pass right by him.

Anyone could end up in that place which, besides for the shopping center, also had many offices and services. All the buses in the city stopped there, as well. Elya didn't approve of those people who absolutely refused, at any price, to go to these places, since it usually ended up being at the expense of others. He could understand that Shloime, with all his preparations for the wedding, or maybe as his father's stand-in, had to come there.

But with all that, something caught inside him. This was about Suri, his dear eldest daughter. True, he checked into the *bochur's* character before entering into the *shidduch*. And yes, he had sincerely promised Devorah that this was the perfect husband for Suri. All this was true. And yet, everyone stumbles occasionally. And perhaps this wasn't a slip-up of Shloime's, but of his own? Maybe he really hadn't checked enough?

When Elya Fuchsman entered his home, he was extremely irritable.

Yisroel Yitzchok had returned before him, ate something and left for yeshiva. Elya knew that it wasn't any love of learning that had chased Yisroel Yitzchok back to yeshiva, but fear of the dressing down he would receive from his father.

"We have to put an end to this," Devorah said. "What's happening isn't doing anyone any good."

Elya sat by the kitchen table and did nothing except breathe – in and out.

"Please bring me something to drink," he requested.

Suri came into the kitchen. Elya, who loved his daughter very much, begged her – silently, of course – to leave him and his wife alone. Outwardly, though, he smiled at her as usual.

"I'm glad to find just the two of you here," she said. "I wanted to talk to you about something. May I?"

"Of course."

Elya regretted that he hadn't asked her to leave. He should have sensed that she was going to raise questions that would drain him.

"When I spent Shabbos with the Bleichs," she began, leaning on the counter. She knew that her parents were listening to her carefully, though each one gazed in a different direction. "It bothered me that the father – my future father-in-law – wasn't there."

"He traveled, didn't he??" Devorah asked. "To take care of things before the *chasunah*."

"Yes, that's what I understood. It didn't strike me as strange. I know that many people travel to America when making a *chasunah* – to collect money, among other things. The truth is I didn't get the impression that that was the reason for the trip. I don't think the Bleichs need to travel around the world in order to come up with some tens of thousands of dollars, but that's not what bothered me."

"Nu?" Elya held out his cup to Devorah for a refill.

"I picked up that the children themselves don't know why their father's not home. As if they hid something from them. I felt uncomfortable asking anybody. I thought that maybe you would have some way of finding out."

"And why should it make a difference to us?" Devorah asked.

"Maybe it doesn't make a difference. The truth is it's hard for me to put my finger on it, but something in the atmosphere was a bit odd. Maybe it was tension. Maybe some kind of mystery. I'm not an expert on atmospheres, but that's what I picked up."

Elya took another swallow of his drink.

"Look, Suri. Every family has its personal matters which remain private even when becoming *mechutanim* with another family. There could be many reasons for the trip to America besides collecting money – and I really don't think that Shaya Bleich is planning on collecting money. Maybe he went to do some shopping?"

"I don't think so," Suri said. "How long does shopping take? Months? A week and a half – two weeks, no?!"

"How do you know he's not on his way home, Suri?" Elya asked, "Besides which, maybe they're the kind of family that doesn't like to talk. There are families like that, where everything is a secret until proven otherwise. Let me explain to you what I believe," he moved his cup aside. "I believe that every person is entitled to privacy, and that everyone has the obligation to help him maintain that privacy. We will not stick our noses into the Bleichs' business, and they won't stick their noses into ours. I think that's decent enough, no?"

• • •

Mendel Lederman pulled himself up from his large armchair and went over to the window. His office was on the seventeenth floor of an office building, and from its window one could see almost a kilometer in three directions.

Shloime Bleich left the building. His steps were quick. At surface glance, he didn't look like someone who had just suffered a blow, but Lederman's sharp eyes could discern his trembling hands shoved deep inside his pants pockets.

Lederman stayed by the window. Shloime waited at the light, crossed the street and receded into the distance. Only after making sure that Shloime was far enough away did he allow himself to leave the window and go over to the telephone sitting on his desk.

He flipped through his phone book. He definitely had the number; the question was only under which cover name.

"Hello," he said quietly into the receiver. "Lederman here. The boy was by me."

Someone on the other side of the line asked something.

"Like an eagle homing in on its prey. He's getting married soon."

The next sentence caused Lederman to sit down abruptly.

"Oh, no. You will not do that – though, between you and me, I got the impression that that would be the smartest thing you could do."

He listened in wonder.

"But you can't. You can't. No, don't say that. Every way has a way back."

When Lederman finished the conversation, he asked his secretary not to let anyone in or transfer any phone calls, only a cigarette to calm him. They were about to make a terrible mistake.

· · ·

Devorah Fuchsman and her daughter Suri stood in the small, home-based store for linen, and tried to choose.

"What do you say about these?" Devorah asked, pointing at a pattern that she thought was pretty.

"Nice," Suri said.

"And these?"

"Also nice."

Devorah gave her a sidelong glance. It was known in the family, ever since she chose dresses for her dolls as a little girl, that Suri had excellent taste. Devorah never went shopping without her, and definitely not to buy the towels and linens she would be using in her new home.

"And these with the stripes, you like?" she tried.

"Yes." No, it couldn't be that she liked the ones with the stripes. Even if they had once been in style, they had gone out very quickly.

"Suri, are you concentrating?" she whispered. The store was small, and the owner was standing five feet away from them.

"I'm... what? Yeah, sure I'm concentrating. See what nice towels they have, Ima."

But Devorah didn't see what nice towels they had. She saw her daughter the *kallah*, who seemed to have faded. It wasn't the same radiant, glowing Suri from after the *tena'im*; it was a different Suri, with a cloud over her face.

*Thicker Than Water* « 173

• • •

Like a blind man in a chimney. That's how Shaya Bleich described himself whenever he thought about his actions in that foreign country, and he thought about it for most of the day.

He would hire a private investigator. On that he was decided. The question was how to go about finding one. Should he hang a notice in shul: "Wanted, private investigator, specializing in the disappearance of relatives, good terms for those suitable."? Or maybe he should ask around in the *shtiebel*? Or – this was another possibility – he could ask R' Nachman himself, thereby assuring himself an immediate answer, along with massive advertising throughout the entire neighborhood.

Shaya Bleich stood and sent up a heartfelt prayer. In normal times, meaning when he was home, the Kosel served as his regular address in such circumstances. But now he was so far away, so disconnected. Maybe his broken-heartedness would rise before *HaKadosh Boruch Hu* and find favor?

Even after *davening*, though, no miracle took place. No bright ideas fell into the room. The telephone didn't ring. No one knocked on the door offering him the wished for breakthrough.

Shaya Bleich sank back down into his chair, full of despair. Should he call Shloime again? He hadn't yet succeeded in making him any smarter. All he managed to do was build castles in the air and find an old letter of Mendel Lederman's under the bookcase.

*Hold on. Just one minute.*

Mendel Lederman. True, the man had kept his mouth completely sealed over the last years, but surely he had connections with private investigators all over the world and could recommend one that would be suitable. Would he refuse that request as well, claiming that he wanted nothing at all to do with the affair? He might, but he might not. After all, he, too, would have liked to close the case, but was prevented from doing so. *He* was prevented, but somebody else wasn't…!

• • •

Suri Fuchsman stood at the corner of the street, watching the passersby and waiting for her future mother-in-law. She was supposed to meet her in order to go together to the jewelry store and choose a necklace, bracelet and earrings set. Suri wasn't such a great fan of jewelry, but, as a *kallah*, she happily accepted her fate.

A taxi stopped on the other side of the street. The door opened and Mrs. Bleich exited quickly, looking around for her.

"Oh, Suri, hello," she said in relief as she saw Suri crossing the street towards her. "I'm sorry I'm late. An important phone call held me up, though, really, you're more important. Were you waiting long?"

They were swallowed up into the crowds rushing back and forth on the sidewalk. The jewelry store was a few blocks away, giving them a few minutes to speak.

"The children don't stop playing with the games you brought them, Suri. How did you know exactly what they like?"

"I didn't," Suri chuckled, "so I took my little brothers along with me to choose. I knew that whatever they liked, the little ones by you would also enjoy. Children are children."

At the bend in the street, Mrs. Bleich met an old friend of hers. Suri knew that her mother-in-law had many friends, and that it would take her a long time to get to know all of them.

"I understand that this is your new *kallah*?" The friend carefully inspected Suri down to her marrow.

"That's right," Chana said. "This is Suri Fuchsman, Shloime's *kallah*." She gripped Suri's shoulders, and Suri felt as if she was trying to protect her.

"How nice," said the friend, "And when is the *chasunah*?"

"In another few months," Chana answered.

"Do you have a date yet?" the friend asked.

"More or less," Chana smiled. "Don't worry, Miriam. You'll be the first to receive an invitation."

After the friend went on her way, Suri wanted to ask why her mother-in-law held back from saying the exact date. Maybe there was a custom in the family to keep the date a secret until the last minute in order to avoid an *ayin hora*? True, she had never heard of such a *minhag*, but each family and its own tradition. On the other hand, when had they managed to create a tradition when Shloime was the first in the family to get married?

She had only formulated the question in her mind when she saw her mother-in-law rummaging at length in her pocketbook. What had she suddenly lost there, in middle of the street, before they had gone into even one store?

• • •

Shaya's fingers dialed the number. The phone rang once, and again. The voice of the secretary answered him.

"Can I speak with the investigator, Lederman, please?"

"I'll take your details and he'll get back to you. He's busy now."

"It will be a very short conversation," Shaya promised, "but it's very urgent. I'm calling from America. I can even wait on the line, if that's possible, but I can't wait until he'll get back to me, you understand?"

"Who's speaking?" Now it wasn't just a technical inquiry, but natural curiosity.

"I prefer to tell him, if possible," Shaya said.

"Impossible. I have clear instructions not to transfer anonymous calls."

"My name is Yeshaya Bleich."

"Yeshaya Bleich," the secretary repeated after him, and her voice reached Lederman's ears through the open door to the inside room, where he sat with a client. "Do you have a file with us?"

"I think that if there is a file, it's in the archives. We're talking about a story of close to twenty years ago." Shaya sighed. This was exactly what he didn't want. Procedure.

"It will be a short conversation," he promised again. "Can you transfer me for just a minute?"

"Sir," the secretary was beginning to lose some of her patience, "I understand you, but it doesn't work that way here. If you're an existing client, I have to mark this call in your file. If you are a new client, I have to open a file for you. I can't just transfer the call."

In the inner room, the client stood up. The secretary heard Mendel Lederman take leave of him and call to her, "Transfer Bleich to me, please…"

• • •

The jewelry store was empty. The saleslady stood up to greet them. She liked such customers, who came in mother-in-law – daughter-in-law pairs. Usually, the mother-in-law wished to give, and the *kallah* felt uncomfortable taking – which made the mother-in-law want to give even more, something which was nicely expressed in her cash register.

"Before a *chasunah*?" she asked pleasantly.

"That's right," Chana Bleich said.

"A diamond ring?" she tried to offer.

"No, we have a diamond ring already. We'd like to see some sets."

The saleslady set some drawers filled with samples on the glass counter and, from experience, turned to a different part of the store in order to allow them to choose peacefully.

Of course, from the corner of her eye she watched the proceedings. The *kallah* gently removed some of the samples and showed them to her mother-in-law. The mother-in-law looked at them and wasn't satisfied. The *kallah* put them back and removed some other samples. The mother-in-law rejected them, as well. Was she the type who forced her opinion on her daughter-in-law?

"Excuse me," called the mother-in-law, "do you have more samples. These are nice, but a bit too simple. My *kallah* deserves gold, just like her..."

The saleslady smiled and pulled out another set of drawers, holding more expensive samples, the kind she usually didn't get to offer.

"What do you think about these, Suri?"

"I don't know," the *kallah* smiled in embarrassment. "I don't know what to say. The things we saw before were nice enough, no?"

"Nice, yes," Chana said, "but not for you. You need something truly special. What do you think about this, Suri?" She picked up a beautiful, heavy, gold necklace. The saleslady discreetly moved away again.

"It's... it's terribly expensive," she heard Suri the *kallah* whisper.

"I'm not looking at the price," Chana said decisively, "and you don't have to look either, Suri. There's no consideration of price here, only of your taste, of what you like."

No consideration of price, Suri noted to herself. And the

truth was, when they finally chose what seemed to be the most expensive set in the store, her mother-in-law wrote out the check so casually, despite the large amount, giving the impression that it really didn't matter to her how much she spent.

Once again, they were on the busy street. The jewelry was wrapped up well in Suri's handbag.

"My mother will be angry," she said laughingly.

"I'll calm her down," Chana Bleich promised. "Please understand, Suri, that this is our approach. You'll see it by Shloime, too, *be'ezras Hashem*. We only take the best, not a drop less. That's how it is when choosing jewelry, an apartment, not to mention a *kallah*. *Boruch Hashem*, the financial consideration doesn't play a role by us."

Oh. Suri swallowed. Now she knew without a doubt that her *chosson's* father hadn't gone to America in order to collect money. The question then remained, why he did travel.

They forged their way between the people. Her mother-in-law removed a notebook from her purse and noted something on it.

"I like to be organized," she said, "to buy everything in advance, to arrange every detail, so there shouldn't be any surprises. I've already done all the shopping – all the clothing for the children, for myself, the shoes – even Shloime's suit is back from the tailor a while already, and hanging in the closet."

"Really?" Suri was amazed. If so, she now received another bit of information: Shloime's father hadn't gone to America in order to shop, since his wife had already done it all so capably. Once again arose the question, even more strongly: why *had* he traveled, specifically now?!

• • •

"Yes, Bleich?" Lederman brought the receiver close to his ear.

Why had he agreed to accept the call? Not because logic dictated it. So, why indeed?

"Hello, how are you? I'm now in America, doing my own investigations. I wanted to know if you could recommend a private investigator here. I'm in New York."

Lederman was quiet for a minute. Thousands of miles away, Shaya Bleich was sure that the pounding of his heart could be heard all the way in Jerusalem. Would he agree? Not agree? Give? Not give?

Lederman, of course, wouldn't tell Shaya Bleich about his son's visit. The ground rule of his job was that nothing was said until absolutely necessary.

"Why did you go specifically now?" he asked, a bit coldly. "Are you afraid that your son has reached the age where he might begin to---"

"Shloime is about to get married," Shaya said briefly. "If not now, then when?"

Again Lederman was quiet.

"If you're asking me," he said, taking Shaya completely by surprise, "if you're asking me, don't be so hasty, and don't do anything irreparable."

"Meaning?" Shaya didn't understand.

"Don't make any wedding before you find his parents."

# CHAPTER 15

"What does that mean???" Shaya was flabbergasted.

"That means exactly what it sounds like. R' Shaya, Shloime is not your son. Let's say you can raise him as you see fit, send him to the yeshiva that you like – but you can't marry him off to whomever you wish. That, in any case, has to be the decision of his biological parents."

"I believe," Shaya said slowly, trying to digest what was said, "I believe that my missing brother and sister-in-law trust whatever decision I make regarding their son."

"Agree with me that marriage is another story," Lederman said. "And besides, even if you had full possession of the boy – which you don't, since you never actually adopted him legally – but even he would be your adopted son in every way, at eighteen he's already his own master."

"Nothing is being forced on him," Shaya stated the obvious, sounding a bit affronted. "I hope that's clear."

"G-d forbid, I didn't mean that. I have no doubt that you're all of one mind here. But you son is very overwrought these days – and I'm saying that as a fact. I suggest that you think the whole thing over, speak to him about it. Maybe you'll find that he, too, doesn't want to get married until his parents are found…"

Shaya was quiet. Too many things in this conversation needed digesting.

"And what," he finally found his voice, "what if Shloime really does want to push off getting married until his parents are found? And if they're not found, as they haven't been found until now? Will he always remain---"

"G-d forbid," Lederman retracted, "I didn't say that. I only requested, suggested, that you think it over. Take into consideration the point of view of someone from the outside looking in. And now, to business, R' Shaya. What did you want from me?"

...

At home, Suri spread the jewelry out on her mother's bed. Devorah Fuchsman's eyes widened.

"That must have cost a fortune," she said. "I hope you thanked her enough."

"It was a little hard to thank her too much," Suri apologized, "because it was such a given by her. She didn't let me take anything cheaper, even though there were some really nice pieces there."

"She's a special woman," Devorah said.

"The money is also special," Suri couldn't help saying. "If you would have seen, Ima, how she wrote out the check, as if we were in a shoe store. They have money, Ima. They're not lacking."

"What do you mean to say by that, Suri?" Devorah threw her a glance.

"I mean to say that their father didn't travel to collect money.

He also didn't go to shop. She said that she already did almost all the shopping here."

Devorah shook her head.

"Abba already spoke to you about that, Suri, right? He said that we don't poke our noses into the business of others, even if they're our *mechutanim* – especially if they're our *mechutanim*. There could be a thousand and one reasons for a trip like this to America, and if we start asking and checking, we won't be helping anyone – not ourselves, and not them. Maybe he went for a family *simcha*? Maybe he needs to undergo some urgent medical procedure? We don't expect them to report to us about everything, right? Besides which, they're not worried, so why do you have to worry…?"

• • •

"Lots of traffic," Shaya said.

"Regular traffic," the taxi driver said and drummed his fingers on the steering wheel.

The meeting with the new investigator, recommended by Mendel Lederman, was set for six thirty in the Hilton. The drive, though, which had actually started out well, had slowed into a traffic jam. Shaya didn't want to come late, especially to the first meeting.

"Don't worry," the taxi driver reassured him. "If he's going to the same place, he's stuck in the same traffic. You'll get there together."

Shaya didn't have much to do, besides staring at those in the cars nearby, who stared right back at him, and riffling through the papers he had prepared.

He didn't have many documents. He mainly had verbal evidence. It was hard to say that this investigator would have it easy.

He would have to start from almost zero.

Wait. Hold on.

How hadn't he thought of it earlier?

Shaya mopped his forehead. "It's a bit hot in here," the driver said, and opened the window. It wasn't the heat, though, that was causing Shaya to sweat, but the thought that the entire meeting would probably be for nothing.

This investigator – Ben Weber was his name – was a friend of Mendel Lederman. They even worked together. Lederman had information. He hadn't wanted to give it to him since someone had warned him not to. He would give this information to Weber, who wouldn't want to pass it along either, for the same reason. The money he was about to pour into this Weber would be for nothing. He would come to the same dead end.

If so, Lederman had made a fool of him. He would wrap himself around Weber, hang all his hopes on him, in order to eventually receive the same frustrating answer.

"I think we should turn around," he said to the driver. "It seems like my meeting is actually unnecessary. I'll let him know that I'm canceling it."

"Look behind you," the driver said to him calmly, glancing in his mirror at the unending line of cars behind them, "and tell me if we can turn back now."

...

The band was deafening. Chana Bleich stood as far away as possible, at the far end of the buffet, and poured a drink for herself.

She was almost revived when she felt a heavy clap on her shoulder.

She turned and saw Brocha Turnheim, who was almost as

wide as she was tall, standing directly behind her. In one hand she held a knish, and the other clutched a glittering evening bag.

"Chana Bleich, as always, doesn't miss a thing, eh?" She bared her teeth in a grin. "In all the frenzy of preparations for the *chasunah*, you have time to dance at the *chasunahs* of others, and to even have a drink."

Chana smiled politely.

"So come, let's hear which band you took for your dear boy, what's his name? Let's see if I still remember from the *bris*. Yeshaya, right?"

"Yeshaya is my husband," Chana said briefly.

"Oh, that's right. So his name is… his name is Zev, right? I knew I wasn't wrong."

"His name is Shloime."

"Oh, Shloime! All right, I wasn't too far off. So when's the *chasunah*?"

"In another few months."

"What do you say, Chana! Another few months! What an exact date. I understand you're keeping it a secret, maybe someone will steal the date?!" She laughed uproariously at her own joke.

Once again, Chana smiled politely. Mrs. Turnheim, however, couldn't tell the difference between a real smile and a fake one. She had no time for that.

"Which hall the *chasunah* will be in, you are saying, or is that also a military secret?"

Unfortunately, a few other women gathered right behind Mrs. Turnheim. Her broad back couldn't hide the fact that they were waiting to hear the answer.

"We still don't know," Chana said uncomfortably.

"Still don't know! You know what, Chana'le? There's something else you don't know. You don't know that the owners of the halls don't exactly sit next to the telephone, until the last minute, waiting for your reservation. If you don't reserve a hall, your Zev will end up getting married on your porch."

"*Nu*, what's so bad about that?" Chana smiled. She wasn't aware that among the group of listeners was a close friend of the Fuchsman family, and what she heard didn't sound very logical to her at all.

• • •

*Not for nothing do* Chazal *say to share your worries*, Shloime thought, as he noticed the open *gemara* lying before him for at least a quarter of an hour, without him really learning one word from it. Thoughts and speculations filled his mind, confusing him, pulling him in all directions. One minute it seemed to him that he understood the entire picture, and the next minute he realized that he didn't understand a thing.

Nochum, his faithful *chavrusa*, was late. Had he come on time, he and Shloime might have lost themselves in blessed learning; in his absence, however, Shloime's mind wandered, absolutely refusing to focus on the lines of the *Gemara*.

Shloime glanced at the large clock hanging at the front of the beis medrash, and then at the doorway.

He saw Nochum hurrying through the wide entrance in a rush to get to his seat. At that moment, a simple, logical idea flashed through Shloime's mind: here was the right address to unload his worries. Nochum was a smart boy, sensible, level-headed, warmhearted and definitely knew how to keep a secret. He was the right person with whom to talk.

"*Nu*, what's doing?" Nochum dove right in, as usual, without much preamble. He sat down and opened his gemara. "Get rid of that cloud on your face, HaRav Bleich," he said gaily. "I know you were really sad that I didn't come. Something urgent held me up, but now I'm here. Shall we beg---"

When he saw Shloime's face, he stopped talking.

"You look like you're carrying the weight of the entire world on your shoulders. What's the matter, Shloime? The hole in the ozone layer? The rain forests? Nuclear war? What's more important than learning a *daf gemara*?"

But Shloime was drained. His mind wasn't up to kidding around.

"I can't learn now," he said in a low voice. "I know I won't be able to concentrate. Nochum," he suddenly asked, "would you be willing to go out with me for a few minutes? Maybe a short walk will improve my concentration."

The two of them went out into the yeshiva's yard. The understanding look of the Rosh Yeshiva met them at the gate, and, with a nod of his head, he allowed them to leave. He didn't have to worry about steady boys like them.

"Something's been hanging over you in the last while. I feel that the learning isn't the same," it was actually Nochum who began.

The conversation didn't meander for too long before reaching the point. As they spoke, Nochum led his friend to a large park, not far from the yeshiva. Shloime needed to air out, and there's nothing like greenery to help one do that.

Precisely then, someone entered the yeshiva gates. He had given the matter much thought, and came to the decision to come and speak frankly with Shloime Bleich, his future son-in-law, in order to ease his basically unsubstantiated suspicions.

However, he didn't find Shloime Bleich anywhere.

Elya Fuchsman went into the study hall, trying to locate his son-in-law's familiar back, the dark yarmulke on top of the light hair. He guessed that Shloime sat at the edge of the hall, and focused his search over there, but Shloime wasn't there.

"Excuse me," he finally turned to one of the *bochurim*, who had stood up for a minute in order to take a *sefer* down from the shelf, "I'm looking for Shloime Bleich. Where does he sit?"

"Over there," the bochur pointed at a specific spot in the left corner of the room.

But "there", there was no Shloime. Fuchsman, a bit uncomfortable, walked up and down between the rows. There were *gemaras* and *sefarim* strewn about everywhere. There were some empty seats, but most were filled. Only Shloime, his dear son-in-law, wasn't there.

Eventually, Elya Fuchsman left the *beis medrash*. Shloime wasn't there.

With slow steps, he crossed the entrance hall. Here and there some *bochurim* passed by him, hurrying to the study hall.

He walked out of the building into the street, and sluggishly got into his car. There could be many reasons for a *bochur* known to be a *masmid* not to be in the *beis medrash* during *seder*, but as sound a reason as there might be, this absence didn't shorten the list of question marks Fuchsman already had regarding his future son-in-law. It only lengthened it.

• • •

"Let's sit here," Nochum said and sat down on a bench under a wide tree. Shloime followed suit. It was all the same to him if he stood or sat or walked.

"Allow me to disperse the clouds," Nochum waxed poetic. "A young *bochur* isn't allowed to have worries. You're about to get married. Soon you won't have any time to be worry free. What's happening, Shloime?"

"Nothing's happening," Shloime said wearily. "I'm bothered by what happened, and by what will happen. I can't do much about what's happening in the present."

"The past is gone and the future is yet," Nochum quoted and smiled. "What's the story? Why did you bring me here, R' Shloime?"

"Do you know my father?"

"Of course I know your father," Nochum was surprised by the sudden turn in conversation.

"No, you don't know him."

"Why do you think that?" Nochum was very taken aback.

"Because I don't know him either," Shloime said. "I don't even know what he looks like…"

Nochum opened big eyes, very big, and looked at his friend, his chum, who, until now, he had thought was completely sane.

"Your father is tall," he informed Shloime, "broad shouldered, with a black beard. He wears glasses. He's usually smiling – at least he was every time I saw him."

"That's not my father," Shloime said, looking with deep concentration at a flower waving in the breeze right next to his foot. "That's my uncle."

Nochum's eyes couldn't open any wider. Instead, the compartment in his mind labeled Shloime Bleich rocked with shock. Had Shloime changed? What happened to the wonderful *bochur*, intelligent and emotionally sound, whom he had known until now…?

"He's my father's brother. My parents disappeared when I was two years old, and they still haven't been found."

"Either you're dreaming," Nochum said, "or I'm dreaming."

"If only it was a dream," Shloime said. "If only I would wake up and say to myself: 'None of this was for real. Now calm down and get back to regular life.' You have to understand, Nochum, they only told me this after I got engaged. Since then, I have no life."

"I don't understand," Nochum tried. "What does that mean, they disappeared? They were sucked into a black hole?"

"Something like that. It seems they fled from the country, for whatever reason, leaving me by my aunt and uncle – whom I know today as my parents – and haven't been in touch since then. My parents tried looking for them in every possible way, but were unsuccessful."

"What are you saying?" Nochum was stunned.

"And now I'm about to get married. To get married, without my parents. And with this mystery that has taken over my life…"

• • •

The taxi in which Shaya Bleich was sitting, desperately wishing that he could turn around and cancel the meeting, moved forward. The traffic finally eased. The taxi driver heaved a sigh of relief and pressed firmly on the gas pedal. Shaya also heaved a sigh, but not of relief. Not at all.

Should he contact Ben Weber now, from the car, and tell him that he's calling it all off? He could, but it wasn't acceptable, or respectable, behavior. Should he come to the meeting and explain to Weber that there was a mistake? He could do that, too. The best thing, though, Shaya's mind knew while his emotions were reluctant to acknowledge it, was to come to the meeting as originally planned, start the ball rolling, pay whatever he was charged, and wait for developments.

The lobby, as he had guessed, was filled with the hum of voices and the clinking of glasses. Shaya found himself a corner from where he could see the entrance. Weber had said he would be wearing a red tie on top of a light blue shirt, paying no attention to the dictates of good taste.

He waited a while, glancing at his watch from time to time.

A polite lateness was reasonable, but twenty minutes wasn't polite anymore.

His cell phone rang. Shaya looked at it with foreboding.

Ben Weber's secretary was on the line, her voice pleasantly lilting: "Mr. Bleich? Oh, I presume they didn't manage to reach you until now. There's been a delay and Ben won't be able to make it to the meeting today. He asked me to let you know. I hope not too much of your time has been wasted…"

"That's all right," Shaya said mechanically. Only after the line was disconnected did it sink in that the secretary hadn't made any mention of a new date for the meeting. That greatly strengthened his assumption that there was no "delay", but that Ben Weber had backed away from the Bleich file at the last minute.

They hadn't managed to reach him until now? Where hadn't they managed? In his hotel room? He wasn't staying in a hotel. In R' Nachman's house? The only telephone number he had given the secretary was that of his cell phone, which hadn't moved from the belt to his pants, which, in the natural course of events, had been on him the entire time.

• • •

The offices of Ben Weber, Investigator were grand. Mendel Lederman's, in comparison, had the appearance of a temporary office on a building site. The heavy carpets in "Weber and Engelberg" swallowed every footfall, as well as a good portion of the voices – though the voices heard there never exceeded a certain decibel level. Most people coming and going from such an office spoke about things that are better said quietly.

At that hour, though, when they weren't really receiving clients, and only one secretary remained from the entire staff of secretaries, Ben Weber paced back and forth, his red tie half-knotted around his neck and a small telephone stuck to his ear.

"It's over between us, Mr. Lederman," he yelled. Simply yelled. The secretary shrank back in fright. "I'm not a puppet! Perhaps where you come from they do such things to friends, but not here…"

The secretary heard Weber slam doors, turn over chairs, bang binders and throw them on tables.

"What were you thinking, Mr. Lederman? What were you thinking?! I took a file based on your recommendation. I know you as an expert and that's why I agreed. Usually, I check out a file thoroughly before deciding whether or not to take it, and here I didn't ask and didn't check. I relied on your recommendation. And what did I get from it? A whole pile of good things. I've never cancelled a meeting with a client, and now I'm about to do that. I've never wasted time. I've never harmed my reputation like this. And never has my blood pressure been higher."

The secretary would have given a lot to hear what was said, or yelled, on the other end of the line.

"I will never do such a thing!!!" Weber shouted. "You know that in our line of business there are plenty of unpleasant things, but the trick is to always come away with clean hands. There may only be a few like me left in the profession – and maybe not that either – who try to remain ethical. And what are you asking me to do, Lederman? To take a file, not in order to investigate it, but in order to bury it? And that's what you call doing my job faithfully…?!"

The secretary heard the call end with a bang of the receiver. A series of additional bangs told her that Weber was slamming his drawers shut, closing his James Bond attaché case and coming towards the office door.

"Close up here now," he told the secretary, "and let my client, Mr. Bleich's his name, know that I won't be coming to the meeting. Give some kind of excuse, I don't know what. I won't be coming. And if someone by the name of Lederman calls here again, tell him not to contact me until I contact him – which will happen in my next reincarnation, but don't tell him that. Good night."

He stormed out, came back for his jacket that he had forgotten, and left again. She summoned up all her courteousness and creativity, got hold of Mr. Bleich on the telephone and gave over the message.

A minute after she heard the door to Weber's car outside slam, the phone rang.

"Mr. Weber, please."

"Mr. Weber isn't here."

"What's that supposed to mean, he's not there? I just spoke to him. I stopped a minute to take a phone call."

"I'm sorry, sir, but he's not here. He just left this minute. Can I give him a message?"

Mendel Lederman hesitated. Ben Weber left? So quickly? Or was he probably refusing to accept his call?

On the other phone, pressed against his other ear, was a very angry Shaya Bleich. He didn't like being played the fool. He didn't call the investigator's office to ask why the meeting was pushed off, but he did call Mendel Lederman in Israel, who had recommended Ben Weber and brought them together.

# CHAPTER 16

"I think that you're the one who's been sucked into a black hole," Nochum said to his friend. Shloime sat next to him on the bench, playing with one of his *peyos*. "Believe me, many *bochurim* would want parents and a family like yours, and you, like an ungrateful little kid, pick up your foot and kick it all away because of some foolishness."

Shloime Bleich lifted a pair of wide eyes.

"You don't believe me, Nochum?!"

"I believe that you fully believe this story, but agree with me that it sounds fantastic. Maybe someone's just trying to pull one over you, and you, like a naïve fool, believe him?!"

Shloime was completely floored. "Nochum, that's what you know me as?! A naïve fool who believes every little thing…?!"

"Not at all. Just the opposite. I know you as one of the most rational people in the world, and that's exactly why I'm so amazed. A steady *bochur* like you doesn't fit with such a story, which seems to be completely made up."

Shloime was quiet. The two of them heard only the chirping of birds and the muffled noise of cars whizzing down the distant street. As the silence stretched, Nochum took out a small gemara from his pocket and opened it.

"My parents themselves told me the story," Shloime finally said in a quiet voice, "so it's impossible to doubt its veracity. Nochum, I'm not one of those boys who, at a certain age, start making up all kinds of stories for fun."

Now it was Nochum's turn to be quiet. Shloime preferred the silence. The light breeze on his face, the natural surroundings that expanded the mind – it was all restoring some of his peace of mind.

"Tell me, your *mechutanim* know about this?" Nochum asked.

"Of course not," Shloime said. "They made a *shidduch* with me as a member of the Bleich family, as my parents' son. They don't begin to imagine that there could be some problem here. And *oy vey* if they did…"

• • •

"How did the stuffed pepper come out?" Devorah Fuchsman asked, her face to the stove.

"Wh… what?" Elya stirred.

"*Oy*, you didn't eat anything," Devorah chided. "You haven't touched your plate, Elya. What's with you lately? You don't eat, you're uptight."

"Of course I eat," Elya said, and speared a piece of pepper with his fork. "Fantastic, this zucchini."

But after a few minutes, when she turned around again, she found only a tiny bite missing from the stuffed pepper. Elya was sitting in the same position, staring at the window, completely disconnected from his surroundings.

"Elya, what are you thinking about?"

He wearily moved his gaze from the window.

"Nothing."

"'Nothing' can't make you go hungry. Don't make me nervous, Elya, tell me what's bothering you and if it should bother me, too."

Usually, he would dismiss such a question with a wave of the hand. This time, however, he didn't.

"If it should bother you… I don't know. Maybe it's just something that got into my head and I have to wait for it to leave. Give me a few more days and it'll be okay."

"Does it have to do with Suri?"

"Suri? Yes, it has to do with Suri. But Devorah, do me a favor. No questions. If need be, I'll tell you. You can believe me."

Yes, she could definitely believe him. But there's nothing that arouses the curiosity of a woman more than a question to which she didn't receive an answer.

"Does it have to do with Shloime?"

Elya was quiet. Just to be sure, he peeked outside to check that the hallway was empty.

"Yes," he said, and heaved a very deep sigh.

• • •

On the steps leading up to the house, Shaya Bleich met R' Nachman, his host.

"How are things, Rav Bleich?" R' Nachman asked jocularly. "From your expression, I understand that you didn't make it big with checks today, hmm?"

"No, I didn't," Shaya said and went inside. His meeting was cancelled, and when Mendel Lederman tried calling the investigator's office to find out why, he found that Weber had already left.

"Your wife called," R' Nachman's wife relayed, "about an hour ago. She didn't leave a message. She just wanted to talk to you. Would you like something to drink?"

"No, thank you. I'll first try to call my wife. Maybe something happened."

Shaya closed himself in his room. It was hard to believe that this phone call would bring him good news.

"I'm on my way back from a *chasunah*," his wife told him. "Believe me when I tell you that I don't even remember whose *chasunah* it was. All I remember is the round face of Brocha Turnheim."

Shaya groaned. Brocha Turnheim spelled trouble.

"She had to know – *had* to know – exactly when our *chasunah* is. And not only her, but a whole crowd of women standing near her, around her, around me – everywhere possible."

"I don't envy you," Shaya said, and meant every word. "How'd you get out of it in the end?"

"I'm afraid I botched it. I didn't give a clear answer, and if there was anyone there with even slightly sharp ears, it must have sounded very strange. We can't know how far this will go, Shaya. If walls have ears, then a group of women has a whole recording studio."

"Oh, you're exaggerating. You don't have to make an issue out of a group of women. One minute they're talking about one thing, and the next minute they're on to something else. As soon as this stops being interesting, it'll be off the agenda. Don't worry, Chana. Our fate, as well as the fate of Shloime and that of the *chasunah* isn't dependent in any way on Brocha Turnheim."

"True, but I'm such a bundle of nerves. I barely managed to get home without getting lost."

"Switch channels, Chana. Maybe say a *k'pital Tehillim*. You definitely don't have to worry. This is the last thing we have to worry about."

As Chana put down the phone, she tried desperately to be convinced, but the thought stubbornly persisted that this definitely wasn't their last worry.

• • •

"Suri, did you see the ad in the newspaper?"

Suri had actually gone through the paper. She had copied down all the numbers of relevant sales and furniture stores. Which ad did her mother mean?

"The large ad, on the first page."

Suri turned the paper over. On the first page was a huge ad, announcing a large, captivating evening for women. Besides that, there were another few small ads.

"You mean this?" she asked, and lifted the paper with the colorful advertisement in its center.

"That's right."

"Why are you asking if I saw it? What does it have to do with me?"

"I thought maybe you'd want to go."

Suri raised an eyebrow. Ima knew she wasn't a big fan of shows. She almost never went to them. What made her mother think that specifically now she'd want to go, especially during this pressurized time before the wedding?

"Perhaps you want to air out a bit," her mother said. "The ad makes it sound as if it will be something special. Why shouldn't you go and enjoy yourself? You need a bit of a change of pace with all the sewing and shopping and other preparations."

Suri didn't know what to answer. Going to a show was a new concept for her. On the other hand, she couldn't ignore the logic behind her mother's words. She also felt a bit of a need to air out.

"You know what, Ima?" she said, a great idea popping into her head, "I'll go if you'll come with me."

"Me? I have no time, Suri."

"But you also need to air out, Ima."

Elya, hearing the gist of the conversation, decided that they were both right. Soon little Ruchie would go to the family that was selling tickets and buy two, one for Ima and one for Suri. They both needed it.

For a day and a half, the tickets hung on the side of the refrigerator. Each time she passed by, Suri was amazed at herself all over again. Devorah, on the other hand, had pangs of regret. Maybe it was a mistake. After all, Suri was at a sensitive point in her life. Maybe it wasn't a good idea for her to meet too many people, who could make all kinds of insensitive remarks. Then again, she fortified herself, it was definitely wrong to pay too much attention to what others said, and there was no need to avoid coming into contact with people because of it.

So, Devorah and Suri found themselves, on Tuesday evening, stepping out of a taxi quite near the hall. Together with them, many, many other women and girls streamed towards the hall. Suri saw some of her friends and nodded hello to them.

"Oh, Devorah Fuchsman!"

Devorah turned around. An old friend of hers, accompanied by her two daughters, was happy to see her.

"It's good to see that you have time to go out while preparing for a wedding," the friend said. "By the way, when is the *chasunah*?"

Devorah told her the date. Had the invitations been ready, she said, there surely would have been one in her purse to give her. But meanwhile, it was a good opportunity for her to write down the exact address, so the invitation could arrive at its destination safely.

"So you do have an exact date?" the friend asked.

"What do you mean?" Devorah wondered. "Why shouldn't we have?"

Her friend shrugged. "I happened to meet your *mechuteniste*, Chana Bleich. She couldn't really say when your *chasunah* would be…"

• • •

Elya paced back and forth between the large bookcase and the heavy curtains. The *bochur* was supposed to arrive at seven thirty. It was already a quarter to eight. True, Devorah and Suri were supposed to be out until at least ten, but time was of the essence.

Finally, the bell rang. Elya hurried to open the door for a slight, ill at ease *bochur*.

"R' Nochum?" Elya stuck out his hand.

"Good evening," Nochum replied, and shook the warm, outstretched hand.

Elya turned on the main light in the living room. Nochum squinted.

"Would you like something to drink?" Elya asked, pointing at the bottles and cups set out on the table.

"It's fine, I'm coming from yeshiva. I assume you haven't invited me here so we can introduce ourselves to one another. By the way, I've heard a lot of wonderful things about you from Shloime. He's really happy to be joining your family."

"We're happy with him, too." Elya cleared his throat. "He's really like a son to us. You're his best friend, I understand."

"I'm a good friend of Shloime's. I don't know if I have the *z'chus* of being his best friend, but we've also been *chavrusas* for a few years." Nochum was most curious to know why Shloime

Bleich's future *shver* had invited him to his house for such a formal conversation, but meanwhile, he held his curiosity in check.

"I heard that you're an excellent *bochur*," Elya Fuchsman said in his forthright manner, "a sincere and smart *bochur*. At least that's what rumor says."

"*Nu, nu,*" Nochum colored slightly, "we know how rumors are."

Elya smiled. "You can trust that I go for the correct rumors… in any event, I wanted to talk to you a bit about Shloime."

Nochum shifted in his chair. He had guessed that Shloime would be the topic of their conversation, but didn't really understand how. Who checked into his *chosson* so long after the *shidduch* was finalized, when the wedding was already quite close?

"I love Shloime as a son," Elya said, "and I have no doubt that he is the best *bochur* I could find as a *shidduch* for my daughter."

"There's no doubt about that," Nochum agreed wholeheartedly, "and not only for your daughter. No girl could wish for herself a better *shidduch*."

Elya nodded. And nodded again. It was obvious that it was hard for him to continue.

"That, in any case," he finally said, "is what I thought when the *shidduch* was made."

Nochum opened his eyes wide. "Meaning, that today you think otherwise…?!"

• • •

"What does that mean she couldn't say when the *chasunah* is?!" Devorah Fuchsman stopped in her tracks. Suri was behind her, so Devorah couldn't see her face which was rapidly changing colors.

"Um, uh," the friend realized belatedly that maybe her words were completely out of place and context, "I guess she was a bit confused. She didn't remember exactly which date the *chasunah* was. It was so noisy and busy there – maybe she did say the date and I didn't realize. But really, why does it make such a difference? The main thing is that it should be at the right time, with *mazal*."

The friend almost forcibly pulled her two daughters and disappeared from there. Suri and her mother remained frozen in place.

"I don't understand," Suri said. "What does that mean, 'confused'? The *mechuteniste* was confused? If you woke me up in middle of the night, I would know the date of the *chasunah*. Everything we're doing revolves around it. What does that mean, she couldn't say the date…?"

"It really does sound a bit strange," Devorah agreed.

"Maybe she did say," Suri tried, unsuccessfully, to calm herself, "and your friend didn't hear, Ima. The *mechuteniste* knows the date of the *chasunah*, so what difference does it make if she said it or not?"

"Maybe she wants to keep it a secret," Devorah tried to understand.

"But why?!" Suri asked. It was important to her to know. Crucially important.

They stared at each other.

"Maybe it has to do with the *shver's* trip to America," Suri said. "And to the tension that I told you I felt in their house."

"I don't think so," Devorah said. "In any event, it doesn't seem to be connected. All right, let's leave it alone. We're going to be late to the show because of this nonsense."

Devorah continued in the direction of the large building, with Suri following behind. Somehow, she felt that her mother, too, thought that "this" was the exact opposite of nonsense.

...

"*Chas v'shalom,*" Elya Fuchsman said, and shifted in his chair. "Not for a minute did I think otherwise. I love Shloime as before, and hold him in the same esteem… but here and there I've been having second thoughts about his fitting in with our family."

*That, too, you should have checked before the shidduch was finalized*, Nochum thought, but didn't say out loud.

"Fitting in, as in what?" he tried to feel his way.

"As in… as in… it's hard for me to put my finger on it. There are a few things that disturb me… for example, is Shloime a *masmid*, learning each day in yeshiva, or can you find him sometimes here and sometimes there?"

Nochum's eyebrows rose. "The question surprises me, Rav Fuchsman. Shloime Bleich is one of the biggest *masmidim* I know. Many nights he stays by the gemara, even after the last of those learning get tired and go to sleep… but you don't have to hear this from me. Anyone who knows Shloime even a little will tell you the same thing."

"No doubt, no doubt…" Elya played with the edge of his beard, "No doubt… but, and I allow myself to speak openly with you since I trust that not one word will reach Shloime, lately I've had chance to see him, specifically during *seder* hours, in all sorts of places outside yeshiva. Among them, places unsuitable for a yeshiva *bochur* to be roaming about… and I'm asking you about this because I sincerely wish to judge Shloime favorably, and I only want to hear how."

Nochum poured a cup of cold water for himself.

"I'll tell you the truth, Rav Fuchsman, what you're telling me totally surprises me. Totally. I know Shloime for years – you could even say that we almost live together. True, we don't follow each other around, but if there was any kind of digression, I would surely have noticed it."

Fuchsman listened attentively.

"Even lately, with the added tension and busyness because of the *chasunah*, it almost doesn't affect our *sedarim* of learning. It could be – and I say this to you frankly – it could be that here and there, there were a few unplanned absences, which could happen to any *bochur*, and surely a *chosson*. But from there to say that there's been a change, I don't think that---"

"No change?" Elya Fuchsman stood by his question. "He doesn't seem to be busy with other things…?"

# CHAPTER 17

"Busy with other things...?"

The memory of the last conversation he had with Shloime, in the park near yeshiva, hit Nochum like a ton of bricks. Of course Shloime was troubled. Troubled? His life was being torn apart. The knowledge of his missing parents had turned life as he knew it upside down. But the *mechutanim*, according to Shloime, knew nothing about it, and weren't allowed to know.

"I didn't notice anything in specific," Nochum said, and played with his cup, careful to keep his face averted so his expression shouldn't ruin the calm atmosphere he was struggling to create. "Of course, it's impossible to expect that a *chosson*, especially a serious *bochur* like Shloime who understands the tremendous responsibility of marriage, would be completely calm between the engagement and the wedding. However, I'm telling you again, Rav Fuchsman, that even with the load he's dealing with right now, he puts in tremendous effort not to miss even one minute of learning. You could even say that---"

"Load?" Fuchsman asked with interest, and Nochum knew that he had said too much. "What load?"

Nochum shifted in his chair. He meant, of course, the fact that Shloime's father was out of the country, but who knew? Maybe the *mechutanim* weren't allowed to know that either?!

"I mean that... that is," *There's no choice, Nochum; you'll now have to cover the hole that you dug.* "The whole load of before the *chasunah*, that is---"

"You surely mean the fact that his father is out of the country," Fuchsman said, unknowingly eliciting a sigh of relief from the *bochur*. So the *mechutanim* did know that. He had to be ten times more careful with every word that came out of his mouth. He had no way of knowing what they did or didn't know. *Shloime Bleich, what did I ever do to you that you're torturing me like this?!*

• • •

"Did you enjoy?" Devorah turned to her daughter as, arm in arm, they left the large hall amongst the stream of women and girls.

"You could say so."

"It was nice, wasn't it?" Devorah tried.

"Very nice," Suri said, and Devorah got the feeling that she was distracted. Her eyes darted about.

"Are you looking for somebody, Suri?" she tried again.

"No, no one in particular," Suri said, but her eyes said differently, roving nonstop among the large crowd.

"I don't think it's possible to find someone here. It's like looking for a needle in a haystack."

"Mmm."

"Are you looking for my friend, Suri, the one we met earlier?!" Devorah dared ask.

For the first time she felt that Suri was with her. "Yes, I want to meet her again."

A sudden tap on her shoulder startled Suri. She turned around and found none other than Mrs. Chana Bleich standing behind her.

"I'm so happy to see you here," the *mechuteniste* said to them both. "It's good that you're taking a break from all the preparations."

As opposed to Devorah, who was truly and sincerely happy to see her future *mechuteniste*, Suri looked somewhat horrified.

"We have to," Devorah said and smiled. "As the date of the *chasunah* comes closer, there's more and more to do. If we don't air out now, later we surely won't have time."

"The date is not a wild bear," Chana Bleich laughed, and Suri perked her ears as she had never perked them before.

• • •

"Yes, I also meant that," Nochum said carefully. "As the oldest, more responsibility falls on him. But he's not someone who will allow that to get in the way of his learning."

"I understand, I understand," Fuchsman said, though his expression said that he had many more questions. "What should I tell you," he half said, half sighed, "I hope *HaKadosh Boruch Hu* will lead us on the right path."

Nochum, seeing that the conversation had ended, said, "I don't see any reason to be so worried, Rav Fuchsman. From knowing him personally, I'm telling you again that Shloime Bleich is the best catch you could have found."

This time, though, Elya Fuchsman didn't say, "of course, of course," nor did he nod his head.

Nochum was scared. Had he said things he shouldn't have

said? Was he, with his own mouth, about to ruin his best friend's *shidduch*? He swiftly replayed the entire conversation in his head. Except for the time that he almost slipped, he didn't find that he said anything wrong. He was beginning to get the impression, however, that there was a lot more here than met the eye – and it was hard to know where the mine was hiding.

Elya Fuchsman stood up, intending to escort his guest to the door. But the guest didn't rise. He couldn't.

"Could you can give me some more details, Rav Fuchsman. What's really bothering you? Maybe I could help you solve the problem if I had a clearer picture of what you're talking about."

But something in Elya Fuchsman's face had closed. He wasn't prepared to share any more.

"I believe all that you've told me R' Nochum; I respect you a lot. You don't have to worry," Fuchsman gave him a friendly clap on the shoulder, and Nochum could feel how non-liberated the clap was. "You're all right. I'm happy that Shloime has a friend like you. How did you put it? He got himself the best catch."

Nochum had to smile, but he wasn't at all reassured.

"You're leaving me with a whole lot of question marks, Rav Fuchsman."

Elya Fuchsman face became grave, not because of the question marks with which he was leaving Nochum, but because he had forgotten to tell him something very important.

"Maybe I didn't stress it enough," he leveled his gaze at the pleasant faced youth, "but not one word of our conversation, as well as the fact that it took place, is to reach Shloime – not even the merest hint. I presume it's superfluous for me to say it, but I'm saying it anyway."

*If you thought it superfluous to say it,* Nochum thought to himself, *you wouldn't say it. If you said it, then you must not find it so unnecessary.*

"Of course," Nochum said wearily.

"I checked into you before asking to meet with you," Elya Fuchsman revealed, "and if they hadn't told me that you're a straight *bochur* who can keep a secret, I wouldn't have invited you here."

Nochum stiffened slightly.

"A straight *bochur* who can keep a secret," he said, "doesn't necessarily negate other characteristics, such as, for example, caring about a good friend and worrying about his fate. Maybe they even go together…"

• • •

"Do you mind," Suri Fuchsman said to Chana, her voice unnatural, "if we go to the side and speak for a minute?"

"The side?" The *mechuteniste* looked around. "Do you see here, in all this chaos, any side where it's possible to speak without being disturbed?"

She was right. All the hallways and rooms were crowded with women and girls trying to make their way outside. "Maybe we should also leave," Suri suggested, "and find a quiet corner outside."

"No problem," Chana said. "Across the street there's a small kiosk. No one will disturb us if we stand behind it. I'll meet you there, all right?" she asked, and turned to someone who wished to say hello to her.

"Fine," Devorah agreed, and pulled Suri by the hand.

"I want to speak to her about the---" Suri tried to explain to her mother breathlessly.

"I understand," Devorah said, "but I think it's better if I speak to her. You go home, Suri."

Suri looked at her mother in surprise.

"You'll speak to her and I'll go home?"

"You're afraid to travel alone?"

*Thicker Than Water* « 209

"Not at all," Suri laughed. "I'm just wondering why it's important that I don't hear the conversation."

"I wouldn't say that it's important for you not to hear. I would say that it's not important for you to hear. You like your *shvigger*, she likes you, and your relationship with her is something that has to last for years. The relationship between me and her is more technical, less emotional. It's better that I talk to her. Go home, rest assured that everything is okay, and I'll come soon."

"How can I know that everything is okay," Suri asked, amused, "before you even spoke to her?"

"What could be not okay?" Devorah steered Suri towards the exit. She rummaged in her purse, extracted bus fare and pointed at the bus standing on the other side of the street, filling up with passengers. "Run, Surele. Tell Abba that I'm coming soon."

Suri ran. But after a few yards she noticed that the bus standing at the bus stop boasted a completely different number than the one she needed. She slowed and leaned against a wide pole to catch her breath.

"So what do you suggest?"

A hushed voice reached Suri's ears. A woman's voice.

Suri looked over her shoulder out of natural curiosity.

The woman stood a few feet behind her. Her head was bent over a small cell phone.

"What do I tell her? You have to tell me what to say…"

Suri glanced behind her again. Lots of women had a dark, styled wig, a small purse and a telephone. Was she mistaken?

"I knew it would reach her, Shaya. I told you that we have to worry about that."

Lots of women had a dark wig, a telephone and a purse, but the number of women who fit that description and whose husband's name was Shaya was very small.

"I told you Shaya. I told you not to travel to America…"

And how many women were there who answered to that description, whose husband Shaya traveled to America specifically now?! The margin of error was getting narrower.

"There's no time to think now, Shaya. The *mechuteniste* is waiting for me behind the kiosk."

All right, so the margin of error was gone. There was only one woman whose husband Shaya had traveled to America, and whose *mechuteniste* was waiting for her behind the kiosk: Chana Bleich.

• • •

"Who's that *bochur* who was here?"

Elya Fuchsman looked up in alarm. Someone had been in the house when Nochum was there, and he hadn't known?!

"I just came in now," Yisroel Yitzchok said, still in his hat and coat, "and I saw a *bochur* running down the steps."

"And what makes you think that he was here?"

"Because a second before I saw him, I heard our door close, and you saying good-bye."

Great. From all the people in the world, Yisroel Yitzchok was the one who had to know that Nochum had been there.

"He's a *bochur* I was speaking to," Elya said briefly.

Yisroel Yitzchok went to hang up his hat. "His face is very familiar to me. He's not Shloime's friend?"

*Oho, Yisroel Yitzchok. I didn't know your nose was so long.* "Yes, he's Shloime's friend."

"What does he have to do with us?"

"What do you have to do with my affairs?"

Yisroel Yitzchok backed off. But not for long.

"I'm just curious," he said. "I understand he didn't just pop in for a visit."

"Well then, you'll just have to control your curiosity, Yisroel

Yitzchok. Completely. There are things that you have no part in, and that's something you should have learned long ago."

Elya watched Yisroel Yitzchok's receding back as he went to his room, somewhat insulted, and knew that he had just saddled him with an order that was too tall for him.

He still stood there, at a loss, when the door opened again.

"Hello," Suri said.

"You came alone?" he was very surprised.

"Yes," she said, and tossed her pocketbook into a corner. "And Abba, I'd be very happy if you could help me understand what's going on here..."

•  •  •

"Come home," Chana Bleich whispered into the telephone. She could see Devorah Fuchsman, without Suri, across the street, waiting for the light to change.

"Come home, Shaya. I'm begging you. Come home already and let's be done with this whole business. I told you right away that the whole trip was unnecessary, and it's becoming quite obvious that I was right."

From all the criticism in the world, Shaya Bleich least liked to hear "I told you so."

"It's still too early for anything to be obvious," he said in annoyance. "If you want me to come home, I'll come home, but it would be a big shame if I didn't finish my job here."

"But who said you're in the right place? Maybe you should be looking in Morocco – or Alaska, for that matter? You're groping about like a blind man in the dark, Shaya, while I'm sitting here and suffering."

"I'm sorry, Chana. You know that we both want what's best for Shloime."

She backed down. She hadn't meant to hurt him.

"I have to speak to the *mechuteniste* now, Shaya," she whispered, moving farther away from those passing by on the sidewalk. "She surely heard about my conversation with what's-her-name, Brocha Turnheim. She'll ask me what's happening with the date of the *chasunah*. What should I tell her, Shaya?!"

"Tell her the date. The exact date. Without blinking. Chana, you hear me? And if she asks you about Brocha Turnheim, tell her that the music at that *chasunah* was so loud, she just didn't hear you."

Chana lifted her head. She didn't see Devorah Fuchsman on the opposite sidewalk. The light must have changed already, and Devorah probably crossed the street and would be next to her in another half a minute.

"And what will be if---" she had to ask, "What will be if nothing moves by then?"

"If nothing moves?" Shaya repeated after her and looked at the empty wall facing him. "If, *chalilah*, nothing moves, and the day of the *chasunah* comes without our finding Naftali and Rochel, we'll see that as the hand of *HaKadosh Boruch* Hu. Just as we've seen everything until now, Chana – and we'll go to the *chasunah* joyfully."

Chana rummaged in her small handbag for a tissue and wiped her eyes. A familiar figure was approaching. She smiled pleasantly. Chana had to shut the phone and appear very calm. The tissue? Oh, that was simply because she had a cold.

• • •

"Abba, could you please explain to me what's going on here?" Suri stood in the doorway to the living room, her face one big question mark.

"What are you talking about, Suri? I don't understand."

"That's the problem. I don't understand either. Ima wants to talk with the *mechuteniste*. Fine. Without me. That's also fine. But Abba, if you would have seen the *mechuteniste's* face, and heard her talking to the *mechutan* on the telephone right before she was to meet Ima, you also wouldn't understand a thing."

"Talking on the phone? About what?"

Elya told Suri to sit down and drink something. She looked distraught. Maybe that's why she was having a hard time explaining herself.

"I was standing next to her," Suri said after she calmed down a bit. "She was going to meet Ima behind the kiosk, which is right near the bus stop where I was standing. At first, I wasn't sure it was really her, but it was. I heard her say to her husband on the telephone that---"

"Saying what?"

"Should I quote?"

"Go ahead."

"She said something like: 'I knew it would reach her.' I know what 'it' is. There was a whole mix-up with the date of the *chasunah*. Believe me, Abba, when I say I don't understand anything anymore. Is there a date, or isn't there a date? How could there be a mix-up with the date? Is that what happens when people get married? How come only we know the date and Bleich doesn't? And why? Why does my whole wedding seem to be getting so complicated all of a sudden?!"

"Suri, Suri. Calm down." He saw that she was on the verge of tears. "I can tell you one thing for sure: It only seems that way to you. It could be that the tension before the *chasunah* is making you feel that way, but your *chasunah* isn't getting complicated. It's only coming closer, making us very happy and excited."

"Us? And not them?"

214 »  *Thicker Than Water*

Elya sighed. "Suri, why are you stuffing your head with nonsense?"

"I'm not stuffing, Abba, it's coming in all by itself!"

"Come, let me tell you something that might reassure you a little," Elya said, and poured a drink for himself. Suri didn't think to ask why there was a tray of drinks and cups set out on the table on a regular day. She was too worked up. "Yesterday, the *mechutan* called me. Did you know that we speak almost every week?"

"No, I didn't know. You didn't tell me."

"Of course. There are many things to arrange before the wedding. Who will I ask which *sefarim* to buy Shloime, which *tallis* he prefers? Who should I talk to about the apartments that I see almost every day?

"Shloime, no?"

"So let me tell you something else," Elya said, and hid a smile. "Immediately after the *tena'im*, Shloime came over to me, a little shyly, shall we say, and asked if it was possible not to include him in any of the arrangements for the *chasunah*. 'I want to use this time to learn peacefully' – that's what he told me. 'I have enough things on my head, so whatever could be settled with my parents, please arrange with them. It's really all the same to me.' Do you understand? He doesn't care which *shas* he gets, he has no opinion on the watch, and it makes no difference to him which apartment he lives in. So it works out that I speak to his father quite a lot."

Suri leaned back in her chair. It was nice to hear these things.

"So you spoke yesterday." In any event, she wasn't letting go of the previous topic. "About what?"

"What did we speak about yesterday…?" Elya scratched his head. "Believe me, I don't really remember the reason for the call. I seem to recall something about the band… and the number of invitations… Anyway, he apologized for being so far away dur-

*Thicker Than Water* « 215

ing such an important time, and promised to return soon. 'I can't wait to see you again – you and my family,' that's what he said. Does that settle your fears, Suri? Does that make you believe that they sincerely want this *chasunah* with us, with you?"

"And why did he travel to America?" Suri still refused to be convinced.

"I didn't ask him. I firmly believe that that's his personal affair, as I already told you."

"And what Yisroel Yitzchok said?!" She found this to be a good time to unload everything that was bothering her.

"What did Yisroel Yitzchok say?" Elya knew the answer, but wanted to hear it from Suri. He wanted to measure the extent of the damage.

"It was a while ago," Suri said, "but it won't leave my head… I keep thinking that maybe he's basing it on something… He said: '*Daven* that you have a *chasunah*,' and believe me, Abba, since then I'm *davening* like a *meshuggene*…"

Elya began pacing the large room like a tiger in its cage. "*Oy,* Yisroel Yitzchok, Yisroel Yitzchok! Yisroel Yitzchok has to be dealt with – and we are dealing with him, Suri – but you absolutely should not pay the slightest bit of attention to what he says. Do you understand?! Not the slightest bit. Yisroel Yitzchok sometimes speaks nonsense. Maybe he wanted to upset you. He… he knows how to push the right buttons. I constantly ask *Hashem* to open his eyes. You can also, Suri. And don't think about it ever again. Do you hear me? Promise me…!"

"But it won't leave me alone…"

"I understand. It's like a mosquito that doesn't go away. Once it's in your head, it just grows and grows, until you can't remove it even if you wanted to. But I'm asking you to make the effort. Do you really think, Suri," he tried a different tack, "but *really* think that if there was a problem we would hide it from you…?"

Suri broke down in sobs. All the fears and worries that had been knocking around in her head almost since the *tena'im* bled from her eyes. All her friends who got engaged and married seemed so happy, so calm, with no strange questions bothering them. Was it just her? Or maybe the others were also keeping their worries well hidden…?

Elya, uncomfortable and at a loss, went to bring a package of tissues. Suri's position hadn't changed while he was out of the room – her head was down on the table and she was crying.

"It's not an easy time, Suri. I know," he said, "and don't think that other *kallahs* have it different. Each one has her fears and her worries. After all, life is about to change. Not just change, but start anew."

"I want to know why he traveled – Shloime's father," Behind all the tears, Suri's eyes were determined. "Something tells me that it all starts from there, that there's where the answer is. Tell me, Abba, please tell me why he traveled."

Elya clasped his hands behind his back and circled the living room.

"I didn't interrogate him, Suri, and I don't plan on doing so now, either. To me, it's a red line that can't be crossed – we don't poke into someone else's private life."

"Not even at the expense of my peace of mind?"

"Not even at the expense of your peace of mind," he said. "You have to understand, Suri. I think that all these feelings are just that – feelings. You can relax; we can help you relax. Everything you're going through is normal. It's definitely not something that has to cause us to break our principles."

"Why did Ima want to speak to the *mechuteniste* without me?!" Suri demanded.

"A thousand and one reasons," Elya shrugged. "You're aware that most things between *mechutanim* are financial matters? Good. And you know that the young couple most certainly doesn't have to be involved in the financial matters? Good. Would you want to be present during a conversation not meant for your ears, for your own good?"

Suri took a tissue from the package. She knew her father was right. But there was a huge stone sitting on her heart. It was hard for her. Her fears were so solid, no reassurance was able to penetrate.

# CHAPTER 18

Making a mistake is never pleasant. And he had erred, Mendel Lederman admitted to himself. He shouldn't have relied on Ben Weber, even though they were good friends. Friendship was one thing, especially if it was a professional friendship, but to agree to do something that seemed not so proper was something else entirely.

Now Shaya Bleich was upset with him – and rightly so. He himself had recommended Weber, and he was the one who had to answer for Weber's sudden withdrawal from the file. He had to find a new investigator for Bleich quickly. Not so much because he cared, but because Bleich couldn't be allowed to dig too deeply by himself. He might come to the correct conclusions, something which couldn't be allowed.

On the other hand, maybe the time had come?! Maybe *Hashem* had worked it out this way so that the Bleich family could finally solve the mystery? And why, in heaven's name, did he, Mendel Lederman, have to decide?!

Absently, Lederman opened his telephone book. There was no lack of investigators, both in Israel and abroad, but he needed to find the right one who had enough sense in his head to understand that the best thing for this file was to bury it.

He turned page after page, name after name. Most names were disqualified at once, some on second thought, and eventually Lederman came to the end of the list without one name in his pocket.

He sighed.

Maybe he should change his mind and tell Shaya Bleich that he was willing to take on the file again, and do the burying himself. Would Bleich realize that he was being led on?

Mendel Lederman sat for a long time, sunk in thought. Had he known from the start that things would get so complicated, he would have shoved this file away with both hands. He had an ironclad rule: If something was bound to interfere on the way, don't even start. But then, on the face of it, Bleich's file had seemed very straightforward. Lederman scribbled forcefully on a blank paper lying in front of him. He wanted to find a solution. Very badly.

Eventually, he stood up, shrugged on his jacket and informed his secretary that he was leaving for an hour.

"You have two meetings shortly," she glanced at his schedule.

"Even if I have ten meetings. There are enough chairs to sit on here; they can just wait until I return."

Lederman stopped the first taxi he saw. He couldn't concentrate enough now to drive. The taxi took him to the Bleich home. He climbed the steps, those which he thought he'd never climb again, and knocked on the door.

"Hello," said the woman of the house. Despite the years, she recognized him at once.

"Hello. Is your son Shloime home?"

"Now?" She was surprised at the question. "Shloime's in yeshiva."

"I see," Lederman said. "When does he come home?"

"Sometimes he comes home in the afternoon, sometimes not. Maybe I can help you?"

Lederman made as if he was hesitating. "I think it's better that I speak straight to him. Can you please tell him that I was here?"

Chana said she'd tell him, and closed the door, burning with curiosity.

Chana Bleich wasn't usually home at three o'clock. That was the time of her regular volunteer work, and it was Faigie's job to greet the children and serve them lunch. When Shloime came home, a piece of green notepaper was waiting for him on the desk in his room.

"Shloime'le, Mendel Lederman was here this morning, looking for you. He asked that I let you know. Have a good day, Ima."

Shloime had to read the note four or five times before being able to digest its contents. Mendel Lederman? Was here? Today? Looking for him? Mendel Lederman?! Hadn't the man solemnly informed him that they were parting ways since he couldn't give him any information? What happened suddenly? Was he now allowed to talk? Had Lederman decided to dissolve the commitment that Shloime hadn't managed to figure out?

He couldn't get any details just then from his mother. When she was volunteering, she purposely disconnected her phone, and it was good that she did. But now he would have to stew in curiosity until Ima came home, or until Lederman called or came again. He wasn't about to pick up the phone and call Lederman. The ball was in the investigator's court; let him call the

*Thicker Than Water* « 221

shot. Lederman was the one who needed him now, and not the other way around.

• • •

The door to the grand office closed silently behind him. Shaya looked around. Ahead of him was a hallway, to the right was a hallway, and to the left was another one. All the rooms there belonged to Ben Weber, his partner and his employees. And where was Ben himself? In an inside room?

"Can I help you, sir?" the main secretary asked politely from behind a huge table opposite the door.

"I'm looking for Ben Weber," he said hesitantly.

"These are the offices of Ben Weber," she confirmed what he already knew. "Do you have an appointment?"

"No, not today." He was supposed to have an appointment the day before, and it had been suddenly cancelled. That's exactly what he had come to check today. "Can I see him for a few minutes? I have an urgent question."

"He's busy now," she smiled. "If you'd like to meet with him, we can set up a meeting."

"I'll explain it to you," he cleared his throat. "I was supposed to meet with him yesterday in the Hilton. Twenty minutes after I arrived, though, they let me know from your office that the meeting was cancelled. I came simply to---"

"Sir," she cut him off, "that's impossible. We don't work that way. We never cancel a meeting after the designated time has arrived."

"I guess there's a first time for everything," Shaya said, "because that's exactly what happened to me yesterday evening."

"Are you certain this was from our office?" her expression couldn't have been more incredulous. "I'm working here for more than ten years, sir. It's an ironclad rule by us, one that we've never broken."

"You're working here for ten years, but I guess you haven't yet learned that rules are made in order to be broken." He ran through the incoming calls on his cell phone until he found the call that came in the previous evening while he was in the Hilton, and the hour it was made. "Check the calendar," he told the secretary, "and you'll see that I had a meeting set up for exactly that time."

Despite her disbelief, she had to do that for him, and she saw that indeed he was right.

"Can you wait here, please?" she pointed to a row of upholstered chairs across the corridor, out of hearing range. "I'll look into the matter."

Shaya sat down. He was becoming more and more convinced that there was more to the story than met the eye. If Weber deviated so grossly from regular procedure, he had to have a good reason. And if there was a good reason, maybe knowing it would make him a bit smarter.

"Sir?" the secretary called to him, "I'm dealing with the matter. It will take another few minutes, all right?"

"That's fine," Shaya said, and removed a small gemara from his pocket.

A few hallways away, Ben Weber sat opposite a loyal client of his. There were clear instructions not to transfer any calls to him in middle of a meeting. No client pushed aside another client. That was his motto. Whoever was on the telephone wasn't any more important than whoever was sitting in the office. Now, though, his telephone was blinking, again and again, the light telling him that it was an urgent call that couldn't be delayed. He apologized sincerely to his client and picked up.

"It's Katie," the secretary said, "I'm sorry to disturb you. There's someone here who claims that he had set up a meeting with you yesterday in the Hilton. After he arrived, he was informed that it was cancelled. Could such a thing have happened?!"

"It can't be," Weber said, remembering at once the previous day's events, "but that's what happened yesterday. Katie, I don't want to talk about it. It's as if it didn't happen."

"But the man is sitting here," Katie said, and gave a sidelong glance at the end of the corridor. The man, who looked to be an Orthodox Jew, was deeply engrossed in a small book. "He wants to clarify what happened. And if you ask me, Ben, he deserves an answer."

• • •

Shloime Bleich didn't have to stew very long.

At three fifteen, Faigie knocked on his door and handed him a fax printout. "This came for you, just now."

Shloime took the paper eagerly. It boasted the logo of Lederman's office at the top, but the actual letter was handwritten – meaning, it hadn't been typed by the secretary, but written by Lederman personally.

"For Shloime Bleich only. I'd like to speak with you urgently. Please confirm at this phone number only our meeting in your house, or any other place that you choose, this evening between eight and ten. Thank you, Mendel Lederman."

Shloime stared at the letter. It was so not like the organized, official investigator who had sat with him not long ago in his office and practically refused to see him! Why not meet in the office? Why was he going about it in such a roundabout manner? Why not pick up the phone? The number on the paper was a cell phone number that Shloime didn't recognize. Most probably a restricted line. Again, why was Lederman choosing not to go through the accepted channels?

Shloime sat there for some time, trying to decide what to do. If he did as the message said, there was a chance that he would be cooperating with something that didn't exactly fit his demands. Otherwise, Lederman would have come forth already then, and not sent him away empty handed. On the other hand, if he didn't answer to the request, he would basically be sealing his last chance to get information about his parents. He couldn't allow himself to do that. At any price.

He'd call Lederman and confirm the meeting. At the same time, he would be on constant alert not to fall into a trap, if indeed Lederman planned to set him up. Where would the meeting be? Not in his house. In yeshiva? Definitely not. Outside? Nah, not at that time.

He needed a different house, the house of a really close friend whom he trusted.

Without hesitation, his fingers dialed the telephone number of Nochum, his best friend.

• • •

"I'll get back to you when I finish," Ben Weber said to his secretary. "Tell him to wait about another twenty minutes."

Katie didn't tell the man to wait twenty minutes. He seemed too involved in his little book for it to make much difference to him if he waited a bit more or less.

The unusual story truly interested her. She got the impression that Ben was quite disturbed by it, and was even losing some of his cool. As the most experienced secretary in the office – she could even be called its administrator – she knew her boss well. One of the reasons for his success was his unshakeable poise.

The sound of a rolling cart came from the corridor. One of

the workers brought a pile of binders he had gathered from the rooms, binders which were kept in special cabinets in the secretary's office. He placed the pile on Katie's desk in order for her to file them.

"Thank you," she said, without lifting her head from the paper she was perusing.

"Before you thank me, tell me if you ever saw something like this," said the worker, who usually didn't speak much. Surprised, Katie picked up her head.

At the top of the pile was a black binder. At first glance, it appeared completely regular.

"Look at this." He lifted the binder and pointed to a crack running along its length. "And at this." He showed her a black and grey striped binder whose edge was completely mashed, as if it had sustained a good blow.

"What happened?!" she asked. "Someone has it in for our supplies? Maybe the binders fell by mistake?"

"They fell a hundred times," the worker said, "and nothing ever happened to them. In order for them to look like this, someone had to have done a good job on them. Look at this," he held up a red binder, "this looks like someone slammed it onto the table, or stepped on it."

"Strange things are happening here today," Katie said. From the corridor she could hear Ben's voice, a bit rushed, taking leave of his client at the door to his room. After a few minutes he returned to his room, and the inside extension of the telephone on her desk blinked.

"Katie, don't send anyone in to me now," he requested.

"And what about the client who's waiting for you?" she asked. "By the way, do you have any idea who ruined many of the binders that just came to my desk?"

"Me," he said impatiently, leaving her openmouthed. "Katie,

listen. There's a question of reputation here. This story will either go through smoothly, or not at all. A lot depends on you. Make as if all is business as usual. I might receive him in a few minutes; I might not. I have to think about it."

He hung up without waiting for a reply.

The client sitting outside, Bleich, deserved all the answers in the world, but that wasn't the real concern. He could come up with some excuse for cancelling the meeting. The truth behind the cancellation, though, the entire truth that Mendel Lederman told him, because of which he did the undoable and cancelled the meeting – did the man have the right to hear it, or was it better that he continue to live without it…?!

• • •

There was a tumult in Nochum's house, as there was each day noontime. All the children, arriving one after another from school and wanting everything at once – to say how their morning went, to eat, but only what they liked and nothing else – made for quite a commotion.

"Nochum," his sister called, "are you here?"

Nochum was usually in yeshiva at that hour, eating lunch and resting in a friend's room in the dormitory. He preferred to forgo the chaos at home, unless his help was needed.

"Nochum!" her voice tried to rise above the din to make sure that he wasn't home. There was no answer.

"Nochum's not he---" she said into the receiver.

"Nochum is most definitely there," the voice on the other end of the line cut her off impatiently. "This is Shloime Bleich, his *chavrusa*, and he explicitly told me today that he would be home this afternoon to rest."

The truth was, it wasn't the rest that Nochum needed, and

*Thicker Than Water* << 227

even if it was, he certainly wouldn't find it at home. He wanted to call the house of a certain Rov who would be able to advise him regarding the complicated story of Shloime Bleich and his in-laws. One could only call this Rov in the afternoon, between two and four. But, as expected, the line in the Rov's house was busy. Nochum took one of the telephones in the house next to his bed and, every so often, dialed again.

"Please check if he's there. Tell him that Shloime is looking for him urgently."

Nochum's sister did as told. She glanced into Nochum's room and found him half resting.

"You have a phone call," she told him. "Please pick up."

"Who is it?" Nochum asked with uncharacteristic suspicion.

"Your friend, Shloime Bleich."

Instead of taking the call, however, Nochum sat up in bed.

"Bleich?" he whispered.

"Bleich, if I heard correctly."

"Tell him that… that I can't now…"

· · ·

Mendel Lederman began to feel obsessive-compulsive. For the third time in five minutes he checked if his restricted cell phone was turned on. He almost never received calls on that phone, because almost no one in the world knew the number. Today, though, he had given out the number to someone in particular, and he was impatiently waiting to hear from him.

But Shloime Bleich wasn't calling. The minutes passed. According to Lederman's calculations, the young Bleich should have returned from yeshiva long ago, received the message that Lederman had come, seen the fax that he sent and gotten back to him. Instead, he was being quiet. What did that mean? That he chose not to cooperate? That he's weighing his move? That he's stunned? Or maybe that he simply hadn't received the message, for some technical reason?

• • •

"What does that mean that he can't come to the phone now?" Bleich refused to accept the message with the confidence of only a good friend who is familiar with every move and intention of his friend. "If he's home, there's no reason for him not to talk to me. Tell him it's urgent."

"I told him," the sister answered. Opposite her sat Nochum, doing nothing, yet motioning to her to absolutely not pass him the phone.

"He's sleeping?" Shloime wanted to know.

"No."

"Eating?"

"No." She was really in a bind. Especially since she didn't understand why Nochum was vehemently refusing to take the call.

Shloime was at a loss. He had to ask Nochum if he would be willing to host the meeting with Mendel Lederman in his house that evening. Nochum, however, for some inexplicable reason, couldn't get the phone, and if he didn't speak with him, then the meeting with Lederman couldn't take place.

"If I come over now, would that be okay?" he asked in despair.

"I think not," she answered, using her common sense. If Nochum refused to speak with him on the telephone, she didn't see why he would agree to do so face to face.

Nochum squeezed his eyes shut. What did Shloime think of him now? He definitely didn't want to hurt his best friend. But he couldn't speak to Shloime about anything until he received guidance and decided on a plan of action. In the morning, when they learned together, Nochum had asked that no topic disturb their learning. Shloime, of course, had agreed. In that way, any discussion about the loaded topic was neutralized from the start. Now, though, wasn't time set aside for learning, and if Shloime had an urgent question, chances were that it had to do with the issue about which Nochum absolutely didn't wish to speak.

"Tell him I'll call him," Nochum said, breathing heavily. He'd try his hardest to reach the Rov. And if he didn't succeed?

"Tell him I'm sorry."

Sorry? Shloime didn't really buy that. He had a strong feeling that Nochum, his best friend and steady *chavrusa* for a number of years, was trying to pull away from him. He didn't want to deal with a "complicated" *bochur*, placing himself in the wide category of *bochurim* who aren't prepared to "be big" and remain faithful to a friend, even when he had problems and wasn't as clear-cut as he had been previously.

*It's a shame, Nochum,* Shloime said silently into the disconnected telephone. *A real shame. I trusted you, made you my confidant. I innocently thought you'd stand by me even during my hard times, and it seems I was mistaken. What will be tomorrow, during seder? Again you'll ask that no topic disturb our learning and slink away like a cat the second we close the gemara…?*

• • •

The small, restricted telephone finally rang.

"Hello," Shloime said. "This is Bleich speaking. I got your message. We can meet this evening, if you want, at 14 Shoshani Street. My father has a small office there which is empty for the time being."

"Excellent," Lederman said. "At eight?"

"Not before nine thirty," Shloime said. It was as if they had switched roles. "Until nine, I'm in yeshiva. And I'd like to hear something about what you're going to tell me."

Lederman cleared his throat. It would be decent to give Shloime that information, even if only partially. "Obviously you realize that it has to do with your parents."

"Yes," Shloime said sarcastically. "I didn't think you were opening a new yeshiva and appointing me to be the Rosh. What about my parents? What are you suddenly allowed to say? What changed since our last meeting?"

"Things have changed, Bleich," Lederman said, "definitely changed. It could be that my approach has changed, too. But I'd like to talk about it in a more orderly fashion. Nine thirty, you said?"

"Nine thirty."

Shloime put down the phone. He didn't need Nochum's favors. His father's small office was a good place. Much better than Nochum's busy house. Better the solitude there than Nochum's dubious friendship.

• • •

Finally, after Nochum, in near desperation, seriously thought of going to the Rov's house and just knocking on the door, he got through.

The Rov, as if he hadn't answered tens of people before him, listened quietly and intently to his question. He asked a few questions, and then was quiet for a long while.

"It's hard for me to give a definitive answer," he finally said, and Nochum's heart sank. If that was the case, then the heavy responsibility would remain on his thin shoulders?

"I would say," the Rov continued, and it was obvious that the answer was difficult for him, "that with something so sensitive it's better for someone who's in the picture to deal with it, someone who deeply understands those involved – you, your friend, his *mechutan* – and could act with the required sensitivity and foresight. I'm too removed to answer such a question."

"So the Rov is saying that I should involve the Rosh Yeshiva, for example?"

"Maybe the Rosh Yeshiva is the right person. Maybe the *mashgiach*. Maybe a different Torah personality who is acceptable to you. I truly think that would be the best thing in this situation."

Nochum thought it made the most sense to turn to the Rosh Yeshiva. He was a wise, very understanding person who would surely shoulder the responsibility. He would go to him that very day, before second *seder*, tell him the whole story and his part in it, and be done with it.

Now the telephone was quiet. Shloime didn't call again, and Nochum dearly hoped that his friend wasn't so angry at him that it would be difficult to patch things up.

# CHAPTER 19

Shloime came to second *seder* as usual. True, they didn't learn together in the afternoon, but they met on the large steps of the yeshiva and said hello to each other.

"You weren't here first *seder*," Shloime said, as if everything was regular.

"Right," Nochum said, also casually, though his heart pounded, "I needed to rest."

"So now you're really refreshed," Shloime said, and Nochum could hear the sarcasm in his voice. "Excellent. You can learn *shtark* with your second *seder chavrusa*. Just don't forget to ask him not to talk about anything else."

Shloime didn't wait for a reaction. Leaving Nochum nailed to the shiny hallway floor, he turned his back and went into the study hall.

Nochum continued to stand there, watching Shloime's stiff, angry back move down the hallway. Shloime was angry at him, and rightly so. If only he could say something in self-defense.

He couldn't say anything, though, until he knew what he was and wasn't allowed to say.

On the right was the hallway that led to the Rosh Yeshiva's room. He decided not to wait – not even one minute.

The door to the Rosh Yeshiva's room was closed. Nochum knocked two, three times, but didn't hear the familiar, fatherly "Yes" from inside.

"The Rosh Yeshiva hasn't arrived yet," someone passing behind him said. "He usually arrives a little later. Try in about another half an hour."

Nochum was overcome by a strong desire to wait by the door until the Rosh Yeshiva came. He wasn't in the mood, nor did he have the patience, to learn even one line while knowing that somewhere in the same *beis medrash* sat a *bochur* very dear to him, who was angry at him through no fault of his own.

• • •

"Send him in, Katie."

Katie, satisfied with the correct decision her boss seemed to have made, told the Jew waiting outside to go into Mr. Weber. At the end of the corridor and right.

"Thank you very much," the man said, as he tucked the little book into the inside pocket of his coat and hurried down the hallway.

"Please sit," Weber said, not looking him in the face. Shaya, though, had plenty at which to look. Weber's office was impressive, filled with eye catching treasures.

"First of all, please accept my apologies for the unusual occurrence yesterday." Weber slapped both hands onto his desk. Shaya noticed that the desk was completely clear of all paper and all writing implements. Was it always that way, or only at this meeting with him, Shaya Bleich?

"I'm truly sorry. I prepared for this meeting and had no reason to cancel it. Suddenly, though, a few minutes before I left for the Hilton, I found out that we won't be able to meet."

Shaya looked at the man. He made a credible impression, but one could never rely on appearances. The man was trying to sell him something. The question was what, and at what price.

"I'd like a more comprehensive explanation," he said.

Weber nodded his head. He had the main points arranged in his head. In his head, and not on paper as he usually did. He didn't want any tangible proof that would connect him to this story. Ever.

"Yesterday, a few minutes before I left for the Hilton, I spoke with Mendel Lederman, the investigator who dealt with this file in Israel. He's my friend, and we sometimes work together. I trust him, which is why I agreed to take this file almost without checking into it first. That was a mistake."

Shaya listened in silence.

"My problem is with Lederman, not with you, Mr. Bleich," Weber said plainly. "I was not in any way opposed to meeting with you, and I'm still not opposed to it. Lederman is the one who wronged me. He wanted me to take the file, but not in order to investigate it."

"Then for what?!" Shaya was mystified. What does one do in an investigations office? Put the files on display?

"In order to bury it…"

• • •

At four thirty, Nochum went to the Rosh Yeshiva's room again. The door was slightly open, a sign that the Rosh Yeshiva was there, but he could hear voices inside.

Nochum understood that the Rav was speaking with somebody. With whom? And how long would it take? There was no way of knowing.

Had it been in the morning, he would have gone into the yeshiva office and asked when the Rav would be available. In the afternoon, though, the office was closed.

Nochum waited five minutes, ten minutes. Meanwhile, his *chavrusa* sat in the *beis medrash*, waiting for him. Eventually, with the conversation showing no sign of ending, Nochum gave up and went back to the study hall. He wasn't focused on the learning, and his *chavrusa* felt it. How could he demand from himself to concentrate when life, in a certain sense, had come to a halt and was waiting for permission to continue…?

• • •

There was silence in Ben Weber's office.

"I gather I've surprised you," Weber said. "I was also extremely surprised. At first, Lederman told me nothing of the sort. He told me about you, told me the story in short and said that he would send me all the material by e-mail. I waited for the material, and meanwhile I set up a meeting with you.

"Yesterday morning, I realized that I still hadn't received even one line from Lederman regarding your case. I called him. I tried reaching him. I didn't exactly succeed. It seemed a bit strange, but I still didn't suspect anything. As I've already told you, I trust Lederman. I know him for years.

"In the afternoon, I finally managed to speak to him. He told me he'd send me all the required material at once. Which he did. But when I looked at the material, I noticed that it was glaringly lacking. Many basic details weren't there. I was very surprised. Had Lederman dealt with the file so amateurishly?

"The whole afternoon and evening I tried to reach him again. But he had planned it such that I managed to get to him only a short time before my meeting with you. Only then did he tell me his true intentions regarding your file: he didn't want me to investigate it; he wanted me to pretend that I was investigating it."

"But why?!" Shaya asked. "He's opposed to the file being investigated and solved?! I don't understand."

"So it seems, Mr. Bleich. So it seems…"

Shaya felt a sudden need to breathe. He loosened the knot of his tie. Weber called for some drinks.

"I'm just… I'm simply learning something new about a man I've relied on," Shaya said. "Almost twenty years ago, when the whole story happened, he began to investigate it and stopped under very unclear circumstances. We understood then that he was under some terrible threat if he continued dealing with the file. We also received such warnings."

Ben Weber was thoughtful, or maybe – Shaya took that into account as well – he was pretending to be thoughtful.

"As soon as I understood his intent, I told him that I'm leaving the file. I was furious at him, and if you would know me at all, you would know that I don't usually get angry, at least not the way I did yesterday."

"I understand," Shaya said, even though he was left with many unanswered questions.

"I had to figure out my next step, to decide whether or not to share the matter with you, and was left with no choice. I had to cancel the meeting, something I've never done and never plan on doing again."

"The meeting is the least of my problems," Shaya said. "The bigger issue is the dead end I've come to once again…"

• • •

At night, too, after *seder*, as if the *satan* was standing between him and the longed for conversation, Nochum didn't manage to get hold of the Rosh Yeshiva.

The door to his room was wide open, and no guest was inside, but the Rosh Yeshiva himself wasn't there, either. Where could he be? Anywhere, really. Had he known that his dear student Nochum desperately needed to speak to him, he definitely would have made himself available. But he didn't know, and there was no way to inform him.

At a quarter to nine, a little before *ma'ariv*, Nochum tried again to find the Rosh Yeshiva. Again he went to his office, hoping that the Rosh Yeshiva was still there, but the door to the office was already closed.

"Hey, Shloime!"

The spontaneous cry fell from his lips before he had a chance to think about it. He noticed Shloime, wearing his hat and coat, headed not towards the *beis medrash* for *davening*, but in the direction of the door to outside.

"Did you want something?" Shloime asked coldly.

"You're running away," Nochum said, and mentally kicked himself. Why was he trying to start a conversation? To get stuck again?

"I have a meeting with someone at nine thirty," Shloime said shortly. "I have to go. Did you want something specific?"

"No, nothing in particular. You're going home first?" Nochum himself didn't know why he was asking such odd questions.

"Yes. I'm in a big rush. Good-bye."

Shloime left. Nochum looked after him as he ran down the steps to the street. He almost didn't feel the tap on his shoulder.

"You're Nochum, right?"

"Right. With whom do I have the honor of speaking?"

"My name is Yisroel Yitzchok Fuchsman."

Nochum paled. Again Fuchsman. Was the family stuck to him like a spider's web…?

"You're looking for your future brother-in-law? He just left. He has an important meeting at nine thirty, so he claims."

"Mmm," Yisroel Yitzchok said importantly, and filed the information in his memory, "but I'm actually not looking for him. It's you I'm looking for…"

• • •

At nine fifteen Shloime left, on foot, towards Shoshani Street. Ten minutes after he left, Chana arrived home.

"Where's Shloime?" she asked Faigie, even before changing into her slippers and taking a drink.

"He left just a few minutes ago. I don't know to where."

"Do you know if he saw the message I left him?"

"I don't know if he saw the message," Faigie said. "I do know that he received a fax from someone this afternoon, while you were volunteering. I know that he wanted to talk to you about it, but couldn't."

"What did it say?"

"He didn't tell me."

Chana was troubled. Mendel Lederman's renewed appearance in their lives, she felt, wasn't good. Was Shloime's present outing in any way connected?

"Where did he leave the fax?"

Faigie didn't know. She hadn't seen it since she gave it to Shloime.

Chana was undecided. Should she go into Shloime's room and look for the fax paper? Would that be an intrusion of his privacy, or something she was allowed to do as a mother who questioned her son's reliability, and was worried about him…?

• • •

Outside, after the draining, unfruitful conversation, Shaya received a phone call from Chana.

"Shaya, I'm worried."

"What now? Brocha Turnheim came to peek into our window?"

"No, no. It's because of Mendel Lederman."

Chana didn't know what kind of dynamite she was lighting with the mere mention of that name.

"Don't talk to me about Mendel Lederman!" Shaya yelled, not caring that people were staring at him. "The man's a crook, do you understand? Because of him I'm here now, chasing my tail. He's playing us like a couple of pieces of chess."

Chana couldn't get out what she had to say.

"I don't want us to have anything to do with him, do you understand? He only messes things up. We'll take a different private investigator. One who will start investigating the story from the beginning. I don't want to hear the name Lederman again. Ever."

"But you have to, Shaya. You don't have a choice."

"Why?!"

"Because I have a strong feeling that Shloime went to meet with him tonight. Who knows what they're saying to each other..."

• • •

If his parents knew where he was then, Yisroel Yitzchok thought in amusement, they would put him under house arrest. His parents, though, didn't know. In general, it seemed to him that lately they were busy with worries of their own, and were less involved with the question of what he was or wasn't doing, and why.

Luckily for him, the streetlights on Shloime Bleich's street somehow weren't lit that day. Under cover of the darkness, he settled himself comfortably in the yard of the building across the street and waited for developments.

Nochum had clearly said that Shloime had a meeting at nine thirty. It was safe to assume that the meeting wouldn't be in a place too far from the house if Shloime had set it for so soon after the end of *seder*. Yisroel Yitzchok believed that Shloime would go home first. These days, so he understood from Suri, his future brother-in-law's father was in America, and he was trying to fill his role. It made sense that, even if he had a meeting, he would first pop in at home, even if only for a few minutes.

The door to the building opposite him opened. A tall *bochur* hurried outside and turned left. He didn't notice the slight figure that waited a bit and then set out after him, wherever he was going.

Whoops, he almost lost Shloime, who turned right and entered an alleyway. At the last minute, he turned in after him, making sure to appear as if he happened to have had to also turn in that direction. He didn't really have to worry. There were few people on the street then, and they weren't too interested in a boy named Yisroel Yitzchok and where he was going. As for Shloime himself – he seemed so sunk into himself that he wouldn't have noticed if a whole convoy of tanks was following him.

Eventually, Shloime entered the gate of one of the buildings, which didn't seem particularly different than the others. He walked past the attractive entrance and went in from the back, to where the storage rooms were.

*What did you hide here, Shloime Bleich?* A small smile played on Yisroel Yitzchok's lips. This *bochur* never ceased to surprise him. He didn't give him a dull moment.

Shloime turned on the light in the hallway, went over to one of the doors and took a key out of his pants pocket. The door, after a slight push, gave in and opened.

Yisroel Yitzchok hid behind the wall. Now there was just the two of them, the light was on, and Shloime could easily discover him. From his hiding place he couldn't see Shloime, but the shaft of light on the floor told him that Shloime had switched on the light in the storage room. Afterwards, he heard the sound of chairs moving – more than one – and then the sound of a faucet running. What was going on there?

There was the sound of water boiling in an electric kettle. The clinking of mugs. A tune that Shloime was calmly humming. Heavy footsteps. It took a minute for Yisroel Yitzchok to realize that the footsteps weren't coming from inside the room, but from behind him. He picked up his heels and raced to the top floor, a second before someone he didn't recognize came to the floor of the storage rooms and followed the light to the room where Shloime was.

Yisroel Yitzchok would have given, without exaggeration, three days of his life to know what it was all about, the identity of the man with whom Shloime (so it seemed) was meeting, and why. As soon as the door closed, he'd circle the building and look for a window into the storage room, to try and hear what was being said inside.

• • •

It was ten o'clock at night. It was a good time to try. True, students in the yeshiva didn't usually call the Rosh Yeshiva on the telephone, but the underlying event wasn't at all usual, either.

"May I speak with the Rosh Yeshiva, please?"

"He's not in right now."

Nochum almost ended the call with a thank you, but desperation welled up in his throat.

"Is there any way to speak with him? I'm a *talmid* in the yeshiva and I have an urgent question. I hope it's okay."

"I can give you his cell phone number," the Rosh Yeshiva's wife said kindly. "He went to greet a donor at the airport. He's on the way now, or maybe he's already arrived. You can try. If the Rav can't, he won't answer and you can try again later."

Nochum thanked her tremendously. The telephone number was there before him. If the Rav was already with the donor, it was out of the question to disturb him. If he was still waiting for him, though, and the flight was delayed, as often happens, it was a perfect time.

The phone rang. Once. Twice. Three times.

"Hello?"

Was that the Rosh Yeshiva's voice? There was a lot of noise in the background, and the connection wasn't clear.

"Hello, this is Noch---"

"Hello?" the voice asked again. It seemed to Nochum that it was the Rosh Yeshiva, but it was a terrible connection.

"It's Nochum, from yeshi---"

He could barely hear the Rav's voice, asking someone near him to try and better the connection. It was impossible, though. The noise was awful.

"Who is it?" he heard the Rav's voice faintly. It was impossible to carry on a conversation this way, definitely not such a serious conversation as the one he wished to conduct. Nochum hung up in despair. It wouldn't be today. And tomorrow…? Would something stand in his way, in the way of him and Shloime both? Nochum believed in one Higher Power. Could it be that he was being held back from Above?!

• • •

"What's this?" Yisroel Yitzchok heard the stranger ask.

"My father's office. He sometimes works here," Shloime said. "Would you like some coffee?"

"Yes, thanks."

Yisroel Yitzchok heard the spoon stirring. The position he was in was far from comfortable – he sat on a shaky gas canister, carefully keeping his head lower than the window, his mouth hanging slightly open in concentration in order to catch every word.

"Will this take a long time, R' Mendel?"

"No, not too long," the stranger said.

"You have new information to give me?"

"You're a bit impatient, Bleich," the man chuckled. "The answer is yes and no."

"I don't understand what that means," Shloime said bluntly. "If you're trying to be vague, then I ask that you stop. If you knew me a little better, R' Mendel, you would know not to beat around the bush with me. I appreciate straight talk that gets to the point."

Yisroel Yitzchok held his breath. He waited to hear what would come next. Specifically those words that seemed to be the key words, however, Lederman chose not to voice aloud, but to write on a piece of paper.

"Your parents are alive," Mendel Lederman wrote, and allowed the huge words to spread throughout the small room. Shloime's ragged breathing reached Yisroel Yitzchok's ears clearly.

"But," the man spoke in a low voice, as if imparting a secret. Yisroel Yitzchok could hear his voice, but not the words. "You asked that I be straight with you. I hope you won't regret that request. I'll state my position clearly: If you take so significant a step as getting married, without them – it's bound to end very badly…"

# CHAPTER 20

"I don't understand what you're trying to say," Shloime raised his voice slightly. "You're telling me not to get married until---"

"Yes, that's exactly what I'm telling you."

"You're telling me not to get married?!" Shloime asked again, in utter disbelief.

"I don't mean, of course, that you should remain single your entire life," Lederman said, "but I don't think it's a good idea to rush into something practically irreversible such as this without them."

"And if it takes years?!" Shloime asked, just as his father had asked when hearing Lederman's advice, "You want me to wait another twenty years?"

"*Chas v'shalom.* One may not lose hope."

Shloime breathed heavily. He didn't like being toyed with.

"So back what you say with action," he said to Lederman. "Help me search. I know you have information."

"I can't," Lederman said in a clear voice.

"So you're not leaving me any way out," Shloime raised his voice. "You're blocking me at both ends! You're telling me to wait and not to get married until---"

Very quietly, in a catlike motion, Yisroel Yitzchok removed his small recorder from his shirt pocket. He didn't know who was speaking, he didn't understand half a word of this conversation, but Shloime obviously took the man and what he had to say seriously. The words he had heard sounded important. Severe. They couldn't be allowed to disappear into the air without a trace. Maybe the recording would serve a purpose and maybe not, Yisroel Yitzchok thought as he pressed the button and held the machine as close as possible to the window. To hear such words, though, without capturing them – that he couldn't do.

"---on the other hand, you're not willing to help me search so that I could get married! Explain to me, please, what you would do in my place, Mr. Lederman…!"

It was silent for a minute. Yisroel Yitzchok remained frozen in place. If he moved now, they would hear him immediately. This conversation couldn't stop, not for a minute. He had to play it back to whoever had to hear it. To his father, who stubbornly refused to hear about anything being wrong with Shloime, to his mother, who might help him convince his father, and maybe also to Suri, so she shouldn't live with illusions about the perfect *bochur* she was about to marry. Yisroel Yitzchok didn't understand what the problem was, what was holding Shloime back, which searching they meant, but it was clear to him that there was something basic there that might prevent the wedding.

"You're right, Bleich," he heard the man say, his voice slightly cracked. Every word was recorded. "You're one hundred percent right. But I'm here only to give you some wise advice, based on the information that I have. I can't offer any suggestions of how to solve the problem."

Shloime took a deep breath.

"You have to understand, R' Mendel," he said. "You don't push off – and definitely don't cancel – a wedding on a whim. I can't come to my *mechutanim*, to my *kallah*, and say---"

A bus roared by. Just then! What couldn't Shloime come and say? Why did it have to be specifically the important sentences that kept slipping away from him…?!

"…You understand that she won't sit in her parents' home and wait for me until she turns white, correct? And besides, as far as my *mechutanim* are concerned, if they would know the slightest bit of what was said here, the wedding would be off."

"I understand."

"So pushing off the *chasunah* doesn't come into consideration," Shloime concluded, "unless you give me some concrete information."

"I wish I could, Bleich. I wish I could."

"Where there's a will," Shloime said, his gaze accusing, "there's a way…"

• • •

Shaya Bleich didn't care that he was standing in middle of the street, that cars were whizzing by and hundreds of people were passing right next to him, almost stepping on him. As far as he was concerned, there was nowhere to continue running. He might even have to go backwards. He stood there paralyzed, the telephone glued to his ear.

"Shloime went to meet with Mendel Lederman?!" he whispered, not because he wanted to speak quietly. He simply couldn't find the strength to say it out loud. "Why???"

"If I only knew," Chana said. "And not only that. Lederman

was here today, looking for him. Lederman himself took the trouble and climbed three flights of stairs and even knocked on the door."

"That's… that's a tragedy, Chana!" Now Shaya was shouting. "That's a tragedy! Our family cannot have any connection whatsoever with this person who only twists us around his finger. You're sure Shloime went to him?"

"Almost. I understood that Lederman sent him a fax today, about a time and place to meet."

"What does that mean, 'understood'? Did he or didn't he send a fax?"

"A fax came," Chana explained, "but it's in Shloime's room. I didn't know if I was allowed to see it."

"Chana!" he reproached her. "You're allowed. It's a matter of life and death. I'm waiting on the line while you please go and get this fax and read to me, word for word, what it says."

He heard her steps quicken. The rustling of paper. His nerves were almost at breaking point.

"I found the paper. It says: 'For Shloime Bleich only," Chana read, "'I'd like to speak with you urgently. Please confirm at this phone number only our meeting in your house, or any other place that you choose, this evening between eight and ten. Thank you, Mendel Lederman.'"

"So polite, this Mendel Lederman. When he wants something, he couldn't be sweeter. This message, though, doesn't teach us much. We don't know when or where the meeting is. We only know that Shloime went to meet with this scoundrel." He sighed so deeply that Chana feared there was no air left in his lungs. "Tell Shloime'le, the second he returns, that he should call me. It doesn't matter what time. You hear?!"

• • •

"I take it that you're trying to make this my responsibility?" Lederman clarified.

"I'm trying to make it the responsibility of whoever is mixing in pretty callously," Shloime said heatedly. "You can't come and say to a man: 'Listen, tomorrow you're going to die, I can't tell you why, and I can't help you, either. Deal with it.' It doesn't work like that, Mr. Lederman. If you want me to take what you say seriously, you have to back it with more information. You might be able to hide behind the fact that you're a big investigator, but that means nothing to me. I need clear information. Here. In my hand."

Yisroel Yitzchok recorder blinked. Could the memory card have run out of room right at that crucial minute? Just then…?!

He carefully moved the machine closer him. His hands were shaking.

"I can't. Please understand me, Bleich. Do you think that if I had a crumb of information that I was able to give you, I wouldn't?"

"I don't know what to think," Shloime said. "I don't know you that well. I heard that you have a good name. I know that in the beginning you wanted to help, but now I'm not so sure."

Lederman looked deeply offended.

"There has to be trust, Bleich. Trust. That's the most important thing. Without it, we'll get nowhere."

"There is no trust," Shloime said shortly, "and anyway I don't see that we're getting anywhere. Correct me if I'm wrong…"

Outside, Yisroel Yitzchok desperately tried to free the memory card from its slot. He had another card in his shirt pocket, and every minute that the machine was off he was missing another few words that who knew how important they were.

"This conversation is difficult for me," Lederman said.

"Would you like some more coffee?" Shloime offered.

"No, I'd like a bit of trust. You should know, Bleich, that I've gone above and beyond the call of duty for your fam---"

A light bang was heard, right under the window. Lederman leapt from his chair.

"Someone's listening to us. Are there any recording devices here?!"

Shloime looked at him, wide-eyed. "What got into you, R' Mendel? You're scared of a cat?"

"Someone's here," Lederman said. "Don't look so innocent." He swiftly leaned over under the table, feeling with both hands for small, hidden recording buttons.

"I'm not as clever as you, R' Mendel. Please, you could even search for a hidden camera. Come to think of it, I'd be happy if there was one."

Outside, three buildings away, Yisroel Yitzchok ran, panting, constantly looking over his shoulder. There was a good chance they had discovered him. That was all he needed. Shloime would know, he would tell Abba, and the story would be added to his case file, which was beginning to get quite heavy.

Only at the end of the street, behind the huge, green dumpster, did he allow himself to stop and catch his breath. And only then did he discover that the small recorder had been left there, between the thorns next to the gas canisters.

Mendel Lederman tore outside and around the building. The window, where was the window? Someone had sat there under the window; there was no doubt about it. If that someone had been sent by Shloime Bleich or not – that still needed to be checked.

He poked around for a few minutes, like someone who knew exactly what he was looking for, and then he removed his scratched hand from between the tangle of thorns. Nestled inside was a small recording device.

"Very nice," he said to the curious Shloime, who stood behind him. "And you claim that this machine has nothing to do with you."

"I don't claim. I'm sure of it," Shloime said with a half-smile. "Whoever left it here did it completely on his own."

There were no identifying features on the device. But Mendel Lederman would take it to his office, open the memory card and remove whatever information it held. From the information, he guessed, he would be able to discover the identity of the owner and plan his steps accordingly.

Shloime wasn't a big maven of recording devices. He just looked on in amusement as Lederman tried opening it in order, so it appeared, to remove something from it.

"There's no card here," he said angrily. "Who's the idiot who records without a memory card? You, or one of your friends?"

Shloime sobered. "Are we getting personal, R'Mendel Lederman?"

Lederman, letting his anger get the better of him, threw the machine forcefully, straight into the thorn bushes. Curse the day he got involved with the Bleich family.

• • •

Yisroel Yitzchok stared at his empty palm in disbelief. How unlucky could he get? A real *shlemazel*! When he started running, he was sure the device was gripped tightly in his hand. Really, it was the tissue he had used to wipe away the sweat dripping from him. Oh boy, was it dripping from him.

He couldn't go back now to take the machine. Shloime and the stranger must have heard the noise and went out to check what it was. If they checked, they probably found the machine and took it. To go back now meant falling straight into their hands.

Angrily, he stuffed the tissue into the back pocket of his pants. Hey, what was that?

His hand hit something hard. It wasn't his keys. The keys were hanging on a key chain attached to his belt. He put the tissue in his other hand and groped in his pocket.

Unbelievable!

Like a boy finding his long lost toy, Yisroel Yitzchok looked in wonder at the memory card that emerged from the pocket. The memory card was by him! By him!!! The important conversation, probably the most important thing ever recorded on his machine, was still with him. The machine itself was now of minor importance. He'd find a way to make up the loss to himself. The precious card, though, with its precious data, was, after all was said and done, by him!

If Shloime or the man found the device, they wouldn't know to whom it belonged, as there was nothing identifying on it. And without the card, they wouldn't be able to get to him. Minute by minute, Yisroel Yitzchok breathed easier. If so, there was a chance that nothing serious had happened.

With firm steps, he left the cover of the large dumpster. He had money. He'd buy himself a new recording device and put the card in it. He would then make a backup of the conversation he recorded, and play it, first of all, to Abba. He noticed that lately Abba was looking at him more and more with a troubled look on his face. Abba was positive that all his suspicions about Shloime were plain nonsense. He was curious to see Abba's face after hearing this conversation. Suri had to hear it, too. Abba and Ima were wrapping her in cotton wool so she would be sure that she was about to marry the next *gadol hador*, an utterly flawless *bochur*. Actually, better that Suri should be first, because once Abba heard the recording, he was likely to forbid him to play it to anyone else.

. . .

"You're an outstanding investigator," Shloime said to Lederman, the two of them still standing knee deep in the thorns. "You really can't know whose machine it is and who was here, even without the missing part?"

"An investigator is human, Bleich," Lederman pronounced, "nothing more than that. I can attain sources of information, cross information, put one and one together based on connections or conjecture. I can also rely on my intuition, which can't be dismissed after so many years in the field, but I can't be a prophet. A machine like this, without any identifying features, is just like one in the store. It could belong to anyone."

"Yes," Shloime said, "but not anyone has a reason to be here now. Only someone who knows about the meeting between us and wants to hear what was said."

"I haven't told a soul about our meeting. If you gave over information, that's a different story – and that's on your head."

Shloime could think of a few possibilities. His sister, Faigie, knew about the meeting, but she wasn't there. Ima, definitely not. Also, they both knew he had nothing to hide, and would wait patiently at home to hear what went on at the meeting. So who could it be? Whom else did he tell about his meeting today?

The more Shloime thought about it, the paler he got. Yes, there was somebody who knew about the meeting set for that evening, and also knew for which time. This somebody, if he had reason to, could have followed him from when he left his house until the office-storage room, and listened outside the window. And there was only one somebody in the world like that.

His name was Nochum. And after the bad feelings between them the last few days, he could already believe anything about Nochum.

"I see on your face that you have a clue," Lederman said.

"There aren't many possibilities," Shloime mumbled. "But I have to check it out. In any event, it's no one that you know, and I don't think it has any effect on us."

"You, Bleich, wouldn't make a good investigator," Lederman said. "There's no such phrase, 'won't have any effect on us'. Every possibility has to be taken into account. As far as I'm concerned, even a bird is a party in the matter."

Shloime carefully lifted the small device from among the tangle of thorns. He had never seen such a device by Nochum, but he couldn't know. Maybe Nochum borrowed it from somebody for specifically this purpose – to record the conversation? But why would he want to do that?

"I'll take this with me," Shloime said, and put the machine in his pocket. Lederman nodded his agreement. "We have to conclude our meeting."

"I don't think there's much to conclude, R' Mendel."

"I meant, where we're headed from here."

"Nothing changed in my direction," Shloime replied in kind. "I'll repeat what I said. Without concrete information from you, I can't move in any direction, so I'll stick with my original plan." He reached into his coat pocket. "You are invited to my *chasunah, be'ezras Hashem,* in another---"

Mendel Lederman took the proffered invitation. It burned his hand like fire.

"Don't do it, Bleich, don't do it," he murmured. "Don't do something you'll regret later on, when it will be too late to turn the clock back…"

# CHAPTER 21

The door to Suri's room was closed. Yisroel Yitzchok knocked on it firmly.

"Yes," said a weak voice. He opened the door. Suri was sitting on her bed, reading a book. Near her, an unfinished dress lay haphazardly on the back of a chair. The sewing machine was open on the table.

"Can I disturb you for a few minutes?"

"Is it important?"

He struggled to swallow a smile. "In my opinion, yes, definitely."

"So for a few minutes." Not that she had anything special to do right then. She couldn't concentrate on anything. Yisroel Yitzchok's presence, though, upset her, and it was best that he be there for as little time as possible.

"I want to play something for you."

Suri straightened up. What did Yisroel Yitzchok have to play for her?

He removed a small recording device from his shirt pocket. "The machine is new," he pointed out, as if it made a difference to her. He pressed here, there and finally brought the machine close to her ear and said: "Listen."

Suri listened.

"What is this thing?" she asked after a few seconds.

"Listen, listen."

"Who's speaking there?!"

"It's Shloime Bleich, who's supposed to become my brother-in-law in another few months – or maybe not, I don't know anymore. Maybe after you listen, you'll be able to tell me…"

The door to Suri's room remained open. At that time of evening, the little ones had already gone to bed, and Ima was busy on the telephone in her room.

"You're telling me not to get married?" she heard Shloime's voice asking. It was Shloime!

"I don't mean, of course, that you should remain single your entire life," Lederman said, "but I think it's a mistake to---"

Yisroel Yitzchok glanced at Suri and was frightened. He really hadn't intended it, but she was white as a sheet. A sheet in the moonlight. Her fingers groped for the off button and the machine fell silent.

"Who… who's the man that Shloime's talking to?!" she whispered.

"Do you want me to continue playing it?"

"No, no!" She gripped the machine with trembling fingers. "I want to know who this man is!"

"I don't know."

"Where do you have this recording from?!"

"It's a long story. I'll tell you another ti---"

"Yisroel Yitzchok???"

Elya Fuchsman stood next to the half open door. He looked

at his son, who stared back at him like a thief caught red-handed.

"Can I know what's going on here?" The truth was, it didn't look like anything special was happening, if not for Suri's face, which looked quite deathly.

Elya took a step into the room.

"Can I have that machine, Suri?"

Without a word, Suri held out the machine.

"Whose is this?"

"Mine."

Elya recalled the recording device he had bought for his son, at Yisroel Yitzchok's request, in the hope that it would improve their relationship.

"This is not yours," he said, after a close look. "The machine I bought you was grey, and this is black."

"Right, it's new." Yisroel Yitzchok kept his answers brief, but Elya had no intention of letting it go.

"Why do you need two recorders?"

"The other one… got lost."

"Got lost," Elya echoed. "Fine. This machine will stay by me for the meantime." Elya slipped the small device into his pocket. There was no limit to the surprises sprung by Yisroel Yitzchok, he thought, each one worse than the one before. But even he didn't imagine how bad.

In his room, behind the closed door, Elya easily turned on the machine. He put it on the night table next to him, and listened.

The voice of Shloime, somewhat muffled, could be heard. Elya tensed. Someone else was speaking with him there. Where did Yisroel Yitzchok get this recording from?! What else was his son doing behind his back…?!

• • •

Finally. Nochum breathed a sigh of relief and stepped through the open door. The Rosh Yeshiva was there, and no one was with him. He wasn't even busy on the telephone. It looked as if he was simply sitting and waiting for him.

"Hello, how are you?" the Rosh Yeshiva said, and invited him to sit.

"I've been looking for the Rosh Yeshiva for a few days," Nochum said, and sat down.

"Really? I didn't know. What for? Something urgent?"

"You could say so," Nochum said, and shifted uneasily in his chair. "Can I close the door?"

"Of course. Would you like something to drink?" the Rosh Yeshiva offered. Nochum looked like a drink wouldn't hurt him.

"No, thank you." Nochum's tongue was actually sticking to the roof of his mouth, but he wouldn't think of bothering the Rosh Yeshiva.

"I'm troubled lately because of Shloime Bleich. The Rosh Yeshiva surely knows that he's about to get married."

"Yes, of course. It's a wonderful *shidduch*. The Fuchsman family. I know the father well, a learned man."

"The Rosh Yeshiva, uh… the Rosh Yeshiva knows that…" The Rosh Yeshiva looked at him with concentration, waiting for him to continue. At the last second, though, Nochum decided not to reveal too much. He would start with what he could, and in the course of the conversation he would try to feel out what was known to the Rosh Yeshiva and what wasn't.

"That is… his *mechutan*, R' Elya Fuchsman, invited me to his home and spoke with me. He had questions about Shloime, questions which are usually asked before the engagement, not after.

"Meaning?" The Rosh Yeshiva narrowed his eyes.

"The *mechutan* wanted to know if Shloime is into the learning enough, if he's focused... Let's say he had reasons to ask about this specifically now. What mainly bothered me about the conversation, though, was the feeling that he wasn't so happy anymore with Shloime as his *chosson*."

The Rosh Yeshiva was quiet.

"And I wanted... I wanted to ask if I'm supposed to pass this information along to Shloime in some way. After all, we're *chavrusas* and also good friends. I don't usually hide anything from him. Especially something so important. It seems to me that it's important for Shloime to know about this. For the past few days I've simply avoided talking to him about anything other than learning, so that I shouldn't mistakenly say anything I'm not allowed to say."

"I understand."

There was silence in the room. Nochum silently prayed that the Rosh Yeshiva would give him a clear answer. That he shouldn't tell him, 'Do as you see fit' or 'You have to ask a *shailoh*' or any other answer that would leave him still confused.

"I've also been watching Shloime lately. And I also feel that he's not the same as he's been. Not that anything is lacking in his learning or behavior, *chalilah*," The Rosh Yeshiva hurried to say, "but I feel that he's troubled. It seems that his *mechutan* also picked up on it, hence his questions. I ascribe it to his engagement. Shloime is a serious *bochur*, and it's only natural for him to take his approaching marriage seriously. In any event, I don't think you should tell him about the conversation with his *mechutan*, because it's quite likely nothing will come of it."

Nochum wasn't reassured. "And the fact that the *mechutan* invited me to his house for an official conversation isn't worrisome?"

No, the Rosh Yeshiva didn't think so. "I know R' Elya Fuchsman. He's a very meticulous, proper person. He had questions, he wanted answers, and this was the most discreet way he could think of getting them. I also know that he loves Shloime very much, and the *shidduch* between them won't dissolve so easily. I don't think there's any reason to let Shloime know about it."

Nochum finally managed to breathe normally. He was relieved.

"And I also think," the Rosh Yeshiva added, "that specifically during this time, which certainly isn't easy for Shloime, he needs a loyal friend at his side, to whom he can talk about anything that's bothering him. Don't pull away from him, Nochum. Stand by him. That's my opinion."

Nochum smiled and rose from his seat.

"And if you have any other questions, don't hesitate to turn to me at any time. It's unthinkable for a *bochur* to look for me and not be able to find me…"

• • •

At exactly eight o'clock in the evening, there was a knock at R' Nachman's door. Shaya Bleich, ready and waiting for the meeting, opened the door and held out his hand in greeting.

"Hi, I'm pleased to meet you," he said and invited the stranger, who was wearing an interesting hat and carrying a large briefcase, inside. "You must be the investigator, Danny Shore."

"What do you mean?" R' Nachman appeared from behind him, "Look again, don't you see it's Sherlock Holmes?" The smile broke the ice. R' Nachman offered them the easy chairs in the living room, and not the dining room table. Before getting down to business, he thought, they had to get acquainted. For the same reason, he brought a whole slew of refreshments to the living room and placed them on the low, wide coffee table.

"It's all right, R' Nachman," Shaya was embarrassed. More

than anything, he wished to be left alone with the investigator.

"Don't worry, I won't bother you," R' Nachman assured him, "but promise me that you'll call me right away if you need anything."

After the heavy door closed behind his host, Shaya moved his gaze from the loaded table and said quietly, "Mr. Shore, it's important to me that you know that you're my last hope."

An hour passed, two hours, and the heavy door to the living room remained closed. Nachman, who until now hadn't attempted to know the real reason for Bleich's being in America, didn't try to find it out now, either. He had arranged the meeting with Shore, a leading investigator, but asked not a word what it was about. If Shaya Bleich wished to inform him, he would do it himself, whenever and wherever he saw fit.

The phone rang in Shaya Bleich's room. Nachman glanced inside and saw the cellular phone on the table blinking again and again. Someone was stubbornly trying to reach Shaya.

Nachman wasn't supposed to answer. It was Bleich's personal phone, which he must have chosen to leave in the room so as not to be disturbed during the meeting. But the telephone didn't stop ringing. Whoever was trying to reach Bleich was bound to get very worried if he didn't answer.

Finally, he picked up.

"Hello?"

"Shaya?" a breathless voice was heard.

"No," Nachman said, discomfited, "My name is Nachman. I'm his host. He's very busy right now and can't answer the phone. Would you like me to give him a message?"

"Oh, thank you so much," the woman on the other end said, "really, thank you for all that you're doing for us. My husband told me a few times that he's so grateful to you for your devoted care."

"It's nothing," R' Nachman said, and truly meant it.

"*Tizku l'mitzvos*. If you could please tell him that I'm desperately looking for him, that would be very helpful.

"I'll tell him," R' Nachman promised.

Meanwhile, though, there was no one to tell. Shaya Bleich was closeted with the investigator Shore, as if they were investigating all the world crises.

• • •

Chana sat in her quiet corner in the kitchen, between the large pantry and the refrigerator, saying *Tehillim*. Shloime had returned a short time earlier, completely overwrought, heeded her request to drink something, but avoided any mention of what happened at the meeting. He only wanted to go to his room and be by himself.

"Shloime, we have some important things to discuss. Abba told me some very harsh things about Mendel Lederman."

"You don't have to tell me anything harsh about Lederman," Shloime said tiredly, pushing the cup away from him. "I can tell you things no less harsh. Do you mind, though, Ima, if we speak later?"

She couldn't refuse. He was worn out.

"Just promise me that you won't go to speak to him anymore, certainly not without running it by me first."

"There's nothing to promise," Shloime said, and stood up with difficulty. "I anyway don't have what to talk to him about anymore."

After Shloime left the room, Chana didn't know whether to be sad or happy about what he had said. On the one hand, he was also completely disappointed in Lederman and didn't want to hear any more about him. On the other hand, what information had he received that had so drained him?

She tried reaching Shaya, but there was no answer. She tried again and again, until it was obvious that he was unavailable at the moment. He'd get back to her when he was able. More than anything, she hated having to wait when she was bursting with information.

The phone rang. Finally.

"Hello," a young voice said. "Is Shloime there?"

"Who's calling?"

"Nochum, his friend."

Chana knew Nochum. She apologized. Shloime was exhausted, and very likely had gone to sleep.

"You're sure he's sleeping?" Nochum asked. No, she wasn't sure. She was assuming.

"Can I come over now?"

"Now?" She was surprised, but didn't have the heart to refuse. "I'll try to see if he's still up, so you shouldn't come for nothing."

She went to Shloime's small room. The door was open a crack. Shloime wasn't sleeping. He was half lying on the bed, staring at the ceiling.

"Shloime," she said hesitantly, "your friend wants to come over. Is that okay?"

"Friend?" he sat up. "Which friend?"

"Nochum."

"No, he shouldn't come."

"What???"

"Tell him that I don't need his favors." Shloime spoke in a loud voice, intentionally, so that Nochum should hear him. He knew his well-mannered mother wouldn't give over such a message.

"Shloime?" she whispered? "I don't understand what's going on."

*Thicker Than Water* « 263

"He suddenly decided that it doesn't pay for him to drop me." Chana was increasingly surprised. This was so not like her Shloime!

"So can he come or not?"

"I don't know anymore," Shloime said wearily. "Whatever you decide…"

• • •

Devorah was summoned from her telephone arrangements to Suri's room.

"Suri'le, what happened? What's all this crying…?"

Suri didn't answer. She sat crumpled on the bed, and only her shaking back disclosed her storm of weeping.

"Suri," Devorah pleaded, and sat down next to her, "what happened? Talk to me!"

Suri, however, couldn't speak. The entire time she had felt that something was happening. Until now she had felt stuck in a vague web of suspicions, but now she had clearly heard. And not from just anyone, but from her esteemed *chosson* himself, that he was weighing whether or not to push off the wedding.

"Don't try to calm me down," Devorah heard a muffled voice coming from the sodden heap that was her daughter, "Just tell me the truth, and tell me why…"

"Why what?"

"Don't tell me you don't know anything, Ima. Don't tell me that. Everyone knows everything. Even Yisroel Yitzchok. And only I, like a fool, believe that everything is really okay…"

Devorah really didn't know what Suri was talking about. It was nearly impossible, though, to get any kind of information from between all the sobs.

"Suri, calm down. Calm down and then we can talk…"

But Suri couldn't calm down. In the doorway, without saying a word, stood Elya.

"Yisroel Yitzchok deserves every punishment in the book," he said quietly. "His behavior has crossed all boundaries. In any event, I think he'll stay in the house for a few days without going anywhere."

"He won't go to yeshiva?" Devorah asked in a low voice. "For him, that's a reward."

"Not so much for the punishment," Elya explained. "I'm simply afraid. It's impossible to know what that boy might do in any given minute. We have to stop him until things become clear."

"Can you please tell me roughly what happened? I understand that Suri received some kind of shock, but from what? What went on here while I was on the phone? I didn't notice anything unusual."

Yisroel Yitzchok, huddled in his room, heard the whispered conversation. He knew it was daring on his part to play the recording to Suri first, but he hadn't been able to forgo the pleasure.

Abba and Ima wanted him to stay in the house. So be it. They thought they'd be able to stop him from all activity, but that wouldn't exactly happen. If Yisroel Yitzchok wanted to accomplish something, in this case to prove to the world that something was wrong with Shloime Bleich, the perfect *bochur* whom everyone held in such esteem, he would do so.

・・・

Finally, the door opened and the investigator, Shore, emerged, followed by Shaya.

R' Nachman hid himself in the kitchen. Shaya and Shore shook hands and wished each other well. R' Nachman guessed that the meeting had already been wrapped up before they left the room.

As host, he hurried to take leave of the guest. A snatched glance at Shaya's face told him that the man was relieved. The heavy cloud that had sat on him for the past few days had somewhat lightened.

"You had a call from home. It sounded a bit urgent," he told Shaya after the door closed.

"Who? My wife?"

"That's what it sounded like. She's waiting to hear from you."

*Boruch Hashem*, he had good news to tell her. The new investigator seemed serious and thorough, wasn't cutting corners and was willing to work hard. He had a good head on his shoulders and, already in their first conversation, he grasped things that would have taken others a long time to realize.

"Shloime came back," his wife said.

"Came back from where?"

"From Lederman."

The mere mention of the name sent a shudder through his body.

"I want to hear everything that went on there. Every word. Please call Shloime to the telephone. I want to hear it firsthand."

"It's not so simple," Chana said. "He closed himself into his room and said he has no strength to talk. All he said was that he doesn't plan on meeting with Lederman again."

"You're not telling me very much. Do me a favor, Chana, and call him."

"He has a friend here now."

"Now?! What time is it by you?"

"Late."

Shaya was annoyed. Big things were happening, and who

was stopping him from hearing about it? A friend?

"Let his friend go home," he raised his voice. "I must speak with Shloime, now!"

# CHAPTER 22

Shloime's door was closed; at least that's what it looked like from the kitchen. When Chana came closer, though, she saw that there was a thin crack between the door and the doorpost.

Through the crack she saw Shloime, more or less in the same position – half sitting, half lying on the bed. Next to him, on a chair, sat his friend, Nochum. They were both quiet.

Assumedly, if they weren't talking, she could call Shloime. Something told her, though, that this silence was more important than speaking.

Shloime heard the sound of her footsteps near the door.

"Ima?"

"Yes, Shloime. Abba's on the phone. He needs to talk to you."

"I'm coming." The bed creaked immediately. Shloime got up and left the room. Nochum followed him with his eyes and didn't move from his place. Shloime took the telephone and went into the small study. The door closed tightly after him.

He stayed in there for a long time. Chana didn't want to think how Nochum was entertaining himself. She preferred to scrub the already clean sinks and wait.

When Shloime finally came out and put the phone back on its base, he told her only: "It's going to be a long time until Abba comes back."

"Really?" The rag dropped into the sink.

"He said that he now has a new investigator who's sunk his teeth into the case. It'll take another few weeks, he said, and then he'll have enough to work with to decide where to go from there."

Chana shook her head. *Nu*, a new investigator. She sincerely hoped something would come from it, and if Shaya was happy – she was happy. The *mechutanim*, though, weren't so happy with this trip, especially since it was all so unclear. And between her and the lamppost, they were right.

"Shloime!" she called.

"Yes, Ima?" He was almost back in his room.

"What did Lederman tell you? Two sentences, Shloime. Ima's asking."

Shloime swallowed hard. Was it possible to sum up that conversation in two sentences? Yes, it was.

"He told me that my parents are alive and well, and that I should do myself a favor and not get married until I find them."

Chana froze.

• • •

Mendel Lederman wasn't taking any more chances. He looked for a quiet place to talk without being disturbed. And he found it. He went down to the underground parking lot of a mall that no one really frequented, a mall that was once the high hopes of the people who started it and over the years became sort of a museum.

"Lederman here," he said into his phone, and was immediately alarmed at the echo that bounced off the walls.

"Just a minute," the other man said, and went into a different room, far from listening ears.

"He was by me," Lederman said.

"I know."

"I wasn't able to convince him."

"All right."

"It's going to be a tragedy."

The man on the other end was quiet.

"Maybe you could do something," Lederman said.

"We don't want to, nor could we."

Lederman fell into a despairing silence. His entire surroundings appeared as he was feeling: dark and gloomy, scary and unknown.

"You're putting your lives in danger!"

"It's too late, Lederman."

Lederman hung up the phone and breathed deeply. Was he expected to do more than that? If people knowingly stuck their heads into the lion's mouth, there was just so much one could do to drag them away.

Lederman leaned against a concrete beam. Above his head he could hear the roar of passing vehicles. In another few months, and he knew the exact date because it was printed on the invitation, something not good was going to happen. Some of those involved were completely unaware, and the others preferred to close their eyes. And he, Mendel Lederman, might be sued in the Heavenly court for the fact that he didn't grab them by the ears and prevent them from doing the deed. And what would he answer then?

. . .

Shloime came back to the room and stretched out on the bed. A metallic clang was heard. Nochum put the *sefer* he had been perusing back on the shelf, and noticed a small grey device that seemed to have dropped from Shloime's pants pocket.

"What's this?" Nochum asked.

"I thought I have to ask you that," Shloime said without looking at him.

"To ask me what this is? It's a device for recording *shiurim*. I meant what's such a machine doing by you? I didn't know you bought one."

"I didn't buy it," Shloime said briefly.

"All right, if you don't want to say more, you don't have to."

The conversation was heavy and loaded. The few words that were said were sharp and stinging. Nochum realized that Shloime was angry at him because of the few days he had kept a distance – through no fault of his own. Shloime was sure that Nochum had decided to do away with their friendship, and now regretted it, for some reason or another.

"I found it," Shloime said finally.

"And there are no identifying features?"

"Nothing."

"So you don't plan on announcing that you found it."

"I still don't know what I'll do," Shloime said.

"Do you have an idea whose it might be?"

"Yes," Shloime said, and his breathing suddenly quickened.

"Whose?"

"Yours."

Nochum was astounded, and stared at Shloime with big, round eyes.

"You surprise me, Shloime Bleich. If this device was mine, I would have just taken it, no?"

"Maybe not. Maybe you have a reason to want that I shouldn't know that it's yours."

Nochum's eyes got rounder.

"Shloime, I don't know you anymore!"

"Of course," Shloime said sarcastically. "In the three days that we haven't spoken, I've become a different person."

"This machine isn't mine," Nochum said. "I have a similar recording device, but it's at home. I don't use it. You know I don't like to record *shiurim*, that I prefer to write them, right?"

Yes, that was true.

"But mainly, I'd like to know why you think it's mine. Shloime, it's a shame. There's no point to this. We can't keep going around in circles. I've come to you with all the good will in the world and you… you…"

Shloime sighed.

"This machine was found next to the window of the place where I met someone regarding my parents," he said. "Someone wanted to eavesdrop on us. Besides for what was said in the conversation, which completely threw me for a loop, I'm also bothered by the fact that someone's following me. I don't need that now. I don't want anyone to have that recording."

"Okay," Nochum said, still not a hundred percent sure that Shloime had stopped believing that he was the mysterious stalker, "but that's not a problem, because you have the machine."

"It is a problem, because when we found it, the memory card wasn't inside. That means that the recording is floating around somewhere. I can't even imagine what would happen if it should reach strange ears – and even more than that, if my *mechutanim* and my *kallah* hear it…"

"There were secrets on it?"

"Most definitely."

Chana, from where she was sitting in the kitchen, was happy to finally hear voices coming from the closed room.

• • •

Danny Shore, veteran investigator, kept spools of all kinds of string in his office desk drawer. Thick, thin, red, green, knotted and untangled. Each time he had to think something through, he would fish out a spool of thread that fit the matter with which he was dealing and try to find the end.

Now, with Bleich's file before him, a number of spools lay next to him. His fingers had already combed them, searching for and finding the ends, and the file was still closed. He had patience, though. He would search until he found the lead he was looking for. The harder the file, the more challenged Shore felt. The story with the cab driver was perhaps the only corner of the case that wasn't completely unlit. Though the story itself seemed to have a thousand and one holes in it, it was still the only thing in the entire affair that gave off a ray of light.

His next meeting with Shaya Bleich was in another few days – and he never came to a meeting empty handed.

• • •

"There's a taxi stand in Manhattan," Shore said, and placed his lighter on the table.

"Really?" Shaya Bleich sat up straight in the armchair. So quick...!

"The name of the fellow who runs the stand is Tommy Black. He had a driver by the name of David Stone about five or six years ago."

Shaya's breath caught.

*Thicker Than Water*

"So you did manage to find him in the end," he said. "I guess investigators have their own methods."

"Their own methods," Shore agreed, "and their own approach, and, of course, money. No one works for free, my friend."

Shaya nodded his head. The hint was well taken. Someone had to eventually pay the bill. That someone would be him, Shaya Bleich, and he'd do well to start filling his pockets now.

"Cab drivers, as you and I both know, never stay in one place for too long. There's usually a high turnover among drivers of any given stand. No one sits behind the wheel of a taxi because it's his dream job. Stone, too, probably drove a taxi for only some time, and left the minute he could – or the minute he had to. You understand that the manager of the stand didn't spare him a second's thought as soon as he left the office after being paid."

"I understand." Shaya certainly did. "So how do we go about finding him?"

"That's why you and I, Mr. Bleich, are sitting here. Mainly me," the investigator chuckled. "There must be things that the manager knows, and for money, wouldn't care if we knew, too. David Stone had friends from the taxi stand. Not many, two or three. One of them still works there today. He knows details that we don't know."

"And how much do we have to pay him so that we should also know?" Shaya asked, only half in jest.

"Everything has its price," Shore replied with utmost gravity. "But if we're scared of expenses, perhaps we should walk away from the whole file. There are wheels that turn only if you grease them well, like the wheels of an investigation."

"Of course," Shaya said. Did he have a choice?

"Good," said the investigator. "Since our last meeting, I met with Tommy Black.

"And?"

"I discovered some very interesting things. Some of which, in my opinion, make us smarter, and some that block us. First of all, here's a picture of David Stone as it appeared in the taxi stand's drivers' index."

Shaya Bleich seized the picture and pulled it towards him.

• • •

"You think there's reason to fear that the recording will get around?" Nochum asked. Shloime's distress touched him deeply.

"I don't know what to think," Shloime spread his hands. "If someone was bold enough to follow me and tape the conversation from under the window, he could do anything."

Nochum's eyebrows knit in concentration.

"I hope the wheels of your brain are turning now," Shloime gave half a chuckle, "because that would be very helpful."

"Not the wheels of my brain," Nochum said, his forehead creased, "but the wheels of my memory. Someone… someone came over to me today in the evening, shortly after you left yeshiva. We spoke about you.

Shloime sat bolt upright.

"Who was it, Nochum? I have to know."

Nochum slapped his forehead, as if to force his mind open and pull out the answer. "Someone… I don't remember. I don't remember…!"

"You have to remember, Nochum. Maybe a cup of tea will help?!"

"A cup of tea?" Nochum laughed. "It will only put me to sleep. I'm almost sure someone came over to me, maybe a *bochur* in the yeshiva, maybe somebody else… or maybe I'm just imagining it…?"

• • •

Shaya studied the picture intently. He didn't notice Shore's eyes watching him carefully in order to see his reaction.

"This??" That was the first word Bleich said.

"Yes, what do you say?" Shore didn't write anything down, but his mind was recording everything.

"I don't know," Shaya said. "It doesn't look anything like my brother. Not the tiniest bit."

"Look again," Shore said, and put one of the pictures of Naftali that Shaya had given him down on the small table.

Shaya took the two pictures. He desperately wanted to find a resemblance. Heaven knew how much he wanted. But he couldn't.

"The beard definitely changes the impression greatly," Shore said. "In the picture you gave me, your brother has a beard, and as a cab driver he's clean shaven. It's very natural for him to do that first thing in order to hide his identity. Besides the fact that it's very identifying, a beard is also a blatantly Jewish symbol."

"I don't believe my brother would want to masquerade as a non-Jew," Shaya objected.

"My friend," Shore held up his hand, "in my profession there's no place for words such as 'believe' or 'don't believe'. There's only 'know' or 'don't know'. You can use intuition, but not rely on it. I, in your place, wouldn't be so quick to dismiss the possibility. When a Jew wishes to hide his identity, first and foremost he removes all outward signs of being Jewish. I'm not saying he started acting like an American inside his home as well, but that's the identity he's trying to portray. Look closely, Mr. Bleich: there's no beanie here, only a cap."

"Maybe the yarmulke is underneath," Shaya said. "Please understand, Mr. Shore. It's just hard for me to believe."

"Again you're using that word," Shore said. "Let's strike it from the books, all right?"

"Okay," Shaya mumbled. He continued to look at the picture, and heard the voice of the investigator: "The eyes are the only identifying feature difficult to change. I believe that, had the manager of the taxi stand allowed it, he would have been photographed in dark glasses. It seems, however, that the picture also serves as some sort of official ID. Now look at your picture. Is there no resemblance in the eyes? In the gaze?"

Shaya looked. True. In both pictures the eyes were dark. The gaze was straight and steady.

"The expression is also confusing you. In your picture he's smiling – could be it's at a family gathering – while in Black's picture he's very serious, even worried, if you ask me, and it seems he had his reasons."

Shaya nodded. Maybe that was why he didn't see it at first. Naftali had always walked around with a smile, as if the smile was part of his face. The serious expression wasn't at all like him, and gave the impression that it was somebody else.

Shaya put down the picture. Shore removed two papers from the folder in his hand.

"This," he said, placing one copy before Shaya, "is David Stone's card from the taxi stand."

Shaya adjusted his glasses.

• • •

"Suri?"

Devorah Fuchsman stood in the doorway of her daughter's room, feeling as if she was paying a visit to the lion's cage. The cage was large and empty, and the lion was huddled somewhere inside, motionless.

"Can I give you something to drink?"

Suri didn't answer. She didn't even move her head. Devorah tiptoed inside and put the pitcher and cup down on the night table.

"Can we talk, Suri?"

Still, Suri didn't move. A few days earlier, she would have answered with a "yes" or "no". Now she was simply silent.

"I have news for you, Suri."

Devorah thought she saw a spark in her daughter's eyes. Encouraged, she sat down on the bed and told the statue standing by the window:

"I spoke with the *mechuteniste* earlier."

Suri shifted. It was an almost imperceptible movement, but it was a movement.

"She asked how you are. She said she wants to buy you a pearl necklace."

Another slight movement. *Please, Hashem*, Devorah begged, *put more of the right words in my mouth.*

"It's enough already!!" Suri suddenly exploded, her shouts matching her earlier silence. "I can't stand this double game. If they want me as their *kallah*, if they want the *chasunah*, they shouldn't say otherwise. If they don't want me, they should stop buying me necklaces…!"

"I see it as a clear sign," Devorah continued in the same calm tone. "If a family plans on, or is even contemplating, cancelling a *chasunah*, they don't continue buying presents for the *kallah*. Do you agree with me?!"

"It's a front!" Suri yelled. "They're hiding something!!! They want to bribe me with jewelry and pearls, but I don't need it! I need to know the truth, Ima! The truth, whatever it is!!!"

Suri collapsed onto a chair and shook with sobs. In the next room sat Yisroel Yitzchok, still under house arrest, listening to every word and every sob. Something in his heart shifted. He really hadn't meant to shake things up *that* badly. He had only wanted to prove that the esteemed Shloime Bleich wasn't so perfect. He didn't mean for him to become blacker than black.

# CHAPTER 23

"What year is this from?" Shaya asked as he examined the photocopy of the card.

"The date is on top," Shore directed him. Shaya glanced at it and did some quick figuring. Yes, the date fit.

"And the date of birth?" Shaya needed a few minutes to remember Naftali's secular birth date. February fourteenth? No, that couldn't be. Naftali was definitely born in the summer, not in February.

"If he wanted to hide his identity, he would change his date of birth, too," Shore said confidently. "He has no reason to give any true information. It makes a lot more sense for him to change it from the summer to the winter than from June to July. And this isn't a birth certificate. It's just an ID card for a taxi stand."

"Married. Number of children: 1," Shaya continued to read aloud. "Taxi number: 72. How does that help us?"

"You can't know," Shore said. "Any information could be helpful, or remain useless. Don't ever make light of details, Bleich."

No, he wasn't making light. By the end of the meeting, he was definitely encouraged. This investigator worked well. He was costing him a lot per hour, besides what he was paying his informants – an unknown sum, in the meantime – but the chance of finding Naftali and Rochel was invaluable. And that chance seemed to be coming closer, more than ever before.

• • •

"Really, Nochum, I'll pay you," Shloime pleaded, "Just remember already!"

"How much will you pay me?" Nochum teased.

"As much as you want!"

"It's not worth it for you. I'll think about the money instead of... of..."

"Come on, already! Who was it? A *bochur*? A man? A kollel *yungerman*? A businessman? Young? Old? Fat? Skinny? What happened to you that you don't remember? What's this mental block?!"

"That's what happens. We forget the important things. I remember what I had for supper yesterday, and what my sisters fought about two days ago, but not who--- who---"

Shloime stood up and left the small room. He felt that his presence was disturbing Nochum's concentration.

The house was quiet. Everyone was already sleeping. Shloime was walking in the hallway when he thought he heard the sound of crying. He listened carefully. It wasn't one of his little brothers. If it had been, he would have already heard the shuffle of his mother's slippers as she hurried to him. It wasn't the cry of a child. It was a different weeping, deeper.

He found his mother sitting next to the gleaming kitchen table, a tissue in her hand. As soon as she noticed him, she tried to hide the tissue, but there was no way for her to hide her wet face.

"Ima!" Shloime was alarmed, "What happened?!"

"Nothing," she said. "What's going on, Shloime? Everything's okay with you two?"

"Don't tell me 'nothing', Ima" he pulled up a chair. "This never happens to you."

"Abba never goes away for such a long time without knowing when he'll be back," Chana answered, and needed another tissue. "It's just a little hard for me without him."

"I'm sorry," Shloime said instantly, and a wave of regret rolled over him. "I should have been in the house more, helped more."

"That's not necessary, Shloime," Chana said immediately. "The best help is for you to learn as usual. The girls help me. But Shloime," she asked, "I want to know everything that was said in this meeting with Lederman. You can't drop a bomb of information on me and leave."

"I'm sorry, Ima, I really am." Shloime felt that soon he would need a tissue. "I shouldn't have done that to you. I should have sat down and told you everything – every word. But I had to speak to Nochum about something important that's connected to the meeting. Something really important."

"Shloime," Chana said, "You're getting me more and more worried. Stop scaring me. What did Lederman say? Shloime, please."

"My parents are alive," Shloime repeated slowly, also to internalize the information himself, "at least according to the information that he has."

"And he first tells you now," Chana understood. "I have a feeling that he knew this for quite a long time and just never bothered saying anything."

"I don't know what's up with Mendel Lederman, Ima. The man isn't investigating this in the usual sense of the word. I think he's holding back more than he's saying, and I don't understand why. He's telling me not to get married, you understand, Ima?! Not to get married until I find my parents. If I don't listen to him, he warned me, it won't be good..."

"Not good?!" her eyes were huge. "In what way?!"

"He wouldn't say. He also wouldn't say where he has his information from. I told him that I refuse to believe him until he gives me reliable sources."

Chana stared at her son. He had the feeling that her gaze wasn't focused on him, but on something else, from the distant past. Her eyes were wide open, dark with a nameless fear.

"Shloime," she said, her voice as if rising from the grave, "Shloime, Mendel Lederman might be a man of intrigue, he hides things, he's leading us on, but there's some part of me that believes him. Believes him very much..."

• • •

In the small hours of the morning, before daylight, Chana heard the phone ring.

"Hello," she heard Shaya say wearily, "I finished the meeting. We have new findings."

Chana listened in silence to the information that Shaya told her. There was no denying it. There was what to work with. This investigator worked seriously, and if he continued in the same vein, they would be able to move forward pretty quickly.

"So much news," Chana's voice was thick with sarcasm. "Mendel Lederman told Shloime that his parents are alive and well, and you're telling me that the investigation is progressing. My heart can't handle all---"

"Don't believe Lederman," Shaya cut her off. "I don't believe it."

"Don't believe?! He said that Naftali and Rochel are alive.

We've waited years for these words and now you don't want to believe?!"

"I don't believe one word that man says, after seeing what he's capable of. In my eyes, he's completely unreliable, you understand?!"

Chana paused, unsure. "I don't know, Shaya. I don't know, I just believe."

"Come, let's not use that word," Shaya suggested. "Let's just leave it out. In an investigation, there's no believing, only knowing."

"Of course you could believe," Chana said. "I don't know how it is by investigators, but women's intuition is sometimes worth even more than solid knowledge. I'm telling you that this time Lederman is saying the truth."

"And maybe you just want to believe this information, because it makes you really happy?!"

"Maybe. But I don't think Lederman would sell us false information when he knows how important his words are to us."

"Chana, by Lederman you could believe anything."

There was silence on the line. This was one topic on which they didn't agree.

"Shaya," Chana suddenly asked, "How much does he take, this Shole?"

"Shore. A lot. He pays everyone who gives him information. Get ready for thousands upon thousands of dollars."

Chana was horrified. "But Shaya, we don't have a bottomless pit!"

"We'll have to tighten our belts wherever possible. Especially now, after spending so much on the *chasunah*."

"Tighten our belts? How will that help? We need a fortune."

"There's one savings plan that's supposed to open now," Shaya said. "And I'll think of other sources. You also think."

Chana couldn't think then. Her tired head dropped back onto

the pillow. Bundles of dollar bills waltzed before her closed eyes. She tried to grab them, but they slipped out of her hands. Pearl necklaces also promenaded in the air. She had to grab ahold of one of them for Suri, her *kallah*.

• • •

"There's something that I definitely remember," Nochum said. "It was a young *bochur*, not a man. I remember his height. He stood next to me. He was a bit shorter than me."

"Then he's not so tall," Shloime said. "Someone from our yeshiva?"

"I have no idea."

"We have to take you to a psychologist," Shloime muttered, "who would get the information from you through hypnosis."

"What?!"

"Nothing."

Nochum shrugged. "You know what? I'll go home and sleep on it. Maybe in the morning my mind will be more awake and I'll be able to remember."

"I really hope so," Shloime said with all his heart.

A quarter of an hour after Nochum left his house Shloime suddenly jumped up.

He had an idea. Fired with enthusiasm, he completely forgot the hour and dialed Nochum's house.

"Listen," he said as soon as his friend answered. "I know what we'll do!"

"We'll go to sleep, I told you already," Nochum chuckled.

"Now we'll go to sleep, yes, but tomorrow we'll set up an ambush."

"What?" The tired Nochum wasn't sure that he heard correctly.

"An ambush. The two of us will take turns waiting for the *bochur* where he lost his machine. If he's a fool, as we believe he is, he'll return to the scene of crime in order to find his machine. He'll keep coming back until he finds it…"

• • •

Chana Bleich didn't usually like shopping at private sales. Even though one could sometimes find cheaper things and the customer service had a more personal touch, Chana preferred the strong backbone of a recognized store, or one that was part of a chain.

This time she deviated from her usual practice. In the next building lived Rochele Klein, a good friend who sold jewelry from her house at relatively good prices. In the evening, Chana went up the two flights of stairs, straightened her snood, rang the bell and waited to be identified in the closed circuit system.

"Chana!" Rochele called in surprised delight. "How are you? How nice!"

Chana, though, wasn't feeling so cheerful. She went into the room that served as the store and asked to see some strands of pearls.

"Please," Rochele said, and removed two-three trays from under the counter. "For your *kallah*, I presume?"

"You presume correctly," Chana said distractedly. The necklaces were nice. Previously, when she was able to allow herself to buy at her usual standards, she would have asked Rochele to put the trays back and show her something truly beautiful, no matter the price. Now, though, she couldn't. She had to buy a pearl necklace for Suri, and it had to be at a decent price. That was why she didn't take Suri with her to the jewelry store to choose, as she had always done, and that was why she was studying these mediocre necklaces with such concentration; she knew she would have to choose from them.

"How much do they cost?" she asked. She knew it was a legitimate question, but for some reason she flushed.

Rochele quoted some prices. Though they weren't low, Chana knew that in a regular store she would have paid considerably more.

"This is very pretty," Rochele picked up one of the samples, trying to gauge Chana's taste. The necklace really was pretty, relatively. Would Suri like it? Would Suri like the fact that she was receiving a piece of jewelry from a box without being allowed to choose?

"You don't have to decide, Chana," Rochele said. Her friend seemed a bit out of her depth choosing jewelry for her *kallah*. How could that be? The engagement had been celebrated a long time ago. "Take a few samples, let your *kallah* choose, and bring the rest back to me, let's say, by the end of the week."

"Oh, really? I could do that?" Chana asked.

"Of course," Rochele said in astonishment. "Everyone does that. You can take four or five samples – leaving a deposit, of course."

Chana was obviously relieved. She wouldn't be putting her *kallah* in an uncomfortable situation. Suri would be able to choose, but only from the samples she would bring her, those that were within their budget – which had suddenly become limited. She wouldn't know the prices. She wouldn't ask, either. Suri was very refined.

"Please wrap this one for me," she laid one strand on the side, "and also this."

"You're sure you don't want this one?" Rochele put her hand on a beautiful strand, its loveliness reflected in its price.

"No," Chana said with a pang, glancing at the almost hidden

price tag, "I don't think my *kallah* will like it…"

• • •

"You would never make a good investigator," Nochum said. The sentence was somehow familiar to Shloime, but it didn't convince him. The two of them stood directly under the window to the office, right where the anonymous person had stood and listened, and then dropped his recording device.

"Here?" Nochum asked in disbelief.

"What's the problem?" Shloime didn't understand.

"Problems, you mean," Nochum corrected him. "First of all, this place is so open that within five minutes we'll be surrounded by all the kids on the block. Besides which, you and I know that the machine fell here, but whoever lost it could think that it dropped anywhere from here to his house. Why should he come here and incriminate himself once more?"

Shloime thought.

"He'll search the entire way, true, and he won't find it. Eventually he'll come here. As for the place itself, of course we won't sit here under the window. We'll find somewhere from where we could watch this place."

"And we'll stand there the entire day?" The whole thing didn't grab Nochum. "And what about our learning? Shloime, I think you should hire a tracking company."

"And you'll pay, right? My parents can't spend an extra shekel right now. Don't take it so to heart, Nochum. I promise you it'll be only two-three days, not more."

"You're an optimist, huh? Or a big *ba'al emunah*?"

"I'm relying on the odds. The boy wants his machine, right? He, or someone he sends, will come here at one point to get it, right? We just have to be here when that happens."

"You forgot to bring a sack," Nochum said, "to throw over the criminal's head as soon as he gets here. How are you planning to catch him?"

Until then, Shloime hadn't given that point a thought. As he thought about it, though, the answer was clear.

"We won't catch him, Nochum. We'll first try to identify him, because chances are it's someone we know. Me, definitely. And if it's someone we don't know, we'll follow him."

"Aha," Nochum said. "Now you're giving us another project."

"Nochum," Shloime pleaded, "it's important…"

• • •

Late in the afternoon, when the waiters were already getting the tables ready for the *simcha* that would take place that evening, the manager of "Simchas Chasanim" sat in his small office adjoining the hall. A jumble of notes, receipts, menus, pens and pencils decorated his desk, but that was nothing compared to what was going on in his head. That season there was a wedding every night, and he had to remember all the special requests of the different *mechutanim*, answer everyone pleasantly, keep track of which price he had given whom, know with whom to be flexible, and with whom not to be and also to fill the calendar of the next wedding season.

The phone rang.

"Simchas Chasanim," the manager answered laconically, shoving the receiver between his right ear and shoulder.

"Hello. I'd like to reserve the hall for the twenty fourth of Av."

The manager was quiet for a minute and then he smiled. He didn't laugh, because the client on the other end of the line was completely serious, but he knew the hall was booked solid until after Succos. The man probably engaged his first child just last night, and was sure that the managers of all the halls were sitting and waiting for his phone call.

"The twenty fourth of Av is taken," the manager said, without even flipping through his calendar. "We're booked until after Succos."

"Are you sure?" the man asked. Not in disappointment, but in a businesslike tone. "Are you sure this date is also booked?"

"I'm telling you without even checking," the manager explained. "The end of Av is a very busy time. The date was locked in months ago."

"I suggest you check," the man said, and there was something in his voice that the manager didn't like. "If you don't mind, of course."

The manager obediently opened his calendar, feeling very foolish. Could there be a mistake about which this stranger knew and he didn't? Could a date have been left open in the thick of the season? Or was someone just trying to string him along?

The pages flew between his fingers. The twenty fourth of Av.

"Of course," he said in relief, "the date is taken, just as I thought. There are no open dates in this season, at least not by me. I suggest that---"

"Can you please tell me who is getting married that night?"

"Why?" wondered the manager, "You think you'll be able to switch dates with them?! I'm telling you, this date has been booked for ages!"

"I'd appreciate it," the man said, and something in his voice warned the manager not to refuse, "if you would please tell me who took the hall for that night."

"The Bleich and Fuchsman families," the manager said.

"All right," said the man. "So I have news for you. It looks like this wedding won't be taking place…"

• • •

*Excellent*, Devorah Fuchsman thought to herself approvingly. It had been a wonderful idea to get Suri out of the house a bit, to make her get dressed nicely and even look in the mirror. Nothing could have moved her to do all that except the explicit request of the *mechuteniste*, Chana Bleich, to "borrow" Suri for the afternoon.

"I'd like her to come choose a pearl necklace," the *mechuteniste* said, "and for a change, I'd like her to choose it by me, at home, without us going out to the store. I brought home a few samples. The children also miss her and want to see her."

She couldn't refuse, of course. She definitely couldn't tell the *mechuteniste* that the esteemed *kallah* was spending too much time in her room, refusing to eat or drink, to wear anything more decent than a robe, and to interact with anyone beyond a simple "yes" or "no".

Devorah came to help Suri choose an outfit. She found her staring at the closet as if she couldn't tell the difference between a white and black suit.

"You can wear this," Devorah pulled a pretty, casual suit from between the hangers. "This looks good on you. Also, the new shoes that we bought go very well with it."

"I have no interest in going," Suri said, as if her face wasn't broadcasting that fact. "What does she want to give me a necklace for? Why does she want me to come there, anyway? Maybe she wants to tell me that the wedding might be off, and she wants to do it in private, not in middle of the street."

"Suri!" Devorah scolded her. "Your imagination has crossed all boundaries of good taste. Get dressed nicely, put a big smile on your face and go to the Bleichs, who want to shower you with good. Why destroy such a nice time with your own two hands?

This time will never return. Every *kallah* has her fears and worries. You can't allow them to take over your life. Go outside, see the ground and sky and birds, and you'll see that everything is perfectly fine."

# CHAPTER 24

"Hold on, just a minute," the shocked manager said, "what does that mean, the wedding won't take place? Who is this, anyway...?!"

"My name is not relevant at the moment," said the voice, and the manager noticed that he had called from a protected line. "The information I'm giving you is not yet public, but it's reliable, and I suggest you lock in the date with another family as soon as possible before it's left open with no chance of filling it."

"I demand to know with whom I am speaking," the manager said forcefully, but the call was disconnected.

The manager of "Simchas Chasanim" shut off all his phones. Now he was annoyed. This had never happened to him. He wasn't in the habit of talking to anonymous callers, but the voice of that man – there was something in that voice that said: "Don't tangle with me too much; I know more about you than you know about yourself." The problem was, even if he chose to believe what the stranger told him, he couldn't cancel the wedding based on that information. On the other hand, to plan the wedding after receiving such information – that he couldn't do either.

What *could* he do?

There was only one thing he could do: feel for information by the Bleich and Fuchsman families. Better he should call Fuchsman. Just the week before he had tried to reach Bleich, to fix the wrong date on the check he had given him, but Mrs. Bleich had told him that her husband was out of the country and she didn't know when he would return. She couldn't fix the date, since the check was from a checking account that belonged only to Shaya.

He'd call the Fuchsmans and feel around. If he heard stammering and stuttering, and didn't receive clear, solid information, he'd know that there was what to rely on, and would demand a definitive answer, in whichever direction. A wedding was thousands of dollars. He couldn't let the hall stand empty, especially during such a busy season.

The manager opened his calendar again to the twenty fourth of Av, took his highlighter and drew a large question mark on the page. He would check it out. As soon as possible.

• • •

"You know what?" Nochum scratched his head. "I just thought of something. I think you're in tremendous luck."

He removed his glasses, which were only for close vision, and gazed with concentration at the top floor of the opposite building.

"I think that apartment belongs to relatives of mine who are now out of the country."

"Really?? And it's not rented?" Shloime wanted to be certain.

"No, it's not rented. They only went last week and they're supposed to return in about a month, as far as I know. If we can get the key…"

"That would be perfect," Shloime said, and shook Nochum's shoulder. "You get the key, Nochum, and we'll have an excellent stakeout without anyone suspecting us. It's a great idea. Get the key today. It's a shame to waste any time."

"Yes, sir," Nochum saluted. He had to check from whom he could get the key, and what possible excuse he could use to get it. True, they weren't planning anything wrong. They just wanted to sit on the porch and catch someone who was doing some secret eavesdropping. He had to come up with a somewhat reasonable story, though, that would cause whoever had the key to give it to him.

"Say that we want to learn by ourselves." Shloime read his friend's thoughts.

"Not in yeshiva?" Nochum wrinkled his nose. "If the person who has the key is who I think it is, he won't go for such an excuse. We have to think of something else."

"Maybe we want to store some things there?"

Nochum shook his head. "No good. First of all, it's a beautiful apartment, and they won't agree to let us use it as a storage place. And besides, if you want to store something, you take the key, put your things in, and give it back. We don't know how much time this stakeout will last. It could be a day or it could take a week. We can't hold the key by us for a week just in order to store things. It looks suspicious."

"And if we take the key, make a copy and give it back?"

Nochum looked at his friend in shock. "Shloime, I think we should forget about this idea. It's sending you off your rocker. If you were your regular self right now, you would never have brought up such a possibility! What's gotten into you???"

Shloime reddened. It was true. He was talking about something clearly dishonest. The wish to move things along, however, was urging him on, chasing him, and really making him insane, as Nochum had said.

"Come on," he said impatiently, "You have to find us a solution, Nochum. You had a good idea. Now we just have to find a way to carry it out. It's obvious that we have to do it, right? So just strain that brain of yours a bit more, and come up with a nice story. Just a bit more…"

・・・

Suri returned in the evening from her visit at the Bleichs. Her mother immediately sensed that the outing had done her good all around.

"How was it?" she asked.

"It was very nice. The kids are cute," Suri told her. "They treated me royally. It was really very pleasant."

"And all your dark predictions…?" Devorah asked carefully. Had the *mechuteniste* really taken Suri to the side in order to "explain" some things to her? Was the atmosphere heavy and frightening, as Suri had been convinced it would be? Were strange things said? Secret hints given?

"The *shver* isn't home, and you could feel it. They didn't speak about him at all, but I felt that it's a bit hard for her like this, alone. Not the technical aspect. Faigie's helping her a lot. It's hard that everything is on her."

"And you spoke about the *chasunah*?"

"A little. The little girls wanted to show me their new dresses, but Faigie suggested that it be a surprise for the *chasunah*. And she gave me this." Suri took a small, prettily wrapped package out of her handbag. Inside the box lay a pretty, delicate strand of pearls, very much Suri's taste.

"I take it that you chose?" Devorah said, "And this was the nicest one?"

"Yes," Suri answered. "You know what, Ima, this time I was happily surprised. You remember when we went to buy the gold set? The *mechuteniste* practically forced me to choose the most glamorous set in the store. And now, I guess she knows me better and realized that I prefer simpler, more delicate jewelry – not in order to save money, but because that's my taste."

"Very good," Devorah said. "I'm glad you're getting along so well together. Believe me, Suri, that's very important in life."

She watched as Suri went down the hall and entered her room. She felt like picking up the phone to the *mechuteniste* and thanking her from the bottom of her heart for taking her daughter out of her self-imposed jail, even unknowingly. Suri had received a beautiful gift that lifted her mood. More than that, though, she had returned to herself and to reality. She felt loved and wanted by the Bleichs, and all the depressing thoughts that had taken over her mind the last few days had now eased. If Yisroel Yitzchok wouldn't do anything else foolish in the near future, it was possible to hope for a complete recovery.

One minute… where was Yisroel Yitzchok?! These days he was supposed to be in the house, and only in the house. Elya had spoken to his Rosh Yeshiva and explained the situation. Yisroel Yitzchok couldn't be allowed to roam about by himself, at least not for the next while. The Rosh Yeshiva, it seemed, was quite happy to remove the responsibility for Yisroel Yitzchok from his shoulders, even for a short time. Throughout the entire day, Yisroel Yitzchok was closed up in his room, listening to music and keeping busy with all sorts of things. Every so often he left the room and took something to eat, but didn't leave the house.

And now the room was empty…!

He was capable of escaping, Devorah knew, but if he did indeed do so, that would be taking things to a new level, or rather, down a level.

"Elya?!" She quickly dialed her husband's cell phone, "Yisroel Yitzchok's not here!!"

"It's okay," he reassured her. "Sorry, I forgot to tell you. I picked him up earlier from the house; he's with me now. I felt that he needed to air out a bit. It's not good for him to stay cooped up in the house for too long. We're together, don't worry. He's under my supervision…"

• • •

"We're up to the next stage," Shore said. This time they sat, for the sake of change, at the edge of the lobby of a huge hotel. The papers were on the small table between them. This time, the investigator's tie was pink. Was that an optimistic sign?

"What is the next stage?" Shaya asked curiously.

"We meet with David Stone. That is, I will definitely meet with him. So will you, if you so wish."

Shaya's heart leaped. This investigator was very quick.

"But where will we meet him? Where is he today? How will we find him?" Shaya didn't understand. The investigator, however, smiled.

"I do my job," he said, "for which you pay me. And about payment, I've been meaning to tell you that we can't move on to the next stage without my receiving full payment for what I've done until now."

"Of course," Shaya said automatically. His heart sank automatically, too. "What sum are we talking about?"

Shore, organized and meticulous as always, pulled out an itemized bill, upon which was detailed all the action he had taken thus far, and their cost. Shaya lowered his eyes to the bottom of the page, and his head swam.

"I can meet you with an easy payment schedule," Shore said

considerately, "but don't forget to take into account that we're very nearly at the next stage, so spreading the payments won't really help. Unless you want to hold up the process, which I don't suggest you do."

"Of course, of course," Shaya mumbled, feeling his entire body sweating under his suit. "I'll get you the money in the next few days."

He had no idea, however, where he would get the money from. True, there was a savings plan that was supposed to open about now, but he didn't remember exactly when. It could easily be in another few months. He would have to borrow a hefty sum. If not now, then in the coming weeks, depending on how quickly things progressed.

There was no question that he was thrilled to have found the right investigator, and that things were progressing well, but the good feeling didn't change the enormity of the sum. Nor did it invent more sources from which he could borrow. And just now, when the facts were so encouraging and it looked like they would be able, with Hashem's help, to celebrate the wedding on time. What would be…?!

• • •

Elya felt his heart twist as he hit the button for the main lock inside the car. He usually didn't lock up, unless he was driving his little children. Now, though, with Yisroel Yitzchok sitting beside him, he felt more secure with the doors locked. When did all this happen with Yisroel Yitzchok? When did he become so unpredictable?!

"Do you have somewhere specific that you want to go?" he asked.

"Somewhere specific…" Yisroel Yitzchok thought about it. It had been a long time since he had been asked such a question.

"Maybe we can go down Shoshani Street?"

"What do you have on Shoshani Street?"

What did he have on Shoshani Street? He had a small recording device that might still be hiding in the thorn bushes, waiting for him. It would be a crime not to take it from there. True, he already bought a new one, even a better one, but why shouldn't he have two?

He couldn't, of course, explain all that to his father. Abba would ask questions; he would have to answer.

"I have a friend," he said, trying to come up with a reasonable story in a fraction of a second, one that his father would find acceptable. A friend that what? That wrote the Rosh Yeshiva's *shiurim* for him on the days he wasn't there? Abba wouldn't buy that. Yisroel Yitzchok wasn't above lying if it worked for him, but not if it made things more complicated. To make up a story that his father anyway wouldn't believe was too dangerous to try.

"A friend that has an interesting disc that I wanted to hear," he finally said.

"Okay," Elya said, "I'll take you there. What number?"

Yisroel Yitzchok almost hit his forehead. He should have thought of that. Abba wouldn't let him get out and walk about alone for even a minute. Even if he was sitting in the car at the foot of the building and waiting for him. Abba wasn't taking any chances; he didn't trust him.

"Forget it, it's not necessary," he said. "It could wait for another time."

Elya, even if he wondered at the quick change of heart, didn't say a word. The car, though, had already turned in the direction of Shoshani Street, and Yisroel Yitzchok's eyes searched for the place. He didn't remember the number of the building, but if he saw the yard with all the thorn bushes growing under the window of the storage room, he would surely remember.

Amazingly, his father slowed exactly as they approached the place, and Yisroel Yitzchok was able to look carefully at the bushes. It had been quite foolish on his part to think that he would be able to see a small machine from such a distance, but…

"How nice," his father suddenly said. Yisroel Yitzchok turned his head.

"Look how nicely they renovated, without ruining the front of the building," his father said. Yisroel Yitzchok was impatient. What interest did anyone have in renovations now?

In order not to arouse his father's suspicions, however, he looked at the opposite building and nodded his head. Suddenly, he caught his breath.

"And look how nice," he said, unable to arrest the big smile that spread across his face.

• • •

The phone rang in the Fuchsman home.

Ima had taken all the girls shopping for new shoes for the wedding. The boys hadn't yet come home from cheder. Suri, who had returned a bit to herself after the previous day, and had even left her room, went to pick up the phone.

"Hello," she said politely.

"Hello, I'm calling from the hall 'Simchas Chasanim'. Am I speaking with Mrs. Fuchsman?"

"No, I'm the *kallah*," Suri said. The words sounded pleasant to her ears.

"The *kallah*. Very good. I just have some sort of question mark here on the calendar… you set the *chasunah* for the twenty fourth of Av, correct?"

Suri didn't answer. The blood drained from her face.

"Hello? Are you with me?"

"Yes," she managed to say weakly.

"I just wanted to receive a final confirmation. I simply have some pressure over here…"

All at once, the black fog settled back on Suri's shoulders. It wasn't only Yisroel Yitzchok who said it. Not only her *chosson* said it – which she heard with her own ears on the recording device. It wasn't only her *mechuteniste* who suddenly forgot the date. Now the manager of the hall, too, wanted to know, because there was some sort of question mark.

"What makes you think that the date isn't final?" she asked. She knew that he could barely hear her hoarse voice. "Why do you have any doubt? Do you call all those who reserve your hall…?"

"Uh, I heard a rumor that---"

By then, however, the call was finished. Not because the *kallah* hung up. He heard a loud thump, as if the phone had fallen to the floor. He didn't hear a busy signal. He hoped everything was okay. He didn't think it was.

"Hello?? Hello??" he called into the receiver. There was no answer.

"Hello???" He felt bad. He was afraid something had happened to her. Maybe it had been a mistake to speak to the *kallah* herself. Perhaps he should have spoken to one of the parents. True, he was only the manager of a hall, but he, too, should show some sensitivity. Sensitivity to what? He himself didn't know.

"Hello…???"

He was talking to the air.

• • •

"How nice what?" Elya didn't understand. He followed Yisroel Yitzchok's outstretched arm. What was he pointing at? The top floor? What was there that wasn't on the other floors?

"Look who's sitting there," Yisroel Yitzchok said. He absolutely couldn't, no matter how hard he tried, take the smile off his face.

Elya strained to see. On the top porch he saw two *bochurim*. Who were they? Friends of Yisroel Yitzchok? Did he know them? And what was causing Yisroel Yitzchok to smile so broadly?

"*Nu*, really, Abba. You don't see who it is?"

Elya tried to make out the face. He must need a stronger prescription, because he absolutely couldn't identify him.

"It's your dear *chosson*," Yisroel Yitzchok said, poison dripping from every syllable, "Shloime Bleich and his good friend, from the best in the yeshiva, Nochum Cohen."

"That's Shloime?!" Elya didn't want to believe it. Yisroel Yitzchok, though, wasn't a fool. He wouldn't make up a story and rely on the fact that his father still hadn't gotten multifocal lenses.

"Yes, Abba. That's Shloime. He's sitting at this hour on the porch, breathing some fresh air. I guess by him it's already *bein hazmanim*, or that he's taking some vacation."

*A bit of respect*, Elya Fuchsman wanted to say, *when you speak about Shloime Bleich*. But he didn't say it. Instead, he was forced to ask Yisroel Yitzchok, who was able to see what he couldn't:

"What's he doing there?"

"I told you. He's sitting on the porch with a friend. He's not even embarrassed to be seen like that, in middle of the day, out of yeshiva – he, the *bochur* who you said is the 'cream of the crop'."

Yisroel Yitzchok didn't stop gloating over his victory for a minute.

"Should we go out and wave hello?" he suggested. "I'm sure

*Thicker Than Water* ⟪ 303

he'll be terribly happy to see us."

"Most definitely not," Elya said forcefully. "We're leaving here and going straight home."

"What a shame," Yisroel Yitzchok said in pretend disappointment. "It's not every day that we meet Shloime Bleich. Maybe we should speak with him; we'll enjoy every wise and wonderful word that leaves his mouth."

Elya's heart roiled within him. He wouldn't, though, take leave of his senses right then and there, in middle of the street. Instead, he started the motor again and began to drive.

Unconnected to Yisroel Yitzchok and his antics, another doubt was added to Elya's list of misgivings. The coincidence disturbed him. What, really, was Shloime doing on the porch of a strange apartment in middle of the day, and, what's more, with his friend who was said to be a refined *bochur* and a big *lamdan*…?!

The car sped through the green light. Elya suddenly remembered something. He swerved sharply to the right and pulled up at the curb.

"Now you listen very carefully to what I'm telling you, Yisroel Yitzchok," he said. "Under no circumstance are you to speak one word to Suri, whether good or bad. Not about the weather. Not about Shloime Bleich, or… or…"

"Or what? Yisroel Yitzchok couldn't resist. "*Chaf dalet* Av? What do you say, Abba, will there be a *chasunah*, or not…?!"

• • •

"Tzipporah Aharonson got a pearl necklace," Rochel Leah, Suri's little sister, related during supper.

"What do you have to do with Tzipporah Aharonson?" Devorah Fuchsman wondered. She poured a cup of lemonade for herself. Tzipporah was Suri's good friend who had gotten engaged not long before.

"Her sister Matti and I passed by a jewelry store today. We stopped to look in the window and Matti showed me the necklace that Tzipporah got. It's exactly, but exactly the same necklace that Suri got."

"Interesting," Devorah said. "Maybe they have the same taste."

"The same cheap taste, you mean," Rochel Leah said. "It was the cheapest necklace in the window. Didn't you once say that the Bleichs like to buy the most expensive things?"

"Rochel Leah, I don't think this is any of our business," Devorah said, and sighed. "And besides, Mrs. Bleich probably understands that our Suri is looking for things that are simple and refined, and not expensive, and therefore brought her specifically such things from which to choose. I actually respect that, that she put her tendency aside and went along with her *kallah's* wishes. That says very nice things about the *mechuteniste*."

"Oh," Rochel Leah said. She seemed to accept the explanation. Later, though, when she was all alone, Devorah Fuchsman thought that the matter wasn't only nice. It also demanded explanation.

# CHAPTER 25

Devorah went into Suri's room, ostensibly to put something in the closet. Really, she wanted to ask her a bit more about the pearl necklace. She sincerely believed what she had told Rochel Leah and, from what she knew of Chana Bleich, she could also believe that her *mechuteniste* would willingly give up her expensive taste in favor of what her *kallah* wanted, but she somehow felt that it wasn't only that. Even a mother-in-law who wanted to accommodate her daughter-in-law's modest taste wouldn't so easily forgo her natural tendency to buy expensively and selectively.

"Suri, the---" She went into the room and stopped short. "What happened? Why are you lying like that – why are you so pale?!"

Suri stared at her without answering.

"Did something happen?!" Yisroel Yitzchok wasn't in the house, greatly lowering the chances of something dangerous having happened, but Suri looked as if she had been hit over the head with a crowbar.

There was no answer. There wasn't even the slightest indication that she was listening.

"Suri, you're scaring me. I want to know what happened," Devorah demanded forcefully. Perhaps the harsh tone wasn't the proper approach just then, but it left her throat without really asking.

"They called from "Simchas Chasanim"," Suri said, her voice cracked.

"*Nu?*"

"And he said… he asked if we're sure about the date of the *chasunah*. They weren't sure, they heard rumors…"

Devorah was struck dumb. From all the people in the world, it had to be Suri who answered that phone call.

"And what did you say?"

"I didn't. The telephone… dropped. I think it cracked."

Cracked telephone or not, it was Suri's fragmented heart that mattered more to Devorah. She sat down next to her daughter and considered what to say.

"We have to check who's spreading these rumors."

"We don't have to check," Suri whispered. "We know. There are only two sides to a *shidduch*, Ima. And if we didn't spread the rumors, then there's only one possibility…"

Devorah Fuchsman was silent. She didn't want to make the slightest mistake, and in such a situation, with such a sensitive *kallah*, every word could be wrong.

"Do you want to drink something, Suri?"

"No. I only want that you and Abba should put an end to what's happening here. Let me know, once and for all, if the Bleichs want to cancel the *chasunah* or not. I don't care what the answer is, as long as it's clear…"

• • •

Mendel Lederman wasn't at peace.

Someone had listened in on him and young Bleich. He hadn't told a soul about the meeting. Bleich, though, could have told anyone he wanted. True, it was hard to believe that he had been such a fool as to publicize the matter, but he must not have kept it as secret as he should have.

But whomever Shloime Bleich had knowingly told should be someone who was looking out for Bleich. He wouldn't have secretly listened to the conversation like some thief and fled the instant he thought he had been discovered. Nor would he have tried to record all that was said. It had to be, then, that this person knew about the meeting from a third party. Not only that, but it stood to reason that he wasn't too interested in the good of Shloime Bleich.

He was looking for such a person.

He hadn't the slightest clue whom it was. The recording device that was now by Shloime resembled hundreds of other recording devices he had seen in his life. It told him nothing about its owner.

Thus, Mendel Lederman adopted the one choice he had: tracking. He, of course, didn't plan on wasting his time, nor his prestige, on long, hopeless ambushes. He wouldn't sit each day in the same forsaken spot next to the storage room on Shoshani Street, waiting for some anonymous person to show up. He *would* do what professional investigators did: he would set up a small camera, completely unnoticeable, in a place that overlooked the corner where the device had been lost. In another few days, he would come and collect the material.

Lederman acted immediately. After he completed the job and returned to his office late at night, he wearily opened Bleich's file again.

The invitation to the wedding peeked out at him. It was

beautifully done. Mendel Lederman tore it from the folder and ripped it to shreds.

• • •

Chana Bleich closed the door behind Suri and sighed heavily.

She never would have believed that she would do such a thing. She, Chana Bleich, before whom jewelry salesladies lined up when hearing that she had engaged her oldest son, gave her *kallah* a present — a pearl necklace that wasn't worthy of even entering her house.

But she couldn't have done otherwise. Luckily, she had a *kallah* with simple, modest taste. Shaya had sounded so desperate on the telephone, so lost, that she couldn't handle it. There was no money, he told her. The investigation was progressing nicely, but it was extremely expensive. They couldn't spend a lot now — and this was just the beginning. The investigation was branching out. They would have to question more people, pay for traveling — who knew to where. They would have to tighten their belts as much as possible.

But she had to buy a present for Suri. She felt that something had cooled in her relationship with Suri; she felt she had to invite her for a visit. Could the *kallah* come to the Bleichs and leave without a present? No, that was impossible.

They also couldn't borrow money. Not a soul knew the real reason for Shaya's trip to America.

She went into her room and closed the door. True, Shaya wasn't exactly in a situation where she could pour out her heart to him, but he would have to understand.

"Hello," in R' Nachman's house they already recognized her voice, "Rav Bleich isn't here now."

"Do you know where he went?"

"Yes, he went to Manhattan with Mr. Shore. He has his cell phone with him."

"Thank you."

Chana dialed the number. Something told her she was making a mistake. Shaya had gone on an important mission. His head was busy with more important things than Suri's pearl necklace. Her fingers, though, refused to stop pressing the numbers.

It took a few long seconds for the connection to be made. The phone rang. Once, twice, three times.

Someone picked up.

"Shaya?" Chana asked. She didn't hear an answer, only some unclear noises. "Shaya?"

Chana strained to hear. There was a conversation going on between two people, maybe three. One of them was her husband.

"Chana!" he suddenly shouted into the receiver, "Chana, I'll call you back soon, but it looks like we probably found him…!"

• • •

Three days later, Mendel Lederman came to the overgrown yard on Shoshani Street to collect the miniature camera that he had left there.

His experienced eye immediately saw that someone had been there not long before. The thorn bushes looked as if someone had trampled on them in the past two days.

When he returned to his office and opened the recorded file on his computer, a look of astonishment spread across his face. The astonishment was slowly replaced with an expression of delight. A boy! It was just a curious boy! He had to be not more than sixteen. Why was he interested in listening to a meeting between two strangers? And anyway, how did he know about the meeting – and what was his connection to Shloime?"

The video ended. Lederman thought about sharing his definite findings with Shloime Bleich. It would be decent to let Shloime know who it was. The information was important to him. Decency, though, wasn't the name of the game – advantage was. And to gain that advantage, he would definitely keep this information to himself.

Slowly, but surely, Lederman set up his plan. It was largely based on chance, but Lederman had learned to trust his instincts, which had proven themselves well.

This boy would return to Shoshani Street. He would come back every so often until he found his machine. He, Lederman, had to draw the boy to him – and being a child made the whole thing much simpler.

He called the Bleichs from his official telephone and politely asked to speak to Shloime.

"I think you should come down to my office as soon as possible," he told Shloime, "and bring the recording device that we found there. I think I have some sort of lead to discover who the anonymous eavesdropper is."

When Shloime showed up with the device, he would sell him some story. As long as the recorder stayed there in his office, locked up in his desk drawer.

. . .

Late at night, Yisroel Yitzchok slipped out of the house. He was choking from the constant supervision. Now everyone was sleeping and he could go outside for a bit by himself, to get some air.

The moon shone on him as he went from street to street, alley to alley. Yisroel Yitzchok knew where he was going. He knew quite well.

On Shoshani Street, in the vacant lot filled with thorn bushes,

*Thicker Than Water* « 311

he didn't find his machine. He did find something else, though: a small green note.

"I'm a friend," the printed letters read. "If you want your recording device, be here tomorrow at exactly eight o'clock. We have a lot to speak about."

Yisroel Yitzchok stood transfixed among the thorn bushes.

Who wrote that note and left it there?! Who knew him, anyway?! Who knew that he lost a recording device?! A chill crept up his spine, just like in the spy stories.

Hold on, maybe someone simply found his machine and, because there was nothing identifying on it, chose this way to return it to him?! Could be, but for some reason, the wording of the message left a different impression. The impression of somebody who knew him and wanted to contact him without any connection to his lost machine.

What could he do, though, being, as he was, under a sort of house arrest? His parents kept track of his every move. They escorted him everywhere. They were afraid he would cause more trouble. There was no way he could come by himself to Shoshani Street and, of course, coming with his father was completely out of the question.

Yisroel Yitzchok took a pen from his pocket and scrawled at the bottom of the green note: "I can't come. My name is Yisroel Yitzchok Fuchsman. Call me at---" He scribbled his home phone number, as he didn't have a different number. He then returned the note to its place and quietly made his way back home, consumed with curiosity.

• • •

Chana's breath caught. She had to know exactly what was going on there. What did Shaya mean?! What did that mean, "it looks like we probably found him"?! Had he already met Naftali and wasn't sure that it was him? Did he not meet him yet? And how could a disappearance of almost two decades end so easily?!

"Shaya, explain yourself!" she yelled.

But Shaya didn't give a clear answer. She heard the sounds of driving and people speaking. She vainly called out to him, again and again. The call finally got disconnected. Chana didn't try to call again. She couldn't hear anything, anyway – or make herself heard.

She did the right thing. Because just at that moment, Mr. Shore and Shaya Bleich exited the car. Shore, noosed in a tie decorated with dollar signs, and Shaya, his entire body trembling uncontrollably, went towards the taxi stand inside which the driver, David Stone should be waiting for them. Though he had left the stand, he hadn't left the profession.

Just before they went inside, Shore stopped Shaya.

"The man doesn't know a thing about us, and definitely not the reason we're here. The person who runs the stand asked him to take over for him for a few hours today, to make sure he'd be here when we come."

Shore had an exact plan, down to the last details. Not for nothing was he paid. While they walked, he instructed Shaya exactly what to say and what not to say, when and how. "The most important thing is not to arouse suspicion," he said again and again. "Even if you're one hundred percent sure that he's the one, don't do anything suspicious."

As they ducked inside, however, Shaya was not at all sure that the calm expression on his face successfully hid the butterflies running riot in his stomach.

They went over to the counter. David Stone sat there. In one hand he held the radio, and a cigar dangled from the fingers of his other hand. His eyes were glued to the screen that showed him where each taxi was located. From the telephone came a constant stream of orders.

"Mr. Stone?" Shore addressed him without preamble.

The man turned to them. His chin was covered with stubble. His jaw was square and firm, and the expression in his eyes was that of an American taxi driver, nothing more.

"Yes, where do you need?"

"To speak to you for a few minutes, if possible."

"I can't," the man said, his voice hoarse from smoking. "I'm alone here now, I can't leave the radio. Come back later, when the boss will be here. I'm just filling in for him today. He went to his son's birthday party. Maybe you'd better speak to him."

And he turned back to the ringing phones.

"We have just one small question to ask you," Shore said. "It won't take even a minute of your time."

"Who are you, anyway?!" the man shot. The cigar sprayed ash on the counter.

"We were told that you once worked for Tommy Black," the investigator sidestepped the question and got straight to the point.

"True, so what? I once worked there. Yes, ma'am, to where do you need?" he continued his nonstop work. He had no time to poke around the past.

"Did you ever come across a man by the name of Bleich? We're looking for him…"

Shaya's blood froze. If this driver, who resembled his brother like a chicken resembled a man, really was Naftali, the name Bleich should shock him.

But the man's look became more and more distant.

"I don't know anything. I don't know what you're talking about," he said crossly. "I was just a taxi driver. And anyway, why are you coming to me? What do you want from me?! Ma'am, the taxi's on its way. Another five minutes…"

314 » *Thicker Than Water*

Shaya tried, in vain, to meet the man's eyes. Stone's gaze wasn't focused, darting about as if he was drunk. He glanced at Shaya only once, his eyes flicking over him the way a lion would look at a fly that was bothering him.

Shaya tried hinting to Shore that they should back off, but Shore didn't seem to get the hint.

"Have you seen him? He was an Orthodox Jew with a black beard. Did you ever drive him?"

The man got annoyed. "Do you know how many Orthodox Jews I drove? That means I have to know all of them?! They all look alike – you can't even tell the difference between them…"

"What a shame," Shore said, seeming to back down a bit, "we thought you knew him. It's very important to us. We were told that you were the most "with it" driver there. We were told that you would sit by the wheel, with one arm leaning on the window, your sleeve flapping in the wind…"

Slowly, Shaya realized the investigator's intent. He broke out in a cold sweat.

"Sleeve flapping in the wind?" the driver knit his thick brows.

Just then, Shaya, as if his life depended on it, dashed over to the counter and swiftly pulled up the man's sleeve.

• • •

Throughout the entire next day, Yisroel Yitzchok waited for the phone call. As if to annoy him, though, that day the phone was constantly busy. Ima spoke with Abba, who was running errands, Suri's friends called. The seamstress called the girls to come for a fitting. They called from the shoe store to say that the shoes arrived. Suri received a fax from her friend with a list of friends to invite. The caterer for the *sheva brochos* had to speak with Ima.

Yisroel Yitzchok couldn't say a word. He wasn't about to say that he was waiting for a phone call from a man he didn't know. He didn't want to be asked questions, nor to give answers that he didn't yet have.

At six thirty in the evening, the phone rang. Yisroel Yitzchok tried to answer, hoping that it wasn't the seamstress again. But when he picked up, he heard that Abba had already picked up the phone in his study.

"Yisroel Yitzchok?" he heard his father ask suspiciously. And then, a thin, high voice, amazingly similar to that of a boy, came from the receiver:

"It's his friend…"

Yisroel Yitzchok knew the voices of all his friends. None of them had such a thin voice.

"One minute," Abba said and called him to the study. He wanted the conversation to take place in his presence. Yisroel Yitzchok put the receiver to his ear. A voice spilled forth, the deep voice of a man, completely different than the childish voice that was heard a moment before.

"Yes," Yisroel Yitzchok said.

"Your recorder is by me," the voice said quickly, "and we have to join forces. When can we meet?"

"I don't know," Yisroel Yitzchok replied. He was stingy with his words so that his father should be stingy with his questions.

"And to speak on the phone with no one disturbing us?"

Yisroel Yitzchok wanted to say 'between two and three in the morning', but didn't, of course. Instead, he began speaking about something else so the person on the other end should understand that it wasn't a good time for him to speak.

"*Daf lamed gimmel, amud beis,*" he said off the cuff. Not good. Abba wouldn't understand why he was suddenly speaking in learning. He would suspect that it was a cover for something else.

"What are you saying there?" the man yelled.

Yisroel Yitzchok couldn't ask "who are you?" even though the question was burning him. Hadn't his father told him it was his friend?

"Do you have a cell phone?"

"No," Yisroel Yitzchok said, "it wasn't written in the sources that they brought."

"Can you be on Shoshani Street again tonight?" the voice asked. "I'll leave you a message there."

"All right."

"And you answer me that way, too."

Yisroel Yitzchok knew that was the only way. "All right."

The conversation was about to end. Mendel Lederman had to know if there was any point to the whole business.

"Send regards to Shloime Bleich," he said.

"Regards?" Yisroel Yitzchok asked, "Maybe a battle call…"

• • •

"I think," Devorah Fuchsman said to her daughter, very carefully, "that the Bleichs are having some sort of financial difficulty right now."

Suri lifted her eyes.

"Financial difficulty?" she tried to understand, "They have no more money? And therefore they want to cancel the wedding? Tell them I have no problem getting married without flowers or a band, and with crackers and herring instead of forty dollar portions. And without hundreds of guests. As far as I'm concerned, just the *chosson*, the *kallah*, and their parents could come. For me, that's enough…"

*Thicker Than Water* « 317

# CHAPTER 26

"*Chas v'shalom*," Devorah said, "I didn't mean that they're in serious trouble. I was talking about something temporary. You know, it could happen to anyone. Maybe some investments that didn't yield as much as they should have or something like that… In any event, it's very possible that the manager of the hall heard something and wanted to check that their financial situation hasn't changed, and that he'll get paid."

"So why did he call us," Suri asked, "and not them?"

"Because he's smart," Devorah said, "and knows that from them he won't get any clear information."

Suri tried to replay the conversation. The truth was the manager hadn't said which rumors he heard. He hadn't had a chance, as the receiver fell from her hand before she even heard exactly what he was talking about.

"Why can't we just speak to the Bleichs and understand what's going on?" Suri didn't understand.

"It would be the most natural thing to do," Devorah agreed,

"but it's not always such a good idea for *mechutanim* to be natural with each other. Sometimes you need to be a little diplomatic. Probably always. We won't ask them such questions unless we think their difficulty could have a direct effect on us."

"You think that the *shver*'s trip has to do with this financial trouble?"

"It's very possible. But we're not going to shove ourselves into their lives, just like we wouldn't want them to poke around in ours."

Suri sat there, digesting it. Financial difficulty? True, she hadn't joined her in-laws' family because they did or did not have money, but it still wasn't pleasant to hear that the *mechutanim* had difficulty fulfilling their obligations.

"Where did we get this information from, that they have financial difficulties?"

"It's not hard fact," Devorah said. She debated whether or not to share with Suri, a young *kallah*, her assumptions, and finally decided that there was no choice.

"Your necklace," she said. "Your pearl necklace. Did you notice that it's much plainer than the other jewelry the *mechuteniste* gave you?"

Suri fingered the necklace she was wearing. Truthfully, she hadn't known that pearl necklaces differed in their value. She innocently thought that all pearls were the same, and all the necklaces cost about the same. She was happy with the necklace, just as she had been happy with each piece of jewelry she had received. It hadn't entered her mind to price it.

"This is a simple necklace," Devorah said, truly sorry to be causing pain to the young *kallah*, "the kind that Chana Bleich wouldn't have even looked at if her financial situation would have been as before."

"So it's good she's cutting back on the jewelry," Suri said automatically, "and not on essentials like furniture or electric appliances."

Devorah smiled involuntarily. How could she explain to Suri that the last thing Chana Bleich would want to cut back on is her dear *kallah*'s presents? And if she did do that, then she must have had a good reason.

• • •

"What are you doing???"

David Stone shot to his feet. This man wanted to attack him! He should have guessed from the start that these two strange men had no good intentions…!

"Why are you pulling me?? What do you want from me???"

At the last minute, a fraction of a second before the cab driver landed his massive fist in Shaya Bleich's face, Shore got the information he wanted.

"I'm so sorry! There's been a mistake!!"

These words were enough for Shaya Bleich to suddenly relax his hold on the man. A mistake meant that Shore hadn't found the identifying mark on the man's arm. That meant that, in one big *whoosh*, all the air left the balloon – and Shaya's lungs. This David Stone wasn't the lost Naftali Bleich – never was and never would be.

"I'm sorry," Shore apologized again and again, pulling the heavily breathing Bleich back around the counter. "There's been a big mistake. My friend, he has some sort of problem, as you can see. He must have mixed you up with somebody else. We're really sorry, you're not to blame. We're leaving right now."

Shaya didn't look back. Had he looked, any lingering doubt whether or not this David Stone was his lost brother would have disappeared. Standing, panting with anger and his eyes shooting sparks, the man reached almost to the ceiling. Naftali Bleich had most definitely not been so tall. Nor had his shoulders been so broad.

"Outside, quickly," Shore urged him. They got out of there before Stone decided to call the police.

He stared after them until they got into their car. Shore sped away from there, allowing Shaya a few minutes for his breathing to normalize.

"That's how… it goes?" Bleich asked, his wits finally returning to him.

"Sometimes," Shore threw him an amused look.

"And it was all a waste." Shaya looked completely defeated. How could all the tracks have led to here, and in the end it wasn't the right man?

"That's our job, my friend," Shore said and glanced at his GPS, "It's elusive work. Sometimes we're successful, sometimes not. In any event, nothing was a waste."

"But we'll have to start all over again from the beginning." Shaya finally gathered the strength to remove a tissue from his pocket and wipe his forehead.

"From the beginning?! Not at all!" Shore exclaimed, "What's wrong with all that we did? Until the last bit everything was perfectly fine. We'll just take one step back and look at additional options. Don't worry, in the end we'll find him. The world is open before us."

*And what about the next world?* Shaya thought in despair.

Shaya finally arrived back at R' Nachman's house. Many draining hours lay behind him, and he had only a few hours to sleep before it would be time to *daven shacharis*.

His eyes closed as he was still saying *kri'as sh'ma*.

The phone rang. Just when he was desperate to sleep! It was probably Chana again, wanting to know what happened – and she was fully entitled. But he couldn't answer. He couldn't guarantee that his words would make sense. He couldn't even string his thoughts along coherently.

He picked up anyway.

"Shore here," a fresh voice informed him, as if he hadn't spent long, tiring hours with him.

"Yes," Shaya said, surprised.

"Something came up that I thought you'd want to hear."

"Now?" Shaya asked, his eyes closed.

"If you ask me – yes."

"I'm listening," Shaya said. "I hope I'm not in too much of a fog to understand what you're telling me."

"Okay. I found out that there were two David Stones who worked for the same taxi stand."

"What?!"

"Exactly that. Two, not one. I'm starting to investigate the second David Stone right now.

"Not now," Shaya pleaded. "Tomorrow morning..."

• • •

Late at night, Yisroel Yitzchok came to the thorns again. He was short on time. Not too many minutes would pass before they discovered that he wasn't home. He gripped a small flashlight in his hand. He had to find a green note there – or any note – and without a flashlight that would be difficult.

There was.

A small note was hidden among the bushes, not too conspicuously, but obvious enough to someone who was looking for it.

"My name is Mendel Lederman. I have valid information why Shloime Bleich shouldn't get married now. Would you be willing to help me prevent him from doing so?"

Yisroel Yitzchok read the short lines once, twice. Who was Mendel Lederman? And why did he want that Shloime Bleich shouldn't get married? What did he have to do with Shloime Bleich?

*Don't be hasty*, he told himself in a flash of awareness. *It's not a good idea to cooperate with someone you don't know – against someone else.*

Yisroel Yitzchok turned the note over and wrote:

"I don't know you. I'm willing to help everyone, but I want to know why you want to stop him from getting married."

He added a line: "P.S. The *kallah* is my sister."

He then stuck the note in the bushes, exactly where it had been before, shut the flashlight and slowly walked home.

...

Only in his office did Mendel Lederman let himself look at the note. He had to admit that the boy's demand was legitimate. He wanted to know why it wasn't a good idea for Shloime Bleich to get married. He was right. But Mendel Lederman couldn't release even a crumb of information.

He would have to make up some story. A cover story. After a few minutes of deep thought, Lederman took a new piece of green notepaper and scrawled:

"I know that you're the *kallah's* brother. You should know that Shloime Bleich's roots aren't clear."

He folded the paper and shoved it into his pocket. He would go that evening to Shoshani Street and hide it there. This whole way of doing things wasn't to his liking. Why couldn't he get hold of the boy in a normal manner? Why couldn't they meet? He made a mental note to check out that point.

At seven o'clock in the evening, Mendel Lederman showed

up at the yard. He made as if the paper fell into the thorns without his realizing it, and continued walking.

On a porch in the opposite building, however, sat two certain *bochurim*, lying in wait for the boy who had forgotten his recording device. Nochum drew Shloime's attention to the man. Shloime looked down and his breath caught. Mendel Lederman. What was he doing there? What was he cooking…?!

"Who is that?" Nochum had to know who that man was, who was poking around downstairs, the sight of whom was causing Shloime Bleich to be unable to breathe.

"His name's Lederman," Shloime said shortly.

"And what's his problem? He's not a pleasant person?"

"He's very pleasant," Shloime said with a bitter laugh. "That's exactly the problem. He does everything so pleasantly."

Nochum lifted the binoculars to his eyes.

"If I'm not mistaken, he threw something into the bushes," he told Shloime. "Something green."

"We're going to take that something green," Shloime informed him. "We'll just wait for him to leave. Something tells me he's not just walking by…"

After a few minutes, when Lederman couldn't be seen anymore, Shloime went down and collected the note. As he walked back up the steps to the building, his curiosity overcame his patience and he took a peek at the note.

Again and again he read the brief lines. And again. He leaned against the wall of the stairwell, his legs buckling.

Seeing that he wasn't getting anywhere by going straight, Mendel Lederman was trying something more underhanded. He was now going behind his back in order to stop his wedding – at any price.

Shloime thanked his curiosity just this once. There was no way he would have wanted to open this note in front of Nochum;

he still wasn't telling him everything.

• • •

When Shaya Bleich asked to continue the investigation the next morning, he hadn't taken into account what time Shore's morning started. And so, when he took his *tallis* bag in order to go *daven*, the ring of the telephone, loud and clear, surprised him.

"We're getting places," Shore exulted. "I hope that by the end of the day I'll have some clear information for you. In the meantime, I have some details. First of all, it's quite clear that the second David Stone isn't in this country anymore."

"So where is he?" Shaya asked, trying to keep up.

"It looks like in one of the Western European countries."

"What was he looking for there?" Shaya wondered.

"I'll tell you what he was looking for there," Shore laughed, though Shaya didn't understand what was so funny. "He was looking for a safe haven. And a haven, my good friend, you look for in the last place they would look for you."

"But a haven from what?!" Shaya asked the real question. "What was he running from? He was such a straight, honest person."

"No doubt," Shore said, even though he heard such sentences fifteen times a day. "I'm working on two tracks. One, to find the man. And two, to discover what caused him to flee – thereby better understanding where he could have disappeared to. Believe me, Mr. Bleich, it's easier to find a needle in one hundred haystacks than to find the lead we're looking for, but the two tracks are intertwined."

"Okay," Shaya said wearily, "I don't know how to find needles and leads. I'll pray."

When he came back from *davening*, a message from Mr.

Shore was already waiting for him.

"We're flying this afternoon to France. We'll be there for at least one night."

*This fellow's quick as lightning,* Shaya murmured to himself admiringly. Except that the money had to be at least as quick. Shore hadn't mentioned money in the message, but it was clear that the previous day's events and the planned flight plus hotel stay would all have to be funded from his pocket, by that afternoon.

"Rav Bleich, you look extremely troubled," R' Nachman commented when Shaya came into the kitchen for breakfast.

"Oh, it's nothing," Shaya said and went to wash.

"A *Yid* who's sad is nothing? It's terrible!" R' Nachman cried. "What's happening with the reason you've come here? Are things moving along?"

"Moving along," Shaya nodded his head and folded back his sleeves. He allowed himself to add in a low voice: "I need money for it to move along the way it should."

Shaya Bleich wasn't the only diner in R' Nachman's hospitable home. Quite a few more guests sat around the table, one engrossed in the newspaper, another in his plate and a third in his thoughts. None of them had to hear that Shaya Bleich was in financial trouble.

"How much?" R' Nachman asked briefly.

Shaya hesitated. He had never intended to borrow from R' Nachman, who, though he took in guests, wasn't rolling in money, but perhaps R' Nachman could arrange a sizeable loan for him through his broad connections.

"*Nu?*" R' Nachman prodded.

Shaya moved over. Someone else was trying to get to the sink. R' Nachman looked at him expectantly. He was waiting for an answer.

Shaya named a sum. R' Nachman heard, nodded his head and said that it would be possible to get the money together over the course of the day. Shaya stressed that he absolutely didn't want any donations. R' Nachman understood.

Shaya ate his breakfast with a lighter heart. After *bentching*, R' Nachman motioned Shaya over with his finger.

"I'm happy to solve the problem," R' Nachman said with his wide smile, "and to remove it completely from your head."

"What does that mean?" Shaya didn't understand.

"This Jew," R' Nachman pointed discreetly at the guest who had washed his hands before and was now sitting and eating, his head bent over a *sefer*, "overheard our conversation. He came over to me afterwards and offered to take on all your expenses."

"What's that supposed to mean?!" Shaya exclaimed. "Who is this man? What does he owe me, anyway?!"

"I also know very little about him," R' Nachman said, though by him "a little" probably meant quite a lot. "He came here only two days ago. I met him in *shul*. From what I understood, he's a *ger* for a number of years already, a very wealthy man. He wouldn't have come to me, to stay by someone he doesn't know, if I wouldn't have begged him to let me have the *mitzvah*."

"He wants to fund my entire---" Shaya couldn't digest it. To be saved like that!

"I believe that it won't exactly make a dent in his fortune," R' Nachman said. "That's how we Jews are, giving each other the chance to do a *mitzvah*."

Shaya had to think the matter over. Should he agree? Not agree? Who was this man, this anonymous philanthropist, who wanted to give such a large sum to someone he didn't even know – and didn't even know for what he needed the money?

He stopped between the kitchen and the hallway as R' Nachman caught up to him.

"The truth is I wasn't supposed to tell you," R' Nachman said, glancing over his shoulder. "He asked that I shouldn't let you know that it's coming from him. I knew, though, that you wouldn't rest until you discovered who was suddenly flooding you with money. Promise me, Rav Bleich, that you won't tell him that I let you know his identity…"

• • •

Shloime sat inside and learned. Finally, he was finished with the dreary sitting on the porch. It was now Nochum's turn. The entire time that he sat looking at the street, there was no sign of anyone approaching the thorn bushes. His eyes hurt already, and it seemed that any minute the thorns would break out dancing.

After opening the *sefer*, it didn't take him long to completely forget about ambushes, thorn bushes and Mendel Lederman himself. The one who didn't quite forget, or couldn't quite forget, was his friend Nochum, because after only ten minutes, a car appeared and pulled up a short distance from the bushes. A young *bochur* climbed out, closed the door and went straight to the bushes.

Nochum backed up to the beginning of the porch where he was out of sight, and raised the binoculars to his eyes.

The boy was familiar to him. It was tickling his memory something fierce. Nochum strained his eyes, trying to catch the face of the boy, but was unsuccessful.

The man in the car stuck his head out the window and called:

"*Nu*, you found your machine, Yisroel Yitzchok?"

That was it. Nochum didn't have a second's doubt: The man was Elya Fuchsman, Shloime's future father-in-law, and the boy was his son.

Things were getting complicated, Nochum understood, not

realizing the full extent of it.

As he watched, his head filled with questions: What was the Fuchsman boy looking for? Could it be that the green note was meant for him? If so, why was his father with him? Since when did a boy that age need such close supervision?

It seemed to Nochum that Elya Fuchsman lifted his eyes to the top porch of the building facing him. He quickly stepped back and tripped over the chair, knocking it over.

"Nochum?" Shloime's voice was heard from inside the apartment, "Is everything okay?"

"Yeah, yeah," Nochum quickly replied.

He should call Shloime there. This must be unbelievably important information for him. Besides which, they had made up to call each other any time something suspicious happened near the bushes – and this wasn't just something suspicious. It was probably the guilty party himself.

Even so, he continued to watch what was happening while Shloime remained inside. He saw the Fuchsman boy spread his hands in disappointment, like someone who was looking for something and didn't find it. He then got back into the car and they drove away.

The minute the car disappeared around the bend, Shloime came out to the porch.

"Something happened?" he asked.

"Uh… nothing special," Nochum answered.

"So why are you standing and the chair is upside down?"

"Uh, it's just… I stood up for a second and the chair fell backwards. The… the chairs in this house aren't balanced very evenly, don't you think…?"

# CHAPTER 27

In the afternoon, Shaya Bleich packed a small case. He was flying to France and would probably spend a night or two there, depending on the developments. R' Nachman pressed his hand and wished him *hatzlacha* with everything. He continued to walk with him out the door and even down a few steps.

"Uh… Rav Bleich," he cleared his throat. Shaya stopped. He sensed that R' Nachman wanted to tell him something more.

"I have to add another detail which I left out this morning because I didn't want to ruin your joy."

Yes, Shaya understood and leaned against the railing. It had been too good to be true. One fine day a rich Jew just decided that he wanted to fund heavy investigation expenses for a Jew he didn't even know? Not likely. Rich people weighed their donations, looking at them through the lens of loss and gain. This unknown person wanted to gain something from the deal, that was clear. The question was only what, and if it was something that Bleich couldn't agree to, thereby causing the whole donation to fall through.

"And what is this detail?" he asked, gripping the iron railing tightly.

"He demanded," R' Nochum hesitated, obviously also thinking that it was an exaggerated demand, "that is, he requested to be included in the process of the investigation."

"What does that mean, to be included?" Shaya put down his suitcase. True, he was hurrying to catch a flight, but there was good reason to think that the flight wouldn't take place. "He wants to fly now with me to France? He wants me to pick up the telephone each evening and fill him in on what's happening? He wants to sit on my investigator's phone line? I don't understand…"

"Truthfully, I don't understand, either," R' Nachman said, and it was obvious that he preferred not to be involved in the story, "but that's what he asked, that you should keep him informed about all developments."

"But R' Nachman, with all due respect to you and this anonymous donor – I don't know him and he wants that I shouldn't know him, yet in the same breath he asks that I let him know about developments?! Does he have some sort of magic wand that can be held at both ends…?!"

"It's a good question, Rav Bleich. I also don't understand exactly how it would work."

"What about through you, R' Nachman?"

"Honestly, I prefer not…"

"I wouldn't want to pull you into a job that you don't want, either. Could you ask him what he meant, and how such a thing would work. That's besides the basic question of whether or not we want to share a personal, private family matter with an outsider. All the more so when we're talking about a private investigation in which secrecy is crucial. I'm really getting a bit nervous,

R' Nachman. I appreciate his generous offer tremendously, but it needs some serious thought and he'll have to understand that."

Still, he picked up his small case from the floor and hurried outside. The flight would take place that day and he'd ask Shore for an extension in order to arrange something. He'd speak to Chana. Maybe he'd even consult with Shore himself.

Sitting on the airplane, though, next to Shore who was decked out in a striped gray suit and typing away with complete concentration on his laptop, Shaya felt that it wasn't the time to explain the matter. He would first have to transfer a substantial sum from his pocket to that of the striped gray suit. Only afterwards would he be able to talk about a philanthropist who wished to subsidize the investigation. The investigator wouldn't want to work with someone who needed charity in order to fund his investigation. He might get scared that he won't receive proper payment on time.

No. Shaya refused a cold drink. Shore had reserved a room in a hotel for them. He believed, even without knowing the name of the hotel – or of any hotel in the entire France, for that matter – that it was an expensive place. What did Shore care to choose an expensive hotel if he wasn't the one paying for it?

At that time, in R' Nachman's house, R' Nachman stood behind the door to his rich guest's room and shoved his hands into his pockets. The conversation with the guest had ended without any real results. The man had refused to offer details; he wouldn't give any even if they paid him. He had only one thing to say: he was prepared to fund all the expenses of the investigation, down to the last cent, on one firm condition – that he be part of each and every stage of the investigation. How would he take part? That was a side question. He could give a fax number, or a telephone number to leave messages. The man and his family weren't interested? No problem; he would withdraw his offer that very minute. They were interested? Very good. Still today, the entire amount would be transferred to their account, wherever in the world it might be, and additional sums would be transferred as the need arose.

R' Nachman tried to draw out from him what was behind his demand. The man, though, wasn't the type that could be drawn out. He remained courteous and friendly, yet resolute. He did make sure to hint to R' Nachman that he wouldn't be in the area long; he would be moving along in the next few days.

And so, without anything real to show for his efforts, R' Nachman left the guest's room. He definitely wouldn't want to be in Bleich's place right then. He might very likely be forced to push away the offer that was being held out on a silver platter. R' Nachman privately felt that the donor was an honest man, even if he was hiding his intentions; the final decision, though, would be Bleich's alone, and it wouldn't be easy.

• • •

That evening, the Fuchsman home received a very strange phone call. Devorah, who was busy cutting a salad, picked up the phone in the kitchen.

"Can I speak to Yisroel Yitzchok?"

"Yes," Devorah answered. She always passed the phone along without asking the caller to identify himself – and taught her children to do the same. Everyone deserved his privacy, she said.

She suddenly remembered that Yisroel Yitzchok wasn't everyone, and what worked for her other children changed a bit when it came to him.

"Who's speaking, please?"

"His friend," a thin voice answered.

Apparently, everything was okay. Something in this friend's

voice, though, made her not want to give the phone over.

"By the name of?" she asked, not liking what she was doing, but having no choice.

"Mendy."

"One minute."

Devorah put down the phone, but didn't call Yisroel Yitzchok. She called his father.

"Do you know a friend of Yisroel Yitzchok by the name of Mendy?"

"No, but I can't know all his friends from yeshiva," Elya replied.

"So what should I do with this phone call?" she whispered. The friend was waiting on the line.

"Let him talk," Elya said. "I'll make sure he's near me while speaking to him."

Elya left the kitchen and Devorah sighed. They had such wonderful children, and so much *nachas* – and only Yisroel Yitzchok stubbornly cast a shadow on it all. They loved him so much and tried so hard, but for some reason he was always positive that he knew better than everyone what was good for him. He was a talented boy. In *cheder* he had always been from the top, but it was as if something had come over him the past year and refused to leave.

She heard Elya relocate to the living room. Next to him was Yisroel Yitzchok, holding the telephone to his ear.

"I didn't find it," Yisroel Yitzchok said and listened a bit.

"Yes, I went and didn't find it," he said again. "No, I can't come again."

There was a short silence.

"Because I have to think about it," Yisroel Yitzchok said.

Mendy tried to explain something.

"Give me a few days to get back to you with an answer," Yisroel Yitzchok said in a low voice. "No, I'm not playing games. I just have to think about the whole business again."

*To think.* Elya Fuchsman was encouraged, as was Devorah in the kitchen. It was a while since they had heard such a pleasant word from their son.

"I'll call you," Yisroel Yitzchok tried to end the call. But Mendy wouldn't let up.

"Yes, I know it's very important."

Yisroel Yitzchok really wanted to hang up already, but it looked like Mendy was trying to keep him on a bit more. And succeeding.

"Which secrets?" Yisroel Yitzchok asked. Mendy told him something.

"I understand that you want to give me a really thick book," Yisroel Yitzchok joked.

Devorah listened intently to the conversation, but couldn't, for the life of her, guess what they were talking about. What did Yisroel Yitzchok have to think about? And what was it that this Mendy was trying to convince him and couldn't pin him down? And what secrets was he talking about?

"Ima," little Bruchie came into the kitchen in her usual noisy way, "I want juice!"

"Shhh," Devorah said automatically.

"Ima!" the little girl raised her voice, "I want juice!"

Devorah dried her hands and went to the refrigerator. "You're disturbing Yisroel Yitzchok on the telephone, sweetie," she said.

"I don't like this telephone," the girl complained. "All day, everyone's talking on it and only I'm not! I don't like it!"

And she hit the telephone sitting on the kitchen table with her little hand – right on speakerphone.

All of a sudden, the conversation that Yisroel Yitzchok was carrying on in the living room filled the kitchen and the friend's voice was clearly heard.

*Thicker Than Water* ‹‹ 335

It was a deep, masculine voice, completely different than that of young "Mendy".

• • •

Shaya Bleich finally found the time to privately call R' Nachman's house.

"What's doing in Avrohom Avinu's tent?" he asked. "I'm in the Connor hotel in Paris. They have a lot to learn from you about *hachnosas orchim*."

"At least they manage to get more out of their guests than I did from my guest."

"Meaning?" Shaya understood that R' Nachman didn't have good news.

"I have no more details than what I told you before your flight. The man wants, and is prepared, to pay all your expenses, down to the last cent, but wants to be kept informed about everything. He could give a fax number, or a telephone number to leave messages."

Shaya sighed. He had to speak to Chana. She was a very smart lady.

"And he's leaving in the next few days."

"But I'm not coming back yet," Shaya panicked, "and I don't know when I will."

"That's okay," R' Nachman reassured him. "You have a day or two to think about it, to ask advice. It's not a simple question."

Except that R' Nachman didn't dream how not simple the question was. Nor did he know that Shaya wouldn't have a day or two to think – or even an hour or two. He was still sitting in the grand lobby, sunk in his thoughts and armchair, when Shore sat down opposite him in a similar position.

"Really," Shore said without preamble, "we should go right

now to the place where, according to my information, someone well acquainted with David Stone lives. But we'll have to wait."

"Wait?" Shaya asked. "Why?"

"Because we're out of gas." Seeing that Shaya didn't understand, Shore explained: "I haven't yet received any payment from you, Mr. Bleich. I have faith in you, but it's not limitless. I'm working nonstop, giving of my time, and believe me when I say that my time is precious."

Shaya didn't like the man's direct approach, or his determination. At the same time, he knew that that determination was what had finally moved things along.

"You're right," he said, and lowered his gaze. "Except that…"

Shore let him explain himself and then patiently explained that it was impossible to continue the investigation like that, and it was a shame to waste their time.

"Give me something," he said. "Go take out cash here, in the hotel's ATM. You have a credit card, no? I'll wait here."

Shaya, completely red, stood up. The man was right. He dragged his feet to the hotel's entrance, next to which stood the ATM machine. But when he got there, he pulled from his pocket – not his wallet with his card, but his small cell phone.

"R' Nachman?"

"Yes." R' Nachman was surprised to hear from him so soon.

"Tell him yes."

"What yes?" R' Nachman was confused for a minute.

"That I'll accept his money," Shaya said breathlessly, "and his conditions."

• • •

"I think we've gone too far," Nochum told Shloime as they stood there on the porch.

"What makes you think that?" Shloime asked.

"What makes me… I don't know exactly, maybe just a renewed understanding," Nochum said. "I have a feeling that that this whole stakeout is for nothing. We're taking too much responsibility on ourselves, responsibility that's not even ours, but Hashem's."

Shloime wasn't convinced.

"You may be right," he said, "but what brings you to say it specifically now?"

Nochum was in a bind. He didn't want to say that he saw the Fuchsman boy and his father coming to search for the note. That could cause an earthquake. And if they came to look for the note, that indicated that it was meant for them. And if that was the case, then there was no point in continuing to watch for someone who probably wouldn't come.

"Nochum, you're a good friend," Shloime said. "You won't tell me the truth?!"

"I don't know what you want." Nochum avoided his friend's penetrating look.

"You have something to say and you're not saying and that's a real shame. It disappoints me," Shloime said in one breath. "Someone was here and you want to hide it from me?"

Nochum marveled for the umpteenth time at the sharpness of Shloime's mind.

"Yes," he said in a low voice.

"Should I guess who it was?"

"Fuchsman," Nochum said and was quiet.

He believed that this information would throw Shloime. He couldn't, however, know how much, as he hadn't seen what was written in the note.

Shloime looked at him with huge eyes. His arms groped for the back of the nearest chair.

"Fuchsman was here to take the note?" he whispered. Only his lips moved.

"Yes."

"Who was it?"

"The father and the boy."

Nochum hurried to sit Shloime down. If he wouldn't, Shloime would find himself on the floor.

"He wants to kill me, this Lederman," Shloime mumbled. "To kill me. But why?? What did I do to him…?!"

• • •

Late at night, Shaya Bleich managed to reach his wife and tell her all the events of the day.

"Someone wants to pay for the entire investigation?" Her eyes opened wide and then narrowed. "Who is this fellow? And what does he want?"

*She grasped in a minute what took me a few hours to understand,* Shaya thought.

"What does that mean, to keep him informed of every detail of the investigation? What, he's from Interpol? I don't understand. What is this, bribery? Explain to me, Shaya. I just hope you haven't agreed to this."

Very slowly, with a sense of defeat, Shaya told Chana the truth.

"He pressured me, this investigator. Do you understand? He really pushed me up against the wall. Either the money or the investigation."

"Shaya," Chana's face was white, "you should have spoken to me first."

"I know, Chana. That was the plan. But understand that I had no choice. You know we don't have a bottomless pit from which to take such sums, or to return loans this size. And here I had a rare opportunity."

"I don't see this as an opportunity." Chana didn't want to rebuke Shaya, but that was exactly what her words sounded like. "I see it as a big trap that we're falling into. I'm not yet sure how, but this Rothschild is definitely dangling bait for us."

"Maybe he just wants to know where his money's going?" Shaya asked innocently. "Many donors check afterwards what was done with the money they gave."

"Fine," Chana said resignedly, "if you believe that, I'll also believe it."

Later, after the phone call, Shaya went back down to the lobby. He had promised Shore to get the money within a few hours, and their outing was postponed until the next morning. Shaya stuck his international credit card into the slot and checked the balance.

A huge sigh of relief escaped him. The donor had stood by his promise. A sizeable sum had been put into his account, more than enough to pay Shore all the expenses until then, and also to cover their hotel stay.

Tomorrow morning he'd pay Shore and then the two of them would travel to their destination. When they came back, Shaya would have another job: to update the anonymous donor. Shore wouldn't like the breach of privacy, but neither would he like not to receive his money. Which of the two would he like less…?

• • •

The deep voice of "Mendy" was enough to send Devorah Fuchsman bursting into the living room.

"Who are you talking to, Yisroel Yitzchok?!" she demanded to know.

"It's… my friend."

"What's his name?"

"Mendel."

"And how old is he?"

Yisroel Yitzchok paused. He didn't know.

"I want you to hang up right now."

Yisroel Yitzchok did as he was told. He anyway meant to finish.

"Go to your room immediately," Elya ordered him.

Yisroel Yitzchok obeyed that, too. Left in the living room were his father and his overwrought mother, whose eyes, for the first time in many years, welled with tears that overflowed.

"He wasn't talking to a friend, Elya. That wasn't a friend. That was a man. I want to know who it was!!!"

Elya was silent.

"Elya, don't be quiet. Say something. Our son is doing things that shouldn't be done. We have to stop this."

"We're stopping it, Devorah. We're stopping it as well as we can, but the boy isn't easy."

"You don't want to check who he was speaking to?"

"I'm not sure that's the right thing to do. Not now, anyway. It can make him rebel against us even more."

Elya's words rang true, causing Devorah's tears to flow even harder.

"Make him rebel? Make him rebel! Against us! Against his parents who love him so much and give him everything. What didn't we give him, Elya? What didn't we give?!"

Yisroel Yitzchok heard the voices clearly from his room. His ears, so used to words of rebuke that they almost didn't hear them anymore, suddenly heard a different sound – tormenting and piercing.

The sound of his mother crying.

He could hold up under talks and explanations, scoldings and persuasion. He shrugged when they tried to bend him. He didn't listen to anyone anymore.

But now there were no more words, only tears.

His door was a little open. No one came to yell at him. It was quiet in the living room. Only his mother's weeping disturbed the silence.

"We love him so much; he's a wonderful boy," Ima murmured, the tissue on her face muffling the words, "why is he doing this to us? Why???"

Yisroel Yitzchok huddled on his bed. What tens of talks and hundreds of scoldings had failed to move, his mother's hot tears melted.

# CHAPTER 28

"I think I'll call him," Shloime said after recovering a little from the shock.

"Who?" Nochum asked.

"That man, Mendel Lederman. The man who wrote this note and tried to give it to our *mechutanim*. The man who wants, at any price, to prevent my wedding – and go know what other steps he's taking to get to that goal, steps I don't even know about."

"What will you tell him?" Nochum asked sensibly.

"I'll ask him what he wants from me," Shloime said heatedly. "Why he's sticking to me like this. His part in the investigation finished long ago. He was involved, he has information, but he absolutely won't tell me what it is. He's suggesting that I cancel the wedding without explaining why. And when I don't agree, he generously volunteers to do the work for me, against my wishes."

"And such a conversation will help?"

"Maybe. Maybe if he sees how much I'm hurting it will move

him and he'll stop hurting me and leave me and my *chasunah* alone."

Nochum thought a bit. "If that's the tactic you want to use, I think you're better off forgetting the phone call. Don't talk to this man like a *nebach* who's suffering. You have to be tough and demand that he stop mixing into your life."

"He said it's for my good," Shloime mumbled.

"If it's for your good or not only you can decide after hearing all the details. No one has the right to decide for anyone else what's good for him."

Shloime buried his head in his hands. The situation was unbearable.

"I'll set up a meeting with him. I have nothing better to do," he said finally. "But you, Nochum, will come with me."

"No way," Nochum said immediately.

"Yes, you'll come," Shloime said, his voice half commanding, half pleading. "I feel so small and weak and helpless. I need someone to back me."

• • •

60 Kleber Street. That was the address. A taxi brought them to the desired house, navigating the narrow streets of one of Paris' crowded sections.

Shaya counted five or six stories. The courtyard was surrounded by a tall gate. Shore went up the steps with Shaya following him.

They were supposed to meet someone who knew David Stone and could give them details about him, thereby helping the investigation. Rather than have this conversation over the telephone, Shore preferred to meet the man face to face together with Shaya, who would know to ask the right questions and decide whether there was a chance that David Stone was his brother, and if there was any point in continuing to run after him.

The man, Valery, hosted them politely in his well-cared for apartment. A number of years ago, he had worked together with David Stone for the same taxi stand. Shaya, of course, didn't touch the refreshments. He sat on the side, trying to find the right way to explain to Shore that there was somebody else who was privy to the closely guarded details of the investigation, without Shore rolling him down all the steps.

The man spoke French and a little English. True, he had been a cab driver in Manhattan, but he had never tried too hard to polish his English. Cab drivers needed to know only a few key words of the spoken language; the rest of the time their passengers preferred them to be quiet. Shore spoke with the man. Actually, you couldn't call it speaking. He interrogated him, in his thorough, meticulous manner, every so often marking down important details in his notebook.

Valery remembered David Stone very well. Together, they had worked for the same taxi stand, and then they had both left Manhattan and the entire U.S. and moved to France. Valery's brother had opened a business there. For reasons that Valery didn't know – and didn't try to find out – David decided to leave the U.S. and try his luck in France, an unusual decision for an American, especially one with a family.

The problem was that all these events had happened long ago, about fifteen years ago. Since then, Valery had managed to settle down properly in Paris, to enter his brother's business and leave, to try to open his own business, to keep it going a bit and then to finally be done with it. It was years since he had met David Stone, but he was sure he lived not far from there. He vaguely remembered visiting him one Sunday afternoon. He even had the address written down. If the sirs wanted, he would take them there – for suitable pay, of course.

"What do you have to say about David Stone after knowing him for so long?"

"He was a very straight man," Valery answered immediately, unconsciously running his hand over his balding head, "very straight. There were some cab drivers – not all, of course, but it was a common practice – who would pick out the tourists who didn't know the city and take them for a drive, collecting a nice pile just from the extra circling around. But David never did that."

Shaya listened carefully. He could understand a bit of what was said, and what he didn't understand, Shore translated for him. This story actually fit Naftali. He was also very straight.

"Did he have children?" Shore asked.

"He had a daughter," Valery said right away. "I remember her. Also a boy, or two boys, if I'm not mistaken."

"Do you recall how old they were?"

"The girl was the oldest," Valery tried to remember. Shaya clasped his hands. It made sense that Naftali and Rochel had a girl after they left.

"Did he wear a hat?" Shaya wanted Shore to ask.

"Yes, yes," Valery grew animated. "He always wore a hat. And if it fell, he hurried to pick it up… I remember. Now that you mention a hat, it's coming back to me."

"The man that we're looking for," Shore said, "is an Orthodox Jew. Did you ever notice any kind of different behavior by David, like on Saturday? Did he drive on Saturday?!"

Shaya leaned forward intently.

"I don't know." Valery wrinkled his forehead. "He had two days off; one of them was Saturday. On Sunday he actually worked, even though most drivers preferred not to work on Sunday. On Friday, I think, I also didn't see him."

Shore glanced at Shaya, his face full of meaning. It seemed that there was a lead here, a nice fat one.

"Ask him if Stone would eat and drink with everyone," Shaya prodded Shore. Shore asked.

Valery needed a few seconds to remember. "We would drink together, sometimes, but not where all the cab drivers would drink – somewhere else. He was very generous and would always pick up the tab."

Valery opened a worn phone book.

"Here's the address. He lives on Rue Paul Violet. It's a few minutes from here. Do you want me to call and see if he's home, my good sirs?"

"No," Shore said. "There's no need. Just take us there."

• • •

Yisroel Yitzchok didn't get back to Mendel. And when Mendel called, he saw the caller ID and didn't pick up.

In the evening, his father came into his room and quietly asked who Mendel was.

"I only know him slightly," Yisroel Yitzchok said in a low voice.

"How do you know him?"

Yisroel Yitzchok wasn't sure what to answer. Lederman had found his recording device that fell when he was following Shloime. That's what he should tell his father?

"It came out that we met through someone else," Yisroel Yitzchok said, and knew that his father didn't really believe him.

"All right," his father said. "I absolutely don't want you to have anything more to do with him. And you know that we know what you're doing even when we're not around." Tremendous pain split Elya Fuchsman's heart when he said this, but there was no choice.

"Okay," Yisroel Yitzchok said, and his agreement slightly encouraged Elya.

Late at night, though, someone knocked on the door and asked for Yisroel Yitzchok. In his hand was a note: "Can we meet? It's very important. Mendel Lederman."

Yisroel Yitzchok stared at the note and then at the youth who stood there, waiting.

"Tell the person who sent you," he finally said, "that I still want to know his intentions. If I receive a clear answer, I'll decide whether or not to renew contact with him. Tell him exactly those words. And tell him, also, that he should please stop seeking me out in all kinds of twisted ways. It won't help anything."

The youth disappeared into the dark stairwell. Yisroel Yitzchok turned around and bumped into his father.

"Can I see what's written in that note?" his father asked and took the note from between his fingers.

Elya read: "Can we meet? It's very important. Mendel Lederman."

"Yisroel Yitzchok," he said, "I want to know what he wants from you."

Yisroel Yitzchok was quiet. He had an answer, but it was shocking.

"He – he," Yisroel Yitzchok tried to answer, but the words stuck in his throat. "I don't know why. He wants that Suri's and Shloime's *chasunah* should be cancelled." There. It was said.

Yisroel Yitzchok looked at his father, who leaned against the wall behind him, his face very pale.

"Do you know this man, Abba?"

"I know who he is. He's known in the community. He has an investigations office."

"Why does he want to cancel the *chasunah*? What does he

have to do with the *chasunah*?"

"It's very possible that you, Yisroel Yitzchok, will be the one to help us find out…"

...

The three of them arrived at the house, a most ordinary apartment building. Valery took the lead with wide strides, followed by Shore with his measured gait, his sharp eyes not missing a thing. Sticking out like a sore thumb in his traditional Jewish garb, Shaya Bleich brought up the rear, not knowing towards what he was walking.

"He lived on the top floor," Valery said, his memory proving to be impressive considering his advanced age and the large passage of time. "There's no doubt about it. He had an attic in which he used to read."

"To learn," the words fell out of Shaya's mouth by themselves.

"What did you say?" Shore asked.

"Nothing, it's not important." It was very important, but not to the actual investigation.

Shore instructed Valery what to say and how to act. They filed upstairs to the top floor.

The door was old and in need of paint. Valery knocked. He knocked again, harder.

Feet moved towards the door. Shaya's heart kept pace with the footsteps.

An elderly woman opened the door. It most certainly wasn't, in any way or fashion, his sister-in-law Rochel.

It was obvious that Valery didn't understand what was going on, either. He opened his mouth, completely disregarding what Shore had told him to ask.

"What's this, David Stone doesn't live here anymore?"

The woman in the doorway fired off a string of sentences in French. Shaya didn't understand what she was saying, or what Valery answered her and what Shore asked, but he did understand that something had gone awry.

•  •  •

When the call came to Mendel Lederman's office, the esteemed investigator wasn't there. The secretary was the one to receive the call.

"Mr. Lederman isn't here," she answered laconically.

"It's very urgent," Shloime said.

"I understand, but even something urgent can't bring him back here if he's not here," she calmly pointed out. All kinds of strange callers were par for the course in her job.

"Where is he?" Shloime asked.

"First of all, I don't know. And secondly, even if I did know, I don't think I would print out a report of his actions for you."

Shloime didn't like the tone of the conversation, but he had to find Lederman, now.

"Can I come and wait for him in the office?" Shloime asked. The secretary raised an eyebrow.

"As a matter of principle, our waiting room is meant for those who have appointments," she said.

"So I'd like to make an appointment."

"Sure." Finally, the conversation was going along the proper tracks. "When would you like? Next Thursday? The Sunday after that?"

"What Thursday? I need to see him today, now!"

"That's impossible. The calendar's full."

"What does that mean the calendar's full? I'm not a line in a calendar, I'm a person, and I need him urgently. It's a matter of life and death."

Nochum, standing on the side, narrowed his eyes. He waited impatiently for the call to end.

"Sir, as much as I understand you, many people are waiting to meet with Mr. Lederman. You can be here on Thursday at four o'clock. I'll also write your name on the side, and if there'll be a cancellation, I'll be happy to let you know. What's your telephone number?"

"Fine, there's no need," Shloime said with a sigh. "If I won't see him today, it doesn't matter anymore when. Many things can happen until Thursday." He hung up and sighed deeply.

Nochum waited for him to calm down a bit and then said:

"I'm not sure you're going about this the right way."

Shloime lifted dull eyes. "Do you have another way to suggest?"

"In my opinion," Nochum said carefully, "this conversation, even if it takes place today, won't get you anywhere. Whatever Lederman didn't tell you until now, he won't tell you now, either. You're only playing into his hands. Instead, try to find out what Lederman won't tell you – in other ways."

"I see you want me to take the change in profession seriously," Shloime smiled bitterly. "From yeshiva *bochur* to detective."

"With your talents and motivation," Nochum assured him, "there's no doubt that you'd surpass Mendel Lederman by far…"

• • •

Yisroel Yitzchok Fuchsman and his father still stood by the front door. Elya rolled the condemning note from Mendel Lederman between his fingers; Yisroel Yitzchok was completely confused.

"You *do* want me to deal with him, Abba?"

"Deal with him? *Chas v'shalom*. This man is a stranger to you. You are forbidden to have any dealings with him."

"So---" Yisroel Yitzchok didn't understand. What did Abba want?

"Here and there I've heard," Elya said in a measured voice, "all kinds of rumors about the *chasunah*. Suri is stressed. Ima doesn't understand what's happening. The whole time I thought it was an *ayin hora* that wanted to ruin this wonderful *shidduch*. Now I understand who's behind everything, who's spreading the rumors."

"But we don't even know this man. Why should he want to act against us?"

"That's what I want to know, too. Something mysterious is going on behind our backs. I would prefer, of course, that you wouldn't know this man at all, but now that he's already made himself known to you, I want to keep on top of his doings. And you, Yisroel Yitzchok, will be my contact and do exactly – but exactly! – all that I tell you to do.

Elya glanced at the note again.

"He wants to meet with you. Do you have any idea what he's planning to tell you at this meeting?"

"He said he has some secrets about our family that he has to tell me. I think that that's how he wants to get me to meet with him."

"I hear. I'm sure he has big secrets in his bag, secrets that even we don't know… Come with me, Yisroel Yitzchok."

Yisroel Yitzchok obediently followed his father to his study. His father took a key and stuck it into the lock of one of the desk drawers. After a brief rummage, he held up a thin string, connected on one end to a tiny microphone, and to a small machine on the other.

"What's that?" Yisroel Yitzchok asked in amazement.

"This little thing," Elya said shortly, "you will attach to yourself when you go to meet with Mendel Lederman. The microphone you'll stick under your shirt in such a way that it's completely unnoticeable. The machine you'll put deep in your pocket, and the string you'll hide under your clothing. This is a sophisticated recording device, and it will memorize for us every word that will be said in the meeting."

"Where'd you get such a machine, Abba?"

Elya smiled. "You thought you were the only sophisticated one, huh?"

Yisroel Yitzchok inspected the device and tried it out. Had things not been so baffling, he surely would have enjoyed the mastery of modern technology that his father was demonstrating.

"And under no circumstances," Elya emphasized, "is anyone in the world to know about this. I know you're quick to speak, Yisroel Yitzchok, and I'm begging you this time to watch your mouth well. I can't stress the importance of it enough."

...

"Why don't you approach your *mechutan* directly and speak to him?" Nochum asked sensibly.

"I don't think that's a good idea."

"Details, please."

"First of all, the less others are involved, the better, besides which---"

"Shloime, I don't think your future father-in-law falls in the category of 'others'."

"I'm not so sure. Meanwhile, I don't have proof that he knows anything about this business. And besides, I prefer not to speak to him about anything that isn't routine. I feel that lately he's not as friendly towards me as he used to be. As if he feels that he made a mistake when taking me as a *chosson*."

"Really, Shloime. You're going to be his son-in-law until a hundred and twenty, *be'ezras Hashem*, and there are bound to be things that will have to be cleared up between you – so I assume. I haven't yet met anyone whose life flows along completely effortlessly. It's a good idea to learn already now how to go over and speak to him."

"You're wrong. After the wedding everything's signed and sealed. Now is like some sort of twilight zone. Not everything that I can allow myself to say and do after the wedding can I let myself do now."

Nochum sighed.

"You're an intelligent boy, Shloime Bleich," he said, "but each time something personally connected to you comes up, you act emotionally instead of using your mind. I think that---"

"Do me a favor, don't think now. My head is already bursting from all this thinking. I want a good angel to come now and tell me that everything will be just fine. One hundred percent fine."

And as if to fulfill his request, steady knocking was heard at the door.

"Your angel has arrived," Nochum said and looked through the peephole. Who could be knocking at the door of his cousin's empty apartment?"

"Actually," Nochum whispered, "I'm not so sure it's a good angel."

"Who is it?" Shloime sat up straight.

"Mendel Lederman. You didn't have to receive a report of his doings. He's here in the flesh," Nochum said and turned the key in the lock.

# CHAPTER 29

"I take it that this isn't the house of David Stone?" Shaya asked from behind Shore's back. "We made a mistake with the address?"

"No, I don't think the address is the mistake. I believe that he lived here, but now he doesn't. Not for a while already."

"And the good friend hasn't checked where his friend is for a number of years already?"

Shore nodded. He had the same question.

"The woman says," he translated for him, "that she doesn't know anything. She's renting this apartment for three years already, and the name of the tenant before her wasn't David Stone, but something else. We have to ask the owner."

Shore took out his notebook and wrote down the telephone number of the owner.

He took out his cell phone and dialed. Shaya leaned against the wall of the stairwell and inspected the expressions of those there. Valery was very uncomfortable, and the woman at the door closed it slowly, a bit at a time, as if to say, "Why don't you leave and stop wasting my time?"

It seemed like the owner answered. Shore spoke to him in rapid French and when he finished, he didn't look too happy.

"This man doesn't remember any tenant by the name of Stone, and he firmly insists that he remembers all his tenants."

"So maybe," Shaya raised a logical assumption, "maybe he bought this house from the previous owner who rented it to Stone."

"Very logical. I also asked him that," Shore said. "The problem is that it's impossible to talk to the previous owner."

"Why?"

"Because he's dead."

"Dead?"

"Completely. A number of years ago."

"What a shame," Shaya said, and felt real distress about the death of a French gentile whom he didn't even know.

"Okay," Shore roused himself, "Thank you, ma'am. We're finished here. I hope we didn't trouble you too much. In any event, thank you. You helped us a lot."

When they were back on the street, on their way back to Valery's house and their car that was waiting for them there, Shaya asked Shore if they hadn't reached a dead end.

"I don't want to hear the words 'dead end' again," Shore said clearly. "If you would know how many dead ends I've come to in my work, you would understand that you're standing next to a bulldozer. If you let yourself get despaired over this situation, you may as well kiss the whole investigation good-bye."

"So what are we going to do now?"

"I'll tell you what we'll do," Shore said and glanced at his watch. "We'll go to the house of that deceased house owner and convince his family to show us his accounts books. There, I believe, will appear the name of David Stone along with other tenants. We'll check who rented the house after him. Usually, whoever rents a house knows a thing or two about the tenant before him – why he left and where he was headed."

Shaya had to admit that it made a lot of sense. "So we'll go today?"

"Right now."

...

"You came to visit me?" Shloime asked, his face a frozen mask. Mendel Lederman stepped inside.

"Yes, I came to visit you," Lederman stressed, "before it will be too late…"

He entered the apartment with confident steps. "Can we talk, young Bleich?"

"We can," Shloime said shortly.

"I mean, without foreign ears listening," Lederman motioned at Nochum.

"I don't consider Nochum Cohen 'foreign ears'," Shloime said. "Anything that I'll hear, he can hear as well."

"I understand," Lederman said patiently, "but not everything that I'll say he can hear. Is he a member of your family?"

"He's my friend who's like a brother."

"I hear," Lederman said and folded his arms. "I'm waiting for him to leave, because our conversation has to be completely private."

"It won't be private," Shloime said with decided confidence. "Nochum will be there, too. You've managed to bring me so low, Lederman, that I need massive support."

Lederman fixed Nochum with an appraising look, as if trying to read him.

"You know what, Bleich?" he said finally, "I'll agree to your request, even though it deviates completely from the way I do things, on condition that I speak to your friend first for a few minutes."

"No problem," Shloime said and shrugged. He guessed that Lederman wanted to check how trustworthy Nochum was. Let him. "I'll go outside. Does anyone want a hot drink?"

No one wanted a hot drink. Shloime poured a cup of tea for himself, not knowing how cold he would soon be. Very cold.

Lederman and Nochum sat in the closed room for long minutes. Every so often Shloime passed by the door, but they were speaking so quietly that he couldn't hear even the slightest murmur.

Finally, after quite a bit of time, the door opened and Lederman called in a loud voice:

"Young Bleich, we're waiting for you."

Shloime neared the room, wondering a little why he didn't hear Nochum.

Upon entering, however, he found Nochum white as snow. His eyes stared straight ahead, focusing on Shloime and darting away. He had heard something earth shattering, that Shloime knew.

"What's doing?" Shloime asked cheerily.

"Nothing," Lederman answered in the same blithe note, "I just told him the whole truth and now he agrees with me."

"Agrees with you that what?" Shloime didn't understand.

"*Nu*, Nochum," Lederman encouraged him, "let's hear what you have to say."

"I... I agree with him," Nochum finally got out. "Shloime, you can't get married now. There's no way...!"

...

Shaya went into his hotel room and locked the door behind him, twice. He then took out his small cell phone from his pocket and, just to be sure, stood far away from the door to the room.

He had a phone number to call in order to leave a message about the investigation's progress. He didn't know to whom he was speaking, he had no idea what would be done with the information he was giving over, but that was the price he had to pay for the investigation to move and for the chance to find his brother.

He dialed the number. As expected, no one answered; there was only a recording.

"Shaya Bleich speaking. As you requested, I'm leaving here the details of the investigation's progress," he said, and briefly summed up the day's events. When he finished, he felt as foolish as one of the towels folded on the bed. What kind of game were they playing with him? To talk to the wall?

The telephone in his hand shrilled. Who was looking for him now? Maybe Chana?

It was Chana. Her voice sounded very worried.

"Shaya, I don't know what's happening here. Shloime came home completely broken. He doesn't want to tell me what happened. He's not eating or drinking. I tried to get him to talk. He just asked that I leave him alone."

"Where did he come from?" Shaya asked.

"I don't know," she answered honestly.

"And he didn't tell you *anything*?"

"He did say a few words." Chana didn't want to say them.

"What did he say?"

"He said something like 'Maybe Hashem doesn't want me to get married. So many things are blocking me' – that's all he said. He then went into his room and hasn't come out since."

"I see. Let me talk to him, please."

*Thicker Than Water* « 359

Shloime's voice, broken, came on the line.

"What's doing, Shloime'le?" Shaya asked. "I heard that you're not having it easy. Someone's making problems for you?"

"No, Abba," Shloime replied. "Everything's fine. What's doing by you? How is the search going? We miss you."

"It's moving along nicely. The investigator that I hired is working like a bulldozer. Give him another three, four days and he'll find your parents – I'm sure of it."

"I'm not so sure anymore if that's so good, Abba," Shloime's voice sounded like it was coming from deep inside the ground.

"Let me guess," Shaya said. "You spoke to Mendel Lederman and he filled your head with nonsense. I told you not to speak to him. That man is a danger to the community."

"Abba, what he's saying is based on real information."

"And what did he say?"

"He said," Shloime almost choked, "that it's not a good idea to get married now, and not to search for my parents. He says to leave it all alone."

Shaya felt a terrific need to smash Lederman's head into the glass window opposite him. What did this person want from their lives?! True, there was a mystery, he tried to solve it and then pulled back from the entire business. They'd had no contact for years. Why had he suddenly woken up?

"He's talking nonsense, Shloime'le. You hear? Pure nonsense. We don't need a stargazer to tell us what's good to do now and what later. If he has what to base his words on – please, let him speak. Maybe we'll believe him."

"But Abba," Shloime squeaked, "he already said."

"He said??" Shaya was astounded. "To you?"

"To my friend, Nochum Cohen. And what he said must have been very convincing, because now Nochum is also convinced that I shouldn't get married now. My last support in front of all these waves – has also been swept away…"

Shaya looked around for a chair. There was no chair where he was standing. There was a wall. He leaned against it.

"What did Lederman say to Nochum, Shloime'le?"

"I would give everything to know, Abba. But he promised Lederman not to tell me."

"There's no such thing," Shaya ruled. His feet finally found the armchair in the room. "Nochum is your friend, and is loyal only to you. If he's joining this *sheigetz*, Lederman, he's not your friend anymore. Find yourself some other friends, Shloime'le. There are enough boys around."

Shaya tried to hear an answer, but what he heard sounded like gasping.

"Shloime?" he ventured, "Shloime? Is everything okay?"

The gasping intensified.

"Shloime'le," Shaya's heart broke, "you're strong. You'll come out of this. When the *satan* tries to stop something, it's a sign that what you're about to do is especially good. Especially important. You'll get through this, Shloime'le. I promise you. We'll get through it together. Don't… don't cry." The last time he said such words to Shloime was when he was four. What had happened to this strong boy of his?!

"Abba," Shloime choked out, "Nochum also said that it's not a good idea for me to know. I have to leave this *shidduch* – that's what he said. To just leave it…"

• • •

"I don't understand what's going on here," Elya Fuchsman complained. "Devorah! What's happening with the telephone?! I'm trying and trying to call and there's no line!"

Devorah didn't know. She had just come home from shopping. No one had been in the house the entire morning. She didn't realize there was anything wrong with the phone.

Elya tried all the phones in the house, both cordless and those with a wire. He heard nothing. Quiet. There was no dial tone.

"Maybe there's something wrong in the whole neighborhood," Devorah thought out loud. The neighbors, though, had no problems with their line. Elya called the telephone company from his cell phone and asked for service urgently.

The company promised that a technician would come soon. Meanwhile, Elya would use his cell phone and waste some more money.

Within forty minutes, a service car from the telephone company pulled up with a screech at the front of the house. Two men in red overalls jumped out and looked for the apartment with the problem.

"Thank you, that was really quick," Devorah Fuchsman said and offered them a cold drink. They poked around for a long while in the main telephone box and, after half an hour, informed Devorah that the problem was fixed. Devorah picked up the phone and heard the pleasant, familiar tone.

"What was the problem?" she asked interestedly.

"There was some wire that was torn," one of them answered.

"All right," Devorah said, "thank you. As long as everything's working now."

And the two men were swallowed back up in the service car.

In the afternoon, Devorah asked Suri if she'd like to go the next day to a sale of linen and robes. Suri said she preferred to go that day, because the next day she'd like to go on a trip to the graves of *tzaddikim*; she would return only in the evening.

Devorah looked at her for a minute.

"Do you want me to come with you?"

"I don't think it's necessary," Suri said. Her eyes were tired.

She was going through a difficult time. She wanted to beg and plead to Hashem to take away all the doubts and complications, and to bring her to the *chuppah* filled with joy and happiness. And no, she didn't need someone to accompany her. Just the opposite. She wanted to be by herself.

"Okay," Devorah said, "but I want you to travel with an official company and to be in constant contact with us, so we shouldn't worry."

Suri had anyway planned to do that. Elya recommended the company "Trips and Tours", which was known for its security and for sticking to its timetable.

Suri called. They had a bus leaving to the Rambam's *kever* the next day at eight o'clock in the morning. From there, they would continue to Amukah and the grave of R' Yonason ben Uziel, and then to Tzefas and Meron.

Suri reserved a place. Devorah looked at her and thought that it really wouldn't harm the girl to get out a bit, and *davening* always helped.

• • •

Under Mendel Lederman's office was a room that was unknown to the public. Lederman privately dubbed it "the room of crimes", but actually, many investigations started moving and came to a successful close thanks to this room.

Now, too, Lederman sat in the room, together with his technician, Shaul.

"The plan went off without a hitch," Shaul said. "Our men cut the wires and then showed up as the telephone company's repairmen and planted the bug on the line. If you want, we can connect now already, and listen. If someone's talking on the phone, we'll hear it. The red light will go on each time the telephone line is in use."

"Connect," Lederman said shortly.

Shaul fiddled with the wires.

"There's a call in progress right now," Shaul said. "Do you want to hear it?"

"Yes."

A push on a button and a voice suddenly burst into the small room.

"Tomorrow at eight o'clock in the morning? Where are you leaving from?"

"From Beis Yisroel Square," came the answer.

"Okay, so please write me down. The name is Sara Fuchsman."

Lederman listened tensely.

"Are you also going to the *kever* of R' Leib ba'al haYesurim?"

"Could be. If there'll be enough time."

"And how much time do you give to *daven* at each place?"

"As much as possible. Just make sure to come on time tomorrow so they don't have to wait for you and set out late. At exactly eight o'clock."

Shaul glanced at Mendel Lederman and saw a smile spread slowly across his face.

"I didn't think we'd make such quick progress," Lederman whispered. "We're being handed our chance on a silver platter."

"How many places?"

"One."

Shaul nodded his head.

• • •

"You look terrible." Shore expressed his opinion of Shaya Bleich as soon as he saw him, first thing in the morning.

"True," Shaya said and rubbed his eyes. "I didn't sleep all night."

"And that's because? By the way, I take it that you don't eat here in the hotel?"

"No, I'll go out to a kosher restaurant here in the neighborhood."

Shore considerately gave up the rich hotel meal and went with Shaya to a small restaurant with an excellent *hechsher*.

"What's going on? You can't sleep? Is there a serious reason?" Shore asked curiously when they were settled at a small table and perusing the menu.

"Serious. Yes. It's connected to the reason we're here," Shaya said, and glanced around. Eavesdroppers could be anywhere. He trusted no one.

Briefly, in a low voice, as he doodled with his pen on a paper napkin, Shaya told Shore about the antics of Mendel Lederman, the private investigator who had ceased to be an investigator and became the family's persecutor.

"He's constantly claiming that he has information that he can't give over."

Shore was interested in the story. Very interested.

"He's a trustworthy fellow?" he asked.

"That, at least, is what we thought in the past. And that's what we understood from the recommendations we received on him years ago," Shaya said. "I must point out that I've never caught him in any sort of lie. Back then, when he retracted from the file, he refused to explain why he was doing so. Throughout all the years, we had no contact. Only now, before my son Shloime's wedding, has the relationship been renewed."

Shore moved the toast on his plate from side to side, deep in thought.

"I'm almost positive that this man has information that we

don't. I would say eight to ten he's in contact with your lost brother, but he's prevented from revealing him so he won't disappear again."

"That means that my brother is continuing to hide wherever he is, for a reason that we don't know, but Mendel Lederman does know."

"Correct. And if you ask me, he'll do everything in order to block us," Shore said, and Shaya could actually see the veins in his neck go taut. He would not surrender this battle.

"He already did, with the first investigator I tried to take," Shaya revealed. "He purposely sent me to an investigator who would try to bury the story. G-d stood by me, and that investigator was too ethical to cooperate with him. He revealed Lederman's motives to me, and then everything ground to a halt. Listen, Shore," Shaya said, his heart pounding, "I know this Lederman. He won't give in easily. He has many ways and means of reaching any goal he sets."

"And I have many ways and means of surprising him from behind," Shore fumed. "I'm not afraid of adversaries. I've already met up with any number of them in dark alleyways."

# CHAPTER 30

A line formed next to the bus that was standing in the square. Suri waited patiently, not pushing. Her turn would also come. She had reserved a place in advance.

Right behind her stood another woman, pleasant, in her forties or fifties. Suri climbed on to the bus and found a place to sit in the back, next to the window.

"May I?"

The pleasant woman requested to sit next to her. Suri willingly agreed.

At first, Suri just stared at the view, her small *sefer tehillim* closed in her hand. Somehow, it was hard for her to concentrate. The woman next to her, by contrast, was deeply engrossed in a "*tehillim mechulak.*"

"Could we open the window a bit?" The woman put her *tehillim* booklet into her pocketbook and turned to Suri.

"Sure," Suri said, and opened the window fully.

"Ah, such wonderful air," the woman said. "It's a nice day."

Suri nodded.

"It might even be a bit chilly in Tzefas, in the *beis olam*," the woman commented. "Were you ever there?"

"Once," Suri replied, "a long time ago."

"Oh. I actually travel there quite often. Every *erev Rosh Chodesh*."

"That's nice," Suri said. She wasn't settled enough to chat with a stranger. The woman picked up on her mood and became absorbed again in her *siddur*, this time with the *Iggeres haRamban*.

The first stop was in Tverya. Suri felt the *davening* to be cleansing, a breath of fresh air. She just needed to *daven*, and everything would be fine. She was so engrossed in her prayers that she didn't feel the gaze of the nice woman, who was never far from her side. Why was she so interested in her? They had never met before that day, and would never meet again. Only the shared seat on the bus connected them.

When Suri went back on to the bus, the woman was already waiting for her in her seat with her pleasant smile. That's how it was? They had to be friends throughout the entire day?

During the ride, the woman sensed Suri's mood and barely spoke. She offered her some fruit and snacks, which Suri politely refused, not more than that.

After Tverya, the bus arrived at Amukah. Suri had been there before, before her engagement, but now she felt even more strongly the need to *daven*. For so many things. Her little *siddur* gripped tightly in her hand, she moved away to a corner where she *davened* for a long time, shedding copious tears.

Her neighbor from the bus, whom Suri didn't notice at all, found a different corner for herself, where she could keep an eye on the girl. She had to do her job fully. That's why she was there. Soon, not yet, would be the right time.

...

The house of the previous landlord, from whom David Stone had rented the apartment, was located in one of the most upper class suburbs of Paris.

"A pity on the person who died," Shore murmured as he parked the rented car at the front of the house. "How long did he plan on living if he built such a palace for himself…? Listen, these people have no idea why we're looking for David Stone. They won't like to know that their father rented the apartment to someone who's disappeared."

"So what do they know?" Shaya asked and slammed the car door.

"Nothing. I told them that I'm a private investigator, and that I have to go through their father's books as part of my investigation. I sent them an official statement that it has absolutely nothing to do with their father, who a completely upright, honest man."

"And they agreed?!" Shaya was amazed. Most people didn't want others poking into their private business.

"Yes. You have to just use the right tone." Shore climbed the steps leading to the grand front door and touched the bell lightly.

The housekeeper ushered them inside and led them to the deceased owner's study. There, on the table, lay the books.

"I don't understand," Shaya asked again, "that's how it works? I mean, they don't owe us anything."

"I didn't finish my sentence before," a hint of a smile danced over Shore's lips. "You have to use the right tone and extend the right bills. After you do that, they already owe you quite a lot."

"I get it." Shore was oiling the wheels of the investigation with a whole lot of money. His money. That is, the money of his unknown donor. He glanced around. There was no one in the room with them, and the door was closed. Now was the right time.

Somehow, though, the words that were arranged nicely in his head refused to leave his mouth. Shore opened the books and began to check them thoroughly. He copied data into his notebook. The opportunity was missed.

...

In the afternoon, while still on the way, Suri lunched on a few crackers. She had never been a big eater, and was now even less so. But she needed strength to *daven*.

The phone of the woman next to her rang. The woman immediately stood up and went to sit somewhere else in order not to disturb her. That was nice of her. Suri's parents also called. They wanted to know that everything was okay with her.

"Everything's great, you don't have to worry," she said. The woman, who had finished her conversation, came back to sit next to her.

At home, though, the Fuchsman parents were not calm. Why had they let a *kallah* go on such a long trip all on her own? They should have insisted on sending someone with her.

"Maybe there's an older woman there who can take you under her wing?" Devorah asked. She felt bad that she hadn't thought twice before letting Suri go. Now she had some sort of premonition.

"Ima, it's fine," Suri said. "I'm a big girl already."

"Even so," Devorah begged, "I'd be calmer if I knew someone was with you."

Suri asked her mother to hold on a minute and turned to the woman next to her with a smile:

"My mother is asking if there's a nice, older woman who could be responsible for me during the trip. She's worried. You know how mothers are."

"No problem," the woman smiled. "I'm also a mother. My name is Leah – tell your mother that I'll take good care of you. If she wants, I'll even accompany you home."

Suri's mother felt more at ease. The bus huffed and puffed its way up the mountain to Meron. Leah smiled at Suri. "Until someone is a mother herself, she doesn't know the meaning of worry. I understand that you're a *kallah*?"

"That's right."

"How nice, *mazel tov* to you. You must have a lot to *daven* for."

"Yes," Suri said, "a whole lot."

But even she didn't know how much.

• • •

"Look," Shore pointed to a specific line in the accounts book of the deceased landlord. "Pay attention to this line."

"I don't understand French," Shaya reminded him.

"Oh, right. I forgot. It says 'David Stone', and here's the date that he entered the apartment and paid a year's rent in advance."

"A year's rent," Shaya echoed.

"Now let's flip forwards," Shore said. "Let's check what happened a year later."

There was the date in front of them.

"It doesn't say here that David Stone renewed the contract," Shore's forehead creased. He flipped back a few pages. A week, a month, until three months earlier he found a new name: Isabella Gutzi. She was listed as a new tenant while David Stone's contract was still valid.

"I don't understand what's going on here," Shore said. "Stone paid a year's rent in advance, and then just picked up and left in middle of the year? Who does a thing like that?"

"Someone who has a reason to run away," Shaya voiced the thought that was passing through both of their minds.

"Oho, here!" Shore discovered a small asterisk that brought him to a lone line at the edge of the page: "Tenant David Stone left the apartment without giving notice." The landlord had written two possible dates, two months apart, and guessed that Stone left the house during that time.

"Do you understand what's happening here?" Shore asked. "Stone paid for a year up front, on purpose, so he shouldn't have to keep in contact with his landlord. At one point he must have felt an urgent need to leave and simply upped and left. The landlord didn't know a thing until he looked for him one day and found an empty apartment."

"So again we've lost his tracks." Shaya's heart sank. How would they find David Stone now? He felt Shore's cross gaze.

"Doesn't it say in your sources: 'Even if you're being threatened with a sharp sword, don't despair'? I'm not the one who should be teaching you, rather you should be teaching me."

Shaya smiled involuntarily and quoted correctly: *"Afilu im cherev chadah..."* He translated into English for Shore: "Even if a sharp sword is placed on a man's neck, he shouldn't cease requesting for mercy".

"All right, so a bit of faith, Mr. Bleich. If G-d brought us to this point, I get the feeling that He has the ability to take us further still."

• • •

Suri wasn't one to cry easily, but now, in the ancient graveyard of Tzefas, her tears flowed like water. She hid her face in her little siddur and tried to hide her sobs. *Ribbono shel olam, make my life continue peacefully like before; that my chasunah should take place with joy and happiness, at the right time. Perhaps I didn't thank You enough for all the good You've done for me, and now I'm being reminded that things don't always go smoothly...?*

As she paused slightly, the nice lady from the bus, the one who took her under her charge, approached her slowly.

"Suri, do you want to go to the *kever* of R' Leib ba'al haYesurim?"

Suri turned her wet face. Yes, she wanted to go. She found it interesting that the woman could read her thoughts. She even remembered her name.

"It's not far from here, just a few minutes. We'll go for a little bit and then come back so they shouldn't have to wait for us."

Suri nodded. She closed her *sefer Tehillim* and went together with the woman, just for a few minutes.

As they walked along, side by side, the woman tried to strike up a conversation.

"I heard," she said, "that whoever comes to the *kever* of R' Leib ba'al haYesurim on a Friday that's also Rosh Chodesh, after *chatzos*, and says the entire *sefer Tehillim*, *Hashem* will give him whatever he asks for that year.".

Suri perked up.

"Where did you hear that from?"

"I don't remember," the woman shrugged her shoulders. "I guess word of mouth."

"These things don't usually have a reliable source," Suri said, "and anyway, there's so many "*segulos*" lately that we tend to forget that the best, most helpful thing is to *daven*. Of course a request could be granted in the *z'chus* of a *tzaddik*, but to attribute all kinds of baseless *segulos* to the great people buried here – I think it's a slight to their honor."

"You're a very interesting girl," the woman marveled, "and

such a thinker… but look, we're here already. Let's *daven* properly because, as you've said, *tefillah* is the best *segulah*."

Suri, influenced by her own words, stood in a corner. Besides them, there was only one other woman there, tall and dressed completely in white, with an elaborate white head covering on her head.

• • •

R' Nachman was thrilled to hear Shaya Bleich's voice. Was he doing all right? Was he managing over there? Was the investigation progressing? Was everything okay?

"Everything's fine, R' Nachman," Shaya smiled, "and thank you for your interest. I have one small question for you."

"Ask, ask, a small question, a big question."

"Your guest, the anonymous donor – is he still staying at your house?"

"No, he's not here anymore," R' Nachman replied, and didn't know what important piece of information he was giving Shaya when he added: "He left the day after you left."

Aha. That was another proof that the man didn't have any business to take care of in the neighborhood. He was simply following Shaya Bleich, and after Shaya Bleich flew to France, the donor flew off as well.

"R' Nachman, I might need your help."

"I'd be very happy."

"What else do you know about this man? I need to know every possible detail about him."

R' Nachman wrinkled his forehead.

"He introduced himself as Avrohom Yisroel."

"And where is he from? Which part of the world?"

"I don't know."

"And who says that's his real name?"

"You're right," R' Nachman scratched his head, "It could be his name is really something else. You know, Rav Bleich, I don't ask my guests for ID. Whoever comes is welcome. The main thing is that he gives me the *z'chus* of *hachnosas orchim*."

"Does he have any family? How old is he? What does he do? Why did he come to the area?"

"I don't know," R' Nachman shook his head and repeated, "I don't know."

"Agree with me, R' Nachman, that it's strange. You usually know a lot about your guests, and about this particular one you know nothing. Absolutely nothing. If he's rich – as he claims and as the sums he's giving me proves – why did he choose to stay in your house, and not in a hotel as befits his status? I'd say eight to ten," Shaya unconsciously copied the esteemed Shore's manner of estimation, "that the man is intentionally hiding everything. He has a specific reason to come stay at your house, and after his goal was reached – he picked up and left."

"I have the chills, Rav Bleich," R' Nachman said, and it could be heard in his voice. "Something not kosher took place in my house and I didn't know…?"

"I wouldn't call it something not kosher," Shaya tried to reassure him, "but rather something mysterious. *Be'ezras Hashem*, we'll manage to solve it all and we'll tell you what it was. Don't worry, R' Nachman."

"I'll start an investigation," R' Nachman promised, and Shaya knew he would do it. "I'm not leaving this alone until I know everything there is to know about this man. He should know that you don't play games with Nachman."

• • •

For a few days, Chana Bleich tiptoed past Shloime's room.

Her heart went out to him. He had suffered a massive blow after his best friend Nochum "switched sides" and became convinced that Mendel Lederman was right, and that the wedding shouldn't take place.

Seeing that the door, which was usually closed, was now open a crack, Chana peeked in. Shloime looked like someone whose future was hanging opposite him. What Mendel Lederman said was one thing; he surely had his reasons and interests. If Nochum, however, his good friend, advocated the same opinion, and he, too, refused to give any details – then Shloime Bleich was alone in the battle. He was one against the world.

The situation at home wasn't too encouraging, either. His father was wandering about the world looking for his biological parents, so far with no results. His mother was trying to function as both father and mother, and to prepare for a wedding whose reality was up in the air.

Shloime sat for long hours, staring straight ahead, as if salvation would come from the wall opposite him. His mother peeked in every so often, offering something to drink, to eat. He usually refused. He knew that his mother wanted to speak, to help him unload, but he avoided it. He couldn't speak about it with anyone in the world. Until very recently, everything was so good. He was one of the top boys in yeshiva, engaged to a wonderful girl from a respected family – and then came the earthquake that turned his world upside down. The fate of the wedding was unclear, and it was very clear what his fate would be if he continued to stay home for days on end without going to yeshiva.

Sometimes Shloime felt as if he was about to lose his sanity. Even if the whole thing came to a happy conclusion – he would probably need some kind of therapy to get back to himself.

One second. Shloime straightened up. He moved his gaze from the wall and looked at the drawer.

Psychologist. That was the word. Once, it seemed like fifty years ago, he had gone to a psychologist in an attempt to extract details of his past from his brain. It hadn't been so successful, and he was left with only a transcript of his conversation with the psychologist. A transcript from which not much could be understood.

Now, though, Abba was working with a new investigator, who, according to what he heard, was smart and efficient. Maybe this investigator would be able to get something from that transcript. Where on earth had he put it…?

Shloime finally found the sheaf of papers under a pile of paper in one of his drawers.

"Where's Abba now?" he came out of the room and asked his mother. She was so surprised to see him out of the room, talking and asking questions, that she forgot to answer.

"Abba? Abba's now… I know he went to France. I don't know if he's still there, and where in France he would be. You can call and ask him. But what happened, Shloime? What suddenly happened?"

"I need to send him a fax."

"Really?"

"Yes. I have some papers here that might be able to help him."

Chana restrained herself with all her might. Had Shloime wanted to show her, he would have done so on his own. And if he didn't – she wouldn't ask.

"Do you want me to check with Abba how you could send him a fax?"

• • •

Suri stood for a few minutes, *davening*. She then picked her head out of her siddur and threw her companion a questioning look.

The woman nodded her head. They had a few more minutes.

Suri, once more deep in prayer, didn't notice the woman dressed in white walking towards her. Had she noticed, she probably would have moved away a bit, and not let her come so close to her.

"Sara, Sara…"

Suri whirled around. Who was calling her name in this distant place?

"Hello, Sara, hello," the tall woman, dressed in white, said in a deep voice.

"Who are you??" Suri drew back.

"Don't be afraid," the woman spoke slowly. 'My name is Miriam."

"Where do you know me from?"

"I don't know you, but I know much about you. Many things that you don't even know about yourself."

A chill ran up Suri's spine and she began to tremble. After a minute, though, she realized that it was just an eccentric, of which there were quite a few in that area. She didn't know her name. She simply called her "Sara", an extremely common Jewish name – only this time it happened to be correct.

Suri rummaged in her purse and placed a coin in the woman's hand.

"Oh, no, not this," the woman said in her slow voice. "I have money. A lot of money. I don't need it, take it back. Soon you're getting married. Take it, so you should have it."

Suri's eyes opened wide. Was this woman really just a "regular" oddball wandering around the area? How did she know that she was getting married?

Actually, though, it made sense to say to someone her age who was *davening* at the graves of *tzaddikim*: "Soon you're getting married." Every girl was going to be a *kallah*, if not sooner, then later. The strange woman didn't know anything about her. She was just rambling, and there was the chance that some of what she said would actually be true.

"Ah?" the woman asked and looked at her so penetratingly that Suri felt that a sharp knife was piercing her. "Ah? You are getting married? Yes? When are you getting married?"

Suri's heart pounded. Again. How did this woman know that the wedding was doubtful? How did she know there was a question regarding the date?

*Nonsense*, Suri told herself forcefully. The thief feels the noose tightening. The woman was rambling again. *She just wants to know when your wedding is, and you're already creating a whole picture based on the doubts eating at your heart.*

"Ah?" the woman rumbled again, "Why don't you answer, Sara?"

"Please leave me alone," Suri said. True, the woman was only getting on her nerves, but it was her right to demand that she didn't stand near her.

"Leave? Why should I leave? It's not good to talk that way. This is a holy place. And you're a good girl. You're the daughter of Devorah."

Suri's heart stopped.

The woman was saying too many correct details to just attribute it all to random rambling. Yes, her name was Sara. She was getting married, *be'ezras Hashem*. Her mother's name was Devorah. That was already too much.

"H-h… how do you know?"

The woman broke into a deep, hollow laugh. "How do I know?? I know everything, Sara, Sara Fuchsman! Everything. You don't ask Miriam how she knows. Your *chatan*, Shlomo Bleich, is in trouble – that, too, I know…"

The horrified Suri looked around, searching for her benefactor, the woman from the bus, the one who took her under her wing and promised her mother to watch over her, and to even accompany her home.

But the woman was nowhere to be seen.

• • •

Danny Shore and Shaya Bleich sat in the hotel lobby and took stock of the situation.

"Is there any reason for us to stay in France?" Shaya asked.

"We have reason to stay here as long as we don't have proof that we have to go elsewhere. You're in a rush, Bleich, and that's not good. Investigations like these tend to be long, drawn out affairs. They can take months, even years. Patience – that's the key word."

"Years??"

"I hope not. But many months is a normal range of time."

This news really depressed Shaya. Shore noticed.

"What's the matter, Bleich? You have some sort of deadline? They're waiting for you at home? You forgot the milk on the fire?"

"Of course, I told you already," Shaya said, wiping beads of sweat from his forehead. "The date of the wedding is approaching. We have to find my brother and his wife by the wedding. Afterwards will be too late. The reason we're searching now is because my son Shloime, my brother's son, got engaged. We don't want him to get married without his biological parents."

Shore looked at him and knit his eyebrows.

"I'm not used to working like this, with people breathing down my neck," he said, "and you have to decide what's more important to you: finding your brother and his wife or marrying off your son, because it's very possible that they won't both happen at the same time. When I begin an investigation, I don't usually stop it. You have the choice of pushing off the wedding, or at least being flexible with the date. Deciding whether or not to find the parents is defining destiny."

"You're right, of course," Shaya said, and loosened the knot of his tie, "but it's not so simple. You don't push off a wedding unless you have a really good reason."

"This isn't a good reason?" Shore wondered. "Do you know of a better reason?"

"Yes," Shaya hastened to clarify, "this reason is definitely good enough for us, but what would we tell all our guests? No one knows the slightest thing about my son Shloime's true story."

"I understand," Shore said wearily and leaned back in the lobby's plush armchair. "We have to conquer the world in less than eighty days. Therefore, already tomorrow we will go check where our dear David Stone headed after he left the rented apartment here in Paris."

"And how do we check that?"

"We try poking around the archives of the border police. If Stone left suddenly, my guess is that he didn't move to the next street. It makes more sense that he wanted to get far away and emigrated to a different country. If he did that, his name has to appear at the border control at that time, and that's what we're going to check tomorrow."

# CHAPTER 31

"If I'm not mistaken, don't we need some kind of official document in order to check the border police archives?" Shaya said, sitting in the car next to Shore, who was driving and grumbling about the awful traffic.

"You're not mistaken about that, but you are mistaken about something else," Shore chuckled. "Of course I would need such an authorization, but people who want to save time don't wait for authorizations." He patted his pocket, which held his bulging wallet. Shaya asked no more. He already understood the system.

"I'm guessing," Shaya said, "that Stone didn't leave France as David Stone, but under a different identity, in order to prevent exactly what you're doing now."

"There's something to what you're saying," Shore commented, "and I must add that you've gotten sharper. It's not so simple, though, to switch identity, even for someone on his own – all the more so for an entire family. Such a thing takes time, besides being a serious breach of the law. If Stone wanted to flee quickly, which is what it seems like from his sudden leaving of the apartment, he had no time for such a process."

"Maybe he prepared an alternate identity in advance, without waiting for the last minute."

"That's also possible. But we'll go the straight route. First we'll search for him under his regular identity. If we don't find him, we'll ask to see all those who left France on such and such date, and look for him based on his picture."

"I think that will be too hard," Shaya said. "To go through all the pictures of all those who left France at that time so that maybe we'll identify him? There's no shorter way?"

Shore stilled the motor. "There are no shortcuts in life, Mr. Bleich. To anything."

...

Suri looked around wildly, gripping her *tehillim* with all her might. She had to get away.

"Where are you running, Sara Fuchsman?" the woman laughed in a terrible voice. "Stay here. I want to talk to you for a few minutes. It's worth it for you."

"I---I don't want to talk to you," Suri's throat was tight. She felt as if she was in a bad dream, trying to yell and failing.

"You don't have to talk," the woman gave a toothy grin. "I'll talk and you'll listen. I'll talk to you about Shlomo Bleich."

"Don't talk to me! Don't talk to me…!!"

"Why are you shouting, Sara Fuchsman?" the woman in white swished her long cloak from side to side. "I'm not doing anything to you. I want things to be good for you. Don't shout; everyone could hear."

Suri glanced about. No one was at the grave except for them. Not far away stood the ancient graveyard, where she would run very soon. In another minute.

"Everyone hears," the woman again smiled her horrible smile. "The Ridbaz, Hoshea haNavi, Rabi Moshe Alshich, Chana and her seven sons…"

"What do you want from me?!"

"I just want to tell you what a big mistake you're about to make," the woman said calmly. "It would be a mistake to have this wedding. And I know what I'm saying…"

"Stop!" Suri yelled. "You're talking nonsense!"

The woman perhaps wanted to say another few things, but Suri wasn't there anymore. She picked up her feet and ran like the wind back towards the graveyard. When she was almost there, completely out of breath, she saw "her" bus, which was supposed to take her home, speeding down the street!

"They left me!" she cried. Her bus had driven away without her! How could that have happened?!

Suri knew that each one was responsible for himself, responsible to keep to the times set by the organizers and finish his prayers on time in order to get back to the bus. She had gone with the woman down to the grave of R' Leib ba'al haYesurim for just a few minutes and should have had enough time to return, but the weird, scary lady had held her up.

And why hadn't the woman who had promised to be responsible for her told the organizers that Suri Fuchsman wasn't there and they shouldn't drive yet?

Suri was no fool. She put one and one together and easily came up with two. The woman had dragged her there, and when the crazy lady had come – suddenly disappeared. She must have gone back to the bus and not mentioned that Suri Fuchsman wasn't there – all so that the lady in white could talk to her, terrify her.

It was all planned. There was no doubt about it. Suri didn't

384 » *Thicker Than Water*

know which mind was behind it, but there definitely was such a mind.

Suri stood in the ancient graveyard. The sun was tilting westward. Soon she'd go up to the city and take a regular bus home. Meanwhile, though, she had to organize her thoughts.

Her parents hadn't worried for nothing. Their premonition had proved itself.

"Aha, there you are…!"

The voice made Suri jump again with fright. She had followed her there, the woman dressed in white…!

"Go home and tell your parents, Elya and Devorah, that you don't want to have this wedding. Tell them that, and then come here to thank me, you hear?"

Suri gathered her nerve, looked the woman straight in the eye and shot:

"Who sent you?!"

The woman faltered. She hadn't been prepared for such a question.

"Me? No one sent me. *HaKadosh Boruch Hu* sent me, on a mission to you. To save you and your *chatan*.

"Tell me who sent you!" Suri demanded forcefully.

"I don't know what you're talking about," the woman said. "You're speaking nonsense."

"Who told you all those details about me? How do you know my name and my parents' names? I want to know!"

But the strange woman suddenly lifted the edge of her long cloak and, with surprising fleetness, fled into the hills.

• • •

R'Nachman put aside all his worries and concentrated on the strange business that gave him no peace: Bleich's philanthropist.

He felt really bad that he had let the man leave his house without getting the slightest bit of information from him. Had he known the matter was so important, he would have kept him in his house at any price.

Go search for one man on the face of the globe, about whom – except for the fact that he came from Uruguay – he had zero information. The man had money. He had no trouble moving from place to place; he could hide anywhere in the world.

And family? Did the man have family?

R' Nachman knew Uruguay like the average Israeli knows the hallways of the White House. He didn't have anyone there. Not even a quarter of a relative. He barely knew where on the map the country was. What language did they speak there? Were there even any Jews there? If he had to, though – and he had to – he would know. He would know everything.

There were four guests then staying under his roof. From experience he knew that the best source of information about what was going on in the world was his guests, who were usually on the road and knew a thing or two about what went on outside the neighborhood.

"They speak Spanish in Uruguay," one guest immediately knew. Spanish?

"And there are a few Jews there, maybe ten thousand or so, maybe a bit more."

"Good Jews?" R' Nachman asked.

"Are there Jews who aren't good?" wondered the guest.

"No, of course not," R' Nachman hastened to explain himself, "I meant Jews who keep Torah and *mitzvos*, or assimilated ones, the kind who barely know what Judaism is?"

This question, though, the guest couldn't answer. This was very important to R' Nachman. The man said he was a *ger*. Was there a *beis din* in Uruguay that converted him according to halachah?

Because if not, the entire picture changed.

"How many years has this man been living in Uruguay?" a different guest asked.

"I have no idea." Too many times, lately, these words left R' Nachman's mouth.

"Because if he lived there ten or fifteen years ago, and was wealthy and well known in the community also then, it's possible that I have a friend who knows him."

"Ask, ask him," R' Nachman begged. He'd be happy with any scrap of information.

The guest, having all the time in the world, dialed his friend.

"A wealthy man, a *ger* by the name of Avrohom Yisroel?" asked the friend. No, he didn't remember anyone like that. There were wealthy people in the community, most definitely, but the kind whose connection to *shul* began and ended with *kaddish* once a year. A *ger* didn't say *kaddish* for his parents. Besides which, something about the story didn't sound right. "Check," he suggested to his friend, the guest, "Check that your host hasn't fallen into a trap. Converts are usually busy trying to catch up, not with making money. It doesn't sound to me like this man is really Jewish. Do your homework well."

R' Nachman's face showed disbelief. The matter was getting complicated. Was it really a *goy*, who, for some mysterious reason, wanted to pay for Bleich's investigation in order to be kept in the loop about it? Had he unwittingly placed Shaya Bleich in the hands of some questionable character...?

• • •

Suri stood at the entrance of Tzefas' ancient graveyard, cell phone in hand. Her parents' fright and panic spilled from the phone.

"You aren't traveling anywhere, Suri'le, not anywhere!" Ima cried. "You're not taking any bus. Who knows what else could happen to you there. You are going right now to the house of my good friend, Tzipporah Schwartz. I gave you an extra fifty shekel, right? Order a taxi that will take you to her door. Not one centimeter away. That must have been so scary. Are you okay, Suri'le?"

Suri was actually calmer now. Devorah was completely hysterical. From afar, everything sounded ten times scarier. "12 Bar Yochai Street, you hear, Suri? Tell the driver. I'm speaking to Tzipporah right now. Sleep by her tonight, and tomorrow we'll come get you. We shouldn't have sent you alone, we really shouldn't have."

In a different place, in a small room under the ground, two men sat. One was constantly busy with dials and buttons. The other was mainly busy with his thoughts. It seemed like the exercise had been successful, though only partially so.

His wife, Mrs. Lederman, had accompanied Suri on the trip. Suri didn't know her. They became friends. Suri agreed to go with her to the grave of R' Leib ba'al haYesurim, where she met the eccentric woman – his wife's friend, who was a good actress. At first, Suri was frightened, but she seemed to be made of stern stuff, and was also blessed with a decent measure of intelligence. Very quickly, she understood that it was a deliberate setup. She demanded that the "eccentric" tell her who sent her, and the latter – in typical female helpless reaction – picked up her heels and ran away.

Now Suri Fuchsman knew that her guess had been correct. Someone had sent the woman; someone who wanted to cancel the wedding at any price. She was more frightened now, as were her parents, but the success wasn't complete. They were likely to decide that they were ignoring all the threats, that they know very well what they're doing, and to celebrate the wedding in style.

What would be? He had tried so many ways already. Shloime Bleich refused to cooperate until he received solid information. He even refrained from all contact with his friend Nochum after the latter "defected" to Lederman's camp. And the Bleich father was roaming about out there, trying to find his brother, Shloime's real father, unaware that the closer he came to his goal – the closer he was drawing to the gaping mouth of a deep pit.

• • •

Once again, Shaya was amazed at the unlimited power of money. He and Shore were shown into a separate room and allowed to study the lists of all those who left France on the desired dates.

"I don't read French," Shaya sighed, and began to feel truly sorry about it. Had he had some knowledge of the language, even rudimentary, he would have been able to help Shore go over the lists.

"It's very good that you don't read French," Shore surprised him, "because you'll go through the pictures without being influenced by what is written next to them. Seven to ten, your guess is correct, and David Stone left France under a fake identity."

"Go through all the pictures? That will take hours!"

"Hours," Shore said and looked at him very meaningfully. "How long are you looking for your brother already? Twenty years?"

Shore sorted the stack of papers and placed a mountain of documents in front of Shaya. "These are the documents of all those who left during the month we think Stone left. Don't just riffle through them. Look thoroughly."

Shaya's patience held for half an hour. Hundreds of faces passed by his eyes. Skinny and fat, pleasant looking and ugly, black and white. He tried to study each one deeply. Had Naftali painted his face black? Maybe he had become really skinny or really fat? Was there any way to know besides guessing?

"It's useless," he sighed. "I see faces even when I close my eyes. Even if there is a picture of my brother here, my hands already automatically turn the pages."

"I'll bring you something to drink," Shore said, "from the cafeteria outside. What do you want? Espresso?"

"I can't drink here," Shaya reminded him.

"Okay, so I'll bring you some water," Shore was becoming somewhat used to his ways.

Shore left, leaving Shaya with the papers and the pictures. He could hear loud voices jabbering in French outside. How did Shore have such a good command of the language? How long did he study it? Twenty years? He'd been looking for his brother for twenty years. A whole generation's worth.

Shore came back. In one hand he held a large, steaming cup of coffee, and in the other a cup of water.

"They don't even have a proper cup here. What a lack of culture, coffee in a paper cup," he grimaced.

"Thanks," Shaya said. The water revived him. Shore put his cup of coffee down on the table. He'd drink it soon, when the coffee cooled a bit.

"Nice, I see you've gone through quite a lot of material," he complimented Shaya.

"A lot of material," Shaya wondered, and pointed to the giant pile that he still hadn't touched.

"Don't ever look at what's left, Bleich, but at what you've already done. The optimist will always look back and feel satisfaction, while the pessimist looks ahead and despai--- watch out!!!"

Shaya, whose spirits weren't especially lifted by Shore's encouragement, moved his hand carelessly and touched the hot cup of coffee. The flimsy cup fell and the brown liquid began to spread over the table, towards the piles of papers.

"The papers!!!" Shore yelled. He grabbed stacks of papers and tried to pull them backwards, to save them from drowning in the puddle of coffee. They were state documents, and they were in his charge!

Frantically, Shore knocked the huge pile to the floor. The papers would get mixed up, but they could be put back in order. Removing coffee stains would be impossible.

"Pull!" he yelled at Shaya. The befuddled Shaya tried to organize the papers in the pile.

"Leave it! Don't organize it now!" Shore dashed over and knocked down the second pile, too. He managed to save it all, except for one ill-fated paper at the bottom of the pile that a rivulet of coffee had managed to reach.

"Oh, good G-d," Shore breathed, "I bribed my way in here, and I think I'll leave totally cleaned out… Things are messing up, Bleich, and that's never good. Why'd you have to spill the coffee?"

Shaya felt very uncomfortable. "I'll pay for everything," he said immediately. "Whatever it costs. But first of all, let's check it out. Maybe the paper can be saved."

Shore gingerly lifted the wet page from the table and turned it over.

"Saved? Even a computer keyboard gets ruined if you spill coffee on it. All the more so, a paper from the archives!"

Shaya nervously tried to restore order to the pile of papers. It had been a bad idea to bring a cup of coffee into the room where they were looking through state documents.

"I believe we'll come out of this okay," he said. He turned his head. Why wasn't Shore reacting?

Shore stood there, the wet, stained paper in his hands.

"How did you put it? Not to despair from His mercy?" he said in an unnatural voice, the page trembling uncontrollably in his hand.

"Look at this document, even though it's wet," he said to Shaya. Shaya looked at the picture.

"It's not Naftali, if that's what you mean."

"But it says here," Shore said, "black on coffee, David Stone…"

• • •

Shloime stood next to Chana as she placed the overturned pages into the fax machine and dialed.

"Yes, Mrs. Bleich," R' Nachman said, "R' Shaya isn't here, but he's supposed to eventually return here. We're in constant contact."

R' Nachman's machine spat out page after page.

"What am I supposed to do with these papers?" R' Nachman asked.

"Pass them along to my husband as quickly as possible," Chana replied.

"Okay, I'll send them by fax to the hotel where he's staying."

The hotel receptionist informed R' Nachman that Mr. Bleich wasn't in his room.

"Can I send him a fax?"

"Certainly. Just note at the top of the fax the name of the person you're sending it to."

As R' Nachman stood by the fax machine, though, about to feed in the papers, one of his guests, who had overheard the conversation, peeked over his shoulder.

"Are these important documents?" he asked.

"I don't know; I believe so," R' Nachman answered.

"Don't ever send important documents to a public fax machine," the guest warned him. "You don't know where they'll end up, and who will use them."

"I'll write at the top of the paper who it's for. I believe that the hotel is a responsible establishment and will give them over directly to the right person. Besides which, what would the receptionists want with this fax?"

"There's never any way of knowing. There might be someone who wants to get his hands on them?"

R' Nachman turned to his guest. "Don't be so suspicious. These things happen only in thriller novels."

Within a few minutes, the fax was on the reception desk in the Connor Hotel in Paris. The receptionist received the fax, wrote Shaya Bleich's room number on it and put it on the side. Soon the service man would bring it up to the desired room.

# CHAPTER 32

In room number 354 in the Connor Hotel in Paris, sat someone who definitely did not look Jewish, yet he listened closely to the words in Yiddish that were whispered into the small telephone in his ear.

"Now?" he asked.

"Right this second," came the answer.

He went down to the reception desk, armed with exact instructions. Pretending to be very interested in the huge oil painting hanging last in a long line of oil paintings, he waited for the right moment.

When one receptionist stood up and turned around, and the other was very busy with a phone call, he sauntered over to the counter and casually slid the sheaf of papers lying there into his hands.

Then he was gone. The elevator swallowed him up and climbed to the top floor, the papers stuffed into the inside pocket of his jacket.

The receptionist ended her phone call and stared at the counter with a troubled look. She was almost positive that a few minutes earlier something had been there, and wasn't now. But what was it…?

...

"Why do you think this is my brother?" Bleich asked Shore.

"Why do you think it isn't? Isn't this the name we've been looking for for so long?"

"Yes," Shaya said. He looked at the picture. He looked and looked, as though if he'd inspect it carefully enough, the stranger in the picture would suddenly smile Naftali's smile. "But he doesn't look anything like my brother."

"And this picture isn't familiar to you from anywhere?"

Shaya wished he could answer yes, but the face in the small, square picture was so foreign, so unfamiliar.

"Look at this," Shore said, and pulled something out of his briefcase. He laid two documents side by side – the coffee stained paper and taxi driver David Stone's employee photo ID.

The cap worn by the cab driver was switched for a beret, and on the shaved chin of the American driver was a small French beard, but you couldn't mistake it.

"That's him," Shaya said, and moved his gaze back and forth from the pictures to Shore. "That's him, all right."

"So I was right," Shore said and sat down on a chair. He was filled with satisfaction, a satisfaction that kept him going for long weeks of empty investigation and injected fresh blood into his veins for the next part of the journey.

"Now we'll finally know where he went next," Shaya exclaimed in relief to Shore, who was studying the document gravely. "I hope that what's written didn't get blurred."

"Yes," Shore said, holding the stained paper very close to his eyes.

"It got blurred?" Shaya panicked. To come so close to their goal, and miss it because of a cup of coffee?

"No, it didn't," Shore said. His voice as if rose from the bowels of the earth.

"We have a long trip ahead of us, my friend," he finally said. "Take a backpack, stick and lots of water. We're on our way to Australia…"

• • •

"I have the material," the man whispered into the receiver.

"Excellent. Copy it. Send me the copy by registered mail and find a way to return the original to its owner. Nobody saw you?"

"Not a soul."

"Okay."

Just before they hung up, the man on the other end asked:

"Did you meet him?"

"No. I've looked into him. He's on the move the entire day. He doesn't come to meals, either."

"Of course not. The hotel isn't kosher. I want you to follow every move of his. For now."

The call was disconnected.

Meanwhile, in the hotel lobby, a small commotion was taking place.

A man from the U.S. – Nachman was his name – called to verify that his fax had arrived.

"Of course, sir," said the receptionist. She glanced at the place where she had put the papers.

They weren't there.

"O… of course, sir," she repeated. The pages had been there.

She was prepared to sign to that in triplicate. She would find them right away. They must have fallen behind the counter, or maybe the service man had taken them by mistake, but they would be found right away.

"Is there a problem?" asked the man on the other end.

"N-n-no," the receptionist said. "Just please hold the line for a few minutes."

R' Nachman didn't understand why he had to wait on the line if there weren't any problems. The receptionist left him to the strains of a full philharmonic band so he shouldn't hear the exchange of words in the background.

"I put here a stapled bunch of papers. Right here on the counter. I'm sure of it, as sure as I am that I work in this place. Actually, maybe not anymore…"

The receptionist scurried frantically from place to place, checking behind and under the computer, behind the fax, under the counter, in the drawers, on the bulletin board. Everywhere. She even peeked into the pockets in her clothing, but the stapled pages weren't anywhere.

"What do I tell this man…?"

Meanwhile, R' Nachman listened to two pieces of the philharmonic band. The third was about to finish, and he was getting impatient.

Additional staff was summoned to help, and a joint effort was made to find the lost papers. The head clerk arrived, and after him also the hotel manager. The receptionist had long since stopped searching, sitting instead on one of the armchairs together with another employee, who tried, unsuccessfully, to calm her with a cold drink.

"First of all," said the hotel manager, his hand on the receiver, "we don't leave our callers hanging. Service is of utmost importance. Hello, sir!"

"Yes!" R' Nachman cried and breathed a sigh of relief. He was already convinced that they were purposely letting him wait. "I'm on hold for a long time already and I don't understand why---"

"Yes, sir," the manager explained, "There's been a hitch with the fax that you've sent."

"A hitch?" R' Nachman wondered. What hitch? The fax was blurry? Cut off? Unclear? He had no problem sending it again if need be. If he understood correctly, this material was very important.

"Yes," the manager cleared his throat. "The fax that you sent arrived, but somehow it disappeared."

"Disappeared???"

"Don't panic, sir. We're looking for it and I believe we'll find it soon."

R' Nachman was beside himself. Those documents weren't his. They belonged to the Bleichs, and he was just a messenger who perhaps hadn't done his job properly.

"I'm trying to understand," R' Nachman said. "My fax arrived?"

"It arrived," the hotel manager said with much embarrassment, "but somehow, it disappeared. Maybe one of the service men took it. I'm positive it will be found quickly."

R' Nachman, though, heard the commotion in the background and wasn't so sure.

"Sir, this is a crime," he said. His guest's warning not to send important documents to a public fax machine rang ominously in his ears.

"I wouldn't call it that," the hotel manager tried to downplay the matter. "You can always send it again. We live in a very sophisticated world."

"Yes," R' Nachman said, "and also a very clever one. Who's to guarantee that hostile forces haven't laid hands on those papers? The hotel administration is responsible for them from the minute they arrived at the hotel."

"I suggest we wait a while more," the manager proposed. "These things sometimes happen, especially in a large hotel like ours. Our service men are very responsible. The room number where the fax was meant to go was written on your papers, sir. I believe they'll find their way to the right address within a short time."

"Enough pretty talk, my good man," R' Nachman said, impatient with the smooth talk. "I'll give it ten minutes. I'll wait on the line. If the fax isn't found by then, I think you'll have a problem on your hands."

"I suggest we wait at least until tomorrow, sir," the hotel manager said.

"I'm sorry, that's not acceptable," R' Nachman said. The French-accented English grated on his ears.

Just then, Danny Shore and Shaya Bleich entered the hotel lobby. They were very tired, very satisfied, and mainly wanted to sleep.

"I get a feeling something's happening here," Shore said. He pointed at the reception desk, where, though they were definitely trying to appear as if all was business as usual, a number of employees were scurrying about nonstop, seemingly searching for something.

"They must have dropped a coin," Shaya commented wryly, "and each one is afraid it will be docked from his salary. Am I free, or do you want to sit down and take stock again?" As he spoke, he approached the counter in order to get his key.

"What number?" one of the receptionists asked him.

Shaya gave his room number. Instead of the key, though, he was treated to very odd looks.

"Can I help you?" he asked and looked around, "and can I get my key?"

But he didn't receive any key.

"Were you here the entire time?" one of the receptionists asked him.

"No, I've been out all morning and just arrived now. Can I have my key so I can put my head down…?"

Shore stood next to him, his sharp senses tingling.

"My key, please?" Shaya asked again. "Why is everyone looking at me like that…?"

The staff was quiet. Each one was hoping his co-worker would relate the story of the fax. Finally, the head clerk told Shaya what had happened. Everyone waited tensely for his reaction.

"A fax? For me? I'm not aware that I'm supposed to receive a fax. Maybe it's from---"

A sudden pain on his foot made Shaya stop suddenly. Shore dug the heel of his shoe hard into Shaya's foot, warning to him to be quiet immediately. Until they knew exactly what was going on, they had to be careful and not just blurt out information.

"Maybe it's from someone I don't know," Shaya vaguely finished his sentence. "Thanks anyway." He took the key from the counter. "If anything new happens with it, I'd be happy to know."

Shore was already by the elevators, motioning to Shaya to join him. Shaya dragged his feet. He had had a long, difficult day. Sleep – that's what he needed now, not any adventure stories.

Shore, though, as usual, looked as if he had just woken up from a refreshing afternoon nap. "Notice the man standing there, next to the armchair," he muttered to Shaya from the side of his mouth.

"Right now I only want to notice my dreams, Mr. Investigator."

"Turn around, please, but very carefully," Shore ordered, "and not now, but soon. The man standing there, with the blue cap, was sent by somebody in order to follow you. I'm sure of it. I've been dealing with investigations long enough…"

• • •

The next day, early in the morning, Elya Fuchsman's car pulled up next to 12 Bar Yochai Street in Tzefas. Two worried parents emerged and were swallowed up into the house.

A short while later, they left the house together with Suri. They disappeared into the car and began to drive.

"I thought about it, Abba, Ima," Suri finally broke the uneasy silence. She gripped the seat in front of her tightly. What she was about to say was very far from easy. "And I'm weighing whether or not to have the *chasunah*."

At the last minute, Elya managed to wrench the car over to the shoulder of the highway, rather than braking in middle of the road and causing a chain accident.

"Suri!!"

"Yes, Abba. So many unpleasant things are happening to us. Maybe they're messages from *shamayim*? They can't be ignored. Maybe because I *davened* so hard, *Hashem* sent me a messenger to warn me against having the *chasunah*?!"

"I have no doubt that you *davened* well, Suri," Elya said after recovering somewhat, "and you're a big *tzaddekes*. Even so, messengers don't just show up from *Hashem*. In the best scenario, the woman was an oddball, and in the worst case, she was sent by someone. You don't cancel a wedding for such nonsense – I hope that's clear to you."

"Not cancel," Suri said. The word scared her, too. "Just to push it off until things become clearer."

"We're not pushing it off," Elya said. "We don't act rashly.

Your *chasunah* will take place soon, *be'ezras Hashem*. Today I arranged for someone to paint the new apartment."

"Just the opposite, Suri," Devorah said. "All these things show that you're on the right path. The *satan* tries with all his might to disturb specifically the holiest things. You have to be strong, Suri, and know that you're doing the best, most proper thing."

About two hundred and fifty kilometers away, someone sat and listened to every word of this conversation. Not only in the Fuchsman house was a bug planted, but also in their car, just to be on the safe side. He sat and listened with great interest, even with bated breath. After all was said and done, it seemed like his small scare tactic had been quite successful.

"No one has the right to control your and our lives," Elya said forcefully. "We are directed by *Shamayim*, not by people, and we do what appears to us to be right. Shloime Bleich is an excellent *bochur*, his family is also excellent, and everything that you call "strange things" is just a bunch of coincidents. Devorah, I'd like to speak about something else," he said firmly and started the car again.

For now, they were quiet. The eavesdropping Lederman waited tensely. Maybe soon they would continue their conversation. Meanwhile, the car glided down the roads of northern Israel.

・・・

"I don't know that man," Shaya said after turning back around.

"Of course you don't," Shore chuckled. "If you did, whoever sent him wouldn't have sent him. Be aware of him and stay away. It's possible that he'll try to eavesdrop on you."

"I'm keeping away from him at once," Shaya said and pushed the elevator button, "and going to sleep."

His footsteps were swallowed up by the thick carpet in the

half-darkened corridor. Finally, he opened the door to his room, went inside and locked it from the inside. For added measure, he looked around to make sure no one was lying in wait for him. *What's happening to you, Shaya Bleich? You're becoming paranoid...?*

Lazily, Shaya bent down to untie his shoes. A difficult day lay behind him, but the knowledge that he had to call that number, the one the donor had left, and leave a detailed message, weighed on him. He'd do it soon. He had promised. What would he say? He'd briefly say that they discovered the trail of his brother leading from France to Australia, and they were on their way there. Australia! Who would have believed? He'd better pack his things as soon as possible. If he knew Shore, early the next morning he'd be knocking on the door with an order: We're traveling!

He started at the sound of knocking.

It was wild to think it was Shore. He was also human and needed to sleep a few hours.

The knocking continued.

"Who's there?!" Shaya called without getting up.

"Personnel," came the muffled reply.

Wearing only one shoe, Shaya opened the door. A uniformed service man took a step inside, holding the door open with his hand. "Here are the papers that were sent for you, sir." He held out a stapled sheaf of papers.

"Oh, very good! They found them?"

The service man nodded his head.

"Thank you very much," Shaya said. The man left, and Shaya closed and locked the door behind him. The contents of the fax interested him very much. He turned on the night light and unfolded the papers.

A second before he began to read, the face of the service man flitted through his mind again and he immediately knew: it was the same man with the blue cap who had followed him that evening in the hotel lobby. He wasn't a service man, and never had been.

Two minutes later, in room 354 in the same hotel, a telephone call was made.

"All taken care of," the man said briefly.

"You photocopied the material and gave him back the original?"

"Correct."

"Was he suspicious?"

"No." Lederman knew he could trust that "no".

"You managed to attach the listening device to the door of his room?"

"Yes. Close to the handle."

"Can it be activated now?"

"It can."

Lederman rubbed his hands together in satisfaction. His man in the Connor Hotel did good work. He cost a lot, but was worth every penny. Soon he would be able to hear every word that would be said in Shaya Bleich's hotel room. Praised be the sophisticated advancement of technology.

Without further delay, he connected to the wiretap. Shaya Bleich's room, though, was quiet. That was understandable. *What did you think, Mendel Lederman, the man talks to himself?*

But suddenly a voice *was* heard. It seemed like Bleich had called someone on the telephone. Lederman tensed.

"Hello," he heard Bleich's voice, "This is Yeshaya Bleich speaking. As per our agreement, I'm passing on what happened with the investigation. And so, today we visited…"

Word by word, Shaya Bleich passed along the findings of his investigation straight into somebody's ear. Lederman hastened to check that the conversation was taped. This information was supremely important!

"…Good night and thank you very much," Shaya ended the call and hung up. Lederman could clearly hear his sigh of relief, and understood that this conversation – wait, it actually wasn't a conversation, he had left a message! – was not to his liking.

Again it was quiet, and Lederman remained sunk in thought. To whom was Shaya Bleich passing along the details of the investigation? And why was he doing it? And what did that mean 'as per our agreement'? Had he made up with someone to pass along the details? What could be the reason for such a report? Shaya Bleich was no fool. He didn't just do things for no reason.

He sat for some time without moving, only his thoughts racing. A new noise suddenly roused him – his line to Shaya Bleich came to life.

"Now let's see what they sent me here…" Bleich murmured. The rustling of papers was heard. "Who sent this, anyway?" he asked himself. Lederman waited. Would Bleich also answer himself?

"Whose number is this? Oh, it says here… R' Nachman? Why is R' Nachman sending me a fax…?"

R' Nachman. Lederman filed the name in his brain.

"Oh, here, there's an explanation…"

Shaya didn't read the explanation out loud. Again it was quiet, but not for long.

"He went to a psychologist… Shloime! Without asking us… without asking our advice… who knows what the psychologist put into his head…" It sounded like Shaya was pacing up and down the room, distraught. "I promised his father to watch over him well. Soon I'm going to meet his father and what will he tell me? 'Shaya, you didn't watch him enough'…?"

# CHAPTER 33

In the morning, his *tallis* bag stashed under his arm, Shaya returned to the hotel. He found Shore impatiently pacing back and forth in front of his room.

"Where were you?" he asked as Shaya rummaged in his pocket and pulled out the key.

"I went to morning services. There's no synagogue in this hotel, as you know. Something happened?"

Shore waited until the door opened and closed behind them, and then said:

"I almost didn't close my eyes the entire night."

"You???" Shaya was astonished. "Why???"

"I wasn't calm. The man with the blue cap wouldn't leave my mind."

A spark of admiration appeared in Shaya's eyes. This must be what made Shore into a first class investigator as opposed to a regular one. His intuitions were usually very well grounded.

His head hanging a bit and in a quiet voice, he told Shore

about the "service man's" visit the day before. Shore jumped up as if bitten.

"He was here??"

"I'm almost positive. True, he was wearing the hotel uniform, but it was his face. Long, with a brown mark over his left eye. I could see it even in the dark."

Shore couldn't believe his ears. "I didn't think he'd be so quick," he breathed and sank into thought. But not for too long.

"Stay here, please," he said, "and don't make any phone calls. I'll be right back."

A bit surprised, Shaya looked at the door that slammed shut after Shore. What was he planning?

When Shore came back to the room, his face was even paler than before. He said not a word, only motioned to Shaya to leave the room, close the door and speak with him outside.

"All right," he released a long breath. "This time we lost."

"Lost?? What did we lose??"

"He's one step ahead of us, that fellow with the blue cap, whoever he is. I went down to the desk and presented myself as a guest who was curious to know what happened in the end with the fax that got lost yesterday. The secretary sighed and said that unfortunately, they still haven't found it."

"So I was right," Shaya said with tight lips. "He wasn't personnel. He was just---"

"Listen to me," Shore interrupted him. "He wasn't 'just' anything. And that's why I took you out here to talk. In my opinion, he was the man who got his hands on the fax that you were supposed to receive. He took it – it's not important now how – kept a copy for himself and returned the other one to you. But not out of good heartedness," he continued, ignoring Shaya's mouth that was opening and closing soundlessly, "but because he had something to take care of in your room. And now we're going

*Thicker Than Water* « 407

to look for what. You can come with me on condition that you keep absolutely silent."

Shaya, still stunned, followed instructions. Shore opened the door to the room and began to search for something – on the door itself. His deft fingers felt the handle, above it, around it and below it. Not two minutes passed before he gripped some kind of small button, the color of the door, and ripped it from its place.

"What are you doing?? You're ruining the door!!" Shaya cried.

Shore motioned to him severely to be quiet. He opened the small button, revealing a mesh of very thin wires. He detached two of them and breathed a sigh of relief.

"I'm not ruining the door," he told Shaya calmly, "I'm ruining somebody's plans – quite a clever somebody, as you see – of listening to every word that is said in this room."

Shaya was thunderstruck.

"That was a bug??!"

"Yes, and I stress the word 'was'. It isn't anymore."

"And the man who came here yesterday stuck it to my door while speaking to me?!"

"So I assume. And I hope that by now you've learned how much my assumptions are worth."

Yes, Shaya had learned. He was a good student, and his teacher was excellent.

"So we have to catch him!" Shaya exclaimed agitatedly. "He must still be here in the hotel!"

Shore shook his head. "I don't think so…"

• • •

Devorah Fuchsman stood by the stove frying pancakes. She desperately wanted to give the house the atmosphere of business as usual, but it was so hard. Almost impossible.

Her Suri, her dear Suri, who should have been – so close to the date of her wedding – a glowing, happy *kallah*, was walking around the house with a frozen face. Devorah missed the days when she would close herself up in her room and cry. Now she wasn't crying anymore. She walked back and forth, her eyes expressionless, putting books back on the bookshelf, taking them off, removing a cup from the cabinet and washing it. Devorah seriously considered professional help for her, but immediately dismissed the idea. Professionals weren't what her Suri needed now, but a happy wedding, on time, to dispel all her doubts and fears.

The children, though they didn't say a word, felt the loaded atmosphere in the house. They approached their parents minimally, barely fought and steered clear of Suri.

Elya came into the kitchen. "Do you know where Yisroel Yitzchok is?" he asked hoarsely.

"In yeshiva," Devorah replied, and felt some warmth steal into her heart. *HaKadosh Boruch Hu* was striking them with one hand and comforting them with the other. Suri's situation was painful and the fate of the *chasunah* was hanging, but on the other hand, Yisroel Yitzchok was showing signs of improvement and was found more and more in yeshiva.

"All right," Elya said wearily, "so when he comes home, please tell him to come to my study. And if I'm resting there, he should wake me."

An hour later, Yisroel Yitzchok quietly opened the door to the study. His father was resting on the couch.

"You wanted me, Abba?"

"Yes." Elya sat up. "A while ago I gave you a listening device. Do you remember it?"

"Definitely." Yisroel Yitzchok said. "It's in my drawer. I didn't do anything with it, because I haven't received any instructions from you."

"Very good," Ely said. He turned on the main light in the room and told Yisroel Yitzchok to sit. Without going into too much detail, he described to Yisroel Yitzchok what Suri had gone through on her trip to the *kevarim*. Yisroel Yitzchok was horrified.

"So that's why she's walking around the house like... like..." he couldn't find a good description.

"Right. It was a very difficult experience for her. But I think there are reasonable grounds to assume that this whole thing was initiated by that fellow, Mendel Lederman. If that's true, then that's taking things to a whole new level. We have to clarify the matter, and we will do that with your help, Yisroel Yitzchok."

A chill ran up the boy's spine.

"I want you to approach him, as if on your own, and say to him that you understand that he has an important goal and you wish to work with him."

"That's what I should say to him?!" Yisroel Yitzchok was again horrified.

"Exactly that. I want him to feel that you're completely on his side."

"He won't believe me."

"That depends on you. If you can convince him that you're interested in helping him, he'll be thrilled, and so will I, because through you I'll be able to get information about him that I'd have no other way of getting."

• • •

"Why shouldn't this man stay in the hotel?" Shaya wondered.

"Why should he run away?"

"It's hard for me to give a definitive answer," Shore said. "I can check it out. But you can't come with me. You'll have to stay here. You attract too much attention by those working at the desk, both because of yesterday's fax and because of your distinctive dress. Wait for me, do something else in the meantime; I'll try to return quickly."

Do something else? Shaya knew that was doomed for failure. He couldn't relax until Shore returned. He could only say *tehillim*. Everything was becoming so complicated.

Meanwhile, Shore went down to the lobby. Not wanting the desk staff to become too familiar with his face, he waited until one clerk stood up to take care of something in the administrative offices.

"Excuse me," he matched his pace to that of the clerk, "I need some help. I lent two hundred dollars to one of the guests here yesterday. He promised to return it this morning, but I don't see him anywhere."

"What's his name?"

"I don't know," Shore spread his hands. "I think he said his name, but I didn't catch it. He wore a blue cap."

"A blue cap isn't much to go on."

Shore spread his hands again. He had no other sign. "You understand… he needed the money urgently. I pitied him. He said that first thing in the morning he'd wait for me with the money at the entrance to the dining room."

The clerk glanced in the direction of the large dining room doors. No one stood there waiting.

"Which room was he in?"

"I don't know," Shore spread his hands once more. "I didn't ask him. I trusted him."

"In the future, don't lend money to anyone without having

some information about him, no matter how pitiful he seems. Why don't you wait until the afternoon? It's possible that he just went out to get the money."

"I can't wait even one minute," Shore had a ready answer. "I must go take care of some urgent matters in another half an hour, and I need every dollar I have."

The clerk couldn't help Shore with so few details, but he had a different idea:

"A blue cap? Maybe one of the receptionists noticed it when he gave in his key, if he indeed left."

Shore waved his hand dismissively. "He could have left without the cap."

"Then I'm really sorry," the clerk said. "I don't think I can help you."

Shore didn't like hearing such statements. He looked at the man meaningfully and withdrew his card from his jacket pocket: "Danny Shore, private investigator".

The clerk's gaze swung like a pendulum from Shore's face to the card that he held in his hand.

"What... what does this mean?"

"This means that there's a need for professional involvement here. I'm following this man as part of an investigation, and I have reason to assume that he has a criminal background. It won't be pleasant for the hotel to become mixed up in this affair, so it's best that you give me any information that you have about the man."

Shore returned the card to his pocket after it made the desired impression.

"I sincerely would like to help you, sir," the clerk said with great deference, "but we don't have any information! If we'd have more details, we'd do everything in our power to find the man who... who owes you two hundred dollars, you said?"

Shore bit back a smile. It wasn't two hundred dollars that the man owed him, but he'd owe him a lot if he continued to stick around and attempt to disrupt his investigation.

"You have information," he said. "Above the main entrance to the hotel is a camera. I saw it. Whoever goes through the door is photographed. If I could see the pictures from this morning, I'll be able to identify him."

"See the pictures from the camera? That's not something that we usually do."

"This instance is not usual," Shore said, and casually moved his hand back towards the pocket which held his card.

"I suggest that you speak to the manager," the clerk said, quite anxious to remove the matter from his responsibility.

• • •

Yisroel Yitzchok Fuchsman had never felt so afraid. He stood before the door to Mendel Lederman's office, five minutes before the appointed time, his entire body quivering.

Mendel Lederman wouldn't take an axe to him. He wouldn't even be cross. He would probably be very pleasant, actually dripping with honey. Yisroel Yitzchok wasn't afraid of him, but of himself.

Would he manage to pretend properly? Lederman was a master of discovery. It was very hard to hide something from him. He could easily expose that Yisroel Yitzchok was sent by his father, and that he definitely had no wish to help Lederman with his odd mission, but rather to help the Fuchsman family be wary of it.

"You can go in," Lederman's secretary said.

Yisroel Yitzchok prayed silently nonstop. The tiny listening device that his father had given him was attached to the inside of his clothing, hidden well.

"Hello, Fuchsman," Lederman said with a friendly smile and shook his hand across the wide desk. "I'm so pleased to meet you again. What brings you to me?"

Yisroel Yitzchok took a deep breath.

"It... it has to do with what you asked me to do then. To work with you---"

Yisroel Yitzchok trembled. He hoped – uselessly, of course – that Lederman didn't notice. Lederman studied him. It was obvious that the young boy was filled with fear of the step he was about to take.

"Now you come to me?" he asked with disapproval. "You needed a lot of time to think, or to decide and then regret it?"

"Call it what you want," Yisroel Yitzchok said, and tried unsuccessfully to steady his voice. "I decided that this is what needs to be done. If you say that this wedding needs to be cancelled, you must know what you're talking about."

Lederman didn't smile. He didn't look pleased.

"You suddenly have so much faith in me," he said, not bothering to hide the skepticism in his voice. "What happened?"

"I don't know," Yisroel Yitzchok said. "At home, there's no night or day... My sister went to *daven* at the graves of *tzaddikim* and met some fortune teller who told her to cancel the *chasunah*... My parents told her it's nonsense, but she's very worried. The whole family is worried because of her. She's afraid to get married. I'm also afraid for her to get married. If this is what's happening before the wedding, who knows what will happen afterwards... So I came to you. Maybe with your ideas and methods we'll be able to cause the wedding to be cancelled."

Lederman gave him an appraising look. Piercing and penetrating.

"What else is happening in your house? And what's happening in the house of your *mechutanim?*"

"At home it's like I described to you… On the one hand, we're waiting for the *chasunah*, and on the other hand, we're afraid of it… My sister sewed so many dresses when she was still happy; now all the clothing is closed up in the closet… I don't know what's happening by the *mechutanim*. I just know that their father isn't in the country."

"Yes, that I also know," Lederman said absentmindedly. He lit a cigarette, and then crushed it into the full ashtray sitting on the desk. He had to think this through deeply. It made absolutely no difference to him that Yisroel Yitzchok was sitting opposite him, waiting to hear what he had to say. When he was sunk in thought, the entire world ceased to exist for him.

"And who will guarantee me," he suddenly asked sharply, "that your father hasn't sent you to keep track of my doings?!"

"My father?" Yisroel Yitzchok gave a short laugh. "My father isn't tracking anything now, Mr. Investigator… He barely gets out to *daven* three times a day. You have to see his study. It's one big heap of papers and mess that hasn't been touched in weeks. And besides, even if my father did want to set up some surveillance, you can imagine that he wouldn't exactly send me…"

It was all true, Yisroel Yitzchok knew. And still. The listening device sat nicely under his clothing. He was curious what other questions Lederman would ask him.

"Yisroel Yitzchok Fuchsman," Lederman said, "are you prepared to do difficult things for the sake of your sister?"

"Yes," Yisroel Yitzchok answered bravely.

"Would you be able to cause her pain?"

Yisroel Yitzchok coughed. He had to answer immediately. "It depends how much, and if I'll be convinced that there's no other way."

"You don't have to be convinced," Lederman said sharply.

"You have to believe me. I have no way of convincing you. You have to decide if what I'll demand from you works for you or not."

• • •

Shaya Bleich chewed his nails for a long time before the door to the room finally opened and Shore stood in the doorway.

"You're invited," he said.

"Invited where?"

"For a short walk."

Shaya didn't know what other surprises Shore had in store for him, but he went along with him. Together, they went down to the ground floor and circled the hotel garden. When they stood behind the huge hotel building, Shore suddenly stopped.

"Look," he said.

"Look? At what?" Shaya didn't understand. Was this a game?

"At the grass," Shore said calmly. "Pay attention. Do you see the trampled grass over here? The entire field of grass is fresh and upright. And only here – under this window – is a circle of crushed grass. What do you think could be the reason for that?"

Shaya tilted his head backwards and looked up. There was a tall row of windows, up to the tenth floor.

"Fine," Shore said with a sigh, "the story's like this: I managed to uncover the identity of the man in the blue cap. That is to say, it makes sense to assume that it's not his actual identity, but some identity under which he registered at the hotel desk. He stayed in this room," Shore pointed up at one of the windows. "We tried calling his room from the desk. There was no answer. At the desk, they claimed that he didn't check out of the hotel. And the fact is the key is not there.

"I was stubborn. 'This man is not a guest at the hotel anymore,' I told them. 'He left with the key, without his suitcase, as if for a short walk. He paid for a week in advance so he could leave the minute he needed to, without leaving any tracks. If you don't believe me,' I told the hotel staff, 'go up to his room now and see that it's completely empty.'

"At first they didn't believe me, but the fear that perhaps their hotel was mixed up with a criminal act finally convinced them. We went up to the room. We banged on the door, but there was no answer. 'He left and will come back later,' one worker insisted. I stood my ground and asked that they bring the spare key.

"We opened the door and, as you can guess---"

"It was completely empty," Shaya said.

"Exactly. There wasn't a thing there. I did all the requisite tests and came to the conclusion that he left this morning. I brought the men over to the window and showed them this circle of trampled grass. I told them that this was where the dear gentleman had thrown his suitcase down, after which he donned his blue cap and gracefully waltzed out of the hotel, collecting his suitcase on the way."

"Why did he do that?" Shaya asked.

"In my opinion, it was a smart move. He didn't know what we know about him, if anything. He did know that it wouldn't do for us to know that he left the hotel. Assuming that we did, perhaps, suspect him, and even knew his identity, we would continue to wait for him to come back to the hotel, not imagining that he was already far, far away. He had a reason to be here – you were that reason. He wanted that somebody should be able to listen to what's going on in your room. That somebody isn't him; it's someone else. I get the impression that he was hired by this someone else and, after completing his mission, simply left. Now, Shaya Bleich, you can try to chase after the wind, if you wish."

"He was sent by somebody," Shaya said pensively.

"Have you any idea whom?"

"I have a few guesses. The first being the man who's constantly trying to wreck the wedding. The private investigator who worked with us in the past, the one I told you about."

"And he reaches all the way to here?" Shore was amazed.

"He's capable of anything…"

Danny Shore and Shaya Bleich walked slowly back to the front of the hotel. Shore's hands were clasped behind his back. He was so deep in thought that Shaya didn't dare disturb him.

"You know what," Shore said, "I think, I have a feeling, that this investigator is making a big mistake."

"Mistake??"

"Yes, mistake," Shore said with complete confidence. "He's working against us, instead of working with us. Today still, you'll find me his telephone number, Bleich. I must speak to him…!"

# CHAPTER 34

"Forgive me for stating my unsolicited opinion," Shaya said, "but I think that contacting Lederman now is a terrible idea."

"Why is that?"

"Because he'll have us going backwards. He doesn't want us to succeed. Look – he managed to find out where we are and send someone to bug my room. He's doing everything in his power to prevent me from finding my brother. How exactly will he help us?"

"Allow me to share a bit of my professional knowledge," Shore said calmly, and paced back and forth on the grass. "A fundamental rule in investigations is – get as much information as possible. It doesn't matter from where, doesn't matter how much, and you could even compromise on the degree of reliability. If this man of yours – what did you say his name is?"

"Lederman, Mendel Lederman."

"And so, if this Lederman is trying to prevent the discovery, it stands to reason that he has information which we don't. Therefore it's important for me to speak to him in order to get this information from him. Simple, no? And if you think that this man can send me backwards, you must not know Danny Shore well enough."

• • •

"Explain to me what you mean," Yisroel Yitzchok suggested, allowing himself to lean back on the chair after the conversation got on the right track. "What do you want me to do to my sister?"

Lederman thought for a minute. "Your father is a bit stubborn," he said. "It's hard to make him do something if he's not one hundred percent sure of it. I want to take advantage of the fact that the *mechutan* is abroad, and the family here is a bit fragile without him. I want to cause them to not want this wedding…"

"And why shouldn't they want it?"

Lederman's eyebrows drew together. "If they would know that this *kallah* isn't suitable for them, for whatever reason, they would pull out of the *shidduch*."

"But she is suitable," Yisroel Yitzchok said, seemingly not understanding.

"Now she's suitable," Lederman explained to him as if to a small child, "but after I make some changes in what they know about her, she already won't be suitable."

Yisroel Yitzchok understood very clearly what he was saying. It was important, though, that he get from Lederman an explicit explanation which would be recorded by his device.

"You mean to give false information?"

"Exactly. I'm surprised at you, Fuchsman. I thought that you're an intelligent boy. Why do you have so many questions?!"

That was all he needed, to make the anyway wary Lederman

suspicious. "I just need to understand how your mind works. This is new for me."

"Well, get used to it quick," Lederman said.

"So what information can you make up about her?"

"There's no lack of possibilities. Look, I really don't want to ruin your sister's good name, so I'm thinking of going with something that will bother only the Bleichs, and not every family. Something that will make them cancel the *shidduch* without thinking twice."

Yisroel Yitzchok thought a bit. "I don't think there's anything that will bother specifically the Bleichs. You know, basic things like *yiras shomayim*, *tzniyus*, the right aspirations – things like that would bother them, as well as any Jewish family."

"Yes, I know," Lederman said wearily, "and yet, I truly don't want to harm your sister. Therefore, you, Fuchsman, have to do a bit of legwork for me and come back to me with an answer – which specific information I can give over, information that will cause Bleich, and only Bleich, to say good-bye to this *shidduch*. That is your first mission…"

• • •

Only in the afternoon did Shaya Bleich have a chance to call his wife and tell her the incredible news from the previous day.

"We picked up Naftali's trail today," he said and gave her a few seconds to recover.

"Really???"

He moved the phone away from his ear.

"I'm running to call Shloime!!!"

"Hold on, Chana, wait a second," Shaya said. "I said that we hit upon the trail. We have a long way ahead of us until we actually find him."

"Where is he?!"

"We don't know. Tomorrow, or the next day, the investigator and I will fly to Australia to continue the investigation there."

"Just come back in time for the *chasunah*!" Chana exclaimed.

Shaya didn't react to that comment. If the long spokes that Lederman was constantly trying to stick in their wheels were anything to go by, the fate of the wedding wasn't so clear.

"It'll be okay, *be'ezras Hashem*. Continue to *daven*, Chana. How is everybody doing?"

"Hanging in there. Waiting for you."

"Keep strong. I hope there'll be good news soon."

When he hung up, Shore turned to him.

"Who's watching your family while you're here?"

Shaya motioned towards the sky.

"Heaven, of course," agreed Shore, "but people see that they're alone, and that's not always good."

"What do you mean?!"

"I don't mean anything. I'm just thinking logically. If this Lederman doesn't hesitate to send his long arm all the way here in order to attain his goals, your family is likely to be a potential victim, too. And when you're not there, they're actually quite easy prey…"

Shaya's heart skipped a beat. Shore was right! Someone had to be with his family!

Maybe they should stay with his parents? For how long, though? You couldn't move an entire family to a different city for an unknown length of time. What would be with school and *cheder*? And the preparations for the *chasunah*?

Maybe his parents should come and stay by them, in their house? Shaya gave it some thought and realized that it wasn't such a good idea. First of all, it wouldn't be easy for Chana to host them right now, when it was anyway hard for her. Besides which, he doubted if there was any point to it. His parents weren't young; they could offer their presence, but not more than that.

"Now you've made me worried," he admitted to Shore.

"I'm sorry," Shore said, "but I think that you need to give this some attention."

Shaya tried to find other possibilities. Someone had to protect Chana and the kids. No other relatives lived in their city, and he was uncomfortable asking friends.

"I'll try to watch over them from here," he told Shore. "I don't have much choice. If something happens, G-d forbid, I'll have to go back, and you'll continue the search without me."

"I hear," Shore replied. "In any event, I reserved tickets for us for tomorrow. I hope Lederman's long arm doesn't reach until Australia. By the way, you didn't give me his phone number."

"Right," Shaya said. "I don't think the idea of joining forces with him is a good one."

Shore didn't like that. "The decision of whether it's a good idea or not, you can leave to me. If you'd like this investigation to progress, we'd better be of the same mind."

"He's not a good person. There's a lot of anger in my family towards him."

"That's what you think. But that's your opinion, not fact. Anger in the family is also emotion, not objective information. If it's true, I'll pick up on it by myself. And even if it is true, I don't negate receiving information even from someone unfavorable."

"You don't understand," Shaya said impatiently. "Lederman won't hesitate to give false information. You can't trust him."

"I, Bleich," Shore answered patiently, "have already learned how to weed out false information. That, among other things, is what you pay me for."

"He's very clever," Bleich said.

"So am I," Shore replied calmly. Shaya couldn't argue with

*Thicker Than Water* « 423

that. "I'd like to speak to him as soon as possible."

• • •

Elya Fuchsman closed all the shutters and switched on the light. Yisroel Yitzchok turned on the tiny machine and Mendel Lederman's voice spilled into the room:

"I'm thinking of going with something that will bother only the Bleichs, and not every family. Something that will make them cancel the *shidduch* without thinking twice."

"Hmmm," Elya made some inarticulate noise.

The two of them listened intently to the conversation. Elya's face turned gray.

"So," he said at the end in a cracked voice, "we have here an explicit admission from him that he plans to spread false information about Suri and ruin the *shidduch*. Good for you, Yisroel Yitzchok, for forcing him to state this very clearly. Now we have to act, because if I know this Lederman, when he says something, it's as good as done."

"Act?! How?!"

"We have to speak to the Bleichs and explain to them that they're going to receive false information, and that they shouldn't pay any attention to it," Elya said. "We have to think how to do that. Maybe I myself will speak to Shaya Bleich, even though he's not in the country. And you, Yisroel Yitzchok, have to continue your mission."

"What does that mean?!" Yisroel Yitzchok opened his eyes wide.

"You have to continue to go along with Lederman. You have to think of a good idea for false information, offer it to Lederman and make sure he accepts it. This way, we'll know exactly which information the Bleichs are supposed to receive and we can prepare them for it."

"But I have no idea what kind of information. What could I make up?! Maybe that Suri had her appendix removed when she was little?!"

"No, no. That makes no difference. Maybe..." Elya tried to activate his wicked genes, which were basically non-existent, "maybe that she doesn't hear so well in one ear...?"

"Doesn't hear well in one ear...??"

Yisroel Yitzchok wasn't sure his own ears were working properly. To give over such information about Suri??

"Abba, such information will destroy Suri. No one will want to make a *shidduch* with her afterwards."

"It's better, though, than saying that there's something wrong with her *yiras shomayim*..."

The two of them were quiet.

"You have to understand, Yisroel Yitzchok," Elya said quietly, almost in a whisper, "Lederman will definitely pass along information. That's bad news for us, very bad, but we have the possibility of sweetening it a bit. We can offer him information that's only a little bad, and not rely on his creativity, which will bring Suri and us all to who knows where..."

"I can't give over such information about my sister," Yisroel Yitzchok declared. And Elya, through the cloud of pain, was encouraged by the steadiness in his son's eyes. *Hashem* both brings people down and raises them up. There was Suri and her suffering on one hand, and Yisroel Yitzchok on the other.

"I have an idea," Yisroel Yitzchok said, "an idea that even Lederman didn't think of. True, it's awful, but it's better than his idea. If bad information gets out about Suri, it will affect her whole life, but if, for example, she fell and broke her leg, the *chasunah* would get pushed off, her leg would eventually get better and no sign would remain."

"Good idea," Elya said, as much as the breaking of his precious daughter's leg could be called good, "but that would only push off the *chasunah*, not cancel it. Lederman wants to cancel it completely."

"Not for sure," Yisroel Yitzchok said. "I'll try to suggest it to him. Maybe, if the wedding got pushed off for a few weeks, it'll be enough to do whatever has to be done so that the wedding could, eventually, take place."

"I'm doubtful," Elya said.

"I'll try to talk to him," Yisroel Yitzchok said decidedly.

• • •

Shaya Bleich had a window seat on the airplane and was thankful for it. A bit of quiet wouldn't hurt him. Shore sat next to him with his laptop, reserving rooms for them in a hotel.

"After we land," Shore said without looking up, "we'll go to the airport administration and ask to see the documents of those who arrived on the date that we more or less have. We'll then rent a car and, based on the information we get, start the search.

"Isn't it better to first rest for a few hours?" Bleich yawned. "It's good to work with a clear head."

"Rest?!" Shore looked at him in surprise. "I thought that the date of your son's wedding is getting closer…?"

"Yes," Shaya said and let out such a deep sigh that the passenger next to them threw him a wondering look. "Who knows what will be with the wedding."

"When is it?"

"In about a month from today."

"That's nothing, a month."

"Right."

"We won't be done by then, unless your brother drops down on us from the sky."

"Well, maybe there'll still be some surprises."

The somber mood accompanied them even after they disembarked. Shaya finally managed to convince Shore to go first to the hotel, and push off the next part of the search for a few hours. He had a reason for that, too.

After they registered at the desk, Shore went to the dining room and Shaya, to his room. He wanted to rest – that's what he told Shore – and indeed that's what he would soon do.

"Hello," he recited into the receiver of his cell phone, "Shaya Bleich speaking. As per our agreement, I'm passing along the present findings of the investigation. The private investigator and I have arrived in Australia, to continue searching for my brother Naftali. Later today, we'll go to the airport administration. I'm taking this opportunity to remind you to deposit ten thousand---"

The door to his room swung open. Shore took a step inside.

"Who were you talking to, Bleich?" A hostile, menacing look replaced the courteous expression Shore usually wore.

The cell phone was still in Shaya's hand. All of Shore's energy was now directed at him. He knew how inadvisable and useless it was to lie to this man.

"I don't know," he said.

"Really." Shore's voice was full of derision. With a few large strides he went over and took the small machine from Shaya's hand.

"It's a shame. It's a real shame that you're breaching the trust between us," Shore said, and you could hear in his voice that he truly felt bad, "but I must do this. If you don't know to whom you spoke, I'll know. Very soon."

• • •

"This wedding can't be pushed off," Lederman dismissed out

of hand the possibility that Yisroel Yitzchok raised. "Delaying it can be harmful. It simply has to be cancelled. I thought of telling the Bleichs that your father went bankrupt."

"My father?!" Yisroel Yitzchok faltered for a minute, "I don't think that will help. The Bleich's want my sister, and my father's financial situation matters minimally to them."

"So maybe a terrible disease that your sister had when she was young?"

"And why would someone else want to marry her afterwards?"

"All right, Fuchsman," Lederman leaned back with a sigh, "I don't think that we can work together. You're very good at asking questions and not giving any answers. I charged you with finding a good idea, and I haven't yet heard even one from you."

"I have to think some more," Yisroel Yitzchok said. That was all he needed, for Lederman to cut off contact with him. Then Suri would be in far greater trouble.

"You don't have much time to think," Lederman said. "Your sister's wedding is in about another month, no?"

"Yes."

"It'll be harder to cancel at the last minute. We have to hurry up."

Outside, the sun shone brightly on Yisroel Yitzchok. He stretched his frozen bones. They had to come up with an idea. Had to, had to. And warn the Bleichs about it and explain that it was made up. Even if they warned Bleich, though, it wasn't certain that it would help. Seeing that they were at the end of their tether, Lederman was likely to spread a rumor about Suri in the street. Even if Bleich didn't believe it – they wouldn't allow themselves to do a *shidduch* with someone whom people were speaking about like that.

The thought sent a shiver down Yisroel Yitzchok's back. He had to talk to his father. They had to find a solution quickly.

They had to!

He crossed the street. A tall, blond *bochur* crossed directly opposite him. Yisroel Yitzchok stared at him. The *bochur* passed by without knowing which fantastic idea he had planted in Yisroel Yitzchok's brain.

He would speak to Shloime Bleich.

• • •

The door slammed shut behind Shore. Shaya sank onto a chair, helpless.

He had hidden from Shore the fact that an anonymous donor was behind the generous payments. He hadn't had the courage to tell him. He was afraid of Shore's reaction. He was afraid he'd be angry that someone else was a partner in his private investigation. Over time, trust had been built between him and Shore, and he hadn't told.

He heard Shore's footsteps receding furiously. What would happen now? Would Shore throw away the whole investigation? Sue him for breach of confidentiality? For leaking information? For deceit?

It was a shame he hadn't willingly shared the information with him at an earlier stage. Shore might have been angry, but he wouldn't have felt betrayed. Now, it seemed, it was too late.

Shore sat on one of the chairs in the hotel yard and leaned back his head. Bleich's small telephone burned in his hand.

Bleich was leaking the findings of his investigation to somebody else. That was, without doubt, a severe breach in trust. Shore felt bad, and at the same time, amazed. He was almost always on the mark, and he had tagged Bleich an honest man. How could it be that he was so mistaken? How could it happen that, with all the time they spent together, he hadn't picked up that something was going on behind his back?!

His fingers jumped on the small machine. He struggled to steady them and marked the last outgoing call.

He wasn't going to try and dial it in order to check who it was. That would give the nameless person on the other end an unnecessary piece of information – that someone else was around besides Bleich. He'd write the number down for himself and trace it. He had his ways.

Almost soundless footsteps could be heard approaching from behind. Shore stiffened.

"Bleich," he said in a loud voice, without turning around, "we have nothing to talk about right now."

He heard Bleich stop.

"I'd like to explain a few things to you," Bleich requested.

"I'm afraid that wouldn't be so smart on your part."

"Even so," Bleich's voice was pleading, "We trust one another."

"Yes, I also thought so until a few minutes ago…"

"We'll speak later?"

"Maybe," Shore said doubtfully, "and even if we do, it won't be a conversation. It will be an interrogation. And I advise you to prepare yourself well, because during interrogations I'm not very nice…"

# CHAPTER 35

Yisroel Yitzchok didn't waste any time. As soon as the idea flashed through his mind, he turned and headed towards Shloime's house.

He bounded up the steps, two at a time. He knocked and waited impatiently.

"Hello," he said to Chana, who opened the door. For a second, he was confused. This was Shloime's mother? He had seen her at the *tena'im* and on other occasions, and she hadn't looked so old.

"Is Shloime home?"

"Yes," she said. "You can come in. One second, you're Fuchsman!"

"That's right."

"Oh, how nice that you came! How's your mother doing, and Suri? Come, come in, have something to eat."

"It's okay," Yisroel Yitzchok said uncomfortably, "I just want to speak to Shloime. It's… it's a little urgent."

Shloime appeared, looking a bit disheveled. His *tzitzis* was on top of his shirt, which was untucked.

"To what do I owe the honor?" he asked warmly.

"I came to speak to you," Yisroel Yitzchok said and didn't exactly smile.

"Please," Shloime said and ushered the younger boy into his small room. "How can I help you?"

"It has to do with your *chasunah*," Yisroel Yitzchok said quickly. Shloime listened attentively as he briefly related what Lederman was about to do.

"Whatever happens," Yisroel Yitzchok concluded, "I want you to know that any information you might receive began in Lederman's factory and is completely untrue."

"But I can't give a hand to this," Shloime said. "No bad rumor about Suri can be allowed to spread, even if it's not true. Even if it's meant only for our ears and even if we ignore it. We have to foil this plot."

"But how?!" Yisroel Yitzchok asked in despair, "I've been thinking nonstop. I'm seriously breaking my head and I haven't found any way out."

For a few minutes Shloime sat there, deep in thought. Yisroel Yitzchok glanced at the walls that were crowded with *sefarim*, and at the modest furniture.

"I have an idea," Shloime said with a sudden flash of inspiration.

Yisroel Yitzchok lifted his head hopefully.

"We'll make the wedding," Shloime said confidently, "not on the date that Mendel Lederman knows about, but beforehand, secretly. With a small *minyan*. By the time Lederman hears about it, it will be over and done with…"

"What do you mean?" Yisroel Yitzchok tried to understand, "You'll get married secretly?"

"Maybe not in a dark basement," Shloime gave a little laugh, "but definitely in private. Besides for my parents and yours, and a *minyan* of men that we'll gather, no one will know about it. And when Lederman wakes up, it will already be too late."

"That's brilliant," Yisroel Yitzchok breathed. "You're a genius, Shloime."

"Don't get carried away. If I was such a genius, I'd have already found a way to completely neutralize him, this Lederman. Can I get you a drink?"

"No, thanks," Yisroel Yitzchok said, "I must run tell this to my father. He'll be very relieved."

And he was out the door. Shloime watched him from the window as he headed home at a rapid clip. The great idea spread through his bones, filling him with happiness, until it reached his brain. And when it got there, Shloime remembered his usual way of doing things: he didn't make any important decisions without first consulting with his trusted friend, Nochum Cohen.

• • •

Bleich and Shore sat facing each other. Not like friends, but like an interrogator and one being interrogated. Shore sat ramrod straight. Shaya squirmed in his chair.

"All right, so I'm on my way to discovering who it was you were talking to," Shore said. To his astonishment, however, instead of Shaya Bleich turning pale and confused, he leaned forward and asked excitedly:

"Really?? Who is it??"

"You don't know who it is?!"

"I haven't the slightest idea."

Shore tilted his head. It was a strange story. In general, Bleich really did make a credible impression. When he claimed he didn't know to whom he was speaking, perhaps he wasn't just offering a dumb excuse.

"So why are you talking to somebody that you don't know?"

"I'm happy you're asking that question," Shaya said, and finally allowed himself to lean back. "For a long time already I've wanted to share this with you, and haven't found the right opportunity – and, truthfully speaking, I was very scared of your reaction."

"Careful, careful," Shore said, and the warning was actually directed mainly at himself. *Be careful not to fall into this honeyed trap. Yeshaya Bleich bought your trust, but that can't be allowed to serve him and cause you to believe his lies.* "I've heard enough stories in my life. My ears don't believe pretty words, only facts. Speak."

"All right," Shaya took a deep breath, "the story's like this. You know that your services cost a lot of money."

"I know."

"Though I'm not poor, I am soon marrying off my son, and the expense of an investigation wasn't taken into account. Heaven arranged that I should meet someone who expressed his interest in funding the entire investigation."

Shore sat without moving.

"I was very unsure whether I should take him up on his offer. What made me decide to agree was the pressure you put on me to pay. The pressure was justified, but at that time I didn't have enough money. I was forced to accept his offer, even at the price that he demanded."

"You're a naïve fool, Yeshaya Bleich. What was the price?"

"The price," Shaya swallowed hard, "was constant updates about all progress in the investigation." Shaya felt like a naughty little boy before Shore's derisive, penetrating look. "Every so often I dial the phone number that he gave me, leave him a message and receive an additional sum of money. That's the arrangement between us."

"And you don't know who it is???"

Shaya felt as though he'd just been crowned the village dunce.

"No, I don't believe it – I don't believe it." Shore shook his head back and forth slowly. "This entire time I'm running an investigation for you, and you go and leak it to someone whom you don't even know?! Listen, Bleich, I've never hit such a record in all my years on the job…"

Shaya was quiet.

"What do you want me to do now?" Shore asked and leveled his gaze directly at Shaya. "I should continue the investigation like this, when who knows to whom you'll leak it tomorrow??"

Shaya had no answer.

"I don't conduct an investigation in such a manner!" Shore shouted and banged on the table in front of him.

"One minute, Shore, just a minute," Shaya tried to calm him. It looked like the cold, calculated man was losing it. Who knew what he would say or do?

"Wait one minute, I have an idea!" Shaya said.

"The best idea is for you to get out of here! I don't want to see you!!"

Shaya recoiled. Shore was beginning to rampage. Other guests in the hotel were looking at them.

"I don't want to conduct your investigation. You're not reliable!! I can't work like this. I made a mistake. I thought you're an honest man. Mistakes like this don't happen to me often, but it did now. Go, get out of here…!!"

Shaya grabbed Shore firmly by his shoulders and steered him into the hotel, as the investigator waved his hands and tried to pull free.

*Thicker Than Water* << 435

• • •

Nochum and Shloime met at the corner. Together they walked until they found a bench, far from the eyes and ears of any passerby.

Shloime unfolded his plan before his friend. Nochum listened carefully. When Shloime finished speaking, Nochum shook his head from side to side.

"Absolutely not, Shloime," he said clearly. "Having nothing to do with whether Lederman knows or not, you cannot have this wedding. I know it's hard for you to hear, and even more so to do, but you have to change direction. Don't keep looking for ways to make this *shidduch* happen; focus on finding a new *shidduch*."

"I don't believe that's what you're telling me, Nochum!"

"That's what I *have* to tell you. I don't have any more pleasant way of saying it, because nothing that's happening here is pleasant."

"Nochum," Shloime's voice was pained, "Lederman's bewitched you. He's completely confused you with all his warped ways. You're my good friend; you can't work against me…"

"I *am* your good friend!" Nochum said sincerely, "and that's exactly why I'm telling you what I am. I'm on your side Shloime, like I've always been, and believe me – I only want what's good for you!"

Shloime shifted to the end of the bench. He buried his face in his hands.

"Shloime?" Nochum asked carefully, "Are you okay?"

Shloime shook his head. How could he be okay if every aspect of his life was unraveling, one by one?!

He sat like that for some time. His shoulders shook. Nochum was helpless. His best friend was crying over his life that was falling apart, and he had no way of helping him.

"Okay," Shloime said after he calmed down a bit, "I think we should go."

"And what are you going to do?" Nochum asked fearfully.

"What I've always done," Shloime said dryly. "Act according to what my common sense tells me. Not like all kinds of "well meaning" people have managed – I don't know how – to convince also you."

"But Shloime!" Nochum called. "Shloime, wait…!"

Shloime Bleich didn't look back, only forwards, firm in his decision to do what seemed best for him, and to ignore all those who were trying to stick spokes into his wedding coach that was rolling along.

"Shloime, no!!!"

Nochum ran after him, trying to grab his sleeve. Shloime shook him off and continued on.

In another month, a little less, was his *chasunah*. Time was short.

• • •

Shaya escorted Shore to his room, ignoring the stares of the hotel guests in the lobby, elevator and corridors. He settled Shore on a chair and disappeared.

Shore would need some time to recover. As he knew him, it wouldn't take too long for him to return to his cold, logical self, and he would be able to weigh his next step – whether he should continue to conduct Bleich's investigation or drop it. If he decided to drop it, Shaya would be in big trouble. They had gotten so far, he could almost see the light at the end of the tunnel. Shore, however, couldn't be convinced of something if he wasn't prepared to convince himself.

With a sense of defeat, he called Chana and told her everything. She actually didn't see things in such a severe light. "First of all, it's very good that you told him," she said. "You couldn't hide such a thing from him for too long. Now that he knows, the decision is in his hands. And even if he does decide to drop it, there are plenty of good investigators around, and you can continue the investigation from where he left off."

"He's a strong man," Shaya said worriedly. "He could completely upset the investigation. He could trip up a different investigator and not allow us to progress."

"You're paranoid because of Lederman," Chana said. "Not every investigator tries to ruin the investigations of a different investigator. It's his right to stop investigating, but he has no right to continue to harm you. We'll pay him the whole amount, and this way he won't have---"

"Chana?"

The call was suddenly interrupted.

"Chana, where'd you disappear to?"

The line hadn't been disconnected. He heard voices talking in the background, excitedly.

"Shaya?" Chana came back to him, "Shloime wants to talk to you. It's very important."

"Yes, Shloime'le," Shaya was happy to hear his voice. "How are you?

"Better than usual, *boruch Hashem*."

"I'm glad. Is there a reason for that?"

"A good reason."

Shloime looked for a quiet, hidden corner in the house, and found it on the utility porch.

"I have a good idea, Abba."

"Let's hear."

"I thought that…" Shloime cleared his throat. "I thought it

would be a good idea to make our *chasunah* secretly, before the official date. This way, Lederman won't be able to prevent us from getting married."

Shaya was quiet.

"What do you say, Abba?"

"Essentially, it's a good idea," Shaya said, his voice low. "It solves the problem of Lederman, but not my problem."

"What's your problem, Abba?!" Shloime wondered. He had been so sure his father would be overjoyed.

"I don't want you to go under the *chuppah*," Shaya said hoarsely, "without your father and mother. They, and you, both deserve to be together at this momentous time. I wouldn't be able to forgive myself if it happened differently…"

"But Abba---"

On the utility porch, between the cartons of grape juice and an old kerosene heater, Shloime sagged against the wall. How much could one young heart take?! He thought he had managed to forge a way to his marriage, but everyone was closing in on him from all directions. Now his father didn't agree to the idea. Abba wanted to find his parents; Lederman wanted that he shouldn't. Abba wanted the wedding to take place; Lederman absolutely didn't. And he himself?! He wanted everything. Everything a *bochur* his age deserved to have: real, loving parents with whom he lived, a wonderful, refined *kallah* and a proper Jewish wedding. Why did his life have to be so complicated…?!

"Shloime?"

"Yes, Abba," Shloime took a deep, deep breath. He needed a lot of air. "I don't know what to say. I think that even so---"

He suddenly heard the sound of a door opening.

"I'll speak to you later, Shloime," Shaya said quickly and hung up.

Shore stood before him, tall and erect as usual. There were

no signs of the storm he had gone through not long before. The recovery had been even quicker than Shaya had expected.

"Okay," Shore said.

"Would you like to sit?" Shaya ventured. Not so much in order to have Shore sit, but to determine his mood.

"I'll sit," Shore said calmly, and Shaya sighed with relief.

Shore looked penetratingly at the closed cell phone.

"I hope you're not hiding anything else up your sleeve, Bleich," he said in a hard voice.

"I have nothing else to hide," Shaya said, turning his pockets inside out, "and I'm very sorry about the one thing I did hide."

"Okay," Shore said again. "So we can summarize."

"Go ahead," Shaya said. His heart pounded furiously. What was coming?

"The first conclusion I've come to, pardon me, is that you're a big fool. The second conclusion is that I was also a big fool for a while, if I thought differently about you. But at least we can take comfort in the third conclusion."

"Which is?" Shore was playing with him. Why?

"Which is," Shore intoned, "that I'm going to use your stupidity for our good. Actually, I've already started to use it."

"I don't understand."

"I'll explain it to you," Shore said, and Shaya noted to himself that the man was reassuming his regular manner. "This donor, who's funding the investigation, isn't doing so for fun. I hope that's clear to you."

"That was clear to me the whole time," Shaya hastened to say. "I tried to find out who it is, to find out what he has to do with me and why he wants to take part in the investigation, but I was completely unsuccessful."

Shore rubbed his hands in satisfaction. "That's because you don't have the tools that an investigator has, definitely not an investigator like myself. But I've already started – and am in the thick of – checking into it, and from what I understand, this man is actually a lead for us. Quite a fat lead, I would say…"

• • •

Mendel Lederman sat in the small room under his office. He had a feeling things were happening in the Bleich-Fuchsman arena, and wanted to keep on top of it.

He pressed the required buttons. Not only was the Fuchsman's phone line bugged, but so was their entire house. The most crucial things were said in private, behind closed doors.

"You look happy," he heard the father.

"Yes," the boy said – Yisroel Yitzchok, the one who had come to his office and made as if he was on "his side" – "and when you hear what I have to say, you'll also be happy, Abba. I was by Shloime."

"Shloime?!"

"Yes. I told him everything that was going on. He said that anyway we couldn't let a bad rumor about Suri get out, and he suggested a great idea."

"Idea?"

"Yes."

Yisroel Yitzchok lowered his voice, as if he was afraid someone was listening.

"Shloime suggested that they do the *chasunah* in advance, privately, so that Lederman shouldn't know and won't be able to mess it up."

Lederman was bent over, almost stuck to the listening device. He couldn't miss even one word now…!

At first he didn't hear anything. Suddenly Elya's voice burst into the room:

"What a wonderful idea! Why didn't we think of it earlier?!"

Lederman clutched his head between his hands. They would do it. They thought it was a great idea.

"And we'll cancel the big *chasunah*?" Yisroel Yitzchok asked.

"No, of course not," his father said. "No one has to know anything. As far as those invited are concerned, it's a completely regular *chasunah*. No one has to know that the couple is already married."

"But by the *chuppah*," Yisroel Yitzchok said. "What will they do by the *chuppah*? They'll make a pretend *kiddushin*? They'll make *brochos l'vatalah*?"

"Don't worry, Yisroel Yitzchok," Elya said, "Every problem has a solution. The main thing is that our Suri should be happy. *Oy*, Suri. Suri…"

Lederman closed his eyes. The Bleich-Fuchsman battle went up a level. He would have to prepare stronger weapons.

"Should I go tell her?" Yisroel Yitzchok asked, his hand already on the door handle.

"No, not yet. I want to tell her myself. I also want to talk to Ima first. The idea needs developing. You know, it's hard to hide from Lederman. We'll have to keep this completely under wraps."

Lederman couldn't help smiling.

"I also want to speak with Shloime, and with his father," Elya said. "Easy does it, Yisroel Yitzchok. *Be'ezras Hashem*, everything will fall into place at the right time."

• • •

"We'll follow up the fat lead your donor has given us," Shore said. "I think he slipped up by giving you his phone numbers."

"You're still leaving me in suspense and not telling me who

he is," Bleich said, allowing himself a small smile to diffuse the atmosphere.

"Right," Shore said, "and meanwhile, I won't tell you. Not until I have full facts in my hand. I'm collecting all the details on him, trying to connect the dots between him and our investigation. When I have grounded information, you'll be the first to know."

"There's a chance he'll advance the investigation?" Bleich asked hopefully.

"A big chance," replied Shore, who wasn't usually big on giving chances.

"And there's a chance we'll be able to have the wedding on time…?"

# CHAPTER 36

"Have the wedding on time?" Shore repeated Shaya's question. "That depends. It could be that your son will be reunited with his biological parents in the next few days, and we may still have a long way ahead of us. In my line of work, it's never possible to know what lies around the bend. One minute."

Shore stopped talking and looked at the beeper attached to his belt. He read the message and smiled.

"Okay," he said, "I think we're progressing nicely. The men I put to the job are making the necessary inquiries, but let's continue to focus meanwhile on our investigation. We came to Australia in order to find your brother, and that's what we'll do."

"Onward, ho."

• • •

Despite serving as his mother for close to twenty years already, Chana had never seen Shloime so broken.

Tears clogged his throat as he told her about his conversation with Shaya. She could hear it. Shloime, her strong, wonderful son, was broken.

"Abba dismissed the idea," he said. "This was the one thing that could have saved the situation. Maybe Abba believes so strongly that his investigation will succeed that he's willing to delay the *chasunah*. I don't know."

She placed a cup of water before Shloime. He sipped from it thankfully.

Privately, she didn't agree with Shaya. She had to talk to him, and soon. Each minute that she was able to lift Shloime's spirits was important.

"Shaya," she said into the receiver of the phone in her bedroom, "where am I catching you?"

"In the government office in Australia," her husband replied. "What's happening? Something important?"

"You could say so. It's about Shloime. I'm sorry, Shaya, but I don't think you're right."

"What are you talking about?"

"I think it's worth making the wedding privately, as he suggests."

"Chana, it's not practical. I can't do such a thing."

"And what were you thinking when he got engaged, Shaya? On what basis did you go through with the *tena'im*? On the basis that you'd find his parents in the few months between the engagement and the wedding when we couldn't find them all these years?"

"It's a good question, Chana," Shaya paused, and motioned to Shore that he was going out for a few minutes. "The engagement was so sudden, we had no chance to prepare ourselves. Things just rolled along, and suddenly we found ourselves breaking a plate – I don't even know how. Fuchsman moved the *shidduch* along quickly; they simply grabbed Shloime."

"True, but if you're so strong in your opinion that he shouldn't get married without Naftali and Rochel, you should have said from the start that Shloime's not listening to suggestions."

"And if I would have done that," Shaya justified himself, "our Shloime's name would have been seriously damaged. What reason could there be for a good, talented boy of the right age not to enter *shidduchim*?"

"I hear," Chana said. "In any event, though, things being as they are, I think it would be cruel to Shloime to push away his idea. If we won't allow him to get married, there will be three unfortunate souls – Shloime, his father and his mother. If we let him, there will be only two. I think that that's our choice."

Shaya had to admit that, no matter how painful they were, her words rang true.

"You know what, I'll think about it," he promised. "The investigator and I are very busy right now."

"I'm afraid we don't have too much time to think about it. We have to decide. Your child is suffering, Shaya, each day, every minute."

"Chana," Shaya tried to stay patient, "moving up the *chasunah* is a possibility, but it's definitely not healthy. A wedding has to be celebrated in a normal fashion, not in a dark cave. Besides which, there's a big chance we're nearing our goal. In the past few days we've progressed quite a bit. You can tell Shloime that. *Daven* – you, him, everyone. There's a reasonable chance that we're about to---"

"Where'd you disappear to?!" Shore appeared behind him.

"Nowhere," Shaya answered, "Chana, I'll get back to you."

"I thought findings interest you at least as much as they interest me," Shore reproached him.

"Oh, there are findings?!" Shaya jumped.

"Definitely."

• • •

"Everything's proceeding according to plan," Avrohom Yisroel said to the man sitting opposite him in the warm lobby of a small, obscure hostel in Montevideo, Uruguay. "He traced me. Someone on his behalf set up a meeting with me."

"Where?"

"He's in Australia."

"And you'll fly all the way there?"

"Yes."

"It's a long trip."

"I guess it's part of my atonement."

He drank from the cup in front of him quietly.

"I did it all on purpose," he said in a low voice. "Had I really wanted to hide, I wouldn't have given a telephone number that could lead to me. I imagined that they had a good investigator helping them."

"What will you tell him at this meeting – or whoever comes for him?"

"I still haven't decided. I believe, though, that I'll tell him the whole story. You know, the past is over, with all the mistakes that were made. I'd be a fool to try and hide information out of embarrassment. The future can't be sacrificed on the altar of the past, especially when we're not talking about just my future, but especially that of the couple that wishes to start their life."

They both sat quietly.

"I've been keeping track of the Bleich family, Yeshaya and Chana, all the years," he leaned back, his fingers gripping the cup. "There was never a time that they weren't under my watch. I did it so I'd be able to get my hands on Naftali and Rochel the minute they found them. But they didn't find them, and gave up searching. Only now, a few months ago, when their son got engaged, Yeshaya left on another, stubborn round of searching and I simply followed him.

"Still to get your hands on them?!"

Avrohom was horrified. "That was a joke, I hope!"

"Of course…"

"Avrohom of yesterday, that is, Mike Lewis, did it in order to get his hands on the people who did him such an injustice, and kill them. But Avrohom of today wants to discover Naftali and Rochel in order to explain to them how right they were, and how much I have to tip my hat to them for what they did. To get down on my hands and knees and beg their forgiveness."

"That won't be simple," the other man said. "After all, we're talking about years and years of anguish that they're suffering because of you."

"I know, and I thank G-d that I have plenty of means to try and make it up to them."

"I'm not so sure that monetary payment is appropriate here. You know, there are things that can't be atoned for with money."

Avrohom chuckled. "You've decided to be my conscience today, huh?"

"No, you have enough conscience of your own. I'm simply trying to prepare you. These people see you as the man who destroyed their lives."

"I know, I know," he put down the cup. "I know. Let me be now."

• • •

Shore held a computer printout in his hands.

"In this year, on this date, your brother lived at this address," he marked the appropriate lines with his pen. "My feeling is he's not there anymore. We may, though, be able to get information from the place, from the people who live there, like we did in France."

"Why do you think he's not there anymore?"

"It's hard for me to explain," Shore said, "but he has the profile of a drifter. Today here and tomorrow someplace else, like somebody who's hiding something and is constantly on the alert to escape."

The two of them sat silently in the small rented car that sped along the streets.

"We're really wandering about," Shaya commented. "I didn't think the search would spread out over so many countries."

"*You're* wandering?!" Shore glanced at him in surprise, "Think about your brother, who went through this in real time together with his entire family – and not for investigative purposes, but because their lives were in danger."

"I cannot begin to imagine the reason he had to flee. Believe me, Shore, my brother never hurt a fly. He doesn't know how to get somebody else angry. In his life he's never caused anyone else to suffer. He didn't even know how to light a cigarette."

"I believe you, but sometimes people are hunted through no fault of their own. It may even have been a mistake, though I find that difficult to believe. You don't chase someone for twenty years without making sure he's the right one."

When they finally arrived at the address, they found a decrepit apartment building in one of the poorer neighborhoods of the city. Filthy steps, rotting doors.

"My sister-in-law wouldn't be capable of living in this place for even half an hour," Shaya smiled.

"Don't forget, we're talking about a long time ago," Shore reminded him. "The building surely looked much better then – and maybe even the neighborhood. Here, that's the door. Do you want to knock?"

"I give you the honor."

An old, bent man opened the door. He could barely reach

the key. Yes, he was the owner of the apartment. He didn't hear so well, so could they please talk louder? Yes, there was a time when he rented the apartment to others, but today he lived in it himself.

What? What was the gentleman asking? If there was a tenant by the name of Stone? He had to remember. At his age that wasn't so simple anymore.

They patiently sat in the man's house, trying to help him reconstruct the past. The old man, excited with the amount of attention he was suddenly receiving, stubbornly went to prepare some tea for them.

"Just so you should know," Shore took this opportunity to tell Shaya, "we have a meeting at the end of the week with his royal highness, your philanthropist…"

Bleich stared at Shore, openmouthed.

"A meeting with my donor???"

"That's right," Shore said and put out his hand to take the cup of tea that their host was serving him. "Are you afraid of him?"

"No." He politely refused his host's offer of a drink. "I'm just a little shocked at your speed."

"Not speed, Bleich, action. Action is the key in life."

"But I need a bit of information about this man before I meet him. Actually, I need all the information you can give me, and I assume that you can."

"We'll speak about this later," Shore promised and turned to their host: "We're looking, sir, for a family that lived here. A couple with children, years ago. They rented the apartment from you. Their name was Stone."

The old man struggled to recall. He had no books where he wrote the names of the tenants. When he was young, he had a good memory; he didn't need to write anything down. But he might have a few papers in the other room. If the gentlemen didn't mind waiting, he'd go look.

Shaya seized the opportunity to continue the previous conversation:

"I don't want there to be any surprises at this meeting."

"I can't promise such a thing. It's clear that there will be surprises. Start with the assumption that this man didn't help you for the fun of it, but because he has some connection to the affair, which he'll reveal at the meeting."

Bleich was quiet for a minute and then said in a voice that wasn't his:

"I have a crazy idea."

"All right, let's hear," Shore smiled.

"Maybe this donor is my lost brother himself…?"

"An interesting guess. I also thought of it," Shore said. "It could be. It sounds too good, though. Let's wait and see."

"I'm afraid I won't be able to sleep for the next few nights," Bleich said.

"Better not to think about it at all, then. It's not a good idea to be tired at the meeting."

"Yes, sir," he turned to the old man who returned empty handed, "You didn't find anything?"

・・・

"I'm going," Suri said, her small pocketbook over her shoulder.

Every day, at about the same time, Suri left to go to the Kosel. She was trying everything to bring a *yeshua*; soon she would complete forty consecutive days at the Kosel and the *yeshua* still hadn't come.

"Why don't you go a bit later today?" Devorah asked.

"Later? Why?"

"Abba and I want to talk to you."

Suri's heart skipped a beat. Abba and Ima wanted to tell her something that would ultimately bury her chance to marry Shloime Bleich. They would do it as gently as possible, but that wouldn't change the bitter truth.

"What do you want to talk to me about, Ima?" she asked, trembling.

"About important things. Don't worry, Suri, everything's fine. Abba will be here soon. You'll go to the Kosel afterwards – it's not so terrible."

No, it wasn't so terrible. It was the conversation that would be terrible.

Abba came home, put down his coat and hat and smiled.

Abba was smiling? Why?

"Devorah, it looks like Suri needs a drink," Elya called into the kitchen, "something hot. She looks frozen."

Devorah brought mugs of coffee and some cake into the study and closed the door behind her.

"What's this party?" Suri asked, confused.

"You'll know soon…"

Elya did a bit of leading up and then threw out the news:

"Your *chasunah* will take place, Suri, very soon. Even before the date that's printed on the invitations."

"What???"

"Exactly that. We decided to push up the wedding a bit."

"Push it up?? But no one will come; on the invitation it says- --"

"That's correct. Really no one will come, except for the immediate family. It will be a small wedding – you could even call it hidden. Secret."

"A secret wedding?!"

Patiently, Elya and Devorah explained the plan to Suri. At

first she was shocked. Very slowly, though, she began to digest the idea that she would dance at two weddings: one authentic, very small one, and the second – a pretend one on the correct date, with lots of guests and celebration.

"It's Shloime's idea," Elya said. "This way, no one will be able to bother us. The first *chasunah* will be two weeks before the second. We'll celebrate *sheva brochos* in secret, too. It'll be a big headache, with lots of confusion and extra expenses, but it's the best solution."

Suri looked back and forth from her father to her mother, tingling with joy.

"So it's final??" she asked again and again. "We don't have to worry anymore? Everything will really be okay?"

*Be'ezras Hashem*, her parents assured her again and again. It all just had to be kept a complete secret. Even the children couldn't know anything – except for Yisroel Yitzchok, who had a hand in the idea.

"Good," Suri said and stood up. "I'm going to the Kosel. I was saved even before I finished the forty days; now I have to give thanks…"

• • •

"Sir," Shore turned to their host, "do you have, by some chance, pictures of your tenants?"

"Pictures of the tenants?!" The old man had strained his memory enough that day, "No, I don't think so. There aren't any pictures."

"How about of the children?" Shore tried. "Perhaps they took some photos with the children in the neighborhood then. Do you know who the neighbors were?"

No, the old man didn't know. He didn't live in the apartment then, and didn't know any neighbors.

"We can ask one of the neighbors," Shore said. "Maybe we'll be lucky."

He stood up.

"Oh, so you're going?" The old man panicked. He didn't know when he'd receive so much attention again. "Wait a bit, wait a bit. I'll search among the old things I have here in the apartment. Maybe I'll find pictures, you can never know." And without waiting for a reply, he shuffled out of the room and down the hall to the storage room.

"I'm afraid he's wasting our time," Shore sighed.

"I'll tell him he should pay you by the hour," Shaya joked. "He'll hear the rate and throw us out of here…"

"Gentlemen," the old man's hoarse voice rose from deep inside the storage room, "there are a few interesting things here. Do you want to come look?"

"He must have found some old newspapers he hasn't read yet," Shore sighed. "You go, Bleich, and if it's really something interesting, call me. I'll rest here on the recliner meanwhile."

Shaya went to the storage room. He was hit by a damp, musty smell.

"Look," the old man said, and pulled out a faded material bag. "Open the bag. Maybe there's something here that will interest you."

Carefully, Shaya peeked into the bag. There was some old children's clothing that could have belonged to David Stone or not, moldy linen, a few broken wooden toys.

"There's nothing here," he said and held out the bag to the old man.

"Look through it," the man said. There were no other bags, and if the two nice gentlemen wouldn't find anything, they would leave, and that would be very sad. "Look well. Maybe you really will find something."

Shaya heard the unspoken plea. He dumped the contents of the bag onto the floor. The clatter could be heard all the way to the living room.

"What are you doing there, Bleich?" Shore called. "Helping him clean up?"

"I'm coming in a minute," Shaya called back. He poked through the things spread out on the floor.

"Hey, what's this?"

He bent down and picked up a small book. He opened it.

"It's a *sefer tehillim*," he said, amazed, and kissed it. It was a sign that believing Jews had lived in the house.

"Oh, you found something?!" the old man asked excitedly.

Shaya went to show Shore what he found and explained the significance of it to him.

"Very interesting," Shore said, and studied the little book from every angle. "Did you find anything else?"

"I found something!" yelled the old man.

"He must have discovered America," Shore said.

Shaya returned to the storage room. What had the old man discovered in the pile of things that he had missed?

"This," the old man held something out with a shaking hand.

"It's an old telephone book," Shaya said and opened it. He froze.

Inside the personal phone book, in script Hebrew letters, in the handwriting of – yes, it was clear as day – of his brother Naftali, were addresses and telephone numbers listed one after another.

"Bleich!" Shore called to him, "Are we moving?!"

No. Shaya wasn't moving. Only his fingers moved. They went from page to page in the phone book. Names of relatives, Naftali's friends from the past. Under the letter *beis*, he found a few Bleichs. One of them was his own name and address.

"Tell me, did you choke on the dust there??" Shore was beginning to get angry. "Why aren't you answering…??"

*Thicker Than Water* « 455

# CHAPTER 37

It was hard to say that Shaya Bleich heard Shore's yelling from the other room. His trembling fingers gripped the phone book tightly, as if it was part of his lost brother's body.

A cross Shore finally appeared in the doorway of the storage room.

"Bleich, you know I charge by the hour. How much will this rummaging through ancient rubbish cost you?!"

But even with Shore standing right next to him, Shaya didn't really hear him. He could hear the voice of Naftali, as if he was speaking from inside the book.

"I never knew that junk could be so fascinating," Shore said, and took the book from Shaya's frozen hands.

"Hmmm, what do we have here…?" he said.

For the first time in close to twenty years, Shaya Bleich felt that he was gripping the end of a rope that was connected to his brother. If he would only tug hard enough, he would bring Naftali to him. And if that didn't work, he'd walk along the rope until he reached Naftali, even if it took another twenty years.

"What does it say here?" Shore asked. Shaya stared at him and then remembered that Shore didn't read Hebrew.

"It's my brother's personal phone book," he said in a strangled voice, his power of speech slowly returning to him. "The names and phone numbers of the entire family are here. It's my brother's. I know. My name is also written inside."

Shore brought a special bag from his briefcase and carefully put the find inside.

"I have to go through it thoroughly," he said. "And if we can mark this place as a definite spot where David Stone lived, then every inch has to be gone over with completely different tools. We'll come back tomorrow."

"You'll come again tomorrow?!" The old man couldn't believe his ears. Could he be so lucky?

"Tomorrow morning," Shore said.

・・・

Now Devorah Fuchsman had two notebooks. The first one, flowered and boasting the large heading "*Chasunah* notebook – Suri" on the cover, had been her faithful companion for the past few months. She got the idea to use a notebook instead of a bunch of scraps of paper from a good friend, and she couldn't thank her enough.

Now, though, that notebook was temporarily relegated to a drawer, and a new one – solid blue – took its place. Nothing was written on the cover, and it wasn't left around unguarded for a second. This was the notebook for the secret wedding, which also had to be arranged properly.

There would be very few people invited, and even that was too many. They needed a *minyan* of men, people who wouldn't leak the secret under any circumstances. Not family members and not friends, who were likely to let something slip, despite their best intentions.

Elya wanted them to be strangers who would sign to secrecy. Devorah shrank a little from that idea. Shloime suggested bringing some very loyal friends of his from yeshiva, and the Rosh Yeshiva would be *mesader kiddushin*.

Where would the wedding be held? Nowhere that would arouse any suspicion. Not in either of the *mechutanim's* houses. Definitely not in any hall. Elya offered his office, which had a small porch that was open to the sky. They decided to go with that.

There was a refrigerator in the small office. Food could be heated up there as well. Devorah would prepare the meal in her own kitchen. There was no need to hire a caterer for so few guests.

Except for the bare necessities, there would be no indication at the celebration that a wedding was taking place. The gorgeous *kallah* gown that was already reserved would be worn by Suri at the big, public *chasunah*.

For Yisroel Yitzchok, this was no simple test. He had to keep the big secret deep, deep inside of him. On the other hand, he felt very complimented that he was included among the adults in the family, and tried to prove himself accordingly. As his father had instructed, he stayed in contact with Lederman in order to ward off his suspicions – forcing him to be that much more careful.

And in the room under his office, Mendel Lederman spent many hours glued to the listening device. He told his secretary to push off everything that wasn't urgent, and completely dedicated himself to the Bleich-Fuchsman project. They were thinking of an early wedding. A logical, expected idea. They thought that whatever wasn't told to Mendel Lederman straight, had no way of being known, eh?

The boy Yisroel Yitzchok tried to act as if all was business as usual. He, though, knew that things had shifted into high gear.

If nothing went wrong, in two weeks Suri Fuchsman and Shaya Bleich would be married. Shloime's Rosh Yeshiva would be the *mesader kiddushin*. No one except for both sets of parents and another few men called for a *minyan* would know about it.

But Mendel Lederman would make sure that things did go wrong. Whoever didn't respond to the carrot would have to be shown the stick.

...

"I canceled all my meetings for the next few days," Avrohom Yisroel said to his friend.

"That bad?"

"I can't concentrate for a minute."

"You've decided what you're going to say to them?"

"I'm afraid that even if I decide, and even if I prepare it in writing, when it comes to it I'll simply fall at their feet and ask forgiveness."

"You're not meeting them directly, though; you're meeting his brother."

"Even so, the brother also suffered tremendously. The entire family. And besides, they're about to find Naftali and Rochel, which means that I'll find them too. And then, only G-d will put the words in my mouth."

"They're believing people, like you?"

"Of course," Avrohom Yisroel said. "In any case, that's how I remember them. I don't believe that they changed. Their faith probably got only stronger after everything they went through."

"If they're believing people," the friend said, "they'll also say what you always say: It's all from G-d."

"True," Avrohom said, somewhat encouraged, "but there's a concept in Judaism that bad things come about through parties that are anyway blameworthy. And if such a terrible thing – to make a family suffer for so many years – came about through me, I guess I must have been very, very blameworthy…"

"But you joined the Jewish people," the friend tried any way he could to encourage him, "and you've erased your past sins. You try so hard to do good for others. Here, you're even funding the investigation that will lead to the couple being found."

"Money, my friend," Avrohom Yisroel said with a deep sigh, "is the cheapest recompense. Can one pay with money?! Can one atone with money?! I can only try. It doesn't always work. And this time I'm afraid that---"

"I'm afraid this is too heavy an emotional burden for you," his friend cut him off, and poured him some water.

"Definitely heavy," Avrohom agreed in a cracked voice. "I don't understand why the meeting was set up for the end of the week. I was told the investigator wants to do some homework about me. And I can understand him, but this homework is eating at my health."

"You can ask him to move up the meeting."

"No, I won't ask him," Avrohom said. "I believe in letting things flow naturally. And maybe it's better this way. At the end of the week people are more relaxed. Milder. Maybe they'll have the patience to hear my story without wanting to throttle me…"

• • •

Shaya Bleich did not join Shore on his return visit to the old apartment where David Stone had lived. Shore said that he'd just disturb him and Shaya was happy to stay in his hotel room and try to organize from there some urgent things connected to the wedding.

Over the phone he could hear the new lilt in his wife's and son's voices, as if someone had poured water on them, reviving them from their faint. The *chasunah*, Chana told him, was set for another two weeks.

"Two weeks?? Chana?? What exactly are these people thinking??"

"I don't know, I---"

"I'm here, far away, deep in an investigation, and they set the date for another two weeks? I understand that I'm not exactly needed at this wedding. It's nice that they at least let me know it's taking place."

"One minute, Shaya, calm down. The *mechutan* said that he absolutely can't get hold of you."

That was actually true. For the past few days Shaya had closed his phone to incoming calls. He had the feeling that the investigation was coming to a close, and he was afraid that someone would mess it up. He therefore shut everything that connected him to the outside world.

"All right," Shaya said, "he couldn't get hold of me. But why in two weeks? What are they thinking, that they could swing me from place to place? What am I, a pendulum?!"

"Don't be angry, Shaya," Chana begged. "Try to understand them. They don't know that you're in middle of an investigation. They think you went to shop for the wedding, or something else that could be interrupted. And besides, it's important to them to make the wedding as soon as possible. Someone's threatening Suri, so they say, and it's a shame to wait even one extra minute."

Shaya was quiet. He tried to digest it.

"Come to the *chasunah*, Shaya. Stop the investigation for a

*Thicker Than Water* << 461

few days and come."

"I can't stop!" Shaya didn't realize that he was yelling. "The investigation is almost over. It's just a matter of time until we find them, and suddenly you tell me that the wedding is in another two weeks…"

Shaya didn't tell Chana about the telephone book that was found. Shore forbade the release of any information.

"I understand, Shaya, but you know that these things take time. Even if the investigation is almost over, we have to think of Shloime and Suri. We want them to get married. I'm sure that Naftali and Rochel would also want it."

"But we can't just stop," Shaya paced back and forth. "If we've already gotten this far - and I tell you, Chana, it's only a matter of time - isn't it worth waiting a little longer with the *chasunah* so we can find Naftali and Rochel, and they can also join in Shloime's happiness just as they deserve?"

"I don't know," Chana said, "and in any case, we can't tell the *mechutanim* to wait. They don't know anything about the investigation and what we're going through. You also have to remember something else, Shaya. Even if you do find Naftali and Rochel, you can't know in what condition you'll find them."

He nodded dumbly.

"I don't think we can ask to change the date that they set," Chana added, "even if we really want to. We don't have a good reason to offer. We can't explain to them all that you've just explained to me, and any other excuse will seem weak. You'll have to leave everything and come, Shaya. There's no choice."

"And what will I tell Shore?" he asked, more to himself than to Chana, "That just now, when things are picking up speed, I'm leaving for two weeks? What will he think of me?"

"Maximum," Chana said, "he'll also stop the investigation for two weeks. Two weeks isn't forever, Shaya. You can always pick

462 ›› *Thicker Than Water*

up from where you left off."

Shaya refused to make peace with the idea. He was almost touching his brother, and he would suddenly have to let go. Logically, he understood the urgency of the matter, but his heart refused to understand.

"We'll discuss it some more," he promised. "I'll try to ask Shore what to do. Later. Now he's very busy."

Danny Shore was indeed busy. Despite the old man's protests, he asked him to vacate the apartment. He stuffed a few large bills into his gnarled hand so he could sit in a restaurant for a few hours and not get underfoot and disturb his work. Now, with the apartment empty, he was able to painstakingly inspect every inch.

A rented apartment, Shore knew, was like a birthday cake: it was built in layers. Each tenant left something of himself in the apartment, even if he cleaned it thoroughly and painted it before he left. Each person has a unique set of fingerprints, not necessarily physical, but rather mental. And Shore's challenge was to uncover this set of fingerprints.

From what, or from whom, was Stone running? He was willing to bet it was from whom. Would he find proof between the walls of the house?

Shore didn't skip a single tile or hole in the wall. And just when he thought he was about to discover something of significance, his cell phone rang. Shore was furious, more at himself than at the phone. He was sure he had shut the phone before beginning the job, but he must have forgotten. Now the telephone was disturbing his concentration.

When he heard who was on the phone, though, his muscles relaxed. Could it be – the anonymous donor was asking to move up the meeting?

The man at the other end stressed that he wasn't asking in the name of the donor, but completely on his own. Being that the man, Avrohom Yisroel, was literally beside himself with impatience, he wanted to ask if it was possible to have the meeting before the planned time. Even that day, if possible.

Shore hesitated. Today? He still had many hours of inspecting the apartment before him. He would definitely be tired and not in top form in the evening. On the other hand, this meeting might yield revelations more important than what he would find in the apartment. It might even do away with the whole need to search the apartment.

"Okay," he finally said. "We can have the meeting today in our hotel lobby. Tonight at eight o'clock."

Before seven, Shore was already back in the hotel. He had finished most of the work in the apartment. If there was any need, he'd continue tomorrow. Even before going to his room, he knocked on Shaya's door.

A few minutes passed before Shaya opened the door, his face creased with sleep.

"Sorry I woke you," Shore said, "but you should definitely get up now and give yourself some time to fully awaken. In a little more than an hour we have a meeting with your philanthropist. Yes, they asked to push up the meeting. You should get ready. He has to see that you're worth all the money he's given…"

"And how did your search go?" Shaya asked, his voice hoarse. "Did you find anything?"

"Actually, yes," Shore said. His briefcase was still in his hand. He asked Shaya's permission to come into the room, and spread his findings out on the small table.

"A few children were born to your brother. I don't know exactly how many. It's quite clear to me that the first was a girl."

"Could be," Shaya said, and was flooded by a sudden wave of longing for Naftali.

"And in the storage room," Shore pulled out a leather folder, into which he had placed some papers that he found, "I found some treasures. What do you say to these?"

Shaya carefully touched some of the old papers. "These are children's drawings. What could you do with them?"

"These aren't children's drawings," Shore stressed. "Turn over the paper, please."

Shaya obediently turned the paper over. On the other side was a printed stream of letters and words.

"I don't understand what you want," he said, puzzled. "These are extra computer printouts. Garbage. My brother's kids colored on them, just like my kids do.

"Nothing is extra," Shore said. He pulled out his pen and marked a few lines. "To me, this printout is a clue to where these papers came from. Chances are they came from David's, or his wife's, work place. And if that's the case, they have a lot to teach us."

"All right," Shaya said with a sigh.

"At least two little boys lived in the apartment," Shore said. "And the girl is the biggest. I found proof of the two boys' births, but not of the girl."

"That's understandable," Shaya said. "She must have been born beforehand. If the search would have been done in one of the earlier apartments, you might have found the proof there. We weren't sure, though, in any of the other apartments, that David Stone was indeed my brother."

"Could be. In any event, it was important to me to find where the family had gone from there. There's no point to the search if it doesn't bring us further along."

"And did you?"

"Not at all."

It wasn't like Shore to admit defeat like that.

"You're sure you didn't?!"

"Completely sure.

"So we'll have to go to the emigration offices again."

"I'm not sure that will be so easy, or at all helpful," Shore said and pulled a cloth bag from his leather folder.

"What do you have there?"

"See for yourself."

Shore's face showed that he had saved the surprise for last, but it wasn't clear whether it was a good surprise or not.

"Just be careful, Bleich. Careful with the papers."

Shaya was careful. He took a sheaf of papers written in English from the bag.

"These look like birth certificates."

"That's because they are birth certificates," Shore nodded his head.

"And this you found in the storage room???" It couldn't be. Naftali had left such important papers lying around?!

"No, not in the storage room," Shore said. "Your brother is a responsible person. Clever, too. He didn't want these certificates anymore, probably because he changed identity, but didn't want to toss them; he hid all the papers in a special hiding place he made in the wall, in case he might need them one day. If he did switch identity, we'll need another miracle to find him – and I'm not so sure we'll have one. Miracles don't happen every day."

Bleich slowly spread the thin papers on the table. Indeed, two sons were born to his brother while he was in Australia.

"But I don't understand," he said. "Even if the daughter was born earlier, her birth certificate should be here. It shouldn't have been left in any of the earlier apartments, unless my brother also created hiding places there."

"True," Shore said. "I was also wondering about that."

He glanced at his watch. It wasn't too late, but Shaya had to get ready and come to the meeting refreshed and put together.

"We'll continue later, or tomorrow," he said, and deftly gathered all the papers gently back into his case. "I'll meet you in the lobby at eight."

...

In the back seat of an expensive, rented car sat Avrohom Yisroel. Next to him lay a black briefcase. His good friend, sitting behind the wheel, wisely chose not to talk too much.

Avrohom Yisroel's cold fingers groped for the briefcase and opened it. There were papers there, pictures and even a small doll.

He took out one picture and studied it. He couldn't stop looking at it. His friend looked at him through the mirror and shook his head.

"Did you bring a bulletproof vest?" he joked. "I hope these people you're going to meet left their weapons in the hotel safe."

Avrohom didn't hear. He was sunk in thought.

"Would you want me to come with you anyway?"

"I don't think there's any need. Bring me to the hotel's entrance."

The car glided down the hotel-lined boulevard and stopped at one of them.

"Here," the friend said. "You're sure you don't want me to accompany you?"

"Positive."

He opened the door for Avrohom and helped him out. He then pressed his hand and wished him all the luck in the world.

"Amen. Pray for me."

Trying to steady his trembling legs, he went inside.

The lobby was crowded. His eyes searched for a person with a black coat and head covering, and found him at the edge of the lobby, together with another man, tall and thin. The two of them were conversing like old friends, glancing from time to time at the entrance.

There was no escape. There was no way back. He went over to them, threading his way between luxurious armchairs and elegant coffee tables. He shook their hands, hoping that the handshake at the end of the meeting would be as firm. Hoping that there would be a handshake. They sat down. He on one side of the table and they on the other.

"My name is Avrohom Yisroel," he began, "and I'm the man who could tell you what happened to Naftali and Rochel Bleich and why they disappeared…"

# CHAPTER 38

Shore placed a small recorder on the table and turned it on. "I hope it's okay with you," he said. Avrohom Yisroel took a deep breath. "Yes, it's fine. Everything I will say is to be heard. I have nothing to hide."

"Then continue."

For Shore, this was another investigative file. For Shaya, this was life itself. What the man was about to say would shed light on the mystery that had colored his life for almost two decades. His heart pounded like a whole group of drummers. Boom-boom, boom-boom.

"And so," the man began again, "I assume you checked up on me and know that I didn't always look the way I do today."

Shore nodded.

"In the past, I was Mike Lewis, one of the world's boxing champions."

Shore nodded again and explained to Shaya, "There's such a sport, boxing. Whoever defeats his opponent with blows is the winner."

"I understand," Shaya said, despite the fact that he definitely did not understand what pleasure people had from hitting just for the sake of hitting.

"I'll tell you a bit about what I was," Avrohom Yisroel said, his gaze fixed on one of the grand chandeliers hanging from the lobby ceiling. "I lived in Australia and, as the continent's boxing champion, I received a high salary from the Boxing Sport Association. I was the darling of the Association and they invested tremendous amounts of money in me. Boxing was almost my entire life. And I say almost because at that time I was already married to my wife, who is no longer with us today. She was killed in a road accident a few years ago. Since then I'm alone."

"You didn't have any children, I understand," Shore said.

"No children were born to me," Avrohom Yisroel said, "but I had a child. And here is where the story essentially begins."

…

Late in the morning, Suri returned from the wig salon. With one hand holding her purse and the other, her *sheitel* box, she barely managed to push open the door to the building. There were a few circulars stuffed in the mailbox. She gathered them and started to climb the steps while looking at an advertisement for exclusive silver jewelry.

Even when standing next to the door, groping in her purse for the key, she didn't lift her eyes from the ad. There was a beautiful necklace that would go really well with Ima's wedding dress. Ima deserved something special; she'd really been through a lot.

Only after sticking the key into the keyhole did she feel the paper.

An envelope was stuck in the crack between the door and the doorpost. Suri's hand, suddenly a block of ice, stuck to the key that was still turning in the hole.

The purse and box fell to the ground. Two fingers managed to grip the envelope. Other fingers, Suri didn't know which, managed to turn the key. Her shoulder pushed the door inwards, her feet nudged her packages into the hallway and her back closed the door behind her.

She leaned against the door and deliberately tore the envelope.

One paper fell out and drifted slowly to the floor, like a leaf falling from a tree.

Suri didn't have the strength to bend down and pick it up. She sank to the floor and pulled the paper to her.

"To the esteemed Fuchsman family," was printed, without any hint, of course, to the name of the writer and sender, "we know that you are planning to push up the wedding and have it on (and here appeared the exact date and place of the wedding), secretly. For your own good, based on the information we have, it's best that you cancel this plan. It can only harm you. Consider yourself warned!"

Suri closed her eyes tightly and saw only black. There had been a bit of light at the end of the tunnel, and now again there was only thick, choking darkness.

She had no strength to get up from the floor. She stretched out her hand to her purse and fumbled for her cell phone.

"Abba," she said, and couldn't continue.

"Suri! Suri'le! What happened??"

"Abba," she said again. She couldn't tell about the letter. She couldn't deal with the fact that again her wedding was being smashed against a hard rock.

"Suri, did something happen?! I'm dropping everything and coming right away, just tell me what happened! Did someone attack you?! Hurt you?!"

"No, yes," there was a large stone in her throat that didn't let the words out, "there's a letter here, Abba... They know about the *chasunah*."

She didn't see Elya's face go white.

"Who's 'they'? Does it say anything?" he whispered.

"It doesn't say. It's them, those bad people who won't let me get married..."

Her voice drowned in a wave of tears. Elya, on the other end of the line, couldn't listen to it. His girl was suffering and no one was with her. He left his office, leaving instructions for those who needed them and said that he didn't know when he'd return. There were times when nothing was important, except for that which was truly important.

• • •

"No children were born to us," Avrohom Yisroel repeated, "and that was the only thing that marred our happiness at that time. We had honor, fame and fortune; we had almost everything we wanted, but only almost.

"After a number of years, we decided to adopt a child.

"We argued, because I wanted to adopt a son while my wife very much wanted a daughter. In the end we decided that we'll register for adoption, and what would come we'd accept willingly, whether it was a boy or girl.

"You surely remember," he turned to Shaya, "that your sister-in-law, Rochel, your brother's wife, worked in the welfare department."

"Right," Shaya said. "Rochel was a social worker. She worked many hours out of the house. I remember that."

"One of Rochel's cases was that of a girl from a family with multiple difficulties. The father was sick and unable to provide for the family, nor could he take care of himself. The mother tried to take care of her husband and her children and to earn a living, and wasn't exactly successful. Eventually, the home situation grew so bad that the children couldn't live there anymore.

"There were two children – a boy and a girl. Rochel, as far as I know, was very devoted to them and became very attached to them. She arranged for the older one to enter a dormitory which would take care of his food and education, and she looked for an adoptive family for the girl, who was really not more than a baby.

"The girl was in a foster home for some time, and then the mother died suddenly. I don't know the exact cause. I do know that Rochel was very broken by it. Now there was no one to take any interest in the girl's fate. She took it upon herself to find a family that would legally adopt her, a family where she would be happy, one that would care for her, educate her properly and be responsible for her future.

"All this took place just when we were trying our hardest to receive a child for adoption. Anyone who knows anything about adoption knows that the adoptive parents' first preference is a young baby. The older the child, the more baggage he has and the more he remembers his biological parents – all of which makes it harder for him to integrate with the new family.

"We knew that if we went through the accepted channels, it would take a very long time until we received a child. The waiting list was long, very long… It's frightening to think, sometimes, that there are parents who neglect their children when there are so many who are desperate for a child… In any event, with our money and connections we were able to bypass the regular route and try to receive a baby quickly, through other channels.

"As in every place, the Israeli welfare department isn't one hundred percent clean, either. It could be that in those days the lists weren't as exact as they are today, maybe there were employees in that office who felt that they could play G-d and decide people's fate, perhaps someone was blinded by the money – in any event, we received information that in Israel there was a baby who fit our requirements, and that we could have her for the right amount.

"I don't know what they told Rochel. I assume they told her something that spoke to her. They definitely told her that they found a family abroad, very wealthy, who would care for the baby in the best way possible. She assumedly was convinced, because the good of the baby was all that concerned her.

"It was obvious to Rochel that these rich adopting parents were Jews. She never dreamed that the Israeli welfare department would give a Jewish baby to non-Jewish parents. It could be that she did ask, and someone gave her false information. Everything becomes kosher when there's a large sum of money waiting at the close of the deal.

"To us as parents, in made no difference if the girl was Jewish or not. It meant nothing to us. True, I was familiar with anti-Jewish sentiments, but my wife knew – most probably a legacy from her parents' home – that the Jews were smart and that it was good to have connections with them.

"Whatever the case, the result was that the little Jewish baby was handed under the table to us, the Lewis family in Australia, for adoption.

"Now, I must add a few details that I left out before so that you can understand the whole story. Besides being the Australian boxing champion, I had another, less public, business. Shadier. I was one of..." Avrohom Yisroel lowered his eyes in embarrassment, "one of the leaders of the continent's criminal world. Outwardly, I was the country's sports "display window", but those who knew the truth about me didn't dare approach the exclusive neighborhood where I lived, or look at my grand house – even in a picture…"

...

On the way home, Elya called Devorah, who had gone shopping out of the city, and told her what happened.

"I'm coming straight home," she stopped and hailed a taxi. "Elya, it's impossible to continue like this. They're destroying the girl. She'll become emotionally unstable like this, and won't be able to get married at all. By then Bleich won't want her anymore, nor will any other family. How did this get out, Elya? How?? We all kept the secret so carefully…"

"I don't suspect Yisroel Yitzchok, if that's what you're trying to say," Elya said firmly. "You know what I suspect – actually quite a reasonable suspicion? I think our telephone line is at fault. I think – I'm almost positive – that someone's listening in on our phone calls…"

The private technician that Devorah Fuchsman called took his head out of the telephone box and nodded.

"You guessed right," he said. "Your line is tapped."

Devorah felt a chill crawl up her back. "Can you know who's listening? Or when this was attached? And how they attached it?"

He shook his head. "I have no idea who attached it. Do you remember if someone 'took care' of your telephone recently? Was something broken or something like that?"

Yes, Devorah remembered. One day there was no line and she had called some technicians and they had fixed the problem in no time. The technician smiled sadly.

"I believe that there was no problem, and there was nothing to fix. Whoever wanted to tap the line caused the problem so that you should call him. It's an accepted practice."

"Accepted practice?" Devorah didn't understand. "Accepted by whom?!"

He was still smiling. "Definitely not by honest people."

"And what did those listening hear?"

"Everything you said on the phone since they attached the bug."

Devorah understood. But something didn't make sense.

"You're sure that that's all they heard?"

"Probably. They're 'sitting' on your line."

"I'm afraid they're 'sitting' on another few things… We know that they have information that didn't go through the telephone, and in no way left this house, either."

The technician heard. It was hard for him to believe, but he was only a telephone technician.

"Maybe, while they were here, they managed to affix some listening chips in your house. For that, though, they have to be very sophisticated. You'd have to bring down a professional to check that. I know that there is such a thing, even though I've never seen it with my own eyes and I've never met someone who used it."

"I'm afraid that they are, indeed, sophisticated. Very…"

Devorah paid the technician and started to go to the kitchen to take a drink. Suddenly, though, she was gripped with fear. Who knew where else there were 'bugs'?! And maybe there was also some sort of electric eye on their refrigerator that would check what Devorah Fuchsman liked to drink, in order to know in which bottle of drink in the grocery to put very sophisticated material that would cause her to speak in her sleep and reveal all her secrets…?

• • •

"Thank G-d, today I'm able to speak in hindsight," Avrohom Yisroel said. "As you surely know, I became a Jew. This process didn't take a week, or even a month. It was a long, many-year process, for part of which Naftali and Rochel are also responsible. But I'm getting ahead of myself.

"The baby made the long way from Israel to Australia. In our large, grand house waited a dream baby room that my wife, may she rest in peace, decorated with all that was needed – and wasn't needed. We were very excited, especially my wife, who wanted a daughter very badly. And the truth is, after I saw the adorable baby, I was also convinced.

"We went through a short time of real happiness. The baby, who seemed to be in great need of warmth and love, accepted all that we showered upon her. She became attached to us very quickly and reciprocated her love. The emptiness in our lives was filled, and the three of us were a happy family, desperately hoping that the happiness would never end.

"It did end, though. Very quickly.

"Rochel Bleich, the dedicated social worker, couldn't separate emotionally from the child whom she had taken care of with such devotion. She knew that for the good of the child, it was best to break ties, but she couldn't do it. Today, I believe it was *Hashem* Who wanted the ties between Rochel and the girl to remain, in order to save the child when the time came.

"Rochel would call us every so often, ask about the girl and make sure that everything was okay. At first, we were happy to cooperate. We told her how cute the child was, how she was acclimating nicely to her new surroundings. Gradually, though, when the calls didn't stop, we began to feel that it was sort of a bother. We adopted a baby in order to be a complete family like all other families, not in order to always remember that our daughter is adopted, and that there's someone who feels possessive about her besides us. We tried to hint gently to Rochel that, now that everything was fine, she could feel free to take care of other children and relax that the child was settled. She said: 'Yes, of course,' and agreed with us, but the phone calls didn't actually stop. Just the opposite, they increased. Almost every week, Rochel would call; it seemed to be out of her control. Today I understand that it was being controlled by *HaKadosh Boruch Hu*.

"At one point we told her plainly that she should stop calling, so that the adoption process could end seamlessly. Of course, she agreed with us, but after a few days she was once again on the line.

"It's possible that by then Rochel already knew the truth – that the girl had been adopted by a non-Jewish couple. She may have wanted to maintain contact in order not to lose the girl, and maybe to lay the groundwork for the next stage, which I'm about to relate to you."

• • •

When Mendel Lederman went down, as he did each day lately, to his eavesdropping room and tried to connect to the Fuchsman home, he found that it was impossible to get a connection.

"They found it," he muttered to himself. "They found it and disconnected everything. Why? Why do people do this to themselves…?"

He sat there for some time, trying to come up with a new plan of action that would prevent this secret wedding. No threats worked on these foolish families. He had to somehow shock them. Sometimes, in order to prevent someone from falling off a cliff, it was necessary to physically pull him back.

The target this time would be Shaya Bleich. His family was alone, without protection. If something happened to him, it would shake them up; they would stop everything until they saw him back home, in one piece.

He looked through his notebook and reached for the phone.

"I have a new objective," he said to his contact. Together, they wove the plan.

• • •

"It seems," Avrohom Yisroel continued his story, "that as soon as Rochel Bleich discovered that her darling was adopted by non-Jews, and would most likely live the life of a goy, she decided to do everything she could to prevent it – at any price.

"Her problem was that she couldn't include anyone in the plan. No official body - and no sane individual, either - would have even thought to try to remove the child from our possession. Whoever inquired the slightest bit, and understood that I was involved in organized crime, dropped it like a hot potato. No one was willing to put his life in danger.

"Besides, it's safe to assume that if Rochel had included someone in her plan, I would have eventually found out about it and made sure that it didn't succeed. She therefore had to do everything secretly, and endanger only her own life. Her husband, of course, didn't let her go it alone, and so the two of them – with unparalleled self-sacrifice – fought for the girl's soul."

Avrohom paused and sipped from the water in front of him. It wasn't easy for him to relive the past events. Shaya Bleich also reached for his cup. His mouth was dry. For the first time he was hearing the beginnings of the answer to the big mystery which overshadowed his life.

"Excuse me?"

Two men stood by their table. Their gaze flitted from one to the other.

"We're looking for someone by the name of Black."

"There's no Black here," Shore said. "Try the next table."

"Maybe Bloke? Blike?" they asked.

"Bleich," Shaya said. What did these fellows want from him?

"Blike, that's it," one of them said dryly. "Come with us, please."

"I'm very busy right now," Shaya said. "I'm in middle of an important meeting. Can I help you with something?"

He didn't notice Shore's eyes boring into the two men like a pair of skewers.

"You can help us only by coming with us."

At this point Shore, fearing that the naïve Shaya would simply go with the two men as they had asked, spoke up:

"Who are you, please?"

One of the men pulled out a police permit. Shore asked to see it. He inspected it carefully.

"Okay," he said, "Mr. Bleich will not go with you without first consulting with a lawyer."

Shaya looked at Shore wide eyed. Shore's look indicated that he sit tight and keep quiet.

"He can consult with a lawyer soon, after the arrest," the other man said impassively.

"Arrest???" Shaya cried.

Shore shushed him. But Shaya had to understand.

"Excuse me, sirs, did you perhaps check if this is a mistake? Because as far as I know, there's no reason in the world to arrest me."

An amused smile appeared on the face of one of the policemen.

"That the judge will decide, Mr. Black. Now you are to come with us."

The bewildered Shaya stood up without a word.

"We'll have to end the meeting now," Shore said and also stood up, "not at all according to plan. I'll go with Mr. Bleich, and we'll be in touch as soon as possible."

Avrohom Yisroel's astonished gaze accompanied the small group that was leaving the hotel lobby. Scenes like these were familiar to him from the distant past. Since he converted, though, and changed his way of life, he knew the word 'arrest' only from the newspaper. What did it mean? What crime did Yeshaya Bleich commit, a man who made such an honest impression?! Was someone intentionally incriminating him? And what would be with his story, which he'd only just begun…?!

# CHAPTER 39

Shloime Bleich stepped into the house. He was alarmed at the quiet that greeted him. True, it was morning, when his brothers and sisters weren't home, but his mother was always there, cooking and cleaning, organizing and making enough noise.

"Ima??"

There was no answer. If Ima left, the door would have been locked, and it wasn't. He was sure of it. He had pressed down lightly on the handle and simply entered.

"Ima??"

Eventually, Shloime came to the utility porch and found his mother there, definitely not in the position in which he had hoped to find her.

Chana sat on the floor, the telephone thrown down near her, staring blankly into space.

"Ima!!" Shloime yelled, "Ima, answer me!! Talk to me!!"

Chana shook her head slightly. She had no strength for more than that.

"Ima, what happened?! Why are you sitting like that on the floor?!"

Chana wanted to answer him, but couldn't. She moved her lips, but no sound came out.

"Ima, just tell me one word!! Something!! Did somebody die? Somebody's sick? Somebody collapsed? Who??"

Chana managed to get out only one word, shrilly:

"Abba…"

"Abba?? What happened to Abba???"

Chana tried to stand up. Shloime ran to bring her a cup of water. When he returned, Chana was leaning against the porch wall, already somewhat recovered. She thankfully took the cup from him.

"They arrested Abba," she said. "He's now being detained."

"They arrested Abba??"

"Wait a minute, Shloime. I'll get you a cup of water, too."

With the strength of a mother, Chana managed to stand.

"Why did they arrest Abba??"

"I wish I knew," she breathed hard. "They just came over to him in the hotel and arrested him."

"And what did they say? What's the reason?!"

She shook her head. "I couldn't understand. I'll talk to Abba later and he'll explain it to me."

"But Ima," Shloime called after her as she went towards the kitchen, "Abba didn't do anything wrong."

"Shloime'le," she called back, "when someone wants to incriminate somebody, it can be done without a problem. One day you're an honest person, and the next you're a dangerous criminal behind bars."

"That means someone wants to frame Abba?"

"I strongly suspect so."

"You suspect somebody specific?"

"Yes," Chana said, "somebody who, for a long time already, is trying to hold us back and his name is Mendel Lederman."

"You think that Lederman arranged that they should arrest Abba?!"

"I think so. Yes."

"Ima, this man has to be stopped."

"It's impossible to stop him," Chana said, and turned to Shloime with sad eyes. "He's without brakes…"

• • •

Surprised at the developments, Avrohom Yisroel sat in the hotel lobby and dialed his friend.

"The meeting ended earlier than expected," he said.

"Why?"

"Under strange circumstances. Very. Can you come get me?"

"Gladly."

A short time later, as the car glided down the dark streets, the friend asked again why the meeting had ended so quickly.

"It was very sudden," Avrohom Yisroel said. "Two policemen appeared out of nowhere and asked Yeshaya Bleich to accompany them. The investigator went with Bleich, and promised to continue the meeting at another time."

"Policemen? Arrest? It doesn't smell good."

"No, it doesn't. At the moment, though, there's nothing I can do except wait for developments."

And as if custom ordered, his cell phone rang. On the line was – Danny Shore.

"First of all, I apologize for the sudden interruption of the meeting, which truly took us by surprise. Secondly, I feel that I must fill you in on the developments."

Actually, more than Shore felt obligated, he knew it was worth keeping Avrohom Yisroel near him. The man was important to the investigation, and constant contact with him was crucial.

"Yeshaya Bleich was arrested because he didn't have a valid visa."

"Really? Very strange," Avrohom responded. "He gives the impression of being very organized. How long is he here? And why didn't he renew his visa?"

"That's just it," Shore said, a bit uncomfortably, "Right now he doesn't have any visa, neither valid nor invalid."

"So how did he enter Australia?! That's impossible. Someone messed up here. Either he, or the customs officers or the police."

"They're looking into it now," Shore said. "Bleich of course claims that he came into the country legally with a visa, and I, of course, know that he's saying the truth, because we came together. Except that meanwhile, this visa isn't around."

"Interesting. Strange," Avrohom said.

"Maybe the visa got lost," Shore said. "You know, we're moving around a lot. One minute of distraction is enough to lose a document."

"Naturally," Avrohom said, though he definitely didn't think that was it.

"I'll let you know about any further developments," Shore said, and left Avrohom Yisroel very thoughtful.

• • •

The door to Lederman's office swung open. The secretary, sitting opposite the door, lifted her eyes in alarm, but relaxed when she saw a yeshiva *bochur* stride briskly inside. The calm didn't last too long, though.

"I want to see Mendel Lederman immediately," the *bochur* demanded.

"He's in middle of a meeting right now."

"That doesn't interest me in the slightest," the *bochur* said forcefully. He went over to the investigator's office, pushed on the handle and went inside, completely ignoring the client sitting there.

"Mr. Lederman," he said, "I demand that you act immediately to call off my father's arrest. We know that you pulled the strings of the---"

To his client's astonishment, Lederman picked up his eyes and said:

"There's what to talk about, Bleich. It's all a matter of negotiation."

"Negotiation?!" Shloime's face was weary. He had no time for jokes.

"Yes, we'll talk about it. I'll just finish with my client for a few minutes. Wait outside, Bleich."

Deflated, Shloime left the room and sat down on one of the blue chairs in the waiting room. He heard murmuring from inside the room. It sounded like the client didn't like the fact that the meeting was interrupted so rudely, and that now it would be cut short.

After a few minutes, though, Shloime saw the client leave holding a black briefcase, and heard Lederman call him inside.

Shloime sat down and gave him a hostile stare.

"I know you're the reason why my father is now being detained in Australia. You and no other reason."

Lederman looked out the window, as if the view of the back yard impressed him. "You know correctly."

"Can I know the reason why you're harassing us without letup?"

"We've already spoken about this, Bleich," Lederman sighed. "I explained to you that I must stop this wedding. If you don't trust me and the information that I have, even though I can't share it with you, I must take the necessary steps."

"Having my father arrested in a foreign country for nothing he did is called 'taking steps'? Have you no limits, Mendel Lederman? What will be the next step? Maybe a booby-trapped car that will, *chalilah*, kill me or my *kallah*, and then you'll definitely prevent the *chasunah*? Excuse me for being so harsh, Lederman, but your behavior is no less harsh."

"You're very worked up, Bleich. This is not a way to make decisions."

"What decisions?"

Lederman stood up and began to pace the room. Shloime looked at the desk and fiddled with his pen.

"Your father will be released today," Lederman said, "if this secret wedding that you're planning is called off."

Shloime didn't ask how Lederman had the information. One didn't ask such things about Lederman.

"You have to understand, Lederman," he said vehemently, "that you can't take responsibility for other people's lives. Nor do you need to. What you're doing now is way out of line. True, my parents hired you years ago to investigate the matter, but with that your part of the story ends. No one asked you to advise us what's proper or not proper to do, and definitely not to take actual steps to cause us to act one way or another."

"I understand," Lederman said, "I understand. In other words, young Bleich, you're standing at the edge of a chasm, and I'm holding out a hand to save you and you're saying: 'Excuse me, that's out of your jurisdiction. No one asked you to mix in; don't try to prevent me from choosing. I want to fall to the depths from my personal choice.' Am I right?"

"No," Shloime said decidedly, "there's a difference. If I was able to see the chasm with my own eyes, I would anyway be careful not to fall into it. This chasm that you're describing, though, is only in your imagination. I don't see it, and I don't have to believe you that it exists. And between you and me, after you dared do such things – to threaten my *kallah* and cause my father's arrest in a foreign country – my faith in you is badly damaged."

"All right," Lederman said briskly, "You have to decide. Canceling the wedding in exchange for your father's immediate release."

"Lederman," Shloime choked, "You're talking like a slave merchant."

"That's because you've left me with no other choice. I can't just stand here with folded arms and watch the tragedy that you're bringing upon yourselves. I don't understand why you choose to see this as evil instead of viewing it as my concern for you."

"A concerned person doesn't act with such cruelty."

"You're mistaken. The more concerned a person is, the less he'll hesitate to cause short term harm for the sake of the long term."

Shloime was quiet. He had no patience then for debate.

"The wedding will not be cancelled, of course," he said.

"Okay, that's your decision."

"And as long as it's not cancelled, my father will remain under arrest…?!"

"Correct."

"What is he, a hostage?!"

"You want to call it that? Call it that."

"You have no heart!" Shloime yelled, and his shout reached beyond the walls of the room.

"Please lower your voice," Lederman said, "and I don't think I deserve such treatment after all I've done for you. You understand that I have no personal interest in this story, and if I was a bad person, I would leave it today, this minute."

"You kill people!"

"No, you're wrong. I'm just trying to make sure that doesn't happen."

"Why? Who wants to kill us?"

"Someone who's a bit more evil than me."

"And you can't tell me his name?"

"His name won't mean anything to you. You don't know him."

Shloime stood up and moved towards Lederman, who stood in the corner next to the small sink.

"If I don't know him, then why does he want to hurt me?"

"Because of a certain thing that your biological parents did in the past." Lederman took a deep breath. He had to be very, very careful now.

"Tell me his name. Tell me his name!! At least say that!!"

"I can't, Bleich. I can't. If I reveal who it is, everything will be revealed. For your own good, it's not worth it. For your sake, for the sake of your *kallah*."

Shloime took a step closer to Lederman. Lederman was up against the wall. He looked into Shloime's red eyes and knew that the normally refined *bochur* was in a state of despair, and was capable of almost anything.

"You said that we'll negotiate, right, Lederman?"

"That's what I said."

"Okay. At this point I'm willing to cancel the wedding if you tell me the name of this man."

"I'm telling you, the name won't tell you anything."

"What do you care? I'm willing to cancel the wedding for this."

"Fine," Lederman said. "Let me think about it for a few minutes."

The drained Shloime went back to his seat and sat down.

Lederman also sat down. Neither of them looked at the other. Lederman took a piece of paper and doodled forcefully on it, trying to measure the danger against the hope.

"Okay," he said finally, and looked Shloime full in the face. "His name is: Mike Lewis. But I'm warning you, the man is dangerous. Very…"

• • •

A large car pulled up next to the gates of the detention house. A tall man emerged, threw a good-bye over his shoulder and closed the door to the car. He was familiar with detention houses, very familiar, but only from the past. Since his conversion, detention houses and prisons weren't on his list of familiar places.

"Should I wait for you?" the driver asked him.

"No, it'll take some time."

He walked down the path and gave his things to the guard to check. In his small briefcase he had a *sefer tehillim*, *gemara*, tissues and a pen. Nothing that he needed to hide.

Soon he would meet Shore and Shaya Bleich. Even though Bleich was being held, Shore insisted that their conversation continue. Yeshaya Bleich could come out for a while and sit with them. The whole arrest still wasn't clear to Avrohom Yisroel, and he had a feeling that he wasn't the only one groping in the dark.

The two of them were already waiting for him next to the small table. They shook hands. Shore was truly happy that he came. Bleich looked down. His hands and feet were cuffed, as was required for every prisoner. Avrohom wanted to ask some questions about the arrest – perhaps he could help – but the expressions on Bleich's and Shore's faces told him to get straight to the point.

Shore's recorder was sitting on the table, waiting.

"All right," began Avrohom Yisroel, "I'll continue from where

I left off. Rochel would call our house almost every week to ask about our adopted daughter, despite our repeated requests that she stop.

"Eventually, when it really began to bother us, we changed our telephone number to an unlisted number. For a while we didn't receive any calls from Rochel, and we were happy to be left alone. After a few weeks, though, she called again, to the new number.

"For us it was a sign that Rochel's interest in the girl went beyond missing her. If she invested so much effort to find our unlisted number, she must have another, more important aim.

"My wife was very angry. She adopted a baby, did everything in order to feel like a normal, complete family, and this annoying woman wouldn't let us forget the adoption and begin a new, wonderful life.

"I told her that we may have to hide the girl, or protect our house in some way. For me, such things were part of life. It was everyday fare. But she didn't want to even hear of it. 'There's no reason for us to do that. We received a baby; we paid no small amount for her. Now she's ours. Why should we have to hide her? Because of some strange Israeli woman's obsession?'

"She stubbornly refused to take any safety precautions, though I tried convincing her. We lived in a private house in a suburban area, where the houses were large distances from one another. The girl's room was on the second floor, and the windows faced the backyard. There were bars on the windows, but there's no bar that can't be broken into. The house was surrounded by trees and thick shrubbery.

"Constant fear nibbled at me. I knew that the way we had gotten the child wasn't completely above board. Today I know that if it had gone through the accepted channels, a Jewish girl would never have been given to a gentile family. Then, I thought that perhaps there was something not so straight about how the girl was taken from her parents, and maybe her parents were the ones sending Rochel to find out about her. They wanted her to maintain contact at any price, so that when the day came – and I didn't know how close that day was – they would be able to have her back…"

# CHAPTER 40

"Even though my wife was strongly against it," Avrohom Yisroel continued his story, "I wasn't at peace. The girl was in danger, and it was our job to do everything possible to protect her. I saw it as an inseparable part of my responsibilities as a father. And so, without my wife knowing about it, I hired someone to come down and safeguard every inch of the house, including the large garden. It was done in a way that my wife wouldn't discover it, and didn't at all disturb the house's appearance. Only after the work was complete did I allow myself to relax, and to calmly watch the girl playing in the yard, my happiness complete.

"I never dreamed that the entire expensive system was completely unnecessary, and that our daughter would be taken from us in a totally different manner.

"I remember that day like yesterday," something in Avrohom Yisroel's face shifted, as if he was living the experience right then, rather than years before. "It was on a Sunday, our weekly shopping day. The sun shone brightly. That week we were to celebrate our daughter's birthday, and of course, the shopping was accordingly festive. We didn't want to buy her just one present, but lots and lots, maybe to make up to ourselves all the empty years and all the children that we didn't have.

We drove our car down the crowded streets. I sat in front, my wife and daughter in the back. During the drive, it seemed to me that a certain car stuck with us constantly. To check it out, I made a few sharp turns one after another and, as I had feared, the white car stayed with us.

"I didn't want to worry my wife. I knew she'd panic. And besides, I had no problem 'neutralizing' this car. In my pocket I had my gun, which I carried at all times.

"'Guard your wife and child carefully' I told myself, 'and at the first opportunity, get rid of this car and its passengers.'

"I remind you again, gentlemen, that crime was my expertise. Just as you set up a business meeting or take a walk in the park, so I got rid of anyone who didn't seem too 'friendly' to me. Life taught me not to be soft. If it looked like someone wanted to harm you, even if it only looked like it, be sure to take care of him first.

"I purposely entered an underground parking lot. It's hard to escape from such a place, while on the other hand, it's easy to do what's 'needed' without too many spectators. The thought of a face to face confrontation with someone who wanted to take something from me – a thought which might send fear through a regular person – made me tingle with expectation.

"I parked the car in a place that had space for only two cars. I expected to see the white car park next to us but it continued on to the lot underneath us, disappearing into the darkness.

"Had my wife not been with me, I would have followed the other car, determined to discover who it was and mete out justice to him. We were all together, though, and spirits were high. It would have been a shame to ruin it because of all sorts of suspicions.

"We made our way towards the stores. My wife wanted to go into the large, expensive toy store in the center of the street. There, she was sure, we could find the nicest birthday presents.

"I kept looking in all directions, scared of every muscleman who passed a bit too close to us.

"'What's with you?' my wife asked. 'You're not focused. Worried about something?'

'No, everything's fine,' I told her, and tried to arrange my face in a relaxed expression. I didn't even want to tell her to watch the child carefully. I was afraid it would spoil the family atmosphere that was so important to us. I promised myself to keep a constant eye on her.

The busy toy store could be seen in the distance. Displayed in front were giant dolls that sang and danced, and many children were gathered around them.

"'Dolly! Dolly!' our little one cried. We were about to go in with her when, right near the store's entrance, I stopped.

"'Let's go,' my wife urged me.

"Why did I stop? Because right there stood a street musician, violin in hand, and he was playing an old, forgotten tune that my mother – whom I had loved and who had already passed on – used to sing to me when I was young.

"'I must hear this song,' I told my wife excitedly.

"'All right,' she said. 'We'll wait.'

"And she stood there, the impatient child in her arms.

"The song was long. Even as I gave myself over, though, to its every line, which brought me back to my mother's knee, the girl and her mother started to lose their patience.

"'Come on, when will it finish already? We want to go inside,' my wife complained.

"'It's already finishing,' I kept answering. The musician, though, seeing my excitement, finished the song and immediately started again.

"'Can't you move from here?' my wife grumbled. 'Just because of a lullaby?'

"'You have to understand,' I said. 'You know how much I miss my mother, and this song makes me feel as if I'm with her once again.'

"My daughter, though, had had enough. 'Dolly! Dolly!' she screamed and cried, as impatient children are wont to do.

"'You know what?' I said to my wife, 'Go into the store with her and I'll stay here for another few minutes.' A frightening thought flashed through my head. I should leave the girl with my wife, who wasn't watching her properly?

"The tune, though, called to me, and I couldn't ignore it. What could happen, already, if I was right next to the store? If someone wanted to kidnap the child, he would have to go through the store's entrance, right where I was standing.

"My wife didn't wait too long. She went into the store, holding the child. I stayed outside, wanting to hear again the song that transported me years back in time, and infused me with a peace and serenity that were so crucial to me, especially now."

• • •

"Did you hear from Abba?" Shloime asked his mother.

"Yes, he was able to call me," Chana replied.

"*Nu*, and?"

"He claims that someone hid his visa. He has no other way to explain it. The visa was on him when he entered the country, of that he's certain. He wouldn't have been able to enter without it. And if he lost it, no one except him should have known about it.

496 »  *Thicker Than Water*

The fact that they came to arrest him for not having a visa, only after which he looked and discovered that it was indeed missing, proves that someone must have taken it from him in order to later charge him with not having a valid visa."

"Just like Yosef HaTzaddik and Binyomin and the goblet," Shloime burst out. "Except that instead of giving him something and claiming that he stole it, they took something in order to falsely accuse him of traveling without it."

"Could be," Chana sighed. "What's clear is that Abba is a *tzaddik* for suffering all this, and whoever did it to him is definitely not a *tzaddik*."

"I was just by him," Shloime said.

"By whom??"

"Lederman."

"You were by Lederman??"

"Yes. An evil man."

Chana wanted to know everything. Immediately.

"He's not willing to release Abba," Shloime said quietly. "He actually admits that he's responsible for the arrest. He only agrees to free him if we cancel the wedding."

"I don't believe you." Chana covered her face with her hands.

"I made a deal with him," Shloime said. "I agreed to cancel the *chasunah* if he told me who's responsible for this whole story, the man because of whom – so Lederman claims – we can't get married."

"You agreed to cancel the *chasunah*??? Shloime, I don't know how many question marks to put after that question!! *You agreed to cancel the chasunah*???"

"Just a minute, Ima, wait a minute. I'll explain. It really does sound terrible, but that was the sensible thing to do. First of all, Abba will be released immediately, and I couldn't bear the thought of his sitting locked up for even one minute. And besides, I want to talk directly to this person, whose name Lederman told me – Mike Lewis. I'm sure that if I speak to him, I'll be able to understand what's going on here, and eventually be able to have the wedding…"

Chana looked at him with huge eyes.

"You made a mistake, Shloime, a big, fat mistake!" she yelled. "Again you acted hastily! Foolishly!! Better you shouldn't have gone to him at all, not made deals with him and not received any names! What will this name give you?! You don't even know who it is, what it's all about, and you're already so sure you can fix the world! Maybe it will harm your parents, Naftali and Rochel?! You're not involved in the story and know nothing about it! Making contact like this could cause tremendous damage instead of helping!!! And in exchange you agreed to cancel the wedding?!"

"And what about Abba?!" Shloime cried heatedly.

"We would have taken a lawyer," Chana breathed deeply. "We would have gotten Abba out of this mess. It's false, after all. We're not in the hands of Mendel Lederman, but in the hands of *HaKadosh Boruch Hu*, Who runs the world."

Shloime's mouth was dry. The notepaper, on which Lederman had written Mike Lewis' name and his address abroad, was sweaty in his palm.

"All right," he said, "nothing really happened. I promised him to cancel the wedding, but I'm only one party here. If Abba and you and the *kallah's* family don't agree, the promise means nothing. There's no agreement."

Chana studied him. Finally, he was speaking sense.

"No *chasunah* is being cancelled," she said quietly, "not because of Lederman, and not because of anything else. A person's match is preordained before he's even created. And if Suri Fuchsman is meant for you, the *chasunah* will take place, no matter how many obstacles pop up along the way. But I beg of you, Shloime," she paused, perhaps to lend emphasis to her words, "I beg from the bottom of my heart, don't make any contact with this person whose name Lederman gave you. We don't know what it could lead to, and what it will do to us and to your parents. Promise me, okay? Do you promise…?!"

...

"The beautiful tune that the street musician played over and over had me bewitched. I threw coin after coin into his violin case to show my satisfaction. It seems he got the message, and each time he reached the end, he started again from the beginning.

"During those minutes, my wife and child completely flew out of my head. In the back of my mind flickered the thought that they were shopping and enjoying themselves.

"I never dreamed that the man holding the violin had never been a street musician, and never would be again. It was only on that day, for that short while, that an entire show was put on in order to take our daughter from us."

"My brother Naftali also knew how to play the violin well," Shaya said longingly. "When he was a young teenager, he would play for the whole family on Chanukah."

Shore looked at Shaya in amazement. Didn't he make the connection?!

"Eventually I realized," Avrohom Yisroel continued, "that I had had no contact with my family for more than twenty minutes. I recovered at once, thanked the musician and hurried into the store.

"'Excuse me,' I asked one of the salesmen, 'where's the doll section?'

"He stared at me without answering. Only then did I realize that he wasn't paying any attention to my question, but rather to the commotion taking place in the store.

"*What noise*, I thought to myself at first. *What yelling! Who's yelling like that?!*

"The customers – and there were many of them – kept moving towards the center of the store. There, I understood, stood a woman I couldn't see, screaming non-stop.

"'Why is she screaming? What happened?' I asked somebody standing near me.

"'She says they took her daughter from her,' the man replied.

"'Took her dau--- *what???*'

"I shot like a missile towards the center of the crowd, forcibly shoving people to the side, stepping on people, trampling toys.

"In the middle of the crowd I saw what my heart told me I'd see, and I so didn't want to see: my wife standing and screaming hysterically. Next to her stood some of the store's employees, trying to calm her, to give her water, to tell her that the girl simply got lost in the large store or, at most, wandered out of the store and into a neighboring store, and that they'd find her right away.

"But my wife didn't want to hear. Deep down, she knew the truth, that the little girl hadn't gone anywhere on her own, that she'd been deliberately taken.

"Police sirens were heard outside. Officers burst into the store, having been called by the managers. It was impossible to talk to my wife. They tried to get me to talk, but I didn't have much to say, since I simply didn't know how this all happened.

"The policemen fanned out through the entire area. I gave them a description of the girl and, together with many volunteers and passerby who were touched by the story, a broad search was conducted, with no results.

"Truthfully speaking, I wasn't at all interested in the presence of the police. The police knew me, and even though just then there was relative quiet between us, I didn't want to wake up any sleeping bears. I had no doubt that they saw the story as more than the mere disappearance of a girl, and suspected that it had some connection to one of my questionable deeds.

"Not many minutes passed and the media began to arrive at the scene. A girl who disappeared from a busy store in broad daylight was a first rate story. I absolutely didn't want to say a single word to the cameras, so I took my wife and we hurried home. We locked ourselves up in the house, fearing the worst – to be alone again, without the girl whom we already loved very much."

"And what really happened?" Shore asked curiously.

"What happened was," Avrohom took a deep breath, "my wife went into the store with the child. They went straight to the doll section, where it seems a saleslady, marketing a new kind of sweet, was waiting for them. She was handing out samples to everyone in store. The girl, of course, wanted to taste, and my wife didn't mind receiving a free packet of sweets.

"This saleslady, though, must have been a saleslady for only one day, just like the street musician, whose job had been to ambush me outside and separate me from my family. The sweets given to my little girl were different than the sweets handed out to the other customers.

"Not too much time passed before the girl, who had been so awake before, began to feel very drowsy. She stopped showing interest in the toys and her birthday presents, and only asked to go home to sleep.

"One of the store's employees, who appears to not have been an innocent worker, but someone planted there, dressed in the staff uniform, came to her assistance. Seeing that my wife was loaded with packages, she offered to go with her to the checkout counter, and to hold the child while the bill was rung up.

"My wife agreed. The child's tired wails must have exhausted her, too, and she only wanted to complete the purchase with as little bother as possible and leave.

"She walked, pushing the wagon piled high with toys ahead of her, while the employee walked behind her, carrying the sleeping child in her arms.

"My wife didn't bother turning around on the way to the checkout counter. She was sure that the employee was walking together with her. When she reached the checkout area, however, she casually turned around, wanting to make sure the worker and girl were with her – and discovered that they weren't. The employee wasn't there, and neither was the girl.

"She looked around, but there was no sign of either of them.

"I believe that the 'worker' disappeared into one of the many turns in the store and smuggled the girl out a back door into waiting hands.

"It was all so carefully planned. Keeping me outside, putting the child to sleep, stealing her outside. I didn't believe that someone had managed to fix me – me, captain of the world of crime. I decided, and I knew that I'd uphold the decision, to hound to the bitter end those who had done this. I'd pay them back and return the child to us.

"I had everything at my disposal in order to discover who had done it. All the crime organizations with their sources of information fell at my feet.

"I set up a special staff to, first of all, uncover the identity of the kidnappers. Not too much time passed before I received the answer I had expected: It had been Rochel and Naftali Bleich, the social worker who had continuously bothered us, and her husband. They were the ones who had followed us, set up a plan – an ingenious one, I must admit – and, with some outside help, successfully pulled it off.

"I was determined to even the score, but, in a way I still haven't figured out, Naftali and Rochel Bleich, together with our daughter, disappeared into thin air…"

...

"Hello, this is Chana Bleich from Israel. Is it possible to speak with R' Nachman?"

Yes, of course. It was always possible to speak with R' Nachman. Despite the fact that Shaya had left his house a considerable amount of time before, R' Nachman still considered him his guest and good friend.

Chana briefly told him the story of the arrest. R' Nachman was shocked. He insisted that it was a shameful libel. There was no reason for someone as wonderful as Shaya Bleich to be detained, except if some ill-intentioned person wished it.

"That's what we think, too," Chana said.

"Do you have any clue who would want to do this?"

"We don't only have a clue, we know who it is. We tried speaking with the man, but he entered into negotiations that I don't even want to repeat. We want to try to free Shaya on our own, and that's why I'm turning to you."

"I'll help with whatever I can," R' Nachman promised, and Chana knew that he would. "But tell me anyway the name of the person behind this. Maybe there'll be someone who can convince him to leave his crooked ways."

"Oh, no," Chana said confidently, "that would never happen. He's tough as nails. We tried convincing him in every way possible, but it didn't help. He even claims that he's looking out for us and doing it all for our sake."

"Really!" R' Nachman was amazed. "All right, in any case, tell me his name."

Chana hesitated. That wasn't why she had called. She truly didn't believe that anyone would succeed where they had failed, and be able to move Lederman. She had only wanted to ask for communal assistance.

"The community is at your service," R' Nachman said warmly. "And there are wealthy, influential people here. We must try all avenues."

With mixed feelings, Chana gave him Mendel Lederman's phone number. He promised to do everything possible. The call ended on an optimistic note; Chana felt that the gloom had brightened a little. Except that Shloime, entering the room with slow steps, punctured her improved mood.

"Who were you talking to?"

"A good Jew from Brooklyn, where Abba stayed a few months ago, at the beginning of his trip. He promised to use all his connections in order to release Abba."

"And you gave him Lederman's phone number, Ima?"

"Yes."

"I'm not sure Lederman will like that his name is being bandied about as the bad man who purposely caused Abba's arrest. And if Lederman won't like it, he'll close himself off to any kind of persuasion, which means that Abba will continue to be detained. I hope I'll be proven wrong."

# CHAPTER 41

No public activists, well connected people or any other person called Mendel Lederman that day, save R' Nachman himself.

It wasn't easy to get hold of Mendel Lederman, but R' Nachman wasn't the sort to admit defeat because of a secretary who screened calls.

"My name is Nachman," he said patiently, "and I must speak to your boss about an urgent matter that can't wait. I'm calling from the States."

"He's in middle of a meeting right now," the secretary followed protocol. R' Nachman wasn't impressed.

"There's no meeting that can't be interrupted," he said calmly. "Please tell your boss that it's a matter that can save many lives, including his own. I'll wait on the line."

The secretary did as he said. R' Nachman listened to the classical music and allowed himself to sing along, despite his croaky voice.

"Sir?" the secretary got back to him, "about which matter do you need him?"

"Bleich."

Not three minutes passed and the esteemed investigator was on the line.

"Hello, Mendel Lederman, this is Nachman from Brooklyn speaking."

"Hello. How can I help you?"

"I can help you. I'm a good friend of Shaya Bleich, who is now sitting behind bars. I understand that you have ways to have him released."

"What's your connection to all this?" Lederman asked coldly.

"Just friendship. I'm trying to help a good friend."

"Then I suggest we end right now. We're talking about something which you know nothing about, so I don't think it's wise to stick your head in if you'd like to keep it."

R' Nachman heard the hostility loud and clear.

"It doesn't suit you, such a leading investigator, to ignore a few crumbs of information that might help you."

"I'll choose my crumbs of information all on my own. Thank you."

R' Nachman, though, didn't let it go. He told Lederman the whole story of his relationship with Shaya Bleich, from when Shaya started staying in his house until he left with the investigator.

"Listen," Lederman said with obvious impatience, "I don't need your information services. Shaya Bleich has been under my constant supervision since he stepped foot out of Israel. All that you're telling me, I already know. Thank you very much, and have a goo---"

"Wait, wait," R' Nachman called. He knew the man was about to hang up and wanted to tell him one more thing, just so he should know. "Just so you should know, a big philanthropist by the name of Avrohom Yisroel is personally taking care of all

Bleich's matters and funding his search. I believe he'll find the money to free Bleich, and if so, all your tricks are superfluous."

"I'm happy to hear," Lederman said sarcastically, "and I ask you to please free the phone line because we're busy with important things. Have a good day."

R' Nachman was left holding a dead phone. The man was definitely not an easy sort. It was hard to believe that something would come of the conversation, but at least he knew that he tried.

On the other side of the world, Lederman slammed down the receiver angrily and strode back to his office, to the client who was waiting there impatiently.

"I understand that this was something urgent," the client said.

"Urgent?" Lederman wiped the sweat from his forehead, "Nonsense, that's what it was. People think that if they're older than you, they must be smarter. They stick their noses everywhere. All right, let's continue from where we left off. So what did we say about---"

But he wasn't able to concentrate. He was angry at himself, that a phone call from some nudnik in America was distracting him so much.

"Should I bring you a cup of water?" the secretary asked from outside the room.

"Yes. It can't hurt."

Lederman sipped the water and raked through the data in his mind. The conversation couldn't be disturbing him for no reason. That usually didn't happen. Even if someone made him really angry, he was able to 'turn the page' and immediately get busy with something else.

There must have been something in that conversation that demanded his attention.

But what?

Lederman was so bothered that he apologized to his client and ended the meeting early. He promised him a new meeting gratis. He was willing to offer two meetings, as well as a ticket to the moon, so long as he was left alone to figure out what in heaven's name was the detail in the conversation that wasn't leaving him alone.

The client finally left. Lederman locked the door behind him.

All incoming and outgoing calls were automatically recorded. He'd listen to the conversation again –he'd listen to it ten times, if necessary, until he discovered what it was.

• • •

"Disappeared?" Shore repeated after Avrohom Yisroel.

"Disappeared completely. I was an expert at finding people who wanted to hide, but in their case, after many attempts, I lifted my hands in surrender. They had done clean, smooth work. There were no tracks. I waited for some mistake on their part, a wrong step that would reveal where they were, but it seemed they knew how dangerous I was and were very careful."

Shaya sat next to the small table, completely forgetting for a minute that he was in jail, and that soon he'd have to return to his cell.

"The only thing I was able to grab on to," Avrohom said, "was their family in Israel. I followed you constantly. I imagined that there was a limit to how long Naftali and Rochel could stay cut off from their entire families, and that they'd eventually try to contact you. Their mission, though, was so important to them, and their fear of me was so great, that they didn't dare make the slightest contact."

"I wish they would have made contact," Shaya sighed. "All the years we waited for a sign of life, and received none. We already thought the worst. At first, we made enormous efforts to find them. We did it very secretly, because we thought if the story got around it could harm them. Until one evening…"

"Yes, what happened one evening?" Shore turned to face Shaya. Was there some detail that Shaya had forgotten to tell him?

"One evening, I remember, I was in the house and someone shoved an envelope under the door. I opened it and inside was a note asking us to stop searching for Naftali and Rochel. Why did you send us that note?"

"Me?! I didn't send you any note. And why should I ask you such a thing? It was at least as important to me to find them. I kept waiting for your search to turn something up, after mine yielded nothing."

"So who sent that note?!" Shaya was floored.

"That's quite obvious," Shore said in his dry voice. "There's only one possibility: Naftali and Rochel themselves got the note to you in some way. It was important to them to tell you to stop searching so Mike Lewis shouldn't be able to find them."

"So why didn't they sign the note?!"

"That's understandable. Had they signed, or given any other indication that it was from them, you would have increased your efforts to find them – which was exactly the opposite of what they wanted you to do. Maybe they wanted you to think the note was from a hostile party and get scared off."

A policeman approached them. Shaya's visiting time was over. Avrohom Yisroel parted from him warmly.

"You'll be out of here very soon," he said. "Everything will fall into place, all things lost will be found and you'll be able to return home, to peace and quiet."

"Amen," Shaya's eyes were wet.

Avrohom Yisroel walked out slowly. Names from the past slipped into his mind, names that were once his world and today were quite forgotten. Names that he didn't want to remember. However, if he wanted to help Shaya Bleich get released from this bizarre custody, he had to remember them again.

In one of his diaries was an old telephone book containing all the names and addresses of all the leading figures of the underworld. Many of them still showed him great deference, even after he turned his back on their world and converted to Judaism. Some calls to a few central personalities would set Shaya Bleich free within mere hours.

Conversely, he couldn't go back and make contact with these people. True, his new, Jewish world was firm, but renewing such a relationship was likely to suck him back in. He was bound to lose much of his progress in Torah if he returned to that dunghill.

To call? Not to call?

Shaya Bleich was sitting in jail and he was able to help him. This help, though, was likely to be to his own detriment. What should he do?!

Avrohom Yisroel paced about his room as if it was a round jail cell. *Those doing a mitzvah come to no harm,* he repeated to himself over and over. *You'll merit doing the mitzvah of* pidyon shivuim, *freeing a captive. Trust that Hashem will help you remain a complete Jew even if you renew contact with those 'friends' of yours.*

Avrohom's lips moved in prayer as he went to dial the first number.

• • •

Lederman listened to the conversation. Again and again, he played the section that bothered him.

"A very big philanthropist… is taking care of all Bleich's matters and is funding his search…"

That was it. Something here smelled fishy. Donors gave

money to good and charitable causes, but didn't usually fund strangers' secret investigations after missing persons.

If so, it must be that this donor had some vested interest. And whoever has vested interest – must be somehow connected to the matter. And if he was in some way connected, he had to be someone from the inside, from within this complicated story called the Bleich family.

Mendel Lederman would discover who it was, without a doubt.

...

With an instinct that remained from those days, Avrohom Yisroel closed all the windows and locked the door, the receiver pressed to his ear.

In another few seconds, when the call would go through to 'Typhus' – his contact man's code name – contact with his old world would be renewed. Two fears weighed on his heart: One, that his soul would lose part of the holiness it had already attained, just by talking to these men. The second was a lesser fear, but more concrete. He knew there were still some unsettled accounts from the past. Though he did try to settle everything and pay whatever was needed in order to start fresh with a clean slate, there were some men who felt that accounts still weren't closed. They were lying in wait for him, waiting to trap him.

The call was connected. Avrohom spoke in a quiet voice, almost unheard. Typhus, on the other end of the line, was very surprised to hear the voice of his old friend.

Avrohom knew that Typhus owed him a favor. An iron rule in the underworld, where justice and integrity of a different sort held sway, was that a favor done received one in return.

Typhus understood the request and promised to take care of

it. He knew what had to be done. Avrohom thanked him. The call should have ended; there was no place for idle chatter. Avrohom, though, wished to say one more thing. To request.

"Typhus," he said, "We haven't spoken. I didn't contact you. Okay?"

"No problem," Typhus answered.

But Avrohom knew that it was a problem. Everything happening here was a problem for him. Typhus didn't owe him anything; there was nothing stopping him from passing along the fact that they had spoken, and the content of the conversation. If he did pass it along, Avrohom Yisroel's name would once again circle among the halls of crime, as one who didn't really disconnect from it all, but left only temporarily.

Avrohom had nothing in his arsenal to prevent the publicizing of the conversation. Right now, Typhus had no reason to repeat it, but if he would have, or if someone paid him for the information, he would publicize it.

"I'm appealing to your heart," Avrohom Yisroel said. It was good that Typhus didn't see the tears in his eyes. Actually, it was a pity he didn't see, because if he had, he would have been completely convinced that Mike Lewis had gone soft – and there were no softies in the world of crime. "I'm asking that the contents of this conversation go no further. Typhus, if there's anything that will get you into Paradise after all you've done in your life, it will be this favor."

Typhus laughed. A coarse laugh, like sewage. "To Paradise? The tickets ran out long ago, Mike." He then sobered. "All right, no problem. We didn't speak. We don't know each other. Even for a million dollars, they won't get anything else out of me."

Avrohom sighed. It was the most he could hope for.

...

A completely illogical idea rose in Lederman's mind. As an experienced investigator, though, he knew he couldn't dismiss any idea, even the most irrational, offhand.

Lederman went down to his special room in order to make this call. He would take all the necessary precautionary measures, since the man he was calling couldn't know where he was.

One ring. Another ring. Connection.

No voice came over the line, but Lederman knew they heard him.

"Marcel speaking," he said. It was years since he used his nickname.

"What do you want?" a deep voice was heard.

"A little information, that's all."

"Information? What information?"

"I want you to tell me how Mike Lewis is doing."

Sewage-like laughter was heard.

"Mike Lewis is dead," said the voice.

"Completely dead?" Lederman asked. He knew that in the slang of the underworld, the word 'dead' had several meanings.

"No, not completely," the voice laughed harder. "Only almost. What do you want to know?"

"Where he is, what he is, who he is."

"Forget him, he's not interesting."

"Not interesting? Really, Typhus, don't pull my leg."

"I'm not pulling your leg. He's out of the picture."

"Meaning?"

Lederman sensed that Typhus didn't want to answer, and his curiosity only grew.

"Five thousand dollars for three short answers," he gave a price.

"Don't try to buy me. I don't want to talk about him."

Lederman knew that whatever couldn't be bought for money,

could be bought for more money.

"Fifteen thousand dollars."

"I have to go, Marcel. Have a good day."

"Thirty thousand."

"What thirty thousand? You're playing games with me?"

Lederman breathed a sigh of relief. Finally, there was an opening. Now it was just a matter of how much.

"Fifty?"

"A hundred."

One hundred thousand dollars for three short sentences!

"Okay."

"It's a deal. Typhus voice was relaxed. "First question?"

"Alive or dead?"

"Alive and well."

"Active?" Lederman asked. He stopped breathing. The man puppeteering the entire Bleich affair and all that extended from it — was he still a threat?

"Not in principle. He left us."

Left?! Was it possible to believe that Mike Lewis, king of crime, found a different occupation "outside"…?

"Last question," Lederman said.

"Go on."

"Is he in contact with Yeshaya Bleich…?"

The name rang familiar to Typhus. He took his Palm Pilot from his pocket and searched for the name that Mike had dictated to him, the name of the prisoner that had to be released.

Yeshaya Bleich.

"Marcel?"

"Yes, I'm listening."

"The answer is yes."

No voice was heard from the other end of the line.

"You know how to transfer payment, right?" Typhus asked.

"Yes, I know," Lederman said weakly.

Shaya Bleich was in direct contact with Mike Lewis!

He felt the blood drain from his face. For years he had invested tremendous effort in order to protect the Bleich family from the claws of this devil, but the Bleichs always thought they were smarter. They bypassed him and his warnings and made contact with Mike Lewis…!

They didn't know that Lewis was lying in wait for them for almost twenty years, and that he had waited so long for just such a moment. Just now, when Shaya Bleich was about to discover the whereabouts of his brother and sister-in-law, Mike Lewis sat confidently with jaws wide open. Soon, when the emotional meeting would take place, Lewis would devour them all in the heat of his revenge.

It was from these jaws that he had tried to save them all this time. *Hashem* knew how much effort he had invested in watching over these Bleichs. It was impossible, though, to help people who didn't want to be helped.

• • •

"Ima?" Yisroel Yitzchok, sitting in the living room, picked up his head from the gemara.

"Yes?"

"Abba's waiting for you. He wants to tell you something urgent."

Something urgent? She stopped breathing.

Elya, though, sitting in his study, actually looked quite relaxed.

"They freed him," he informed his wife.

"Freed whom?" For a minute she was confused.

"The *mechutan*, Bleich. He's out of jail."

"Really?! How did it happen?"

"I have no idea. He called before to tell us."

"Very nice. And when is he coming home, did he say?"

"No. I'm not sure he knows himself. He said he has a few more things to take care of."

"All right," Devorah spread her hands. "I just hope Suri isn't listening behind the door and getting depressed again…"

# CHAPTER 42

"So really," Shaya Bleich said to Shore, the two of them sitting in the white car, rolling down the street, "Avrohom Yisroel didn't bring us any further. He told us the past, but he has no more information about the present than we do. He's also looking for Naftali and Rochel, groping his way just like we are."

"Right," Shore said. "True."

Shaya opened the window and breathed in the air of freedom. Again Mendel Lederman emerged empty handed; he had planned on keeping Shaya locked up, but Avrohom Yisroel managed to have him released within half a day. What he wouldn't give to travel straight to the airport and get on the first plane that would bring him to Eretz Yisroel, to Yerushalayim, to his beloved family and regular life! His mission abroad, though, still wasn't completed, and wouldn't be until he found his lost brother and his family. He felt that Naftali was within hand's reach, yet he was still unable to touch him.

"So where do we continue?" he asked.

"From where we left off," Shore said. "Your brother's trail led us here, to Australia. We'll gird ourselves with patience and continue."

Patience. Perhaps Shaya would manage to be patient, but not his family in Eretz Yisroel.

"You must come to my son's wedding," he told Shore.

"When is it?"

"In two weeks."

"And if you don't find your brother by then?"

"Then we won't have a choice," Shaya said. He had already come to terms with it. "We'll have to have the wedding in any case. The bride's family doesn't understand what's going on with us."

"I'm glad that's what you've decided," Shore said and looked at the street. "It's enough that your son's past is shrouded in mystery. There's no need to put a question mark on the future, too. If it's good for him to get married, let him get married."

"Yes, it's the right thing to do. But it's a painful decision."

"Everything has its price. Good things have a higher price. That's the way life works."

They traveled a while in silence.

"I'm still praying for a miracle," Shaya said suddenly. "I believe that if it's wanted on High, we can find Naftali in a week, in a day."

Shore, contrary to his skeptic nature, actually nodded. Spending so much time in the believing Shaya Bleich's company must have moved something in him. "Right, Bleich. It's not worth building on, but you can't deny that sometimes miracles do happen. Pray – it's proved itself until now…"

• • •

A small case with *tefillin*, some *sefarim* and a few necessities

– that was all Avrohom Yisroel took with him to the airport, on his way to spend two days in Eretz Yisroel.

He'd planned to visit the Holy Land for a while already, but never found the chance. His business sent him all over the world, but Israel wasn't on his map. He was angry at himself for choosing to focus his business in all kinds of foreign countries and not in the land of the Jews, his nation.

On the other hand, he was a bit afraid of a direct meeting with the Holy Land and with such a large concentration of Israeli Jews. True, he was a *ger* for many years already, but that didn't prevent him from feeling like a stranger among his own people. Somehow, he found it easier to be a Jew among gentiles, than a Jew among Jews.

Now, though, he had an important reason to visit. Two days earlier, he received a telephone call from Israel. An unfamiliar voice, speaking English with an Israeli accent, asked him:

"Have I reached Avrohom Yisroel?"

"Yes."

"My name is Mendel Lederman."

Avrohom Yisroel didn't remember right away who it was. The name tickled his brain, but that was all.

"Remind me," he requested.

"I investigated the Bleich file close to twenty years ago."

All at once, Avrohom remembered. Yes, this man had been in his sights for a long time. The Bleich family had hired him to find Naftali and Rochel, but he withdrew from the case as soon as he realized that Mike Lewis, terror of the entire world of crime, was involved in it.

This Lederman, so Mike Lewis had felt all these years, knew where Naftali and Rochel were. He absolutely refused, though, to reveal that information to Yeshaya and his wife. If they discovered Naftali and Rochel, Lederman knew, Mike Lewis would immediately know, too, and then their fate would be sealed. For all these years, Lederman kept the keys to the search securely by him.

Avrohom Yisroel remembered how he had promised himself, many times over, to take care of this Lederman, the brave man who looked out for his clients' welfare even at the expense of endangering his own life. Each time he seriously thought to do him in, though, he changed his mind and decided that the time hadn't yet come. *Who knows?* He thought then. *This Lederman has information that's too important for me to send him from this world. Maybe one day he'll still be useful?*

And now that same Lederman was on the line. Much water had passed under the bridge since then. Mike Lewis was no more. Avrohom Yisroel was born in his stead, full of remorse for the past, and possessing a fierce drive to do better in the future. Naftali and Rochel Bleich had been sucked into a black hole. He was no longer angry; he understood that nothing happened down below without it first being determined up Above.

"Yes, I remember you."

Lederman cleared his throat. "You understand that if I approached you with your present name, I've followed your tracks down your entire journey."

"I understand."

"Avrohom," Lederman said, "we have important things to discuss. Crucial things, I would say."

Avrohom caught his breath. Did Lederman mean to reveal his information? Now that it was clear that he was coming peacefully, was Lederman able to finally tell him where Naftali and Rochel Bleich were…?!

"You… you mean to tell me all that… all that you know?" Avrohom stammered, from excitement, or shock, or perhaps the two of them together.

"I want to meet with you," Lederman said without answering directly. "We have what to say to each other to advance the Bleich affair to the benefit of all parties involved."

"Fine," Avrohom said, "We can meet."

Throughout the conversation, Lederman tried to get to the bottom of who the man was. A small pocket of suspicion still remained in his heart. His mind refused to accept that the man had made a one hundred and eighty degree turn, completely changed his spots and became a *ger tzeddek*. He knew quite well from experience that miracles didn't happen every day.

He wanted this meeting in order to confirm the wonder face to face. He wanted to be convinced beyond a shadow of a doubt that Mike Lewis was no more, and that the danger had indeed passed.

"I'll come to Israel," Avrohom said. "I've planned to come for a long time. Today or tomorrow, I'll give you the time and place of the meeting, and *Hashem* will help us."

"Amen," Lederman said, and fervently hoped so.

Three days later, at nine o'clock in the evening, a round faced Jew, looking slightly out of place, entered the lobby of a well-known hotel in Tel Aviv.

Mike Lewis would never have dared meet like that, in public, in a centrally located hotel. Now, though, Avrohom Yisroel relaxed in an armchair, perusing a small gemara. He looked up to see a man in a long black coat hesitantly approaching his table.

They shook hands. Lederman couldn't control the trembling of his hands. The tremendous fear he had formerly felt towards this man wasn't completely gone.

"I'm pleased to meet you," Avrohom Yisroel said honestly, and showed the other man the inside pockets of his jacket. "I know you came to check if I still carry a weapon, Mr. Lederman.

Your fear is justified. So here, you can frisk me."

Lederman was embarrassed. "*Chas v'shalom.*"

"No, no," Avrohom said, "If I was you, I wouldn't believe me so quickly. You, more than anyone, know how dangerous I was. You should know that I think very highly of you. You could even say I admire you."

"Admire?!"

"You could say even more than that. You have a large part in the fact that I chose to join the Jewish nation."

"I don't believe it!" Lederman exclaimed.

"Oh, yes," Avrohom nodded. "At the time I was completely amazed at you. The Bleich family hired you to find Yeshaya's lost brother. You, a talented investigator, quickly solved the case, but instead of going over to them and saying: 'Listen, fellows, I cracked the case – now pay me and have a good day,' you chose to take responsibility, even if it meant acquiring lifelong enemies instead of friends. Not wanting to give the Bleichs into my hands, you informed them that you're stopping the investigation, without revealing the hiding place. At the time, I was angry at you. I was burning with rage. The entire time I had been following you and the Bleichs, waiting for you to discover Naftali and Rochel. Later on, though, along with the anger in my heart, I also found admiration. I didn't know anyone, not in my close circles nor in my broader surroundings, who would have acted so responsibly and considerately towards strangers. This amazement at you joined with the amazement I felt towards Naftali and Rochel, who put themselves in danger for a child who wasn't at all related to them.

"Later, when I wanted to know *why* I was investigating the Jewish people and contemplating joining them, I understood: I wanted to know the nation in which each person feels such a great responsibility towards another, only because they're both part of the same nation. Such a thing doesn't exist anywhere else in the world, only by the Jews. And you, with your exemplary behavior, made me notice this and want to be a part of it."

Lederman discreetly groped for a tissue in his pocket. *If this was the only reason you've shouldered responsibility for the Bleich family for so many years,* he said to himself, *only in order to bring such a fine person under* kanfei sh'chinah – *it was already worth it. A person never knows where his actions will have an impact.*

"Tell me," Avrohom Yisroel almost pleaded, "Tell me where Naftali and Rochel are. Is there any chance I can meet them and ask their forgiveness…?!"

...

Late at night, Lederman returned to his office. He fumbled in his pocket for the key, went inside and sat for a few minutes in the dark. The light in his heart was bright enough.

He dialed the Bleich home without even looking at the clock and asked to speak to Shloime.

"He's sleeping."

"So please wake him up, because this is something beyond urgent."

A few minutes passed. He heard footsteps approaching the telephone.

"Hello?" Shloime's voice was sleepy. "Who's speaking?"

"Mendel Lederman."

"What do you want?"

Lederman swallowed hard. The hatred was palpable.

"To give you some news."

"I don't need your news," Shloime said. "Until now, you've only given me bad news, and now you're even waking me up for it. I only managed to fall asleep not long ago after tossing and turning because of you."

Lederman understood the force of the pain of the refined boy. If he could bring himself to speak so harshly to him, it seems he didn't see Lederman as human, but as a form of evil.

"Listen to me for a few minutes, Shloime,"

"I don't want to."

"Do you want to get married?"

"I want to, but I can't. Because of you."

"So now you could."

"What...???"

"Just what you heard. The danger has passed. Now you can make the *chasunah* without worrying."

"What suddenly happened?" Shloime asked suspiciously.

"I thoroughly looked into the matter and came to this conclusion."

"Fine," Shloime said. "Can I go back to sleep now?"

"I thought you'd be happy, Shloime," Lederman said disappointedly.

"What do I care what you thought?"

"I thought that if you tell a *bochur* he can get married after being in doubt for so long, it should make him happy. Perhaps I was mistaken."

"You were mistaken. I never had any doubts, and I planned on having the wedding in any case."

"I know. But I thought that a stone would roll off your heart, as it rolled off mine."

"You know what stone you're talking about. I don't. You wouldn't tell me why I can't get married, and now you're not telling me why I can."

"For the same reason that I couldn't tell you why not, I can't tell you why yes. But soon," Lederman promised, "soon you'll know."

Something in his voice, Lederman felt, did encourage the broken youth.

"Soon I'll know from you?"

"No, not from me."

"So from whom? Again you're hiding information?"

"You'll know, Shloime, you'll know, *be'ezras Hashem*. Do me a favor, smile – just for a minute. I want to know that you're happy."

"I'll smile after I know that I'm out of your hands."

"Okay," Lederman sighed, "Good night."

Lederman's second phone call was all the way to Australia. He prepared himself for an outpour of rage, almost protecting his head with both hands. The mere mention of the name "Lederman", let alone the voice of the evil one himself, was enough to make Shaya Bleich unleash all his tremendous pain.

"R' Shaya," he said, "this is Mendel Lederman speaking from Eretz Yisroel."

Thunderous silence.

"There's nothing for us to speak about, Lederman."

"Why?" Shore asked from the side. "Don't ever say that. It's always possible to receive another bit of information. Don't lock open doors. Ask him what he wants."

"What do you want?" Shaya asked, left with no choice.

"To tell you that there's nothing preventing you from making the *chasunah* at the agreed upon time."

"We really need you to marry off our children," Shaya said scornfully. "You're the fourth partner in creation, I understand."

Lederman ignored the derision. "I'm doing my part. I checked the matter and realized that the danger was removed. You can make the wedding without fear."

"Thanks for the permission," Shaya said. "It's just a pity you checked it now and not earlier, and made our children miserable for no reason."

Lederman swallowed the insult.

"What did he say?" Shore asked curiously.

"What's the difference?"

"It makes a big difference. This Lederman is a key figure in the whole story."

Shaya burst out laughing. "Key figure? The key has long been thrown into the ocean. He dealt with the investigation many years ago and dropped it, and since then hasn't stopped causing us trouble."

"He actually gives the impression of being a good man. What did he say?"

"That we can make the wedding."

"I wonder why," Shore murmured. "What changed?"

"My private investigator is asking if we can receive some explanation as to the sudden change," Shaya said into the receiver.

"Explanations will come, R' Shaya," Lederman said confidently. "What's important right now is for you to leave everything and come to your son's *chasunah*."

"Leave everything? Why? We have an investigation that's progressing beautifully, *boruch Hashem*, and there's no reason not to carry on with it."

"There is reason to take a break and be a little happy," Lederman said.

"It's nice that you're worrying about my happiness, for a change…"

• • •

At six in the morning, Chana Bleich and Shloime, his face sporting a more mature look, arrived at the airport.

"So my parents will remain a mystery," Shloime said to Chana, as they stood opposite the screen showing takeoff and landing times, waiting for Shaya's plane to be announced.

"*Chas v'shalom*, not at all," Chana said. "Abba's just taking a break. We're in no way stopping the search. Especially after they've come so far."

"I know how it is," Shloime said. "When you stop, you lose the momentum and it's very hard to get back into it. Especially since Abba will probably stay a little after *sheva brachos* to help with all the arrangements and get somewhat back to himself."

Chana knew he was right. She did have one ray of light, though, to offer him: "Abba's investigator, Shore, is coming with him. And if he's coming, the investigation is also coming. He'll push Abba to go back with him and continue the search."

At exactly that time, a taxi was making its way towards the airport. Avrohom Yisroel sat inside, his small case resting at his feet and his emotions mixed.

He came to Eretz Yisroel for an important meeting. The meeting took place, but he was leaving disappointed. He had hoped to hear from Lederman where Naftali and Rochel Bleich were, but Lederman wouldn't say. They spoke about the investigation, about Shaya Bleich's chase all over the world after his brother – a chase that Avrohom Yisroel was funding. They spoke about the Bleich family, about the son who was about to get married, and of course they also spoke in learning. The secret, however, Lederman refused to divulge.

"When I'm able to," he said, "I'll tell. And I believe that it will happen soon."

"You know where they are?!"

"Yes," Lederman said plainly. "I know, and I've known the entire time."

"So why can't I just meet them?" Avrohom asked, half rising from his chair.

"I still haven't received permission to pass along the information," Lederman said, "and as you know, with me, what's confidential remains confidential. All secrets will go to the grave with me."

"I have the impression that many people will want to open your grave after your death…"

• • •

Tall Shloime noticed a black hat weaving through the crowd.

"I think Abba's coming," he said. "*Oy*, he looks so tired."

Wordless, Shloime fell into his father's arms. Shore, decked out in a blue and white tie, surveyed Shloime with great interest and then pressed his hand.

"I feel like we know each other a long time already," he said. "Just like I know your biological father, though I've never met him. But don't worry, we'll soon find both him and your mother."

"*Be'ezras Hashem*," Shloime replied.

"Hello," someone next to them suddenly said. Shaya and Shore turned towards the familiar voice.

Avrohom Yisroel!

"I'm here for just two-three days," the man said, "and I'm on my way back home. I didn't know I'd meet you here."

"No, no," Shaya said excitedly, "you're not on your way home. Shloime here is getting married in another two weeks, and it's out of the question for you not to join us at the wedding."

"What do you mean?" Avrohom laughed good-naturedly, "Thanks for the invitation, but my business awaits me."

"It'll wait a bit longer," Shaya said, "because its owner has to take part in a Jewish wedding in Eretz Yisroel." He gripped

Avrohom's hand warmly and led him back in the direction from which he came.

# CHAPTER 43

One more phone call, most crucial of them all, remained to Mendel Lederman.

Now that he knew the danger had passed, there seemed to be no reason to do it in secret. Naftali and Rochel had nothing more to fear; they could openly reveal themselves, and he would be truly happy to be the first to let them know.

But he couldn't. The decision whether to come forward or remain hidden was Naftali's and Rochel's alone. They would be the ones to check if the time had indeed come for them to come out of the hiding that was forced upon them for the past twenty years.

Mendel Lederman couldn't expose them against their will, even if he knew there was no more danger facing them.

He sat in his locked room, unsure whether to give Naftali and Rochel the incredible news over the telephone, or to write them a letter and send it by registered mail. The importance of the news perhaps demanded a letter. On the other hand, a letter could always fall into the wrong hands. Besides which, he really wanted to tell Naftali in person, to hear his reaction and share in his happiness.

• • •

When R' Nachman heard Shaya Bleich's voice on the telephone, he immediately understood that something good had happened.

"Where are you calling from, my friend?" he asked jocularly.

"I'm at home, in Eretz Yisroel," Shaya replied, "and I wanted your address so I can send you an invitation to my son's *chasunah* in two weeks."

"*Mazel tov, mazel tov!*" R' Nachman cried. "What's the date? I must come!"

Shaya gave R' Nachman the date and the address of the hall, and warned him that even if the invitation didn't come on time, he must join the celebration.

"*Avada!*" R' Nachman said. "What's the question?"

After hanging up, Shaya turned his attention back to the final preparations for the wedding. Only the invitations of those friends who lived in the neighborhood remained on the table. Those would be hand delivered to their mailboxes either that day or the next. Shaya made a list of those who needed to be invited personally over the phone.

Shloime sat on the couch, staring as if the whole thing was removed from him.

"Shloime'le," Shaya said, "come, there are a few invitations here that need a personal written message. Would you like to do it? People would be very happy to see your handwriting on their invitation. You know how everyone loves you."

"As much as they love me, I know that my parents love me

more," Shloime said intensely. "I'm sitting here, trying to imagine my *chasunah*, and I think that what hasn't happened until now is about to happen – I'm about to break…"

Shaya stood up at once and went over to Shloime. He wanted to give him a reassuring hug, but it seemed too late: Shloime had already burst into hacking sobs, his broad shoulders bent with pain.

"Every *chosson* has parents," he said between sobs, "and if he's an orphan, he has a grave to go to, to invite his parents to join in his happiness. But I'm hanging somewhere in midair. An orphan with live parents."

"Don't speak like that, Shloime," Shaya begged. "I don't want you to talk that way. Your parents are alive and well – Mendel Lederman himself promised us that, and Ima claims we can believe him. You remember? Even if they won't physically be with us at the *chasunah*, I'm sure they'll be there in their hearts. And who knows," he dared say what he had said to Shore back in Australia, "in the short time left to us, miracles can happen. *Yeshuas Hashem k'heref ayin* – *Hashem's* salvation can come in the blink of an eye."

Shloime wiped his eyes with the back of his hand. "I'm trying very hard to be strong, but it's not working. I'm afraid of what will happen to me under the *chuppah*. It's a time of joy, the greatest time of my life. Instead of feeling happy and uplifted, I'll probably do what I'm doing now," and again he wiped his eyes, this time with a tissue.

"I'm sure you'll be perfectly fine," Shaya said with full confidence. "You just have to be a tiny bit stronger and believe a tiny bit more that it's not we who run the world. You know, Shloime," he told him, "while I was abroad, there were times when I felt I was chasing after the wind. Once, it seemed as if we were almost there, and then suddenly all leads evaporated. On the other hand, sometimes things just seemed to fall down from Above at the least expected time. This entire time, I tangibly felt how we were like little pawns on the *Ribbono shel Olam's* game board, how much we didn't know why He chose to make one move instead of another. To accept His decree with love – doesn't mean to make peace with the bad that Hashem brings on us. Just the opposite – it means to know that there's nothing bad here, only eternal good, even if we really don't understand why."

Shloime looked at his uncle-adoptive father, who gazed back at him lovingly.

"And it will be okay?" he asked pleadingly.

"More than okay," Shaya promised, and enfolded him in a fierce hug.

• • •

Chana came out of her room at nine o'clock PM, looking very troubled.

"Maybe a smile or two?" Shaya requested. "Aren't we marrying off our dear son very soon?"

"Fuchsman called," she said and sat down.

"*Nu?*"

"They want to speak to us about something important."

Shaya's face grew serious. "What?"

"I don't know. I hope there are no new troubles. It seems like every problem in the world has to happen on the way to this *chasunah*."

"*Chas v'shalom!*" Shaya exclaimed. "Don't talk like that, Chana. It's clear that the *satan* dances when a good, G-d fearing couple wishes to get married. The holier something is, the harder he tries to upset it. But why are you thinking of new troubles?"

"Because if they had something regular to tell us, like about mattresses or quilts or which model washing machine to buy, they would have just said it over the phone, no?"

"Probably," Shaya nodded his head. "Do you have any idea what they want to tell us?"

"Maybe something's wrong with Suri?" she thought out loud.

"What could be wrong? Maybe she doesn't feel well?"

"Maybe," Chana said. "Anything could be. I think that this *chasunah* epitomizes the rule that whatever could go wrong, will…"

"If Suri and Shloime are meant to get married, they will get married, because that is what is decreed upon them. And if, *chalilah*, not, then that's also decreed upon them. Come, let's not take over *HaKadosh Boruch Hu*'s job."

Chana fell silent, a pensive look on her face. Her imagination was off and galloping.

"Come, let's not think about it," Shaya suggested. "Did they mention who should be at this meeting?"

"Us and Shloime."

"And who will come with them?"

"Only them."

"Not Suri?"

"No."

"Very interesting," Shaya said. "When is this meeting?"

"They asked that it be at a time when no one else can hear."

"Where, here by us?"

"No, not by us and not by them."

"So where?" Shaya wondered. "Outside?"

"No, not outside. They said they'll let us know where to go."

"What should I tell you," Shaya said quietly. "I'm beginning to get nervous. Just today I promised Shloime that everything will be fine. Now I hope I didn't make a mistake by telling him that. When is the meeting?"

"Tonight."

"We have to tell Shloime," Shaya said and sighed. What else did this dear boy have to go through?

"You let him know."

"Oh, no. Chana, do me a favor."

"I can't. I can't face him and tell him that something else went wrong."

"Chana, have pity…"

They were both quiet. Shloime's footsteps were heard behind them. They turned and saw him smiling, holding two new shirts over his arm.

"Great, I wanted to ask you both which shirt is better for the *chasu*---" He broke off when he saw their strained smiles.

"Don't tell me something's wrong," he said, all the fear in the world in his voice.

They looked at each other and remained quiet.

"Meanwhile, everything's fine," Shaya finally managed to get out. Chana's gaze was pleading. "We're supposed to meet the Fuchsmans tonight," he added.

Shloime grabbed hold of the edge of the table. "Who's 'we'?"

"Ima and you and I."

"A meeting? For what? Did something happen?"

"Until we hear, we won't know," Chana said in a low voice.

Shloime looked at the two of them for a minute, and then his gaze steadied.

"I won't come to this meeting," he said decisively. "I don't have the strength. You go and tell me afterwards. Maybe hearing it secondhand will temper the bad news a little…"

At a quarter to eleven, Shaya and Chana left the house.

It was quiet outside and a cool breeze blew, but failed to refresh them.

Chana turned around to see if Shloime was still standing by the window, watching them.

"He's still there," she whispered to Shaya.

"It's a shame he didn't come with us," he replied. That was his original stand. Up until they left, he tried to convince Shloime to join them, but Shloime stood firm in his refusal.

"To stay home and torture yourself with doubts is worse than coming with us and hearing – whatever it might be," Shaya claimed. Shloime, though, protested that he didn't have the emotional strength to face bad news again. He'd stay home, he'd try to learn something – maybe he'd even go to sleep.

The three of them knew he wouldn't be able to fall asleep. It was doubtful if he'd be able to concentrate on a *sefer*. Shloime wasn't a boy anymore, though, and they couldn't argue with his decision. Shaya gave him the address if he wanted to join them later.

Now Shaya studied the slip of paper in his hand. "Ten Gurtal Street. Do you know where that is?"

"Of course. Gurtal Street is five minutes from here."

"What's there? A hotel? An office? Where do they want us to meet them?"

Chana thought. "This address rings a bell. It's not familiar to you?"

"Familiar? You know someone who lives there?"

Chana didn't remember. "Let's just go and we'll find out."

They turned right, and then left.

"My heart is pounding like a ten pound hammer," Chana confessed. Shaya completely understood her, as his heart was pounding, too. Not like a hammer, like a sledgehammer.

As soon as they turned on to Gurtal Street, Shaya stopped.

"I can't believe it," he said and smacked his forehead. "How could I not remember?!"

"*Nu?*" Chana asked expectantly.

"This is where Mendel Lederman's office is. I don't understand how I forgot that...!"

"So that's where we're going?!"

"So it seems. Yes, this is his address. Ten Gurtal."

"Why should Fuchsman choose to meet us in Lederman's office?"

Chana's knees were weak. She had had a big enough helping of Mendel Lederman over the past two months. Each time his name was mentioned, her blood pressure rose a bit more. The name Mendel Lederman meant trouble, problems, investigations, complications.

"He'll also be there?" she asked.

"I have no idea."

The two reached the building and stopped. Shaya glanced at his watch.

"It's time," he said.

"And here they are," Chana said.

The Fuchsman couple was drawing near. Mendel Lederman was nowhere to be seen. Chana noticed that they weren't happy to see that Shloime hadn't come.

And indeed, Elya Fuchsman's first question was: "Where's Shloime?"

Shaya chose to be diplomatic. "He was very tired. He ran around all day. He asked that we tell him all that was said at the meeting. I hope that's okay with you."

No, it wasn't at all okay, Chana picked up. The Fuchsmans looked extremely disappointed.

"Would it be possible to call him?" Devorah asked.

"I think he went to sleep," Shaya said. Shloime probably hadn't gone to sleep, but if they called him now, it wouldn't convince him to come. He didn't like to be pressured.

*Thicker Than Water* « 537

"So maybe we should push off the meeting for a different time," the *mechutan* suggested. Shaya and Chana were surprised. They hadn't thought that Shloime's presence was so necessary.

"All right, if it's so important to you, I'll try to call him," Shaya said. He moved to the side and dialed home.

Faigie, though, told him that Shloime wasn't home. He had gone out.

"I'm really sorry," Shaya returned to the *mechutanim*. "It's impossible to reach Shloime now. If that causes a change in plans, we could maybe---"

But it seemed the *mechutanim* had changed their minds and decided to go ahead with the meeting in any case.

Elya Fuchsman went to Lederman's office, located on the first floor, took a key from his pocket and opened the door. He switched on the light and invited everyone inside.

There were enough chairs to go around. Elya sat down, looked around and knew he had to start speaking. The silence was so thick, though, he couldn't bring himself to break it.

"Did something happen to Suri?" Chana asked tensely.

"To Suri? Not at all. *Boruch Hashem*, everything's fine. She's a happy *kallah* and is counting the days to the *chasunah*."

Shaya and Chana breathe a deep sigh of relief.

"So to what do we owe the honor of meeting with you today?" Shaya chuckled, a laugh that attempted to cover up the tension.

Devorah Fuchsman looked at her husband. He looked at her, as if they were each trying to roll the ball to the other's court.

Finally, Devorah opened her small purse and removed a picture.

Shaya and Chana follow her movements with bated breath.

Devorah handed the picture to Chana.

"Look," she said. Her voice was thick and choked.

Shaya and Chana almost grabbed the picture.

"It's Shloime," Shaya said, "when he was a baby. And these are his parents, Naftali and Rochel, for whom we've been searching for so many years---"

It was too late. He wished he could stuff the words back into his mouth. They were Shloime's parents. They, the *mechutanim*, Shaya and Chana Bleich, and none other…!

He looked at Elya Fuchsman, terrified. Fuchsman, though, looked sunk deep within himself. Mrs. Fuchsman looked lost in the picture, as if trying to draw strength from it. Had they not heard? Had they not grasped?! Or maybe they knew the truth, and were only pretending not to know?!

"Devorah," Chana suddenly asked, "who gave you the picture? Shloime gave it to Suri…?"

Devorah didn't answer. She returned the picture to her purse and took out another one.

"This is also Shloime," Chana said, "when he was really little. He looks about a year, maybe. He's cute."

Chana clucked her tongue, but beneath the pretty words raged a mighty storm. Why was her *mechuteniste* suddenly showing her pictures of Shloime as a baby? Is that what she had to do two weeks before the wedding, just to pass the time…?

"Interesting," Shaya said and took the picture into his hand, "I've never seen this picture. Where did you get it?"

Elya and Devorah didn't answer. It seemed to Chana that something huge and terrible wanted to burst from their hearts, and couldn't. Without realizing, she gripped the edge of her chair with her fingers.

"I'm sorry Shloime's not here," Devorah said, "because he's the first to deserve to hear this."

Shaya wanted to apologize again, but Chana took a different tack.

"Why is he first?" she asked.

Elya and Devorah looked at each other. Shaya felt an urgent need to move things along.

"Is there something you want to tell us?" he asked gently.

"Certainly," Elya said, "we didn't arrange a meeting with you for nothing."

"So let's hear."

But nothing solid left the throats of the Fuchsman couple.

"I think," Chana said and smiled, as much as the circumstances allowed, "that they're hoping we'll understand on our own what they want to say. Am I right?"

Devorah Fuchsman nodded her head.

The whole thing seemed a bit odd to Shaya, but he decided to go along with it.

"Why didn't Suri have to come?" Chana asked.

"Because we're not dealing with her right now," Devorah replied.

"And you are dealing with?" Shaya asked.

"With Shloime, with us and… with you, of course."

Chana thought. "There's something the three of us have in common, that has nothing to do with her?"

"Right," Devorah said.

"In common?" Shaya echoed.

The Fuchsmans nodded.

"You're speaking in riddles," Shaya sighed. Whoever heard of calling a meeting with respectable people and not explaining the reason for it? He wondered what Shore would say about it.

"If Shloime would be here," Chana said, "I have no doubt he'd solve the riddle. His straight thinking always hits the mark."

She tried to make sense of it all, but couldn't.

"Can you give us some more hints?" she asked.

It was clear that, though the Fuchsmans wanted to help, they simply couldn't.

"Can you at least tell us what it has to do with? What topic? Good news or bad? Some kind of change? Something?" Shaya asked, almost begged. He had had enough with riddles. For too long he'd been trying to figure out what was beyond him.

"It has to do with... with... Shloime's parents," Elya finally said.

"Really?!" Shaya and Chana jumped up. Their shock was greater even than the realization that their big secret was known to the *mechutanim*, and that it may have been known to them the entire time. "You have information about Naftali and Rochel?! So why didn't you say so?!"

Though Elya and Devorah seemed satisfied with the conversation's progress, there was still tremendous tension in their faces.

"Clear information?" Shaya demanded to know.

"Very clear," Elya said quietly.

"What kind of information?" Shaya was sorry Shore hadn't joined the meeting. "Documents? Eyewitnesses?"

It was possible that they had done their own investigating, Chana thought. They also wanted to discover who their son-in-law's parents were. It was their right. Maybe they found something that the Bleichs had failed to uncover.

Again, though, the conversation stalled. Elya didn't answer. Devorah was quiet. She removed a tissue from her purse.

Suddenly, there was a knock at the door. The knob turned, and none other than Shloime stepped inside. His face was tired, as if he had just returned from a long journey.

"I was standing by the window the entire time – you didn't notice me," he said to his parents and his in-laws together. "I can't understand how you didn't figure out the big secret, which the Fuchsmans are simply incapable of expressing in words..."

And without further explanation, he went over to Elya Fuchsman, his future wife's father, and fell on his shoulder. Elya embraced him fiercely, tears streaming from his eyes.

"Shloime," he sobbed, "Shloime, my Shloime'le, my beloved *bechor*…"

# CHAPTER 44

The room seemed frozen in time. Shloime was enfolded in Elya Fuchsman's arms, refusing to leave. Mrs. Fuchsman was crying loudly, intensely. It was unclear whether she was crying from pain or happiness. Shaya looked at each of them in turn.

"Do... do you understand what's going on here, Chana?!" he managed to croak.

Chana stood nailed in place, handing tissue after tissue to Devorah Fuchsman and refusing to understand what logic dictated that she understand.

Shloime removed one arm from Elya Fuchsman's shoulder and extended it towards Shaya.

"Abba..."

"Shloime'le, I... explain to me, it can't be that---"

Shloime pulled Shaya into the embrace.

Chana looked very hard at Devorah Fuchsman's face. It was now swollen from crying, but she had seen her so many times lately, with so many different expressions: excitement, worry, friendliness, attentiveness. It couldn't be that so many times weren't enough for her to identify her.

She stepped closer to Devorah and stared directly into her eyes, as if there she would find the answer.

"R... Rochel...?!"

She looked tensely at her *mechuteniste*.

Devorah Fuchsman slowly nodded her head.

"Rochel Bleich???"

Yes. Yes.

Chana grabbed Devorah's hand, as if touching her would help her find that it really was her.

"And you...you were here the whole time...?!"

Chana's voice was choked. The woman before her didn't look at all like her dear sister-in-law, whom she had last seen almost twenty years earlier. She tried imagining that Rochel twenty years older, but the result was completely different.

Shaya, too, studied Elya Fuchsman's face at length and didn't understand.

"You... you don't look at all like Naftali," he said, his tone reserved, "and I know what I'm saying. I've been searching for Naftali nonstop, and, together with my hired investigator, constructed a likeness of Naftali's face how it should look today. There's no resemblance."

Elya nodded his head. He was still holding on to Shloime, refusing to relax his grip.

"We owe you long explanations. Very, very long," he said, "as long as our forced separation..."

There was an odd atmosphere in the room. It wasn't how Shaya had imagined meeting his brother. He had dreamed of many possibilities: Naftali would be found in a musty cellar, or at the top of some mountain, on an isolated island, or even among some remote tribe in Africa. The whole time, the image of the beloved brother he remembered stood before him – a bit older, but still Naftali. He tried to imagine the changes he had undergone: graying hair, lines etched into his forehead, a longer beard. Now, though, a different man stood facing him. The hair was a completely different color. Yes, the beard was longer, and his face was lined with age, but it wasn't the same face. Only the eye color was the same, but millions of people had brown eyes.

Shloime had been very little when he was separated from his parents. Their image wasn't etched in his brain. He didn't have to bridge the gap between a familiar picture and this completely different reality. He could simply hug his father and be wholly happy that the big mystery of his life was solved.

"It's an extremely long story," Elya said, and at that moment Shaya felt the first connection to the man: his voice. True, it was older and deeper, but it did resemble Naftali's voice as he remembered it. With the face so different, however, he found it hard to convince himself that it was the same man. At most, it was possible to note that the voice was very similar.

"We'll tell you the whole story, *be'ezras Hashem*," Elya promised. "I'm sure you have many questions." *Yes*, Chana thought, *there was a stack of questions higher than Mt. Everest.* "Meanwhile, though, my dear brother Shaya, let me give you a sign that will help you out."

And Elya Fuchsman unbuttoned his cuff and pulled up the sleeve.

Shaya's eyes were fixed on the arm that was slowly being uncovered.

Right above the elbow was a birthmark, shaped remarkably like a peach pit.

• • •

Suri cut the thread with her teeth. That was it. The last stitch of the last button of the last dress was finished. What a shame Ima wasn't home to rejoice with her.

Actually, where was Ima?

It was already late. Her parents sometimes went out for a short walk in the evening. Lately, they had actually been going out quite a lot, whenever they wished to speak undisturbed. This time, though, the walk seemed very long; twelve o'clock at night was late enough.

"Yisroel Yitzchok, where are Abba and Ima?"

"They went out."

Suri was a little worried. She tried calling her father's cell phone, but heard it ringing in the next room. Abba had gone without his phone, and Ima probably did, too. They didn't want anyone to disturb them.

Suri went to shut the phone ringing on the dresser. Just before going out to the porch to see if her parents were talking downstairs, she turned back. Something caught her attention.

A yellow, folded paper, old and a bit creased, sat on top of a pile of documents next to the telephone. Assumedly, this paper wasn't any different than other papers floating about the house, but for some reason, Suri unfolded it and took a peek.

It was a document from the Interior Ministry. A birth certificate. Interesting. All papers of that sort were neatly organized in a specific drawer in the house, together with the vaccination records and all medical papers. If this document was removed, there must have been a reason for it.

Suri surveyed what was written. Family name: Barnett. First name: Sara. Father's name: Yitzchak. Mother's name: Matilda. Nationality: Jewish.

Suri wondered who the girl was, and what her birth certificate was doing in their house.

One minute. The identity number of the mysterious Barnett baby was very familiar to her, and the birth date also sparked her memory. This girl was born the same day that she was born, in the same year, and their identity numbers were identical. Could there be such a thing – the same number for two people…?

Suri went over to her purse and took out her ID card. No, she wasn't mistaken. The number and date was the same.

"Yisroel Yitzchok," she called, "come see something interesting."

Yisroel Yitzchok straightened the paper and quickly scanned it.

"Who's this?" he asked. "You know someone Sara Barnett?"

No, Suri didn't know. They had no relatives or friends by that name.

"So what exactly is so interesting here?"

Suri pointed to the date and ID number. "That's exactly my number, and I was also born on that date."

"What do you say!"

Yisroel Yitzchok studied the paper intently, as if a line that he hadn't seen would suddenly jump out and reveal the secret.

"Mmm, I wonder what it means."

"And it's not clear what it's doing here."

Yisroel Yitzchok thought hard. Suddenly, his jaw dropped. An awful idea struck him.

"What?" Suri prodded him.

The notion was so outrageous, so illogical. *Again you're looking for adventure stories, Yisroel Yitzchok. After you've finally changed for the better and became more settled.*

If even one small percent of this idea was true, though, he couldn't tell it to Suri, not even hint to it slightly. Poor Suri. She had gone through so much in the last while. Her nerves were completely raw, and each small thing shook her up. She wouldn't be able to face such a thought without collapsing.

Yisroel Yitzchok shoved the idea out of his mind. It was so groundless. The day Suri was born, thousands of other babies were born. The name Sara was one of the most common names in the world.

And the ID numbers? Each person had only one identity number. No two people had the same number.

Suri sensed that Yisroel Yitzchok had an answer to the riddle. She couldn't bear his silence.

"Yisroel Yitzchok, you have to tell me what you're thinking," she pleaded. Her voice rose hysterically, and Yisroel Yitzchok had the feeling that she, too, knew deep down what the story was and wanted to hear from him that that wasn't what he was thinking.

"It's silly," he said. "Believe me. It's too bad I read so many detective stories."

"It's not silly," her voice rose, "It's not silly! You have to tell me! I'm your big sister, Yisroel Yitzchok, and you have to listen to me…!"

*You're my big sister, Suri…? I'm not so sure anymore,* Yisroel Yitzchok wanted to say, and forcefully bit his lips.

Suri started to cry. Yisroel Yitzchok, had he not felt the need to be strong for both of them, would have joined her. He couldn't drop such a thing on her. Definitely not now.

"It can't be!!" Suri yelled, "It can't be that this girl is me!!! Tell me it's not true, Yisroel Yitzchok, tell me…!!!"

Yisroel Yitzchok continued to be quiet. He couldn't be the one to say it.

Suri fled to the other room, and the yellow paper fell to the floor. Yisroel Yitzchok picked it up. It was a bad dream. His big sister Suri couldn't be anything else besides his big sister. If it was true, how had Abba and Ima managed to hide it all the years? And why? Why had Abba and Ima adopted a girl even before they had children of their own? Did they think they wouldn't have children? What had made them do something so drastic...?

From behind her closed door, he could hear Suri's sobs. Suri was bright. She, too, must realize that this discovery was connected to the big, uncomfortable mess of her whole engagement. And it had to happen now, just when things seemed to have settled down.

There was a knock at the front door. Abba and Ima had returned.

Devorah and Elya knocked and knocked, but nobody opened the door. Suri was in her room, crying bitterly – she hadn't even heard the knocking – while Yisroel Yitzchok stood uncertainly between the door to Suri's room and the main door. Should he try to calm Suri down before opening up for his parents? Should he open the door and be the one to explain why Suri was crying? Or should he ask Suri to open the door herself?

A long, shrill ring echoed throughout the house. Abba and Ima didn't understand why they had to wait outside. They could see the house was lit up, and knew that not everyone was sleeping.

Yisroel Yitzchok went over to the door and opened it.

"What's going on?" Devorah asked, "What happened? We had to wait for such a long ti---"

The question died on her lips. An old, yellow, creased paper lay on the floor in middle of the room. She looked at Yisroel Yitzchok's pale face.

"Suri's in her room," he said quietly. "She saw this paper. She's very scared. I don't know what she's doing there."

Devorah and Elya exchanged looks. Yes, they had purposely put the paper in an obvious place, but was it good that Suri had found it when they weren't with her…?

Yisroel Yitzchok picked up the paper with his fingertips, as if he was afraid it would bite him, and put it on the table.

"It's… it's true?" he asked.

"What's true?" Elya asked.

"This… this is connected to us, this paper? To Suri…??"

Elya took a deep breath. "Yes," he said.

Yisroel Yitzchok looked at the paper as if it was dynamite, and looked back at his father.

"I don't understand. Who is Sara Barnett…?"

Devorah went over to Suri's room and pushed open the door.

"Suri'le?" she said softly, "We want to talk to you. We want to tell you a story…"

• • •

## >>AUSTRALIA, 1989

When little Sara Barnett awoke from the heavy sleep induced by the drugged candy she had eaten in the toy store, she found herself in a small, unfamiliar room.

She sat up in bed, trying to figure out where she was. No, she hadn't suddenly fallen asleep in playgroup. The place didn't look like a playgroup, but like a house – a house, though, that she didn't recognize. It wasn't her new room, in her new father and mother's house. That room was large and colorful, and this room was small and not at all pretty.

"Mommy, Mommy!" she called.

In the next room, Naftali and Rochel Bleich sat and spoke quietly, trying to plan their next move. It was clear they couldn't stay there. The long, deadly arms of Mike Lewis would catch up to them, take back the girl and ruthlessly punish them for what they had done.

The local morning newspaper lay on the small table. The main headlines screamed in big, red letters:

"Sara, where are you?" A sweet picture of little Sara Barnett was spread over almost the entire page.

"Mike Lewis must be grinding his teeth right now," Naftali commented. "The last thing he would want is for the story to be publicized. But you can't expect the media to give up this scoop – it has everything a good newspaper article needs. The police are on our trail, but I'm less afraid of them. Mike Lewis and his gang scare me much more. The police just want to catch us. He wants to catch us in order to kill."

The scent of death hovered in the air. In the next room, the little girl began to make noises. She had no idea how many people were hopping because of her, and that Rochel, her beloved social worker who had suddenly appeared once more, had put herself and her husband in mortal danger just for her sake.

"We're going to have to do something drastic," Naftali said and folded the newspaper.

"What, run away…?"

"Of course we have to run away. That's not what I meant."

"So what?!" Rochel whispered.

"We'll have to switch identity. To make ourselves completely into different people. We have no other choice."

"It won't help," Rochel said and opened the newspaper again. A picture of the terrible Mike Lewis stared out at her, the "father" of the little girl, who swore revenge on the people who kidnapped his daughter and ruined his family that he had finally managed to build. "Even if we go by a different name, he'll catch up to us and lay his long, cold fingers on us."

A chill crawled up her spine. She didn't regret for a minute the step they had taken in order to rescue her little charge from this gentile. However, despite the fact that they had done their

*Thicker Than Water* « 551

homework well and prepared themselves for every eventuality, nothing had prepared her for this tangible, deathly fear.

"Rochel, don't cry. We have to be strong. We can't give way now. We have to think calmly."

But Rochel did dissolve in tears.

"Don't worry, Rochel," he couldn't watch her cry. "*HaKadosh Boruch Hu* brought us this far with such clear *hashgachah pratis*. We can trust that He'll continue to accompany us. Sara will be okay. We'll be okay."

Rochel nodded. Her tears continued to flow.

"I wasn't thinking about Sara now, or about us," she said and choked up. "I was thinking about Shloimy."

The name of their little boy, with his pure face and glowing smile, echoed in the room.

"Don't think now," Naftali tried to say, but his voice also broke.

Up until the last day, they had tried to use any and all connections to get little Sara out of Mike Lewis' grasp, but they found that there wasn't anyone who cared about some unknown little girl the way they did.

Naftali thought of the kidnapping as a fanciful, far-out possibility. He didn't even share it with Rochel. It was obvious to him that she wouldn't agree to it.

Very quietly, he worked out the plan. He put a lot of thought into it, planned it down to the last detail, and then stowed it away as a farfetched last resort in case nothing else panned out.

The morning before that night when they left the sleeping Shloimy with Shaya and Chana, and fled without any explanation, Rochel got up the nerve and called Mike Lewis' house one more time, asking after little Sara's welfare.

The phone rang and rang, but no one answered. Finally, the answering machine picked up and the voice of Mrs. Lewis asked to leave a message.

Rochel decided to try.

"Hello," she said pleasantly, "this is Rochel Bleich from Israel speaking, Sara's social worker. I wanted to know how she's doing, how she's acclimating by you, and to hear that everything's okay. Please call me back at telephone number---"

Rochel was about to leave her phone number when a voice suddenly ripped through the line:

"Bleich???"

"Yes," Rochel said. It was the voice of Mike Lewis himself.

"I'm telling you for the last time," his low, intense voice penetrated her ear. "If you call here again, you low down woman, you, I will hurt the girl. I don't stand for others mixing into my affairs, and if I see that the girl has such a bothersome caretaker like you, I'll be rid of her – and I don't care how. There are many other children in the world just waiting for me to take them. For your own good, if you're worried about the girl, if you don't want her to be hurt, this had better be the last time you try calling here, you hear??? Hello, you heard me?"

Rochel didn't answer. After a few minutes she heard a loud bang and the call was cut off.

Naftali, returning home in the afternoon with Shloimy, found her in the same frozen position.

"What happened???"

Rochel repeated the conversation and the threat.

Naftali sat down. His knees, too, began to shake.

"What's clear," he said quietly, "is that he can carry out that threat at any given time, even if you don't call. It's impossible to know what he'll get into his head to do. If one day he'll decide that he doesn't like her anymore, or that she's too Jewish for him, or that she's simply extra – he'll get rid of her without thinking twice."

"What does that mean?"

*Thicker Than Water* « 553

"That means that the girl is essentially his captive. Simply a captive."

"But he loves her. He wants her. Why should he harm her?"

"In the underworld, Rochel, there are different rules. There, there are no friends, and no love. He could spoil her today, and toss her tomorrow. We've already learned a thing or two about him."

Rochel shook her head slowly.

"I think that this is really… really a life or death situation. We might be obligated to get her out of there…"

The decision was made that same day.

Naftali shared his plan with Rochel. It was a dangerous plan, a frightening plan – definitely well-constructed, but completely dependent on *siyata dishmaya*. It was the only plan.

About one o'clock in the morning their taxi stopped in front of Shaya and Chana Bleich's house. They asked the driver to wait and went upstairs, Naftali carrying Shloimy's bag and Rochel – the sleeping tot.

"You're sure it's okay that we didn't say a word to them first?" Rochel whispered.

"It's not okay, but it's what we had to do. Had I called Shaya earlier, he wouldn't have let me make such a move without telling him why, without insisting that I consult with someone first. I wouldn't have been able to tell him: 'I'm bringing you my son and I can't explain to you why.' It also wouldn't have been right. But now, when we're coming at such an hour, with the taxi honking downstairs and the plane about to take off without us, they'll understand the urgency and that there's no time for questions."

Rochel looked at the sleeping Shloimy, brushed an unruly curl off his face and refused to believe that she was about to part from her baby for an indefinite amount of time.

"Rochel, come," Naftali whispered when he saw her hesitating.

"I can't," she murmured brokenly.

# CHAPTER 45

Rochel sat down on the bottom step with the sleeping Shloimy in her arms. Naftali hesitated a minute and then continued up the steps and rang the bell.

It was close to one in the morning. It made sense that it would take some time until the door opened. They were probably sleeping. Each minute, though, was a shame. He pressed the bell again, its shrill ring echoing in the quiet building.

"Just a minute!" he heard the voice of Chana his sister-in-law. She quickly opened the door, and her eyebrows rose in surprise.

"Hello!"

"Call Shaya," Naftali said abruptly.

"He's gone to bed already!"

"So wake him up. Immediately."

Chana ran to the bedroom. Naftali shifted uncomfortably. His sister-in-law was such a refined person, and she always treated them so warmly. And here he suddenly appeared at her house in middle of the night and began issuing orders.

He heard Chana urging a sleepy Shaya to get up. Another few minutes, and Shaya, too, realized the urgency of the matter. He could hear the shuffling of slippers. Naftali closed the front door behind him, went into the living room and perched himself on the couch.

"I'll be right there," he heard Shaya's hoarse voice from the bedroom. "What's doing, Naftali?"

"I'm waiting for you. Come as you are. As quickly as you can."

This announcement caused Shaya to leave his room dressed in a shirt and striped pajama pants, his rumpled sleeping yarmulke almost falling off his head.

A worried Chana offered strong coffee. Naftali refused and asked her to leave the living room and close the door, despite Shaya's critical stare.

Shaya took a chair and sat down opposite him. He wanted to know what was going on.

At that critical moment, when Naftali had to put an entire life into three sentences, and put forth his request without too much emotion, his throat suddenly closed. He wanted to speak, but only managed to grab his brother's hand and jiggle it back and forth, his eyes imploring Shaya to understand.

Shaya was bewildered. He put his hand on Naftali's shoulder. He wanted to encourage him, but didn't know about what.

In stages, Naftali finally succeeded in opening his mouth and explaining to his brother why he had come and what he was asking. To travel abroad, for an urgent, vague reason, and to leave his only baby by them.

He couldn't guess the extent of their shock. He had no time to guess, anyway. He opened the door and called to Rochel in a whisper to come upstairs right away.

Afterwards, everything happened quickly. Chana dragged a

playpen into her work room, and made it up with a sheet and blanket. Rochel went inside and stayed there for a few minutes.

Naftali waited behind the crack in the door. They were in an indescribable rush, but he saw his wife's shaking shoulders. A month or two was a lot of time to be away from one's baby, especially a first baby. He wanted to hurry her, but instead of speaking, he pushed open the door and joined her in the dark room.

Shaya accompanied them downstairs to the taxi. Chana remained in the house with the sleeping Shloimy, watching from the window.

The taxi's motor was running and its lights were on. Naftali and Rochel climbed in and slammed the doors shut.

And then, in a flash of reason, with the driver already pressing on the gas pedal, there was a sudden wild pounding of fists. Shaya banged on the window, almost breaking it. What did that mean, leaving a baby with relatives in the dead of night and disappearing without any explanation?! What happened to asking for help? If you got tangled up in something, what was family there for if not to help?! Why keep everything a big secret and run away?!

"Naftali," he yelled, his hoarse voice filling the silent street. Naftali waved good-bye.

"Naftali, Naftali," Shaya bellowed frantically, "Give me a phone number, an address, something…!!!"

Naftali made a helpless motion with his hands, as if to say: "I have none." A second later he gave in and opened the window. Shaya pounced on it.

"Don't search for me in the meantime," Naftali begged, "at least not for the next few months… I don't know what will be, but I do know that it could harm me, us. You promise?!"

Naftali knew that if he said anymore he'd break down. Without waiting for Shaya's promise, he firmly closed the window and urged the driver to go. The taxi moved forward and then sped down the empty street with a roar of its motor.

Naftali and Rochel had never flown to Australia; they now had three days to spend traveling. As if in a trance, they went from airport to airport. Most of the time, Rochel cried; the separation from Shloimy ripped her apart. Had she been able, she would have called Chana and asked to at least hear his babbling over the telephone, to send him kisses, but Naftali forbade her to do it. If anyone knew where they were headed and why, there was a big chance the information would reach the wrong ears.

During those crazy days, Naftali was mainly occupied with running around, and calming Rochel between each round of running. They flew from country to country, not believing that until two or three days earlier, they had been living a regular life.

Rochel begged Naftali, almost falling at his feet, to allow her to make one phone call, just one, to Chana. Naftali, his heart bursting no less than hers with longing for his son, was forced to refuse again and again.

"That man is monitoring our every move," he explained. "By now he's discovered that we've been away from home for too long, and is keeping close tabs on Shaya and Chana's telephone. Please understand, Rochel," he tried explaining to her, "this man is like a deadly octopus. If one of his many arms manages to reach us, our fate is sealed."

When they arrived, they rented a small, one room apartment and refined their plan. They needed the cooperation of a few outside people. Money, though, as Naftali claimed, tended to open people's hearts and close their mouths. Therefore, before they left, he had freed a savings plan in the bank and deposited all the money in his account. If there would be any need, he'd be able to draw cash, no matter where in the world he might be –

and the need indeed became obvious.

The plan could have failed on so many accounts. It depended completely on *siyata dishmaya*. There wasn't much to stop someone from messing the whole thing up, or worse: causing them to be exposed by the devil himself.

But the plan succeeded. Now the girl was with them, in the tiny apartment, and the story of the kidnapping was making waves throughout the country. They both knew that Mike Lewis wouldn't rest, combing every house in the entire continent if necessary, until he discovered who and where the kidnappers were. Naftali felt he would do it less for the girl than to take revenge on those who succeeded in tricking him and trampling his honor.

"To switch identity?!" Rochel asked again.

"Absolutely. We can't be Naftali and Rochel Bleich anymore. We have to completely erase our identity."

"But this… this criminal knows our faces. Can't he can find us even under a different name?"

"Could be," Naftali said, and truthfully, he was quite sure of it.

"So what should we do?"

"We'll have to---"

Sara's crying from the next room made them jump up. Rochel went into her. The child, who had gone through so much since seeing her last, refused her outstretched arms. She called for her mother, for Mrs. Lewis.

"Sara, Sara," Rochel tried persuading her, smiling at her, hugging her. The girl was still somewhat foggy, maybe from the drug induced sleep. Rochel knew that the renewed connection would take some time, but time they had. The girl wasn't meant to change hands anytime soon. She would remain with them, *be'ezras Hashem*, always.

"To switch identity, to erase Naftali and Rochel," she whispered to her husband. "You know what that means?!"

"Yes."

"That means that we won't be able to see---" a huge lump stuck in her throat.

"We won't be able to meet---" she tried again. The lump was blocking. Words couldn't leave, air couldn't get in.

"To meet --- to meet ---" she choked. She succumbed.

Shloimy.

Naftali stood in the doorway, blocking the light. He saw his wife sink to the floor.

"You --- you --- this is what you had in mind when you cooked up this plan?!" she cried out like a wounded animal. "This is what you planned?! And you didn't tell me???"

He wanted to say the truth, that absolutely not. When he had planned everything, they had been far away, far from the yawning jaws of danger. He knew it was a dangerous mission, but didn't realize how dangerous. He thought they would be able to take the girl and hide until the search for them died down, until the man would realize that there was no point in searching further. The full extent of the danger, though, became known to him only now. Fire looks scary from afar, but only from close by could one feel how much it burns.

He now knew that the original plan wasn't enough. Based on what they'd been hearing about Mike Lewis, the story clearly wouldn't end in a month or two, or even in a year or two. Mike Lewis didn't belong to the class of people who forgot. He was from those who dug into the ground like a snake, camouflaged, and patiently waited for an opportune time to strike and sink their fangs into their prey.

Had he known that from the start, he would have obviously planned it all differently. Saving a child's life was extremely important, no doubt, but there was a limit to what they could sacrifice for her sake. Now, if they wanted to live, they needed to cut off all contact with their family, with their oldest child, and become new people with all that came along with it - including changing the structure of their face and their outward appearance – for an indeterminate amount of time…!

The childish crying of the frightened Sara, who didn't know why and how she had been taken from her adoptive parents arms and brought to this musty apartment, suddenly stopped. Not because she had calmed down, but because different sobs filled the room. The sharp, stabbing sobs of a woman who had had everything, and now had to tear her former life to pieces and forget her beloved son.

Naftali went over to her, praying from the depths of his heart that *Hashem* put the right words in his mouth.

"Don't worry, Rochel," he said. "*HaKadosh Boruch Hu* sees everything. We took pity on a Jewish child, and He'll take pity on us. You'll see, Rochel, the day will come when, *be'ezras Hashem*, we'll be rejoined with our Shloimy. You'll see…".

Time worked against them. Each additional day that they stayed there – with their original identity, with the girl – presented a very real danger to their lives.

Naftali began to weave a plan, but, as before, didn't tell Rochel about it and didn't start carrying it out. According to his plan, they would have to shed their names and history, adopt new ones, and rejoin the world as completely new people.

He knew he would have to include in the plan another, inevitable part, even though it was hard for him to even think about it:

They would have to undergo plastic surgery.

He never would have dreamed of taking such a step. The two of them, a young couple for whom the whole criminal world never existed even in their imagination, would be forced to undergo surgery, to move the nose a bit upwards, the cheekbones a bit downwards, to stretch, to straighten… he was afraid to even mention the idea to himself.

Without even realizing it, Naftali ran his fingers over the bridge of his nose, his forehead, his beard. He felt his ears and his eyebrows. He had never given them much thought. The last time he had carefully studied his appearance was when he chose a new pair of glasses before his wedding.

*However, Naftali Bleich, you would do well to look in the mirror one more time, in order to say good-bye to your face. It'll never return.* If Shaya and Chana showed Shloimy pictures, he would etch the features of his parents in his memory, but wouldn't be able to identify them upon meeting them. They would look completely different.

Who would have believed? *Who would have believed?!* The thoughts tore at his mind. From a quiet, peaceful family, they'd become wanderers, hunted fugitives on the run. A person could know how he started something, but could never guess how it would end. Within such a short time they'd parted from Shloimy, flew to the other end of the world and were now in mortal danger.

• • •

David Stone, the most colorless name in the world, was the name Naftali chose upon his arrival in the United States. David, perhaps as a reminder of his Jewish identity, which he also needed to keep under wraps. It was impossible to strike roots in a Jewish community under a false name. All Jews know each other, or at least know someone who knows the other. People would very quickly become suspicious of him, something which was likely to shorten Mr. Lewis' way to them.

Rochel pulled herself together and demonstrated supreme

strength the entire way. Before the storm, when they had lived a peaceful life in their safe apartment, Naftali hadn't guessed what sort of physical and emotional strength she possessed. The upheavals they had experienced, however, and the trials they had been forced to undergo, released inner strengths of whose existence even she hadn't imagined.

One of the most painful moments had been when they removed the bandages from her face after the surgery. Rochel asked Naftali to bring her a mirror. He tried to refuse.

"You don't look good yet," he said, "You're still swollen, with blue marks."

But Rochel insisted. She wanted a mirror. Naftali had no choice. He brought her a small, round mirror.

Rochel silently inspected her face in the mirror. Her hand fluttered hesitantly from the forehead to the eyes, from there to the nose, lips and chin. And then Naftali heard her cry – a quiet cry. She didn't want to move her sore face; the crying was heard from inside, as if her very soul was weeping.

For the first few days after their surgeries, Naftali and Rochel couldn't look at each other. They felt like they were strangers. In addition, they had to get used to using their new names. They couldn't use their real names at all, not even between themselves when no one could hear, for fear that they would slip out also among strangers.

This difficult adjustment lasted for a few months, during which Naftali and Rochel arrived in the U.S. with the plan of settling there. The money from the savings plan, which they had been using all along, ran out, and Naftali had to find a job.

He looked for the most obscure workplace possible, where he wouldn't be able to stand out even if he wanted to. On the other hand, he had no diplomas or especial talents. The choice he was left with was rather dismal, especially for such a bright, scholarly young man as himself: to become a cab driver.

Slowly, he and Rochel got used to their new life. Sara kept her name, as it was used by both Jews and gentiles. Rochel didn't work, dedicating her time to taking care of Sara and the new baby that was born to them.

The entire time, Shloimy didn't budge from her heart. He accompanied her day and night, in her dreams and while awake. She tried to take comfort in the fact that she had left him in good hands, but her heart was torn to shreds.

Every so often, when Naftali returned in the evening from his exhausting job as a cab driver, he would find Rochel sitting in a dark corner, crying bitterly. Then, even though he very much wished to join her, he had to be the strong one and strengthen her, too.

"Don't worry," he would repeat his promise over and over, though he hadn't the faintest idea how it would be realized. "The day will come when we will be reunited with Shloimy. We'll go back to being one family. We just have to believe that everything – everything – is from *Hashem*, and to *daven* constantly."

After being in the United States for a while, Naftali felt secure enough to release a bit of the breath he'd been holding. It looked like the great operation had succeeded and Mike Lewis had lost their trail. One day he even dared voice this thought out loud to Rochel.

"So we can now go back to Eretz Yisroel??" Rochel jumped.

"Go back?" Naftali was shocked. "To Eretz Yisroel?! Don't you know that man's heavy hand is waiting for us specifically there?? How did you even think such a thing?"

"But Naftali and Rochel don't exist anymore," she maintained. "He can't find us. We're now the Stones. Why should he discover us??"

The thought of possibly being closer to her Shloimy stunned

her senses. True, she wouldn't be able to meet him, because he was still being closely watched. If she revealed herself to him, they would both be swallowed whole. Perhaps, though, she'd be able to see him without him seeing her... She wouldn't be able to ask Chana to bring him somewhere so she could see him, but maybe she'd be lucky... maybe they could live near Shaya and Rochel and bump into Shloimy in the street...?

"You're fantasizing," Naftali said firmly. "Even if I would agree to this dangerous plan, as the non-Jewish Stone family, we wouldn't be able to live in the *chareidi* community where Shaya and Chana live. It would be impossible. In any event, though, returning to Eretz Yisroel would be an absolutely foolhardy, reckless move. We can't make the wrong decision just because we miss Shloimy, even though it's driving us insane..."

After that conversation, Rochel went through some very difficult days. Naftali knew that she had felt close to Shloimy for a few minutes, and was heartbroken at being forced away from him again, even in thought.

"Be happy that we have it peaceful," he told her, and he was right. They had decent living quarters, and Naftali's job supported them adequately, even if not in style. They had charming children. They couldn't live openly as Jews, something which tore at them, but at least they were alive and well, and could breathe.

This idyllic time, though, didn't last too long.

One morning, Naftali left for his job as usual. Rochel stayed home, busy with her usual chores – cooking, cleaning and taking care of the little ones. Suddenly, she heard a knock at the door.

She peeked through the peephole. An unfamiliar man stood there.

"Who's there?" she asked.

"A neighbor," the man said. Rochel didn't know the neighbors very well, but she didn't remember seeing his face in the area. Thinking that maybe she hadn't identified him properly through the peephole, she opened the door.

The man was very friendly. He introduced himself as a new neighbor in the building, and asked if he could ask her a few questions.

Rochel wasn't too happy about it, but common courtesy made her answer his questions. She couldn't bring any suspicion upon herself, and throwing someone out of her house was bound to raise questions.

The man wanted to know a few ordinary details. Who were the neighbors in the building? How many years were they living there? Where were they from? Where was the grocery? How did the transportation work?

Rochel answered briefly and waited for him to leave. Luckily, he didn't stay too long and left after a few minutes.

Towards evening, when Naftali returned, the story was already a hazy memory in Rochel's mind. She told it to Naftali as she served supper.

The fork slipped from his hand and clattered to the floor.

"A new neighbor???"

"Yes, that's what he said."

"I know all the neighbors. Describe him to me."

Rochel tried to remember. She described the man as well as she could. Naftali listened carefully and shook his head.

"If what you're saying is accurate, there's no one who answers this description in this building. You can be sure of it. I've learned who everyone is, and I watch all of them."

"So what does that mean??"

The fork remained on the floor.

"It means it demands explanation."

"Who could it be?"

They were both quiet. The silence was so thick it could be cut.

"It could be someone who hit upon our trail." With difficulty, Naftali voiced the thought going through both of their minds.

"No," Rochel said. The idea was like a black wall approaching them with terrifying swiftness. "How on earth could someone have found us? Even I sometimes forget who I really am…"

"Not for nothing is the criminal world called the underworld," Naftali said. "It has dark, crooked ways of reaching everywhere."

It was cloudy outside, and gloom descended on the small house of the Stone family. If someone discovered their trail, the nightmare was starting again from the beginning. Again they would have to run away and hide, switch identity, begin everything all over again…!

"Naftali, maybe we should wait a bit, maybe it will turn out to be a false suspicion."

"We don't have the luxury of waiting," Naftali said, "because it it's true, every minute that we remain is a ticking time bomb. We can't afford even the slightest bit of complacency."

He went over to the window, trying to draw some air, to fill his weighted lungs. Rochel went and stood next to him.

A figure could be seen roaming about the yard.

"Hey, one second," Rochel whispered, "that's him, the 'new' neighbor! Look…!"

Naftali strained to see. There was no doubt about it: this man wasn't one of the neighbors, and never had been.

# CHAPTER 46

With two small children, it wasn't simple to go away for even a two day vacation, let alone travel with them to another country and begin a new life.

Naftali and Rochel fled to France, where they had to start all over again. Rochel insisted on not switching identity again. She claimed it wouldn't be a problem for them to disappear into France even if they remained the Stones. Naftali, who anyway wasn't positive that flight was crucial, and not merely precautionary, granted her that.

Rochel had a hard time with the French, and continued to use English. The children, however, acclimated right away. Again Naftali looked for work, and again he found the job that was, for him, a sort of protective umbrella – a cab driver. The two things demanded of him were a driver's license and courtesy, and he excelled at both.

He was careful not to become too friendly with any of the other drivers, earning himself the reputation of a loner – which suited him just fine. He couldn't, however, prevent the friendship with Valery, who had worked together with him in Manhattan and had also moved to France just when he and Rochel were running for their lives.

Rochel liked the new apartment up on the top floor of an apartment building on Rue Paul Violet. Very quickly, with her talented touch, she managed to turn it into a warm, homey place. She prayed that they be able to stay there for a long time, and not have to run at the slightest noise.

One day Naftali returned home all worked up. Rochel hurried to serve him a drink and asked him what happened.

"I met Mr. Ludwig Mortimer," Naftali said. "He suddenly climbed into my taxi. I got so scared."

Ludwig Mortimer was one of their long time neighbors in Manhattan. "He came to visit his sick sister here in Paris. I took him to the Salpêtrière Hospital."

"Did he ask you where you disappeared to?" Rochel asked.

"Yes. He was very surprised to see me. I told him that our rental contract had run out and the owner threw us out, so we took the first plane to France, to live with relatives until we settled ourselves."

Rochel had a good laugh.

"But I didn't only give information; I also received some," Naftali added. "I hope his information is more reliable than mine was. I spoke to him about that 'new neighbor'. You remember?"

Of course she remembered. They were where they were because of that 'neighbor'.

"Well, he really was a new neighbor. Even though he hadn't yet moved in, he already paid for his apartment, so he took the liberty of calling himself a neighbor."

"Ah," Rochel said very contemplatively.

"I felt so relieved," Naftali said. "I don't regret that we left, as it was a necessary precaution, but in retrospect, it's good to know that no one was following us."

Rochel continued to think quietly.

"What are you thinking about?" Naftali asked. "You want to go back to the States?"

"No," Rochel said resolutely, "I have no such plan. We've moved about enough. The U.S. doesn't speak to me any more than Paris does. I'm thinking about something else."

"I know what you're thinking," Naftali said. "You're thinking that if really no one's following us, that means we're free. And if we're free, we can start thinking about Shloimy."

"Exactly."

They were both quiet.

"I'm sorry," Naftali said, "but I don't think we can allow ourselves to go near him."

"Why? *Why??*" All the pain in the world was contained in Rochel's voice.

"Because not enough time has passed. I'm sure Mike Lewis is still looking for us, and that one of his main traps is in Eretz Yisroel. He's waiting for us to return. True, it's very hard to identify us now, but it's still dangerous. Dangerous. You have to understand. He's no fool. He knows that we'll miss Shloimy, so he's keeping close tabs on him. If we'll live in Shloimy's neighborhood, there's a good chance we won't be able to control ourselves and we'll try to approach him some way. That's exactly what Mike Lewis is waiting for – for new people to be seen around Shloimy. We can't fall into this trap, and bring Shloimy down with us!"

"Not enough time passed?" Rochel repeated. "It's been almost two years!"

"That's not a lot," Naftali said.

"So how many years will we have to wait?!" her voice choked.

"What's the measuring stick? And how will we be able to verify that it's really safe? Until the man's dead we'll never be able to be sure."

Naftali lifted his arms. "It's all from Above," he said. "A person's steps are dictated by *Hashem*. Come, let's look at the good in our lives." That had always been his approach. "Sara is with us, we're alive and well, life is calm, we have a delicious son, and *HaKadosh Boruch Hu* is watching over us with exceptional *hashgachah pratis*. We'll continue to *daven* and to hope that one day we'll be reunited with Shloimy and with the entire family."

Half a year went by since their arrival in Paris, and everything seemed to be going well. Nothing prepared Naftali and Rochel for what happened one Thursday morning.

Naftali had a fare to Charles de Gaulle Airport with a pleasant family, loaded with suitcases, who didn't stop chatting the entire way. Naftali guessed they were going on vacation.

When they arrived at the airport, Naftali helped his passengers unload their suitcases and then slowly glided down the street, looking for a fare back to the city.

"Taxi," a man raised his hand.

Naftali pulled up next to him and stepped out to help him put his luggage into the trunk.

Suddenly, the blood froze in his veins.

Two steps away from him, another person was leaning into a different cab. Something about his movements, his profile, caused Naftali's heart to stop.

"Sir," he heard the voice of his passenger, who was already sitting inside the taxi and waiting, "is everything okay? Can we be on our way?"

"Of course," Naftali said, and with arms of stone he slammed the trunk and slid into his seat, not moving his eyes from the taxi behind him.

The man who had such an electrifying effect on him made himself comfortable in the seat next to the driver's, while the driver loaded his luggage onto the back seat. Naftali began to drive slowly, his eyes glued to the mirror. It couldn't be him, but he looked so much like him that it had to be him.

To avoid upsetting his passenger, Naftali increased his speed. To his joy, the taxi behind him also set out, and he was able to continue studying the man as he drove.

He was positive beyond any shadow of a doubt: It was that man. Mike Lewis. And he was now in Paris. There could be many reasons why he came. Many, many. But one of them could be that he received information about Naftali and Rochel Bleich and came to verify that information.

Shortly afterwards, Naftali burst into their house, panting heavily.

"We're leaving right now," he called to Rochel. "We don't have a minute to spare. We must run."

"But why?? What happened??"

"Mike Lewis is here. I saw him. I'm sure it's him."

Rochel's entire body started to tremble. "He recognized you...?"

"No," Naftali said, "but I'm not sure he didn't notice me. Just imagine," he went on without taking a breath, "had I waited one second longer, he would have entered my taxi. Thank *Hashem* that you still have a husband."

"You're living with too much fear," Rochel said. "I'm sure he's come for different reasons. He doesn't have to come personally in order to catch us. He has enough henchmen who would agree to 'meet' with us."

"You're wrong," Naftali said. "He might have received information that we're here, and wanted to come kill us with his own hands." Not a muscle in his face moved as he said it.

"So now what?" Rochel looked around uncertainly.

"We have to flee. Quickly. It's rotten, but that's what we have to do."

"Flee?? To where??"

"To somewhere where he won't look for us."

"Where is that?!"

Naftali thought for a minute. He had an idea. "I know where," he said. "It's a place where he won't look for us anymore, because he's completely convinced that the search there has been exhausted."

"*Nu*, where is that?"

"Australia…"

"We'll go to *Australia*?! We ran away from there!" Rochel was wide eyed with wonder.

"Right, we ran away from there, and I'm telling you he combed every inch of land on that continent. He's positive we're not there – that's why it's the safest place for us."

The news was too much for Rochel. To pack up everything and go with the children such a long distance, again, to a new country…?!

"I really understand the curse of Kayin," she said, no tears falling from her eyes. Not yet. "There's no worse punishment than being forced to wander around. People don't realize the tremendous gift of a permanent place to live. It's an anchor, a rock – and whoever doesn't have it tosses about crazily like a boat in a stormy sea…"

They told the children they were going on vacation. They told the same thing to the neighbors, their few acquaintances and Naftali's boss. If anyone began to wonder about the vacation that was lasting longer than expected, it would be too late, as they would already be far, far away.

As they sat on the airplane, holding the little ones on their laps and looking at the ocean spread out underneath them, Rochel whispered:

"I don't understand. Why do we have to live in constant fear that this man might be on our tail? Maybe we can keep tabs on him, always know where he is, and then we can be more relaxed!"

"I thought of it," Naftali whispered back, "and it's too dangerous. If we follow him, he'll sense it. He has excellent sensors. We'd basically be signing our own death warrant. But don't worry. We're not in Mike Lewis' hands, nor in the hands of anybody else. We're only in *Hashem's* hands."

Another baby was born to the Stone family living in Australia. Their happiness was greater than that of a regular family. Each additional baby healed them a bit more, comforted them – even though they never stopped missing Shloimy for even one minute.

At least, that's how Naftali felt as he held the tiny baby in his arms. Rochel, the new mother, also felt flooded with joy for the first few days. As the weeks passed, however, her good mood evaporated and she sank into a depression.

Naftali thought that the birth was causing her to feel low and to miss Shloimy more. He made sure to be at her side as much as possible, to make her happy, to help her take care of the other children and to make sure she was okay.

But she wasn't okay. Not even after two or three months. She took care of the baby mechanically, without the natural happiness typical of other mothers. She barely paid attention to the other children. The house, which she had always worked so hard to take care of, lay neglected. The bare minimum of household chores was carried out with difficulty.

Naftali hired cleaning help, and tried cooking the little that he knew how. He hoped the difficult time would pass and the positive, cheerful Rochel would return to herself, to her family and to her home.

But it didn't pass. Naftali slowly understood that it was something more serious: Rochel had fallen into a serious depression. She lost interest in everything. She didn't care if her precious children ate or bathed, and she spent most of her time in bed.

Naftali was at a loss. They had no family to help them and he couldn't leave his job. He was also afraid to consult with anyone. Their family couldn't be too exposed. The pitiful appearance of Rochel lying in bed, though, and the children running about, brought tears to his eyes.

"What can I do for you?" he asked in despair. "What can I do to make you come out of this, to go back to what you were, what we were?"

He didn't expect an answer. Lately, Rochel wasn't in the habit of giving answers – at the most she gave a grunt or two. To his surprise, however, she turned around and said in a low, but clear voice:

"There is something you can do for me."

Naftali jumped up.

"Nothing will be too hard for me," he said passionately. "It doesn't matter how much it costs. Just tell me what…!"

"It will be too hard," Rochel said, even more quietly. Almost in a whisper.

Naftali thought he was beginning to understand. He folded himself back onto the chair.

"You won't have the strength for such a trip," he told her.

"I'll have the strength to travel around the world seven times," Rochel said, her voice a bit firmer.

They both knew what they were talking about: If Naftali would agree to move to Eretz Yisroel, to live near their beloved Shloimy, even without seeing him, it would breathe new life into Rochel.

Could it be?! Naftali asked himself. He looked at his wife lying there like a rock, and knew that he had the power to light up her life, or – if he refused her request – to cause her to sink even more into depression and despair.

He couldn't refuse. But he couldn't agree. He missed Shloimy no less than Rochel, and maybe even more. "As a father has mercy on his son," Shlomo Hamelech said. A father, not a mother. However, he had no less mercy on the rest of his family, and was responsible for their welfare. Traveling to Shloimy meant teasing danger.

The two possibilities swung before him, as if on two sides of a scale: removing the extended, intolerable depression of his wife, and endangering his entire family.

Naftali had his own reasons for wanting to go to Eretz Yisroel. The education his children were receiving was not to his liking. He desperately wished to be part of a Jewish community, something which he hadn't merited in such a long time.

Secretly, without saying a word to Rochel of course, he had cooked up a daring plan.

According to the plan, they would once again become a completely *chareidi* family and live in one of Israel's main cities, as part of the community. They would change their name, of course, and introduce themselves as a family that moved from a different part of the country. The little children would quickly forget their tumultuous past and begin a new, good life in Eretz Yisroel.

The plan, though, was shoved deep down into the inner recesses of his heart and the door locked. Maybe in the future, Naftali thought, maybe in another ten years, when enough time had passed, he would find enough nerve to carry it out.

Now, in light of Rochel's pitiful state, the door to that room opened a crack. Maybe all his fears were unfounded? Maybe Mike Lewis wasn't even following them? Maybe he gave up on them, and they were running and hiding for no reason, like people hiding deep in the forest without knowing that the war had finished long before…?

*No!* Naftali yelled at himself. *You can't let down your guard and allow the silence to trick you! You're still in Lewis' sights; he won't hesitate to shoot when you appear on his radar screen!*

*Don't fall into the net, Naftali; don't let your strong emotions conquer your good sense! Rochel's situation isn't simple now, the solution seems to be in your hand, but if you're not at peace with it – don't do it…!*

"I'll think about it," he finally said and stood up to go. He had to get some air, to pray that *Hashem* help him reach the right decision.

That day, for the first time in months, Rochel managed to sit up in bed and talk pleasantly with the children. The children were so happy that Naftali, watching the scene, wiped away a tear. Towards evening, she even managed to fry an egg for them, after the cooking utensils had already started gathering dust in the cabinets. It was an astounding jump in her state of health. Naftali had no doubt that just the thought that the trip to Eretz Yisroel may be closer than ever, put her on her feet. If that was the power of the mere thought, the trip itself would definitely make Rochel into a new person.

He went through some terribly difficult days of uncertainty. Rochel wisely didn't bother him with questions. From day to day she improved, as if someone was injecting her with some reviving potion. She bathed the baby, sang songs with the children and did laundry. These simple activities, which had once been part of normal life, were literally a prize now. Naftali saw this and his heart tore. The future depended on him. If he told Rochel 'yes', the situation would improve more and more. If he said 'no', the situation would deteriorate at once to what it had been, if not worse.

After a few days, when Rochel was standing at the sink washing dishes, Naftali said:

"I think I've decided."

Rochel froze.

"I decided that yes."

She lifted shining eyes.

"But I have a few conditions," he added, "and only if you faithfully promise me that you'll keep them, can we carry out the plan."

The first condition, of course, was to avoid any connection whatsoever, neither direct nor roundabout, with Shloimy and with the family. Naftali's second condition was that the children start fresh. They were still young enough to forget the past. They had to know that they were born and grew up in Eretz Yisroel as completely religious Jews; there could be absolutely no mention in the house of their wanderings.

Third, they couldn't let slip even the slightest hint that Sara wasn't their daughter.

Rochel gave an immediate, firm 'yes' to all three conditions. Only after Naftali was convinced that she was saying it rationally, and not out of eagerness to be on the way already, did he agree to lay out his new plan before her.

Their new name would be Fuchsman. Their first names would be Eliyahu and Devorah. The children had been given Jewish names at birth, names that hadn't yet been used. Sara would remain Sara and be called by the nickname Suri.

Almost three years after fleeing Eretz Yisroel in a panic for "a month or two", the Bleich couple returned home. No one was capable of recognizing in the pleasant Fuchsman family, the young couple Naftali and Rochel Bleich.

They set up their home in Yerushalayim. The children learned Hebrew quickly, and it didn't take long for them to become an inseparable part of the community. Suri went to kindergarten, and the boys went to kindergarten and to *cheder*.

The years passed. More children were born to the Fuchsman family. Life was so busy that Naftali and Rochel themselves forgot that they had once gone by the names Bleich and Stone. The names Elya and Devorah Fuchsman became so ingrained that "Naftali" and "Rochel" became a dim, distant memory.

One person, though, was never forgotten.

Shloimy.

# CHAPTER 47

Rochel-Devorah kept her promise. Naftali-Elya knew she would; otherwise, he wouldn't have put the plan into motion. She didn't say a word about Shloimy, and tried very hard not to think about him either. She took comfort in her beautiful, growing family, and in the fact that Shloimy was the shortest possible distance away from them and in the best possible hands.

To say that she didn't sometimes imagine bumping into him? That she didn't hope to see him in the street or in the park? She couldn't say that. As soon as they arrived, she was overcome with an uncontrollable desire to see him. Shloimy should have been about five years old then, and each boy that age that passed by in the street was treated to a penetrating look. And if one of them would be Shloimy? Would she be strong? Would she manage not to fall on him with fierce hugs, on her son whom she hadn't seen for so long? Would she manage not to go over to him, not to give the slightest hint that he was her oldest son?! No, she wouldn't manage. She prayed two conflicting prayers: to meet

Shloimy, and not to meet him. She knew she wouldn't withstand the test, and asked *Hashem* not to test her, but she so badly wanted to meet him.

Slowly, though, the urgency lessened. Shloimy remained in a specific part of her heart, in a corner of constant yearning, and the rest of her heart was available to contain her new, full life. Elya joined the business world and learned half a day in a kollel for businessmen. The children grew. Suri finished elementary school and entered the excellent community high school. The boys also did very well in their studies and joined excellent yeshivas. The Fuchsman family became known as a wonderful family that excelled in their children's quality upbringing, their beautiful *middos* and their refined ways.

On Suri's seventeenth birthday, when her younger brothers joked that next year they'd celebrate her *chasunah*, Elya and Devorah were the only ones who didn't smile. Their faces were very grave. They didn't have to exchange one word in order to know that the exact same thing was going through both of their heads. The exact same.

There was one *chosson* that they wanted. Only one. If that boy joined their family, they would receive not only a son-in-law, but also a lost son. Their son, Shloimy Bleich, would be Suri's *chosson*.

They couldn't, though, carry it out. There was nothing more dangerous.

In secret, behind closed doors, Elya and Devorah allowed themselves to whisper. The idea, which was as brilliant as it was dangerous, wouldn't let them alone.

If Suri, their dear adopted daughter, would marry their son Shloime, they could be closer to him than ever. They could bring him into the family, without him or anyone else knowing that he really belongs to the family. However, if he built a home with someone else, he'd sail away to his new life as the definite son of Shaya and Chana, his wife would be their daughter-in-law, and the incredible opportunity would be lost forever.

They both knew, however, that it wasn't practical.

Under the *chuppah*, it would be impossible to keep up the pretense that Suri was their daughter. Her biological father had a different name. In order to marry her off, they'd have to let their *mechutanim* – whoever they might be – know the truth about her. True, they wouldn't have to say the entire story; it would be enough to say that Suri came from a family that fell apart due to overwhelming difficulties, and was adopted by Devorah, who was a social worker. They would have to tell her story, though, even before setting up a *shidduch*. It wouldn't be fair to spring the truth after they were engaged. On the other hand, it would be an awful shame to present Suri as anything but the top quality that she was. She deserved a good *shidduch*. Her background – and her parents knew this very well – didn't detract the slightest bit from her excellence.

There was only one top *bochur* in the world, Elya and Devorah knew, who would take their Suri as she was and not see it as settling, but rather as receiving the finest of the fine. And that was only if they told him the entire story, from beginning to end.

Shloime.

If they revealed the truth to Shloime, and to Shaya and Chana, the *shidduch* would go through with tremendous joy on both sides. Shloime would no doubt be thrilled to marry the girl who grew up in his parents' home, and to at once become both son and son-in-law to his lost parents.

There could be no greater happiness than that.

But they couldn't do it.

Even if they told the Bleichs the truth in absolute secrecy, behind locked doors, there would be many guests at the wedding listening to the reading of the *k'subah*. It would be impossible to hide the fact that Suri was the daughter of a different father. Eyebrows would be raised and tongues would wag. Could it be?! The well-regarded Suri Fuchsman wasn't the daughter of Elya and Devorah?! What did that mean?! And if Suri's background was indeed problematic, why did the perfect Bleich family agree to the *shidduch* – especially as they were talking about their oldest son, Shloime, apple of their eye...?! And mainly, it would be impossible to hide the truth – that Shloime wasn't the son of Shaya and Chana...!

Well-meaning souls wouldn't rest until they discovered the truth – for themselves, all the guests and the entire world, including the evil ears of Mike Lewis. Such a chain of events was liable to turn the joyous wedding into a huge tragedy.

The only way, suggested by Devorah, they could carry out the wedding, was to do everything secretly. That is, to have a quiet *chuppah*, in which Shloime and Suri would be married before two witnesses, with only the family in attendance. Afterwards, at the official wedding, they would stage another *chuppah*, with a fictional *k'subah*, in which Suri's name would appear as it was known in the community.

Obviously, to do such a thing they would have to share their secret with the Bleich family. Elya and Devorah held different opinions on the topic for a long while. Devorah claimed that they could wait until the last minute to reveal themselves. A day or two before the wedding, they would approach the Bleichs and let them know about the secret wedding. This way, they could keep the danger to a minimum. Except for the immediate family, no one would know a thing.

Elya tended to agree with her, though he was still consumed with fear. The thought of letting their big secret out of the house made his blood run cold. That was one of his conditions before they moved back: not to make any contact with Shloime whatsoever. And here, not only would they be making contact, they would be telling the family the entire story…!

Unable to decide, Elya left the question open, until one day a well-known *shadchan* called up with an excellent suggestion for Suri – a fantastic boy from a wonderful yeshiva and a good family.

Elya respectfully heard him out, blessing the telephone that didn't disclose his shaking hands. The suggestion truly was wonderful, but he knew he couldn't accept it, or any other suggestion. Whatever would be would be. He couldn't let Suri enter *shidduchim* without receiving a clear *p'sak* from a *rav* that he was allowed to hide her background in order to get a good *shidduch* – and it was clear that he wouldn't get such a *p'sak*.

He thanked the *shadchan* profusely and promised to look into it and get back to him soon. That same night, he and Devorah held an urgent consultation. They couldn't wait any longer.

"If only we had someone who could estimate the danger for us," Devorah said, "who could know if we have to be so very careful or not…"

But no man in the world was privy to their secret. Or, at least, that's what they thought.

There was one man – only one – who knew every detail of the story. His name was Mendel Lederman, a brilliant private investigator whom Shaya and Chana had hired shortly after Naftali and Rochel had disappeared.

Mendel Lederman worked quietly and thoroughly, as always. In ways known only to him, he sniffed out the lost trail of Naftali and Rochel, and tracked them down.

Slowly, he uncovered the sad story. Naftali and Rochel had traveled to save a young girl, and found themselves fleeing for their lives. Lederman understood the tremendous danger to the entire Bleich family if the hiding place of Naftali and Rochel should be revealed.

Lederman was stuck: he had been hired by Shaya and Chana Bleich, and apparently had successfully completed the investigation. His conscience, however, didn't allow him to share his findings with them. They thought it would be great if they knew where their brother and sister-in-law were; he knew that it would actually be terrible.

When Mendel Lederman decided to tell the Bleichs that he was quitting the investigation, he never dreamed that his desire to help would make him into the family enemy for the next twenty years or so.

He couldn't explain what happened to Naftali and Rochel, and he couldn't explain why he couldn't explain. Lots of anger and bitterness were dumped on him for assuming unsolicited authority, and deciding in the Bleich's place what was and wasn't good for them.

And Lederman endured it all. He quietly absorbed the anger, the looks of hatred. He silently followed Shloime's upbringing by his aunt and uncle, and kept contact – one sided, of course – with the Bleich family that changed its name to Stone, and later to Fuchsman.

From the minute the Fuchsman family entered the country, Lederman couldn't relax. Had they asked him, he would have told them in no uncertain terms not to come near the country. The Fuchsmans, though, knew nothing about him, and never guessed that there was someone keeping tabs on their every move.

Lederman smelled trouble. Besides waiting, though, he couldn't do much. He was very well aware of Mike Lewis' reputation, and was gripped with fear no less than the Fuchsmans themselves.

However, the multi-talented, very thorough Mendel Lederman made one mistake: He refrained from following the movements of the terrible Mike Lewis. The man was so fearsome that Lederman accepted it as immutable fact, much like a terrible tiger that would never change its stripes. And truthfully, it would have taken an extra-large measure of wild imagination to think that perhaps Mike Lewis had ceased to be "Mike Lewis" and was now a convert by the name of Avrohom Yisroel, worlds away from his previous existence. Had such a possibility been put forth to Lederman – who had already seen it all – he would have laughed it out of town.

The night that Shloime Bleich and Suri Fuchsman got engaged, Lederman was beside himself with fear. What had happened to the Fuchsmans, who had been consummately careful for so many years?! Had love for their son addled their minds? Maybe the fear that Shloime would become part of a different family pushed them to endanger themselves and their daughter so that he should remain theirs…?!

That was the first time, in almost two decades, that Lederman contacted the Fuchsman family and revealed to them that they had been closely followed by him all those years.

The terror that overcame the Fuchsmans is difficult to describe. Someone did know about them!! The solid wall they had built around themselves for so many years was in fact cracked! Who knew, maybe just like this Lederman traced them, the terrible Australian, or one of his men, had also traced them…?!

Lederman reassured them as much as he could that no one besides him knew their secret. But, he said, he had come now to warn them to absolutely not go ahead with the marriage to Bleich. Even the engagement was a big mistake. There may have been some harm caused already, but meanwhile people weren't talking. They must back down from this dangerous idea – at any price.

The Fuchsmans, though, were hard to convince. After many attempts to talk to them, Lederman concluded that their love for Shloime was blinding them. They explained their plan of having the real wedding secretly, a day before the official *chasunah*, in order to keep the danger to a minimum, but Lederman didn't want to hear about it. Danger, danger, danger, he kept repeating.

When he saw that the family insisted on entering the lion's jaw with their eyes open, he couldn't rest. His sense of responsibility didn't allow him to let things continue; he was determined to go to any length in order to prevent the dangerous wedding from taking place.

At first, he tried nicely. He tried talking to Shaya Bleich, asking him to trust him, to listen to him, even if he couldn't explain his motives to him. Bleich, however, became increasingly angry at the investigator. *You didn't agree then to give us any information, you refused to help, to tell us what you know about our lost brother and sister-in-law – so why should we listen to you now, when you want to hurt us again and prevent us from having the little bit of nachas that we deserve – to see Shloime marry a wonderful girl and build a home?! Go away, Lederman! We don't need your favors!*

Lederman also tried speaking to Shloime. Maybe Shloime's young heart would be more open to listening, to accepting. But Shloime saw Lederman only as an enemy who wished to destroy his happiness. He wouldn't give information about his biological parents, and now he wanted to ruin the wedding.

Mendel Lederman had no choice but to try to foil the wedding. Though he knew his intentions were good, he did so with a very heavy heart. Sometimes, he told himself, you have to hurt someone so that he shouldn't get hurt more.

He marked Yisroel Yitzchok Fuchsman, who was going through a slightly low period, as a good source of help. Yisroel Yitzchok had a hard time accepting the talented and successful new *chosson* who had captured the hearts of the entire family. With his narrow, immature view, the younger boy refused to accept that all the attention being showered upon Shloime was temporary, and that things would return to normal after the wedding.

Even before Lederman contacted him, Yisroel Yitzchok set out all on his own to prove that Shloime Bleich wasn't the perfect *bochur* everyone made him out to be. He did it so thoroughly, so diligently, that he managed to arouse the suspicions of Elya Fuchsman himself.

Elya, whose sole desire was to be reunited with his beloved eldest son, was devastated when he began to suspect that maybe Shloime wasn't the excellent *bochur* he had heard that he was. After all, he didn't know the Shloime of today. He had to rely on others for that information. He loved his son very much, but maybe Shloime wasn't fitting to be Suri's *chosson*…?

Elya didn't just follow his heart. He invited Shloime's good friend Nochum to his house to check the matter out thoroughly. He wasn't at ease until he made certain that Shloime was indeed the *chosson* he desired.

Mendel Lederman tried getting Yisroel Yitzchok to work with him. The boy's penchant for adventure, fearlessness and typical boyish judgment could be helpful. He was unlucky, though. Yisroel Yitzchok's conscience began to bother him, and his father "won" him over to his side in order to help frustrate Mendel Lederman's schemes.

Lederman was left to fight alone. But he didn't give up. Shaya Bleich had gone on a major search throughout the world, and Lederman didn't stop watching him for a minute. He tried tripping him up at every step, even asking the private investigator to bury the story. This only boomeranged against him, as not only did the honest investigator refuse to go along with the scheme, he even revealed it to Shaya, whose animosity towards Lederman only increased.

Throughout the entire engagement, Elya and Devorah held their breath. They couldn't say a word to anyone. Not even to Suri, for whom what should have been a joyous time became an extended nightmare. Lederman didn't stop at anything. He started a rumor that the Bleich family was pulling back from the *shidduch*, causing the hall manager to call the Fuchsmans and scare Suri terribly. He sent his wife to join Suri on her trip to *kivrei tzaddikim* and try to frighten her.

It was decreed from Above, though, that nothing should come of all Mendel Lederman's efforts, and that the *shidduch* should continue.

And what of Mike Lewis?

The wealthy gangster indeed lost track of Naftali and Rochel after they changed their name and faces and fled from him. He had no idea where they were, and was furious. He continued keeping close tabs on the Bleich family in Israel. He guessed, rightly so, that one day the longing would be too much and Naftali and Rochel would want to be reunited with their son. He waited patiently.

A few years down the road, however, the entire picture changed.

A fatal road accident claimed his wife's life. Mike, who dealt each day with the knowledge that there were those who wanted to do him in, and who had their home protected in the best way possible to prevent an attempt on his or his wife's life, was broken specifically by what seemed to be the chance death of his wife.

He investigated the incident thoroughly and the conclusion was plain: it was innocent. The people involved in the accident weren't sent by anyone. They simply veered out of their lane – it wasn't clear why – and hit his wife. She didn't stand a chance.

Mike called it fate, but the description bothered him.

His wife was the only person in the world who had an emotional connection with him, therefore being the only person whose death pained him, and whose loss he felt keenly. *Why?* He asked himself again and again. Why did it have to happen? There was no point to her death. No one and nothing gained from it, so why did it happen?

For a change, Mike began to think. He closed himself up in his house for days, sunk in sorrow and thought. His business in the criminal world was neglected, but he didn't care.

There had to be an answer, he told himself, losing all interest in anything else. He found comfort in thrashing out the matter, though he knew that nothing would bring his wife back.

His basic characteristic that had stood by him in all his dubious dealings stood by him now as well: he was always prepared to take something to the very end, without compromise. Now, too, when trying to clarify the meaning of death and life, he didn't flinch from taking it all the way.

Had he known that his search would eventually bring him to join the nation of Naftali and Rochel, his daughter's kidnappers, would he have even started?

Avrohom Yisroel, too, asked himself this question many times, always giving the same answer: Yes, without a doubt. After learning about the existence and meaning of Judaism, he knew that here, too, he would go until the end. If this was the truth, he would live by it.

Lewis' friends didn't understand what happened to him. "What, you've become spiritual?" "You're depressed?" And they were justified in asking, as Mike Lewis was the last person in the world they'd have suspected of leaving the criminal world for Judaism. But it happened.

Mike Lewis converted.

Along with his conversion, Mike Lewis – Avrohom Yisroel – began to understand what he had done to Naftali and Rochel Bleich. He understood the importance of a Jewish child to the Jewish nation, and found himself admiring the people who had agreed to put their lives on the line for the sake of little Sara. And together with the understanding, there spread through his heart a tremendous regret that gave him no peace. For close to twenty years, the Bleich family was suffering because of him – terrible, constant suffering!

His first urge was to find Naftali and Rochel and ask their forgiveness. That, however, was impossible. Naftali and Rochel had disappeared, and no one knew where they were to be found!

Avrohom Yisroel had no choice. He continued his close surveillance of Shaya and Chana Bleich's family, not with the hope of trapping Naftali and Rochel and taking revenge on them for kidnapping the girl, but with the fierce desire to meet them and try to ask their forgiveness. His craving for forgiveness was ten times greater than his previous longing for revenge.

He knew about Shloime Bleich's engagement to the daughter of the unknown Fuchsman. He presumed – correctly – that now Shaya Bleich would go on a desperate search for his brother, hoping to find him before the wedding. From the minute Shaya Bleich left Israel's borders, Avrohom Yisroel dogged his every step, like a shadow, waiting for the moment Naftali and Rochel would be found. That was the reason he offered – still incognito – to fund all the expenses of the search. He hoped that Shaya would be desperate enough to agree – which indeed was what happened.

That whole time, Avrohom Yisroel couldn't find the nerve to go over to Shaya Bleich and say: "I'm the one. I'm the wicked man who made your family miserable for close to twenty years. I've left my evil ways. Now I'm a Jew, a *ger*, and hope for your forgiveness." The need to do so hounded him. The terrible mortification stopped him. And, he didn't deny, he shrank from the anger of the Bleich family. After all, abuse of many years is very hard to erase with one request for forgiveness.

He followed Shaya Bleich's and Danny Shore's travels with bated breath. Once they reached Australia, he knew it wouldn't be long before they uncovered the tracks of Mike Lewis – and that Shore, the brilliant investigator, would also uncover the fact of his conversion. He gathered his courage and set up a pivotal meeting with Shaya and Shore, in which he began to lay before them the entire truth.

• • •

"Did you understand the story, Suri'le?" Devorah Fuchsman asked gently. Elya stood in the doorway to the room, large tears falling into his gray beard.

"Do you forgive Abba and Ima?" Devorah asked. "So many times lately I've tossed and turned, hearing you cry from the next room and crying with you. But we couldn't do otherwise. We couldn't let out the secret, not even to you. Forgive us."

Suri didn't answer. She looked at the people who, for so many years, endangered their lives for her sake, and asked herself if biological parents would have been so devoted.

Someone knocked at the door. Soft knocks.

"I know who it is," Elya said and opened.

A tall, smiling *bochur* stood on the threshold. Elya rubbed his eyes.

For a minute, the tall figure blurred, and in its place stood a small boy, two years old, clutching his teddy bear, exactly as he did on that night.

"I had to come again," Shloime whispered. "For so many

years you've been waiting for me to come, to return home…"

"And here you've returned, Shloime'le," Elya said softly. "Look at the wondrous ways of Hashem. For years we thought we've parted from one child, and in the end we gained two."

The invitations to the wedding lay on the table. Shloime touched one of them. He looked at the names. These were his parents, and so were these. His marriage wouldn't bring him into a new family. It would join his two families together.

He felt blessed.

In another few days, his two fathers would lead him to the *chuppah*. His two mothers would lead the *kallah*. Grandparents would be told the amazing story behind the mystery of so many years. Good-hearted people would wipe away tears along with them. Praised be the ways of Hashem.

And under the *chuppah* would reverberate the faith-filled promise that his father had uttered each day, every year: "The day will come when we will be reunited, when we'll become one family again."

The promise was fulfilled.

One family.